PRAY FOR JUSTICE

A Chance and Choices Adventure

SARDA BOOKS

Lisa Gay

This book is a work of fiction. The names, characters, places, and incidents are either the product of the author's imagination or used factitiously. Any resemblance to an actual person, living or dead, business establishment, event, or location is entirely coincidental.

ISBN-13: 978-1-945858-04-8
ISBN-10: 1-945858-04-4

Those involved in these incidents:

Place of Origin - Harmony, Arkansas

Ann Williams– the oldest sister
Stephanie Williams– the middle sister
Sally Williams– the youngest sister
Tom Yates- the owner of Yates Mercantile
Hattie Yates– deceased wife of Tom Yates
Eli Yates- son of Tom Yates
Smithfield Wyman- sheriff/livery owner/ blacksmith (Smitty)
Mara Wyman– Smitty's wife
Earl Carpenter– farmhand, living in town/ undertaker
Clara Carpenter– Earl's wife/beekeeper
Horace Devine- tinker
Betsy Devine- Horace's wife/schoolmarm
Lawrence Gridley– doctor (Doc)
Nellie Gridley– Lawrence's wife/nurse
Laura Gridley– Lawrence's daughter
Clyde Eggleston– carpenter
Patty Eggleston– Clyde's wife
Zachariah Eggleston–Clyde's son/carpenter/ farmhand

Joseph Pinckney– saloon/inn owner (Joe)
Samson– Williams' large draft horse
Dusty- Williams' horse sold to outlaws

Place of Origin – Indian Territory (Oklahoma)

Noah Swift Hawk- Native American in Harmony
James Williams- Ann, Stephanie, & Sally's uncle/original owner and builder of the Williams Farm
Algoma Williams– James' wife
Arabella– Noah's horse

Place of Origin – Various/unknown

Hank Butterfield– leader of the Butterfield Gang
Roy Butterfield– Butterfield Gang member
Gus Hutchinson - Butterfield Gang member
Benjamin Rowe - Butterfield Gang member (Ben)
Alvin Ives - Butterfield Gang member (Al)
Charlie Cobb - Butterfield Gang member
Pete Drake - Butterfield Gang member

Place of Origin - Clarksville, Arkansas

Lemuel Slade– sheriff (Lem)

Elmer Baker– doctor

Mable– boarding house owner

Cyrus- bartender

Stable Hand- no stated name

John Freeman– Boat owner/operator

Moses– barber

Place of Origin – Fort Smith, Arkansas

Richard Atwood– judge

Edith Atwood– Judge Atwood's wife

Warren Lampson– lieutenant - U.S. Army

Jeremiah Pratt– private - U.S. Army

Jesse– private - U.S. Army

Will– private - U.S. Army

Ernest– private - U.S. Army

First Floor - Woods (⇧)

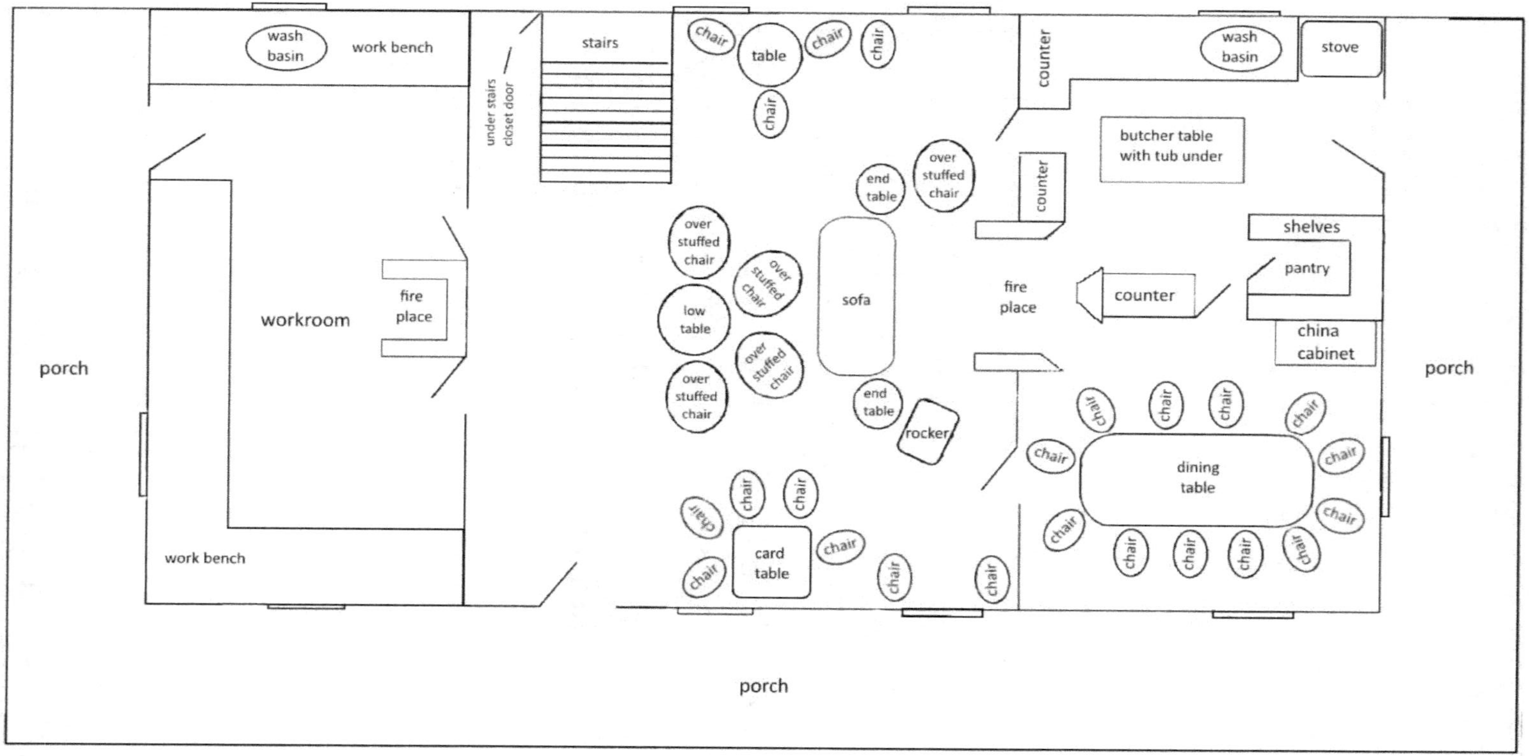

Second Floor - Woods (⇧)

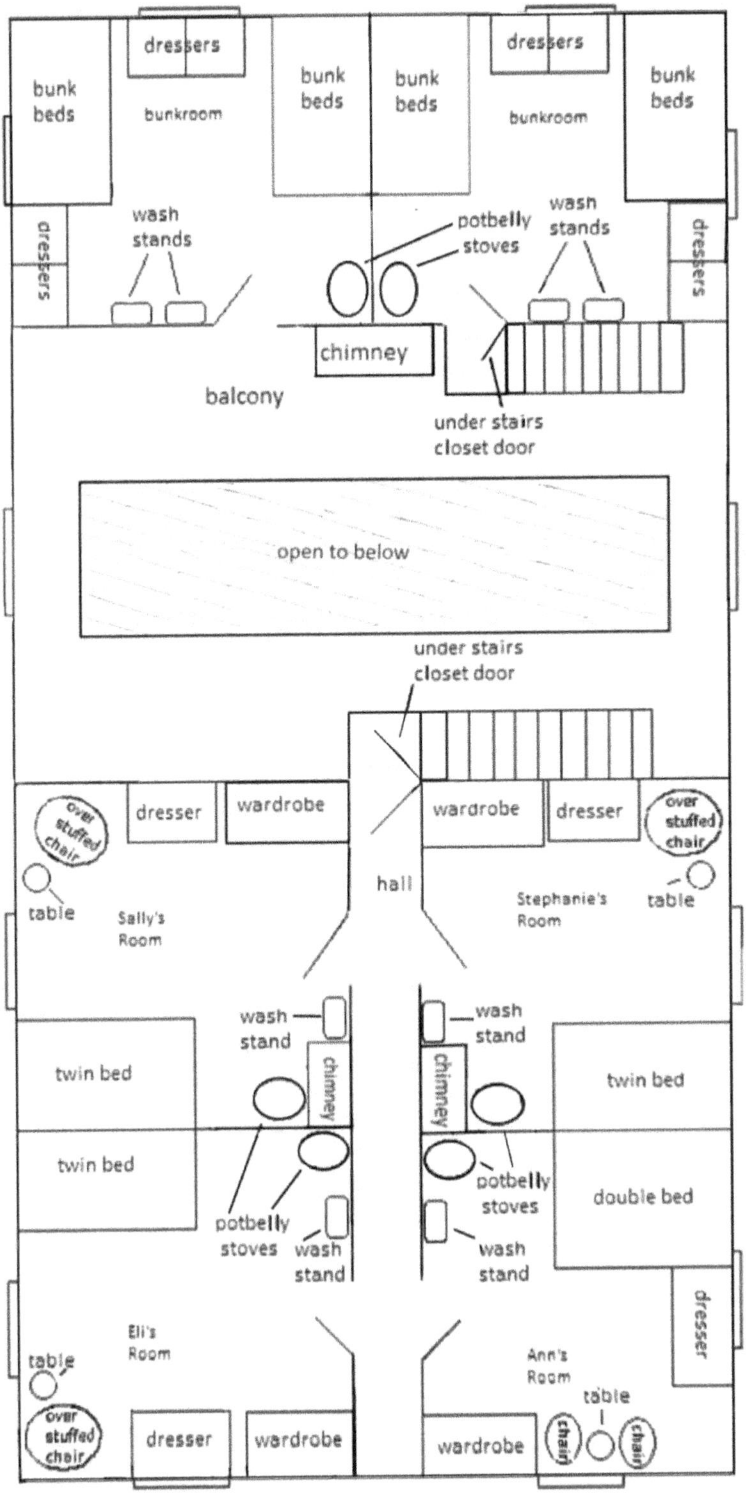

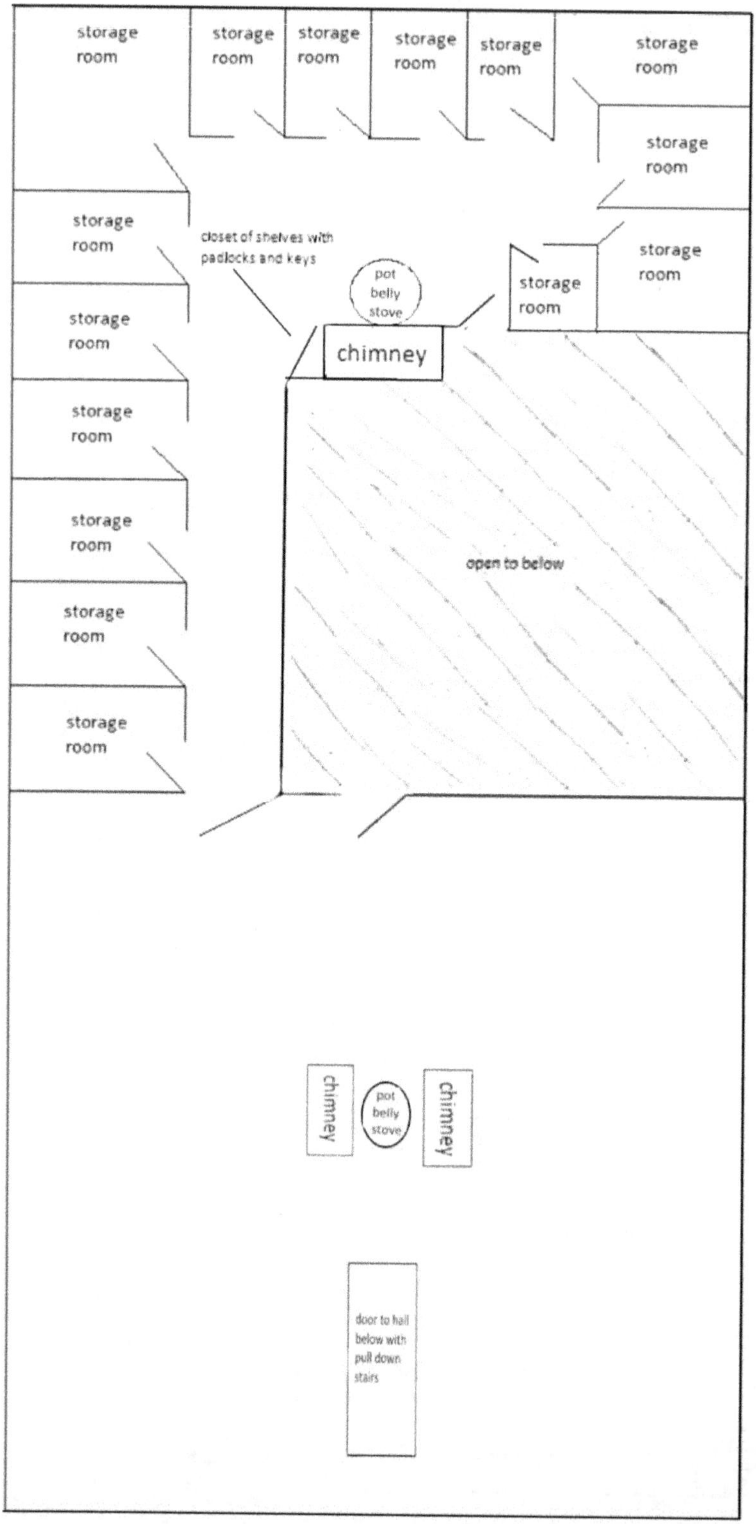

Third Floor - Woods (⇧)

ONE

"Get the rifles! Lock the shutters!" Sally's chair clattered across the floor.

Her sister threw open the glass windows. "What's happening?!"

"They're going to kill us!" Tears streamed from Sally's eyes.

Ann pulled in the outer shutters. "Calm down! Who is it?"

"People!" Sally screamed.

The third sister, Stephanie, hurried to the rifles above the front door. "What people?"

"People. On horses. They have hats! They're men!" Sally grabbed the powder horn that hung beside the door. "It's going to be a horrible death!"

Stephanie placed a rifle in her sister's hand. "Check the powder in the pan." She stretched up for the other gun.

"You're overreaching. Not every stranger

is a killer." Ann slammed the thick iron bar into the latch that secured the heavy wooden boards. She hurried to the fireplace and scooped the brass telescope from the mantel. "Sally, get the shutters in the kitchen and dining room. Stephanie, close the rest."

Concealed at the side of the front window, Ann peered at the approaching riders. "Don't close the front shutters. I'm going to take a chance."

Sally poured powder into the rifle pan. "Are you out of your mind?!"

"Two men are riding double with saddles strapped to their backs. I think I can sell them horses."

"No! I love our horses." Sally handed Stephanie the powder horn.

Ann spoke calmly. "Would you rather have the horses or money to buy food?"

Stephanie looked into her sister's teary eyes. "I had to tighten my belt another notch this morning. If we don't get more food soon, death by starvation is sure. Besides, you know we don't have enough hay to feed all three horses until the grass comes up. Probably these men only want to buy horses and not to hurt us." Stephanie hurried off to secure the shutters anyway.

As the oldest, Ann felt it was her responsibility to protect her sisters. She decided there wasn't any reason to make it easy for the men to get at them, and the strangers were too far off to see what they were doing. She hurried to the far end of the house and locked all the shutters, even the one at the front. She took another look from her post by the one open ground-level window. "They're almost here. Both of you go up and stand on the balcony. If any of them tries to get in the door, shoot them!"

As the men drew near, Ann watched their lips through the telescope. She whispered the words of a man riding double. "I heard there's just girls here 'cause their folks died. Why don't we have some fun with 'em?"

The man on the lead horse replied, "If you get off your horse or say even one word, you'll answer to me."

The rider, with the man wanting to do as Sally had feared, warned, "Shut your bone box! Don't cross Hank. The other one will come out."

Hank dismounted at the foot of the few steps up to the porch. Everybody else stayed where he sat. Boots clomped across the veranda. The butt of a gun rapped on the door twice before the man slid the weapon back into its holster.

Behind the stone wall, Ann stood to the side of the door and waited the amount of time she thought it would have taken her to walk over from her rocking chair. She drew a deep breath, put a smile on her face, and then opened the door.

"Howdy, ma'am. As you can see, my men and I have a right strong need for horses. Do you have two you would sell us? I'll pay you handsomely."

Sally drew a bead on the left eye under the hat. Across the balcony, Stephanie set her rifle to take out the other.

Get as much as you can. "We need all our horses here on the farm," said Ann.

"I'd pay you enough for three." The man stepped closer to the door.

Sally squeezed the set trigger of her rifle. She shifted her finger to the firing position.

"It wouldn't make any sense to sell ours. We'd have to go all the way to Fort Smith to get more. You go there and buy some."

One foot of the tall, handsome man stepped away as he twisted to the side and swept his hand toward his men and horses. "I'll pay you twice their worth. Our horses are plumb worn out from carrying two of us and our saddles."

"Mine are very strong."

"Well, then I'll give you fifty for each."

"Not our draft horse. I'll sell you the other two." Ann held out a hand. "In gold or silver coins."

"Much obliged!" The man counted out gold coins.

"I'll put this on the table." Ann signaled her sisters to go to the window. "Wait here. I'll get them." Completely exposed, Ann stepped out the front door.

Upstairs, her sisters kept their rifles ready. Stephanie whispered, "You see the man with the sneer on his face? The one on the palomino?"

Sally answered, "Yes," so softly Stephanie barely heard.

"If we have to, take him out first."

A minute later, Ann led two strong farm animals out of the barn. A tear fell from her eye. "Treat them well." She didn't want to see the horses she loved leave her life, and the look in the eyes of the man with the round face, the one who had wanted to have 'some fun' with her and her sisters, sent shivers of fear up Ann's spine. She hurried to the house. Once inside, she quickly dropped the heavy iron to bar the door.

TWO

Hoping to set into motion a path to a better future, the two younger sisters climbed into the driver's box of their farm wagon. The wagon creaked as their remaining horse pulled them out of the barn. The air, cooled by the blobs of snow that lay on the grassy land, as well as life without two of their horses, felt chilly to the sisters. Lost in their thoughts and concerns about the future, the girls traveled four miles to the small town of Harmony, Arkansas.

All three sisters knew it wasn't likely that they would be able to achieve what five people had barely accomplished. They also knew they had to pull themselves together and try if they were to have any chance of making it.

In the early spring of 1839, Stephanie halted their horse in the dirt road between two short rows of homes and business establishments. She and Sally stepped onto the raised wooden boardwalk in front of Yates Mercantile. The bell on the door jingled as the girls entered the store that smelled of bacon.

Dusting boxes of bullets, the store owner, Tom Yates, stood behind the long counter on the left side of the room. Bolts of cloth, neat piles of premade clothes, boots, and hats sat on the shelves behind him. Stacks of paper, boxes of pencils, jars of canned fruit and vegetables, all kinds of tools, and just about anything else you could ever want, filled the store. Barrels of pickles and lard, along with sacks of grains, sat on the floor beside the barrels of bacon. Very little of it was going home with the two sisters. The shopkeeper turned toward the sisters. "Welcome."

"Hello, Mr. Yates. We've come to buy supplies." Stephanie handed the man the list of items she and her sisters had meticulously calculated to be the best choices to get them on the road to survival.

A different person might not have noticed anything wrong, but Mr. Yates had known the girls all their lives. They were late for their usual spring visit. He had been worried that they hadn't survived the harsh winter on their own.

Stephanie picked up a fifty-pound bag of flour. Mr. Yates saw the outline of her shoulder bones through her shirt. He feared that she had lost too much weight to carry the heavy sack. Before he could say, 'let me get that,' she went out the door. Mr. Yates hollered to his son. "Eli, come in here."

Eli turned the outside corner of the store. *Stephanie is here. I'm so glad she's all right.* If the oldest sister had walked out of the store in front of Eli, he wouldn't have known whether or not the girls had made it through the winter. Ann hadn't been in Harmony since she was a child of ten. That was nine years ago. He had no idea what Ann looked like now, and it wasn't likely that he would spot a family resemblance. In his opinion, the two sisters he did know didn't look alike.

Stephanie was tall with crystal blue eyes and straight blond hair cascading down to the small of her back. A delicate nose and slightly plump lips adorned her oval face.

Sally's mane of chestnut waves framed her heart-shaped face and bounced down below her shoulders. She looked at the world through hazel eyes flecked with gold, green, and brown. Her full rosy lips matched the shape of her face. However, the girls did have a few characteristics in common. Long days of hard work had made them muscular, and the last exceptionally difficult year had left them both much too thin.

Eli hoped some of what had transpired the last time Stephanie had been in town would not happen today.

***

It had been after a heavy rain. Horses had

stomped the dirt street into a pit of mud. Stephanie had been carrying flour on her shoulder that day too. Instead of looking where she was going, she had been looking at him. As she stepped off the boardwalk, she had lost her footing and done a belly-flop into the mud. Eli had rushed over and held out his hand to help her out of the mire.

Embarrassed and flustered, she had slapped his hand away. "I don't need any help." She had gotten herself up from the mud and then hollered at her sister. "Sally, get in the wagon, now!" Stephanie had grabbed the flour sack from the mud while Sally climbed in as fast as she could. As they had ridden away, Stephanie's eyes had filled with tears. She had felt like such a fool falling into the mud and had done so right in front of Eli, of all people.

Just outside of town, Sally had realized that they had forgotten something. "Stephanie, did you pay Mr. Yates?"

"Oh no, I didn't! I can't go back there.

Sally, take him the money for me. I'm sorry I yelled at you. Please?"

"I think you should go and apologize to Eli. He was only trying to help you."

"But he saw me looking at him when I fell into the mud. He doesn't even know I exist, and now he's sure to think I'm an idiot."

"Of course he knows you exist. He's been putting supplies into our cart for years."

Tears had cut channels through the mud on Stephanie's face as she held out the money to her sister. "You know what I mean. He thinks I'm a little girl, and now he thinks I'm one who can't even walk. I'm begging. Please take it."

Stephanie had such a pitiful look in her teary eyes that Sally had consented. "I'll do it, but I still think you should apologize. Besides, he can't possibly think you're a little girl. He's seventeen, just like you."

Eli had stood on the porch of his father's store as Stephanie sat in the wagon with her head hung down. Even though he had only been looking at her back, he could see that she was crying. Until then, Eli hadn't considered Stephanie as anything other than one of the Williams girls. That day, however, Eli had seen Stephanie watching him. It was the day he had started wondering about her.

Sally had run into the store, paid Mr. Yates, and gone back out. Eli stopped her. "Come over here." Sally walked the few steps to where Eli looked down the street at Stephanie. "Tell her that I just tripped over a sack I had only a second before put on the ground."

"I'll tell her." When she returned to the wagon, Sally passed on Eli's message. Stephanie turned and waved. Eli waved back before the girls went off. "I think Eli is a very nice person to say that to you."

"Me too, and I think he's very handsome. Did you see the muscles in his arms?"

"I think you're in love."

"I am not in love! I just think he's very nice-looking."

***

That had happened the previous fall. On this spring day, Eli entered the store shortly after Stephanie. Instead of her looking at him, he watched her gather items from the shelves as he crossed the room to his father. Her beautiful golden hair and shapely, but very slender, body captivated him. Even in trousers and a blouse, she was the most beautiful girl he had ever seen. "What do you need, Pop?"

"Load two sacks of seed corn in the wagon out front."

Stephanie reached for a jar of canned peaches on a high shelf. Eli stopped in his tracks. "Hello, Stephanie. May I help you with that?"

"Yes, and I appreciate you being kind last year when I fell off the porch."

Eli stood beside Stephanie. Only inches away, his dark brown eyes looked into her light blue eyes. So close to her face, he saw how truly beautiful she was. His heart pounded. "How many?"

"Ann said I may have one jar." Stephanie

blushed and looked at the floor as she took the peaches. "Thank you, Eli."

"You're welcome." Eli went out the back door with his mind racing. Other than Stephanie, he had never seen a girl able to sling a fifty-pound sack of flour onto her shoulder. The doctor's daughter, Laura, who lived in town, was also their age. He had tried to have a conversation with her once. Laura had said that she had more important things to do than talk to a store boy. She and Eli had lived in the same town all their lives. He thought it was ridiculous for her to believe she was any better than anybody else. In his opinion, they were all just people.

Stephanie wasn't like that. She was always friendly, and in a few minutes, she was going to ride away. Eli saw how much the girls needed help when he noticed that he could see the shape of Stephanie's hip bones through her trousers. He picked up two dusty hundred-pound bags of corn and took them to the wagon.

Stephanie stood in the wagon, packing their other supplies as Sally handed them to her.

"Could you girls use any help at the farm? I know it must be hard getting everything done."

A smile lit Stephanie's face at the thought of having Eli at the farm. "It's not up to us. Ann is the one who would decide, but come and ask her."

"Don't go anywhere. I'll be right back." Eli hurried back into the store. "Pop, I think I need to make a living on my own someday. Don't you?"

Not knowing what his son had in mind, Mr. Yates replied, "Of course, son."

"Why not now? I know this is sudden, but I want to help the Williams girls. You know they need the help. I can go out there now and ask Ann."

"I always knew this day would come. I had hoped it would be much later. I won't try to stop you, but you better visit me every chance you get." Mr. Yates hugged his son tightly. "Go get your things, so you'll be ready to work when Ann hires you."

"I won't be far away, and I'll visit as much as I can. I'm going to miss you." Eli went to his room and packed his few personal belongings and all the clothes he owned. He went back into the store and hugged his father again. "I love you, Pop." He wiped the moisture from his eye, went out the door, and threw his bag into the cart. "All right, girls. Let's go."

THREE

In the farmhouse, Ann took a pan of cornbread from the oven. She placed it on the counter beside the wood cooking stove and thought about their dire situation. *We've got long, hard days coming up trying to plant corn with only one horse, us three girls, and very little food. I doubt we can do it. It's probably going to be a slow death as we have fewer and fewer resources and less ability to create more.*

Ann shuddered, walked to the far corner of the kitchen, put a log on the fire, and then went through the door into the living room. She sat in her mother's rocking chair. *I miss you, Papa. How did you and Mama get influenza anyway? I don't want everything to be my responsibility. Sure, I got us through a whole year, but I'm not doing a good job, and it's your fault, Papa. You're the one who said, "Don't trade the cow to the doctor." If only I hadn't listened to you and had gone sooner. There must have been something I could have done, and you'd still be here. You always knew what to do. I don't. Now, we're starving.*

I should have bucked up and done something last spring after you died, but all I did was lay around and cry. Papa, if I give up the farm, what would we do instead? Where could we go? I don't know how to find your family back east.

I wish you'd think we did a good job. All on our own, the three of us got in the volunteer corn God gave us, but we got that corn to market so late we didn't get much money. Even though I spent every penny on food and hay, we still don't have enough, so you think I did terrible, don't you?

Mama, I'm much obliged to you. You taught me how to cook and take care of the house. We ate and canned a lot of that corn and every pawpaw we could find in the woods. We gathered all the hickory nuts and black walnuts, just like you showed us. We've also been hunting. I know you didn't like it when Papa took us hunting and showed us how to use the rifles. If you're looking down from Heaven, you can see that Papa was right. I sure wish I could hear you say that you love me to the moon and back. I miss you both so much.

As she thought about their circumstances, Ann heard the sound of the returning wagon crossing the flat land in front of her home. She stepped onto the porch, looked across the meadow, and thought that early spring felt refreshing after the bleak, frigid winter they had spent missing their parents.

Not many days after they had sold the horses, Ann had sent her sisters to Harmony with the money from the sale and a list of what to buy. She hoped it would be enough to get them through the summer if supplemented with the vegetables she planned to plant and the wild game they could hunt.

Eli spotted the dot on the horizon that was their destination. As they approached, he could see a woman standing on the porch. She was the person who would decide if he would be staying or not. Drawing closer by the minute, he looked at her and contemplated his chances of getting the job.

Ann looked like a practical woman. Like her sisters, she wore a blouse, boots that could take a hard day's work, and her belt had a new hole punched through to keep her loose pants on her body. She was several inches over five feet with long, loosely curled, almost-black hair. Her hair was tied back in a ponytail, but small soft curls escaped and framed her face. Mostly, he noticed that her green eyes looked like emeralds.

Ann saw a third individual sitting in the wagon with her sisters. "Why is this person with you?"

Stephanie replied, "Well, you know, I was thinking, there's a lot of work to get done, and maybe we can use the help. Eli is willing if you think we can hire him."

The young man quickly jumped off the wagon and reached up to help Stephanie down.

Ann knew almost nothing about the people who lived in Harmony. She did at least remember that Eli was the store owner's son. She wanted to know not only what Eli would say but also how he would act. "What do you have to say about this, Eli?"

Eli stood calmly in front of Ann and looked squarely into her eyes. "I'll work hard. I'm strong, and I can work all day. Pop and I have known your family ever since I can remember. Pop always thought so much of your folks. We hate that you have to work so hard, and Pop can run the store without me."

Ann wondered about Eli's expectations. "You do know that we won't be able to pay you?"

"Yes," was all Eli could think to say. During the hours they had ridden together to the farm, he had been thrilled to be with the girls. They had talked about everything under the sun, except that particular fact, which he did know but hadn't thought about.

Ann stood silently on the wide porch as the tension mounted. She noticed the way Stephanie looked at her with pleading eyes. The fact that her sister had obviously enjoyed Eli helping her off the wagon entered Ann's mind. She wasn't sure if she should be happy or alarmed. Sally stood on the wagon behind them and waved her hands as if to shoo them into the house. Ann finally spoke. "Sally, bring the wagon to the kitchen door. Eli, since you're here, you might as well eat with us. Help get everything inside."

Ann rounded the right corner of the porch and continued to the kitchen door. Sally drove the wagon over. Stephanie and Eli walked across the front yard.

Stephanie whispered as Ann passed to get supplies, "Thank you."

"Don't thank me yet."

Stephanie told Eli, "Grab a load and follow me."

Eli followed Stephanie through the door directly into the kitchen. He didn't know what was cooking on the big cast-iron stove to the right of the door, but an appetizing aroma filled the room. He suddenly felt hungry. "Something smells delicious."

Along the same wall as the stove, a long counter ran to the end of the room. Light streamed through a big window on the back side of the house, and a washbasin filled a hole cut through the counter. To Eli's left, as he entered, a short wall ran about six feet and then turned away farther to the left. Straight across the room, Eli could see through an open door. A short counter filled the space from the door to the fireplace in the left corner, where a fire burned to drive off the chill in the air.

Stephanie placed her items on the butcher's table in the middle of the room. "Eli, put yours here."

He turned left, placed his packages on the table, and looked through another open door.

Across the adjoining room, he saw another large window letting in the sunlight that gleamed off the big, black-walnut table and the matching chairs surrounding it. He wondered why they had so many chairs for their small family. He turned to get another load and saw that the short wall he had passed coming in was the side of the small room that was their pantry. He helped get the supplies as Ann put them into the pantry.

Because their mother had always sung *Amazing Grace* when she had put away their supplies, Sally sang it as they worked. Many years before, Sally had asked her mother why. Her mother had told her it was because they should be grateful that God had again supplied them with what they needed. When all the supplies were in, Ann told Stephanie what she wanted her to do next. "Show Eli where to put the seeds, then put up Samson and the wagon. I'll get supper on the table."

"Come on, Eli." Stephanie led Eli away. Ann noticed the smile on Stephanie's face that had been missing since their mother had taken her last breath.

Sally started to follow them. Ann stopped her. "Sally, will you set the table, please?"

"Sure." Sally sashayed to the china cabinet in the corner of the dining room. She always insisted that they eat together like a proper family. Sally loved to set the table. Even though she was sad to set out two fewer plates, Sally still enjoyed it. This day, Ann heard happy humming. She turned and watched her sister. Sally practically danced around the table to set the plates, then the napkins, silverware, and glasses. Ann's heart lifted. Both her sisters were happy. It didn't take a genius to understand why. She decided Eli would be staying.

FOUR

Eli helped Stephanie onto the wagon and got on with her. Stephanie's quick flick of the reins set Samson in motion. The horse knew food, water, and rest waited in the barn. He headed that way as soon as he got the signal to go. Stephanie stopped next to the stall they had cleared out the day before. So Eli could help her get down, she got off the wagon on the side where he stood. "Put the corn in this stall. I'll unharness Samson."

As soon as Stephanie took the harness off, Samson went to his stall. She followed the horse with a big pitchfork full of hay. "Eli, we need to draw water. Did you notice the well we passed?"

"Sure did. Where is the bucket?"

"The buckets are hanging on the pole just

to the right of the door. Fill them both. Give the chickens water first then give the rest to Samson."

Eli wanted to be a good worker for two reasons. His father had taught him always to do his best, and he wanted the girls to see him as valuable and hire him. He put the two sacks of seed into the stall, picked up the buckets, and walked to the well. Stephanie gave the chickens some of the cracked corn she had bought, put the rest away, and then went into Samson's stall. Samson loved the care he received. Stephanie loved everything about the horse: his strength, his smell, the way his sorrel-colored hair gleamed, and the way he nuzzled her as she brushed him.

Eli connected the bucket pole to the rope at the well and lowered both buckets simultaneously. He let the rope out a long way before he heard the splash. The double pulley over the well made retrieving two full buckets easy. He unhooked the bar from the rope and carried the buckets to the barn across his shoulders. He poured fresh water for the chickens and the horse. "If you have another brush, I'll help you."

"I would love for you to help. The tack room is the last stall." Stephanie was glad Eli wanted to help. Taking care of the horse would help them bond, and she wanted them to like each other. Eli returned quickly with a brush in his hand. He slipped up to Samson beside Stephanie. The horse usually didn't take to new people quickly, but Samson was familiar with Eli and welcomed his attention. "He's beautiful, isn't he?" Stephanie gently brushed the giant horse.

"He sure is. I've thought so every time you came to the store. We used to load so much on the wagon I was sure he would die pulling it home, but he was always there the next time you came."

"That's why we call him Samson. When we were little, Papa read us the story of Samson. Since Ann worked with the horse pulling, plowing, and carrying, she knew how strong he was. She asked if Samson was as powerful as our draft horse. Papa said the Samson of the Bible would have been much more powerful. I said we should call our horse Samson anyway. We all agreed, and that's how he became Samson."

"I never heard the story of Samson."

"Haven't you read it in the Bible?"

"No, Pop put ours up when my mother died."

"Do you remember your mother?"

"Not much. I was only five when she passed. It's strange; even though I don't remember much about her, I still miss her."

"It's not strange. I know just how you feel. Nobody can take the place of your own mother."

In silence, they brushed Samson, both thinking of their missing mothers and taking comfort in being together, knowing that the other felt the same. After they completed their task, they put up the brushes and walked across the open field to the house. Eli admired the beautiful fieldstone house. "It must have taken a long time to gather enough stones to build your house."

"We weren't here when my uncle built it. However, since the house is forty-eight feet long, twenty-four feet wide, and twenty-four feet high, I'm sure it must have taken a long time. The sad part is, even after they used all those stones to build the house, the ground is still full of rocks."

"What happened to your uncle? How did your family come to be living here?"

"Papa said Uncle James sent a letter to his parents that said he was leaving with his wife, so if anybody from the family came west, he would give them his land and house."

"This is a great place. Why on earth did your uncle want to leave?"

"I was told that it all started when Uncle James married an Indian woman. At first, it wasn't a problem. Then more and more white people came who didn't want Indians or their children around. They got the government to force them to move to Indian Territory. My uncle didn't have to go, but his wife did. When Uncle James wrote to his folks, he said that nothing was wrong with his wife or any of the rest of the Indians and that no piece of land was worth his family.

"Papa told us that none of his brothers' wives wanted to come out here, so he went to Mama and told her that he could own a hundred acres of land and a house out west if he would live on the farm. Papa held her hand, told her that he loved her with all his heart, and asked her to marry him. He told her he would try his very best to make her happy if she would go with him. Mama said 'Yes,' so they got married, packed up, and came here."

Stephanie finished the story as they stepped onto the porch at the west end of the house. They entered the house into a twelve-foot-deep room that spanned from the front to the back of the house. Three large windows flooded the room with light. Except for the wall directly across the room where a fireplace stood between two doors that opened into the rest of the house, a workbench as deep as a person's arm ran around the room. An old harness and a broken chair lay on top of the workbench. Packed under the workbench were containers and materials. Eli glanced over the tools that hung on the walls and perused the repair materials on the shelves below. *I'll look more thoroughly if I got the job.* "This looks like a great place to work."

Stephanie walked to a washbasin fitted into a dropped-down section of the workbench under the window on the backside of the house. She poured half a pitcher of water into the basin and picked up a neatly folded cloth. After she washed the dirt from her face, arms, and hands, she reached into the pool of water and pulled the cork plug out of the hole in the bottom. "Give me one of those towels, please."

Eli handed her a towel and watched the water drain from the basin. "Where is it going?"

"It goes out a wooden pipe, down the incline, and then out behind the pines." Stephanie stuck the plug back in and poured the remaining water into the basin before she handed Eli the washcloth.

"Pretty smart. How did your uncle think of that?"

"I don't know. James was gone before we were born, but he left us an instruction book. It says to use only water and never to empty a chamber pot in it. It sure would be nice if we could. I hate carrying that to the Johnny house, especially in the winter."

"Fascinating." Eli pulled the plug and again watched the water leave the basin.

They walked out of the workroom into the main entry hall. To Eli's right was the front entry door where Ann had stood when he arrived. Above him, the ceiling continued for three feet, then opened all the way to the roof for five feet before the ceiling resumed. To their left, stairs led up through the opening to the second floor. At the second floor, a balcony encircled the open space between the first and second floors. A person could take the balcony walkway to the left to the two bunkrooms above the workroom or follow the walkway on the right to the door into the hall between the family bedrooms over the house's main living area.

Beyond the entry hall, in the sitting room, four furniture arrangements lent themselves to separate gatherings and looked inviting. Eli walked with Stephanie across the room. As in the workroom, two doors stood on either side of a large fireplace in the center of the far wall. He noticed that the fireplace opened not only into the living room but also at the back left and right corners. "What's going on with the fireplace?"

"Come over and look. It opens into all three rooms so one fire can warm them all. The chimney flues go up through the second floor into the attic and then out the roof. We have wood stoves in the bedrooms above that connect to the chimney, and there are vents in the floors of each bedroom, so the heat from down here can rise into our rooms."

Through the fireplace, Eli heard Sally humming in the dining room and Ann working in the kitchen. Being careful not to get his hair into the small fire, Eli held onto the walnut mantel, bent over, and looked into the fire pit. He could see through the fireplace into the kitchen on the left and the dining room on the right. As Eli and Stephanie walked into the dining room, Stephanie called out, "We're back."

Eli looked at the table with lovely dishes, "How nice."

Sally beamed with pleasure that Eli appreciated something important to her.

Ann carried in a steaming pie. "Sally, where do you want people to sit?"

"Ann, you sit at the end, Stephanie next to

you in front of the fire, Eli next, and I'll sit here closest to the kitchen."

Eli could almost taste the smell. "Sure smells good."

"It's squirrel pie." As well as anybody can cut up a slightly runny pie, Ann cut the pie into four pieces. She scooped one part onto her plate before she passed the pie to Stephanie. Ann took a bit of cornbread to sop up the gravy, swimming with chunks of squirrel meat. Next, because she didn't want to overpower the flavor of the stewed apples, she spooned her small portion into a separate bowl and then passed the fruit.

Eli's father had taught him to watch the host and follow suit. He took food just as Ann and Stephanie had, then put the food next to Sally's plate. Sally poured steaming sassafras tea into their cups before taking the last portion of squirrel pie and stewed fruit.

Eli had always eaten domesticated animals. Even though it smelled good, he didn't feel very hopeful about the flavor of squirrels. He cautiously tried a bite. The gravy had a nice flavor of sage from the herb garden and was quite good. The cornbread was dry, just like when his father made it, but it was fine once he covered it with the gravy. He saved the fruit until he saw Sally add crystallized maple sugar.

Sally sat the sugar bowl on the table beside Eli. "This is from two years ago. It's all we have left. We need to make more. Don't we, Ann?" Sally tried to point out why they needed Eli.

Stephanie didn't know Ann had already made up her mind and only needed to discuss the details with Eli. "She's right, and we need to dig up more sassafras roots."

"I guess we should tap the maples soon. We have a harness that needs repairs, a chair that needs to be fixed, and we always need to chop wood. I noticed that the house needs repointing on the west side. Sometimes, the wind blows the dust so fiercely that it grinds out the mortar between the stones. Eli, what can you do about any of that?"

"I'm good at fixing harnesses, bridles, and pretty much anything leather. I'm sure I can also repair the chair. I can't even tell you how much wood I've chopped. You'd have to show me how to tap maple trees and repoint the wall, but I learn quickly, and I'll work hard." The two younger girls looked at Ann with hopeful eyes as she quietly contemplated her decision.

"Girls, help me take the dishes into the kitchen. Eli, would you excuse us for a minute? Also, would you put the teapot on the hanger in the fireplace?" Ann picked up the empty plate and pie pan in front of her. Sally and Stephanie picked up the other dishes except for the cups and saucers. Sally pushed the cork stopper into the hole before they placed the dishes into the washbasin.

"I know we can use the help, and I see that Eli is a nice young man, but we don't have any money. All we have to offer until after the harvest is a room and food, and you know how little food we have. We would have to divide it by four. We'd have to find a way to get more. When we sell the corn, we couldn't pay much."

As if they had any excess food, Stephanie tried to get her sister to see that it could work. "I don't mind eating less, and we're going to hunt anyway."

Sally stated what was in her heart. "We aren't strong enough to do everything. We need to have a man around. You know Eli would be a gift from God. Besides, God took Papa and Mama. He owes us. We should have somebody back."

Ann gently rebuked her. "God doesn't explain why He allows these things to happen. He doesn't owe us anything, but we do owe Him everything."

Sally stuck to her opinion emphatically, "He does too owe us!"

Stephanie added passionately, "And you should hire Eli!"

Ann knew they couldn't divide their food with another person, but God had gotten them through a whole year when they hadn't had enough. It was unlikely they could accomplish everything on their own, so she decided that God would make hiring Eli work. "Girls, I already thought we should. I want to be sure you understand the situation."

"You were?!" Stephanie put down the kettle of hot water she had poured into the basin and hugged Ann.

They went into the dining room, where Eli stirred the coals in the fire pit. Even with the door closed, he had heard everything. Eli was sure he could have heard from the living room as well. He hadn't known what to do, but since the sun was down and the coldness of night had set in, he had poked at the fire.

The pot of sassafras tea was hot again. Ann refilled their cups, put some crystallized maple in hers, and offered the spoon to Eli. "When you get yours fixed like you want it, come into the sitting room." Ann walked away. She didn't sit in her favorite rocking chair. Instead, she sat at the end of the long sofa facing the fire.

Usually, Stephanie went along with Ann's plans. She believed her sister never did anything out of spite but made her decisions with love after careful consideration. Right now, however, Stephanie wanted Eli and Ann to know that he was a member of the group and not an intruder. She thought about where she should sit to ease the tension of the situation and then sat at the other end of the sofa. Stephanie motioned for Eli to sit between her and Ann. She glanced at Ann to be sure her sister noticed that she would not let her make Eli feel uncomfortable.

Ann wasn't trying to exclude Eli. She was trying to gauge the extent of Stephanie's concern and engagement with the welfare of their guest. Eli filled in the last spot on the sofa. Oblivious to the maneuvering that had taken place, Sally plopped herself down in the overstuffed chair at the other side of the fireplace.

"Eli," Ann turned slightly to face him, "I appreciate your concern. I don't know if we can succeed on our own, but we might with your help. However, please don't feel obligated because we can't offer you much. Until we bring in the harvest, all we can give you is a room and food, and we'll have to hunt to get enough food for all four of us. Then, we'll pay you ten dollars a month for the time you have helped us." She waited for Eli's reply.

"That's a fair offer. I want to add one request. Once a month, I want to take two days to visit my father. I would gladly pick up or take anything when I go and conduct business for you in town."

Ann asked for the opinion of her sisters, "Well, girls, what do you say?"

"Deal," Sally firmly agreed.

"Deal," Stephanie smiled.

"Well, Mr. Eli Yates, I think we have hired you." Ann and Eli shook hands to ratify the agreement.

FIVE

The following morning, Ann assigned Eli his first task. "Fill up the water barrel in the kitchen." Eli dumped the second round of buckets into the empty fifty-gallon wooden barrel. It still looked empty. He realized that it was going to take many trips. He appreciated the two-bucket system even more. Sally drew water for the horse and the chickens with the other set of buckets. Before she gathered the eggs, Sally gave Samson hay, and the chickens cracked corn. Also in the barn, Ann loaded equipment into the wagon.

In the house, Stephanie cut a loaf of bread into eight thick slices. She placed one on each of four plates and then poured the hot grease from the bacon on them. After she covered the slices, Stephanie went to the china cabinet and got a glass. She used it to cut a circle out of the center of the other four slices. She plopped them into the pan she had used to cook the bacon.

Sally came into the kitchen and set eggs beside the stove before she went into the pantry. When she came out, Sally set a picnic basket beside the grease-soaked bread they needed to supplement their lean wild meat diet. She put the greasy bread slices into the bread pan, covered the pan with the napkin, and tied a string around it. She placed the pan in the basket beside another napkin filled with four handfuls of dried apple slices.

Sally wiped up the precious drops of grease still on the plate and sucked it off her finger while Stephanie cracked eggs into the holes in the bread.

When Eli finally filled the water barrel, the wagon was ready for the day's excursion. The small mid-day meal was packed. Stephanie set eggs cooked in slices of freshly baked bread, fried bacon, and hot sassafras tea on the table.

After breakfast, they rode north through the forest of oak and hickory trees toward the bare stone cliffs of the Boston Mountains. High in the sky, a small formation of Canada geese honked their encouragement to the goose leading the way. As they moved along, Samson's harness jingled, warned away, and prevented the squirrels and chipmunks from becoming pie.

Stephanie brought the wagon to a halt. Ann picked up her primed rifle, cocked it, and pulled the set trigger. Overhead, the geese approached. Ann took aim but waited for a clear shot. As if suddenly aware of the danger below, the geese veered away. Ann fired. A bird plummeted from the sky.

Sally jumped off the wagon. "I hope we can find it. A goose to eat would be such a blessing." They tied Samson's reins to a tree and went in search of the supper that Ann had brought down from the sky. When they approached the area where they believed the goose had fallen, the growl of a cougar stopped them short.

Disappointedly, Stephanie whispered, "I guess we gave a cougar a meal."

"Why stop at the goose? I say, let's eat the cougar too." Eli held out his hand. "May I have the rifle?" Ann passed him the weapon. Eli got a wadding patch from the bag and popped it into his mouth. As he chewed, he measured and loaded a fresh charge of powder into the barrel. He took the patch out of his mouth, wrapped it around the lead ball, and forced them down the barrel with the help of the ramrod. When the ball was in place, he reattached the rod to the ferrules of the rifle. "Since we want to be sure we have a dead cougar, not an angry one, we should clean out the touch hole. Do you have a vent pick?"

Ann fished the pick from the bag and handed it over. Eli cleaned the vent, put the primer powder in the pan, and closed the frizzen. With the rifle in the half-cocked position, he and the girls quietly crept forward until they saw the cougar observing the goose, actually geese. Ann's shot had only winged the bird. No longer able to fly, it had plunged to the earth. The fall had not killed the goose, so its mate stood guard.

Stephanie whispered, "Too bad we didn't bring both rifles. We could have gotten a cougar and two geese."

"I want to try. Get the wadding around the shot. Measure the powder and have it ready to load. Hold the ramrod." Eli cocked the rifle, aimed, pulled the set trigger, and then squeezed the firing trigger. Nothing happened. He knew what to do. His rifle had failed to fire before. It was what he had tried to prevent by cleaning out the touchhole. Eli kept the rifle pointed in the direction of the cougar. Thankfully, the cougar hadn't heard the click of the trigger and still crouched, observing the geese.

Suddenly, the rifle fired with a loud

report. The cougar dropped before it knew what had happened. The goose, however, flew off like a shot. Eli quickly reloaded. When the goose circled back toward its mate, he was ready again and fired through the trees. Unfortunately, he missed. The healthy goose decided to leave its dying mate to its fate, flew off, and didn't return. Eli gave the injured bird a quick death.

Stephanie made short work of gutting the bird, then stood with goose in hand and watched Eli remove cougar innards. Ann stood guard in case the cougar also had a mate. When they returned to the wagon, they loaded their take. Sally had never liked the bloodiness of hunting and commented on the lack of messiness as she looked at the carcasses in the wagon. "I'm glad they're not getting blood all over everything."

Stephanie remembered something. "Ann, do we have time to show Eli the cave?"

Eli thought going into a cave sounded exciting.

"What cave?" Sally asked.

Stephanie explained, "Many years ago, we went to the maple grove with our parents. We were too young to help much, so we played close by and discovered a cave. The light filtering in from the entrance only dimly lit the cavern, but we went in anyway.

Ann asked, "Stephanie, do you remember why we never went back?"

"Yes, but we were little then and didn't know it was there. We're older now, and we know what we're going to find, so it won't be a shock. Sally and Eli, do you like a mystery?"

Sally felt slightly concerned. "Why? What's in there?"

Eli replied, "I love a mystery. Let's discover as we go. Unless you think it would be a problem."

Ann didn't want to force Sally, but she encouraged her. "Nothing from the past has any effect on the present. Will you be comfortable with that?"

Sally wasn't sure, but she wanted to be brave. "I think so."

At the base of the cliffs of the Boston Mountains, they came to the stand of black maples nestled among the post oaks and shagbark hickory trees. At the higher elevation, it was much colder, but Ann had brought the needed clothing. She gave Eli her father's greatcoat and then passed out the other coats, mittens, and hats before they poked into the undergrowth at the base of the cliff.

Stephanie's stick didn't touch stone. "Here it is."

Ann called out, "Everybody, come to the wagon. I brought everything we need. Eli, use the machete to cut the brush away from the cave entrance. When the area is clear, hang one of the coils of rope across your chest. Stephanie, secure the end of the other rope to a tree just outside the entrance. Sally, light the lanterns."

Last, Ann tied the other end of Stephanie's

rope to herself and the others with enough slack between them to move independently for a short distance. They squeezed through a short crack into the mountain. The sides opened just beyond the narrow passage into a vast cavern, most of which was to their right. They walked down the bowl-shaped slope of the cave to the bottom not far below, held up the lanterns, and tried to determine the shape of the cave. They could barely make out that they stood inside a gargantuan hollow rock orb.

The small lake in the center of the cavern reflected the image of the deposited minerals that hung in waves from the ceiling like multicolored sheets rippling in the wind. In the distant past, when the water had dropped to its current level, colored minerals formed into a ledge of rock at the edge of the geode in which they stood. The ledge completely encircled the shallow lake. Stephanie saw a cave poles apart from the one she had experienced as a young child. "It's very different than I remember, but I couldn't see much back then. I didn't realize it was one big room."

Eli stood in awe. "The shell of this cave must have originally been one huge hollow bubble that cracked. It reminds me of an egg broken across the long way with the halves close but not quite fitting."

"An earthquake probably broke it." Stephanie had read how earthquakes broke and cracked the earth in a book her mother had brought west with them.

"That would do it." Eli walked to the crack to look at what resembled curly, thin, white worms. He touched one. "These are hard."

"What are they?" Stephanie walked over and examined the formation.

In case it was dangerous, Sally used the tip of her pointer finger and barely made quick contact with one. "Strange." She walked to the pool of water. Small, white fish darted here and there. She squatted down to look at one remaining close to the edge. "Come look at this fish. I can see its insides and bones right through its skin." They all went over and squatted beside her at the water's edge. She informed them of something else she had noticed about the creature. "It doesn't have eyes."

"It doesn't need them. Eyes wouldn't work down here in the dark." Eli stood up. "Let's go farther."

Ann authorized the exploration because she wanted to examine the place. "All right, we'll go until we're out of rope. Eli, lead on."

They walked along the mostly red-colored shelf of solidified calcite to a structure of red, orange, black, yellow, and white minerals. The stalactite growing from above had joined the stalagmite building up from below and formed a single thick column from floor to ceiling. Eli wrapped his arms around the column to keep out of the lake and held on tightly. His feet barely found space on the narrow path that remained.

Ann and Stephanie both took hold of Sally's hands to prevent her from following. As he disappeared behind the column, Eli let out a shriek. Not knowing what had happened, Sally screamed in reply. Stephanie and Ann laughed. Sally indignantly asked her sisters for an explanation, "What's going on?" She didn't wait for an answer. "Eli, are you all right?"

Eli regained his composure then answered with a slightly peeved tone. "I'm fine. I guess I did say I wanted to discover as we went."

Ann and Stephanie replied in unison, "Yes, you did!"

Stephanie wasn't entirely sure she wanted to revisit what was on the other side. "Is it as horrible as I remember?"

Curiosity set in. Sally stepped up to the tiny space Eli had navigated to the other side. "What is it?"

Eli thought about it. *Should I prepare Sally? She already knows it's something scary due to my response. I'd rather not give away the surprise.* "Come around and see, but be prepared."

Sally looked at Ann and then Stephanie. "Should I?"

Ann repeated what she had stated earlier, "It's from the past, and can't do anything now."

Sally wanted to see what was on the other side without actually going around. She clung to the column, inched forward, and looked down the path. "I don't see anything."

She turned her face and gasped in shock. Forced by an instinctive repulsion to the vicious humanoid carnivore that dripped saliva as if craving satisfaction for its hunger, her brain firmly issued the command to run for her life. Like her sister years before, she stepped backward. Her foot went into the water.

A second later, it registered that Eli bravely stood next to the creature's side. She more calmly focused on the being that dwelt on the back side of the column. The flesh had long before rotted away and left bare bones subject to the water that deposited its crystallized mineral cargo as it ran to the floor. In the same way that the cave had built the massive column they had just rounded, the water dripped from above and worked to encase a human's remains.

Ann went around next. Stephanie joined them last. Stephanie told the story from years before, making sure her voice sounded as scary as she could. "This is a true story. Ann and I were eight and seven when we found this gloomy cave. We crept along this barely visible path up to this very column that blocked our way, but we were determined to go on. Ann looked back at me and held my hand as we bravely and skillfully made it around. Since Ann wanted me safely away from the water, she moved me over to the wall to continue."

To add life to her story, Stephanie quickly grabbed Sally and Eli's arms and loudly declared, "Something grabbed me."

Sally, Eli, and even Ann jumped.

With desperation in her voice, Stephanie continued the story. "I saw what had tried to grab my arm. A skeleton stood up in the darkness. It gnashed its sharp teeth and tried to eat us alive. In a panic, I pulled back."

Demonstrating what had happened years before, Stephanie stepped back on the path. "My foot splashed into the pool, and I lost my footing." To increase the drama, she screamed, "Ahhh!"

Stephanie held out her hand. Ann took it with the appropriate look of concern and fear to accompany the story. "Ann caught my hand and narrowly saved me from drowning in the bottomless pool."

Stephanie let go of Ann's hand and furiously ran in place. "With the little-girl-eating skeleton inches behind us, we ran as fast as we could to the faint light that was the exit. We scrambled up the incline and darted out."

With her story finished, Stephanie stopped running in place and wiped her hand across her brow. In a calm voice, she commented on the event. "It was the scariest thing ever. I could barely sleep for months. The only time I was able to sleep was in bed with Ann."

"And I was glad to have you there. I think what you said earlier is right. He's not frightening at all."

Stephanie turned her eyes toward the subject of her story and pondered the mystery. "Look at the way it's standing. I wonder what happened to him."

"With its back to the wall holding out its arm like that, it looks like the person was trying to keep something away." Sally's brain was once again in a calm state. She stepped closer to examine the remains. "Look at its skull right here."

Stephanie was genuinely surprised. "That looks like a hole was bored into its head, and the bone started to grow back. I'd never have thought people back then would have had the knowledge to do that."

"Unless they were trying to kill the person." Ann took her turn up close. She held her hand under the cold liquid that dripped from above on its way into the man-made hole. The coldness made her shiver as she looked at the skull that still sat on top of its neck bones. Petrified tears clung to its large empty eye sockets, ran down its bony cheeks, then dripped off the lower edge of the top jaw making small but sharp stalactite teeth. Ann looked down. The lower jaw lay on its owner's skeletal feet.

Ann imagined the evil look that would have been on its face. After a second, she felt pity for a poor soul who took his last breath alone without a single person to comfort him. "Maybe, instead of trying to keep something away, he was trying to hold onto something."

Eli contemplated the mechanics of a dying person's body. "I'm surprised the skeleton is still standing. It seems like the person would have slumped down or fallen over when he died." They looked at its head tilted slightly forward as the body leaned against the column.

Ann had an idea. "Maybe its arm is out because it was resting on something that held him against the wall. His head leaned forward when he died, but his body was held in place by something heavy that eventually dissolved away."

"Like what?" Sally couldn't imagine anything.

"I guess there's no way to know." Ann moved away from the bones. "Whatever happened, it was a very, long time ago." Hoping they would continue along the stone ring around the pool, Eli already stood a few steps farther up the path.

Sally stepped away from the mysterious skeleton. "He must have been a Quapaw Indian." The four intruders left the skeleton to its solitary existence.

The rope skimmed across the water as they explored the path that curved around the pool. At the end of the first hundred-foot rope, they stopped to tie on the second. Sally examined what looked like milk poured over the path. She bent over to swipe her finger through what appeared to be a thick layer of white liquid. The shiny substance was solid, like the hard crystal threads at the entrance. "I could have sworn that was milk, but it's as solid as Eli's worms." She stood up. "I don't think there is anything in the world as beautiful as this cave."

"I agree." Ann looked toward the entrance.

Eli feared that she wanted to go back. "I think we can go all the way. If we can't, we can return this way."

They were close enough for the light from their lanterns to illuminate the back of the cave. Ann studied the path that rose before them. She couldn't determine the width of the high ledge almost perpendicular to the place where they stood. She thought about whether they should keep going or not. Eli obviously wanted to circle the whole cave.

Stephanie and Sally also seemed to be enjoying the excursion, and she was enjoying it immensely. She decided to continue. "It shouldn't take very long. Lead on."

Spectacular and strange formations continued to amaze them. Coming down from the ceiling, they saw hundreds of short to very long hollow tubes the size of the reeds growing by their creek. After accidentally breaking one of the very fragile tubes, they carefully avoided those that were long enough to be an obstacle.

The next time they stopped, Stephanie inspected a stalagmite flattened down smoothly at the top. "It looks like a fried egg laid out over here."

Somewhat farther along, Sally examined a different mineral growth. "This looks like spilled popcorn."

They were just about at the end of the second rope when Eli stopped. "We're out of line, but we've passed the farthest point. I think we're getting closer to the entrance."

Ann stepped to the front and looked

ahead. "The cave is much higher back here. It has to be over fifty feet to the ceiling."

Sally asked, "Is that a waterfall? It must be at least as wide. How can it be that I don't hear it?"

"It's not water. It's solid," replied Stephanie.

"Let's keep going." Ann assumed they would be able to get around, just as they had at the first obstacle. "I want to get close enough to see the colors. It'll be spectacular." They pressed forward up the incline.

At the waterfall, streams of ruby, black, gray, yellow, brown, orange, green, white, and a myriad of other colors mingled as they flowed toward the lake below. The beauty astounded them. Unfortunately, the rock over which the waterfall had formed completely blocked their way.

To their right, a thin translucent sheet of crystallized minerals hung in front of the cave wall like a tapestry. The water droplets that made the waterfall dripped onto their heads and splashed into the pool below the sheer drop-off to their left. Long before the pool below filled, those water drops had splashed on the cave floor and formed a mass of razor-sharp mineral deposits. Ann felt awed. "God is incredible to make a place like this!"

Eli stated his opinion, "I think it's the water that's making this place."

Ann chose not to argue about who or what was making the cavern. She held her lantern to the veil of solidified minerals. "I guess this is as far as we go."

Eli unhappily agreed. Stephanie, however, felt a tickle of moving air and thought, *maybe not.* "Do you feel that?"

Ann stepped closer to the cavern's wall to feel whatever her sister felt. "I do, but where is it coming from?"

"I think it's coming from behind this veil." The light from Stephanie's lantern passed through the thin sheet of colored minerals that hung from the ceiling. Water ran over it, dripped off the bottom edge, and grew the veil that had not gotten all the way to the ground but had stopped a few feet above the path. "It isn't solid at all. I can see space back there. I can go under and come up on the other side."

Ann gave her permission. "Don't go any farther than right on the other side."

"I promise I won't." Stephanie lay parallel to the bottom of the veil and rolled to the other side. "Hand me my lantern." She reached out. "I'm in a narrow space between the wall and the veil. I see the crack above that's letting the water in and the crack in the wall that we've seen all the way. It looks like it goes far into the mountain back here. It's much wider. Maybe a little higher than the lantern is tall." She held the light to the fissure just behind the waterfall. "It looks like we might be able to get through if we wiggle on our bellies."

Ann and Eli, both being very curious, together asked, "Can I get in there to look?"

"It will be tight." Stephanie squeezed to the back. They all gathered behind the veil and examined the opening. Eli, as he had from the second they had entered the cave, wanted to go forward. "It would be exciting to crawl through. If it does go all the way to the other side, it will be quicker."

Stephanie knew Eli wanted to go through the tiny hole in the mountain. "Let's go through. If Eli is willing, he could go first and find out if we can make it. If not, we'll go back the way we came."

"Do you want to?" Ann didn't want Eli to feel pressured into something he didn't want to do.

"Yes. I should be the only one tied to the rope, but you all need to keep a tight grip on it. If I get through, I'll tell you to come on. If you can hear me, answer back. If I don't hear you, I'll pull the rope twice if it's safe or three times to say don't come."

Ann wanted to be sure that Sally would feel comfortable. "We don't have to go. We can go back."

Sally informed Eli of her conditions, "If it's too hard or scary, you can't tell us to follow. You have to come back."

"I promise to honor your request." Eli crossed his heart.

Ann knew they still had a problem. "Since the rope will have gone through the tunnel, it won't be able to go with us the rest of the way."

"It isn't much farther. It looks safe. We can pull the rope back when we get to the entrance." Eli pressed for the option he wanted.

SIX

Ann untied the rope from her waist. Eli slid his lantern into the fissure and started in. There wasn't enough space to get up on his hands and knees to crawl, so he slid across the smooth downward surface on his stomach. The slope helped him move forward but made his lantern continually try to fall over. He managed to keep control of the lamp and made it to the far side, where he pulled himself into the open cave at the level of the pool. He stood up. It felt good to be back in what seemed like unlimited space after the restrictive tunnel. "I got all the way through. Come on."

Ann spoke into the crack, "We hear you." She turned toward her sisters. "Who wants to go next?"

Stephanie saw the concern on Sally's face.

To give Sally double assurance that it was safe, she offered to go next. Stephanie tied the rope around her waist. Ann verified that the knot was secure before she let her sister disappear into the tunnel's darkness. Stephanie kept close to the left wall and inched forward until she saw Eli's smiling face. Eli pulled her out of the fissure and held her against his body to ensure that she stood securely on her feet before he let her go. Then, to control the thoughts going through his mind, he very intently worked on the knots at her waist. Stephanie encouraged and warned her sisters. "It's fine, kind of fun like a slide, but it's a slope, and your lantern will try to fall over. Be sure to hold it tight."

Ann pulled the rope back. "You next, Sally. Are you sure? You and I can still go back."

"I'm not a baby. I'm capable of everything the others have already done. I'm going the same way that Stephanie went."

"I would never think you're a baby." Ann tied her youngest sister securely and double-checked the knots. She hugged Sally and then kissed her on the forehead.

Sally climbed in. She kept the lantern ahead but found it difficult to move forward and hold the light. After only a short time, Sally wanted to go back. She felt the mountain above her was about to collapse and crush her. The void to her right threatened to pull her into the abyss. Monsters hissed at her from the darkness.

Sally summoned her determination. Holding the lantern upright with her right hand, she pushed forward. She brought her right knee forward in the few inches of available space, rose on her left hand, and dragged herself along. Her mind screamed that she would never make it, and fear demanded that she give up and retreat. Time slowed. Only minutes after she had entered the tunnel, she felt as if she had been inside for an eternity.

She knew she couldn't possibly be going straight across but was instead making her way into the mountain. She felt to the left to assure herself that she was where she should be. There was no wall. Her mind accused her; *you crawled into the mountain!* Panicking, she shifted radically to feel farther over. Her lantern careened sideways, rolled into the emptiness to her right, and went out. Complete blackness engulfed her. No words, only hysterical shrieks ripped out of her body.

"Sally! What's happening?" Screaming was the only reply Ann heard. "I'm coming in! It's going to be all right!" She crawled in without tying on the rope.

"I'm coming." Eli started in from the other side. He tried to scramble up the slope but couldn't get traction on the smooth upward slope. For every few feet Eli moved forward, he slid back two. He barely made any progress. Neither he nor Ann could see any light from Sally's lantern. They definitely heard her.

Ann pulled herself recklessly into the

small space illuminated by her lantern. She tried to reassure her sister, "I'm coming. I'm coming! I'm almost there!" Ann knew she was nearing her sister because her panicked shrieks in the echoing tunnel grew shriller. She feared what she would find. "God, You already took Mama and Papa. Please, please, don't take Sally." Ann squirmed with the utmost speed.

Finally, she saw Sally. She didn't look injured. "I'm here. You're safe." Ann put her arm around her sister. "I'm here." Ann turned Sally's face to force her to look directly at her, but she didn't see any recognition in her sister's eyes. Not even a tiny corner of Sally's mind could hear Ann as terror overwhelmed her. Ann knew she needed to do something drastic. As well as she could in the tight space, Ann gave Sally a hard spank on her butt and demanded compliance in her best imitation of their mother's sternest voice. "Sally Williams! Stop that screaming right this instant!"

Sally's eyes focused. "Mama?"

"No. It's Ann."

"Ann, you're here!" Sally started sobbing.

"Yes. You're safe. It's going to be all right." Sally clung to her sister as Ann stroked her hair and silently thanked God. "I'm with Sally. We're safe."

Eli wanted to know if he should keep trying to get to them. "Do you need help?"

"I don't think so." Ann believed there was nothing to do but comfort her sister.

"I'm going to wait here before I back out." Eli had barely gotten anywhere. However, he didn't give up his progress in case he needed to get to them.

After a long time, Sally choked back her sobs. "I'm sorry, Ann. Thank you for coming to get me."

"Of course, I came to get you. I love you with all my heart. I will always come for you. Do you hear me? I will always come for you, and I'm sorry I let us get into this in the first place. It was stupid of me. You had every right to be scared. There is no need to be sorry." Ann held her sister lovingly until she thought Sally was comforted enough. "Do you think you're ready to go the rest of the way?"

Sally begged, "Can't we just go back?"

"Eli, I can barely see the light of your lantern. How far are you from the end?"

"I was only able to get a little way. I'm very close to the end."

"Sally, it's shorter to go forward than back. It's only a little way, and I'm with you. You can do this."

Sally was still terrified and was sure she couldn't do it alone. "Promise you'll stay right beside me."

"I promise. There is no way I'm going to leave you."

Together, Ann and Sally made their way forward. Sally blamed Eli for what happened. When she saw him, she told him, "You lied to me! You said it was fun and easy."

Eli knew he had pressured the others to

go through the tunnel and felt guilty. "I'm sorry. I didn't have any problem. What happened?"

Ann vetoed discussion, "Leave it alone, Eli."

Eli backed to the exit and slid out. When Sally got there, he tried to help her out. She slapped his hand. "Get away from me!"

Stephanie had hated standing helplessly. The second Sally was out; she hugged her so tightly that Sally complained. "Stephanie, I can't breathe." Stephanie let her sister go and then untied her from the rope. Even though she knew it wasn't possible, Sally wanted the security of being tied together. "I guess we have to go on without the rope."

Trying to reassure her sister and herself, Ann said, "I think we'll be fine. I don't see anything but an easy path from here." Having not convinced herself that everything would be fine, she issued operating instructions for the rest of the journey, "Be careful. Everybody pay attention."

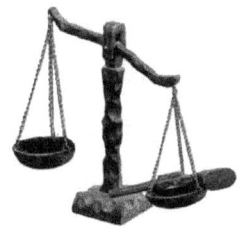

SEVEN

They continued along the path that once again rose from the cave floor. Even though they encountered more fabulous formations, Sally no longer saw anything good. They had almost circumnavigated the cave when they encountered a chasm.

Stephanie looked at Ann. "Now what?"

Sometimes, Ann just hated being responsible for everything. "Why do I have to come up with all the answers?"

Eli redirected the conversation back to the issue at hand. "It looks too wide, and we're much too high to jump."

Sally didn't need anybody's opinion about the gap ahead. She was not going to jump or let any of the others try it. "It's obviously too wide. The water didn't look deep. We should go back to the pool and wade across." Suddenly, she wondered if going into the water would be safe. "Do you think there's anything dangerous in the water?"

Eli looked over the edge. "From up here, it's hard to judge the depth, especially with the reflection from the ceiling. Stephanie, what happened when your foot went into the water when you were little?"

"Nothing, but we'll have to wade all the way across. We'll get much wetter, and the water will be icy cold."

Ann considered everything. "We should try wading. There's no way we can jump, and I don't want to spend all the time it would take to go back the way we came."

Sally sat in the path. "I'm not going into that tunnel. I'll sit here until I starve. I'm almost starved to death already, so it shouldn't take very long."

As if she had forgotten, Eli reminded Ann, "It's uphill from this side and too slippery to get through. We can't go that way."

Even though Ann didn't want the responsibility, she decided for them because she didn't see any other choice. "We'll try wading."

They went back to the fissure through the column, squatted beside the pool, and tried to determine the possible hazards of a voyage through the water. Ann saw no sharp formations that would make it impossible to wade. "The bottom will probably be uneven. We'll have to go slowly and feel the floor at every step. There might even be underwater sinkholes. I don't want anybody to drop into one. We should take off our pants and stockings and cross in only our boots."

Eli stepped into the cold water with his rolled clothes in one hand and a lantern in the other. Sally stopped him, "Wait." All heads turned toward her. "God, I haven't spoken to you since you took Mama and Papa. If you aren't too mad at me to listen, please get us safely out of here." Everybody joined Sally's, "Amen." Eli then carefully led the way to the crunching demolition of tiny underwater stalagmites.

Just as they feared, the water got deep. It ran into Sally's boots. She stopped walking. "The water went into my boots. It's freezing."

Ann encouraged her, "Keep coming. We're almost there."

Sally tried another step. "I can't. My foot comes up, but my boot stays down."

Eli wanted to do something to make amends. "If you'll let me, I'll carry you."

"I'll let you, but I'm not forgiving you."

"Give me your clothes." Stephanie took the clothes bundles from Sally and Eli. "Yours too, Ann, and hold this for a minute." Stephanie swapped her lantern for Ann's clothes. She put all the clothes together. So nothing would fall out, she ran her belt around them and pulled it as tight as she could. She attached Eli's belt to the bundle and made a loop that Eli lifted over her head. The strap crossed her chest. The bundle rested in the middle of her back.

Eli squatted slightly. "Get on."

As Sally climbed on, her feet were left bare. "Oh no, I've lost my boots."

"Don't worry. I'll get them." Stephanie pushed up her sleeve and reached into the freezing water for the first boot. She dumped out the water and one little, see-through, eyeless fish. After she slid it onto Sally's foot, she got the other. "We're ready."

Ann handed a lantern to Stephanie. "Eli, I'll go first. I don't want you to slip. Both of you could be severely cut." Sally held the lantern to light the way for Eli. Stephanie brought up the rear. After only a short distance, the water sloshed into Ann's boots. She knew the water would do the same to all of them. She needed to find a way for them to keep going. Ann silently prayed, lifted her foot only enough to take the weight off, and then pushed her foot forward. The breaking stalagmites in the pool made a tinkling sound. She laughed.

The other three asked, "What's so funny?"

Ann turned and faced them. "I was wondering how we would continue if the water got too deep. I prayed for God to send His angels to help us. Exactly that, 'Send Your angels.' I decided to push my foot forward instead of picking it up. The sound was just like the tinkling of angels. I laughed because God sent His angels just like I asked."

Eli replied, "I didn't hear angels. It's just the sound of you breaking what we're walking on."

Stephanie said, "I believe you, Ann."

Eli strongly encouraged them to get on with the trip. "Let's go. I'm carrying Sally."

Ann saw no reason for Eli to continue to carry Sally. "Put her down."

Sally countermanded Ann's instructions, "What? Eli, don't you dare!"

"Sally, your boot will be full of water, but you can lift your foot just a little and push your boot forward."

"I'll try one step. If it doesn't work, Eli

absolutely is carrying me." Sally slid off Eli's back into the frigid water up to her thighs. She sharply sucked in her breath. "This is really cold!" She tried Ann's suggestion. "I think I can make it on my own this way. Even though I'm mad at you, Eli, it means a lot to me that you carried me." To the sound of the accompanying angels that even Eli was then compelled to hear, they scooted their boots across the pool bottom in water deeper than they had guessed. Sally hiked her coat above her hips as the water rose. She became sure that the cave had them trapped. "It's getting too deep. I can't make it."

Ann disagreed. She had felt the water level change again. "Come on. You can do it. The last few steps, the water hasn't gone as far up my legs." Sally waded the last few yards with the others and breathed a huge sigh of relief as they stepped out of the water below the entrance. Ann took the clothes bundle off Stephanie's back. "Wait a little bit and dry before you put on your clothes."

"I've got an idea." Eli unbuttoned his coat. "I wore three layers, and I have this coat. I'll take off my inner shirt. We can use it to dry off and get back into our clothes quicker."

"Good idea. I'm freezing." Stephanie held the greatcoat and looked away. Ann also faced away as she loosened the belt around their bundle of clothes. As if it might disappear if she stopped looking at it, Sally kept her eyes riveted on the way out. In one fell swoop, Eli pulled all his shirts over his head. He quickly pulled out the inner shirt and laid it on Stephanie's shoulder.

Ann knew Eli was dressed in only his unmentionables and boots. "Make haste getting back into your clothes." He pulled the rest of his shirts back on and got back into his coat.

Stephanie held his inner shirt out behind her back. "Dry yourself first. We can wait. Lean on me."

Eli held onto Stephanie's shoulder, took off his boot, and ran the shirt over his leg and foot. Because she was shivering quite violently, he tossed the shirt onto Sally's shoulder. "Sally, start drying off. Ann, I need a sock." Ann held one out behind her back. Eli pulled it over his slightly damp skin as quickly as he could.

Sally took hold of Stephanie's other shoulder, dried one leg and foot then held the shirt out toward Eli without looking. Ann handed Sally a sock. Since everybody was looking away from him, Eli requested what he needed next, "Trousers, please." He laid the drying shirt on Stephanie's shoulder for Sally to take. Ann again held Eli's piece of clothing behind her back. He got one leg in, then slipped his foot into his empty but wet boot as Ann handed Sally her trousers. They took turns giving the shirt back and forth while Ann doled out the correct piece of clothing as instructed. They made short work of getting dresses so Stephanie and Ann could do the same.

Stephanie sat down and emptied both her

boots. She dried her legs and feet, handed the shirt to Ann, and quickly pulled on her pants and socks. Once dressed, she put her hand down and pushed herself up. Something slimy squished under her hand. "Yuck. What was that?" She tried to wipe the slime onto the ground.

Eli was the first to look at the small, pale-yellow mound of slime. "It has legs, but it doesn't have eyes. I think it's a salamander of the cave kind."

Already dressed, Ann came over to look. She held the shirt out to Stephanie. "Go wash your hand in the pool." Stephanie smelled the slime, wrinkled her nose, and took the shirt. Ann picked up the rope. She drew it back with one arm, then reached forward with the other and pulled. It didn't come. "I think the line is caught."

"Let me try." Eli pulled but did no better.

Salamander-slime free, Stephanie said, "Let's all pull."

The four of them pulled, but the rope didn't budge. They tried again with the same result. Ann decided to give up. "We don't have time to go over there to free it up. We'll get it some other day."

"You sure you want to leave it?" Eli asked.

"Yes."

"Let's get out of here." Sally led them up the slope to the light above.

EIGHT

Eli stepped into the air, warmed by the midday sun. "Except for what happened to Sally, I'm glad I got to have this adventure with you." He put out and then carried two of the lanterns to the wagon.

"I think that's enough for me for quite a while." Ann brought the other lantern.

Stephanie put Eli's wet shirt into the wagon. "One thing's for sure; we'll never forget it."

Ann saw Sally hang her head with a very troubled expression on her face. "Stephanie, come help me get the dinner basket." As they retrieved their meal, Ann chastised her. "What do you think you're doing?"

"What?"

"Saying we'll never forget it."

"I won't. What's wrong?"

"Do you think Sally wants to remember that terrifying experience forever?"

"I'm sorry. I didn't think about that. I'll go apologize."

"No, leave it alone. That'll only make it worse. Just think about what you're saying."

"I will. I certainly don't want her to remember that."

Safely out of the world of the cave, they drank cold sassafras tea and ate dried apples with bread saturated with congealed bacon fat. They leaned against the maples and looked down into the world of the forest that they had happily traveled through that morning.

After eating, they put the empty dinner basket in the wagon and got the tools to tap the maple trees. Stephanie showed Eli how to drill a hole through the bark and gently tap the spout into the tree just far enough to get into the layer where the sap flowed. Sally stuck close to Ann and drilled upward-angled holes about three feet from the ground before they tapped in their set of spouts.

They put three or four taps in all the big trees and hung the collection containers. Next, they secured a cloth over all the spouts and buckets to keep out falling debris and insects. Once they had completed the task that was the main reason why they were there, Ann, Stephanie, and Sally hitched up Samson and loaded the tools. Eli got the goose and cougar bodies from inside the cave entrance, where he had put them to keep them fresh during the day. He loaded their hunting trophies into the wagon. They rode down the mountain with a goose, a cougar, and—good or bad— an adventure they would never forget.

NINE

"Eli, hang the cougar on the wall pegs over there." Ann pointed to the appropriate place inside the barn. She handed the goose to Sally. "Get the pots ready."

Stephanie and Eli got Samson settled in for the night while Ann unloaded the wagon. Ann called for Stephanie and Eli. "Come over here and get an armful of wood. Please get the fires going. We need to cook the goose, and we need to heat lots of water. We don't know about the water in the cave, so we should all take a bath."

Eli held out his arms. "And because I'm covered in maple juice." Ann loaded him up. Eli wanted to take his armload of wood directly to the appropriate location. "Where do you want the fires started?"

Stephanie stepped over to let Ann fill her arms. "We need a fire in the stove and the kitchen fireplace." She and Eli started to the house as Ann loaded up with more wood. Inside, Stephanie leaned over next to the fireplace and let the logs roll off her arms. "Put yours by the stove." She joined Eli with the tinderbox. Stephanie handed over tinder, then kindling when the fire was ready. When Eli had a nice flame going, she passed him a few logs from the stack by the stove.

While they got the fire roaring in the stove, Sally filled the four big pots she hung on the hooks in the kitchen fireplace. Ann pulled a big tub on wheels out from under the butcher table in the middle of the kitchen and then proceeded to pour bucket after bucket of water from the barrel into the tub. She was still pouring buckets of water into the tub when Eli and Stephanie had the second fire blazing.

Eli looked into the water barrel he had filled that morning. It was almost empty, but the tub was full of water that was much warmer than the icy water in the well. He went to the workroom to round up materials to mend the harness.

While Sally bathed, Ann and Stephanie scalded and plucked the goose. Sally got out of the water and dressed. Stephanie washed as Sally and Ann boiled rice with onions and chopped dried apples. They seasoned the stuffing with sage and thyme they had harvested from their herb garden the previous fall and salt and pepper they had purchased at Eli's store. The other two girls stuffed the rice mixture into the goose and slid it into the oven while Ann bathed.

Meanwhile, Eli examined the harness and decided on the best plan for its repair. He cut replacement leather until he heard, "Eli, get some clean clothes. It's your turn." He left everything on the bench, got his clothes, and went to the kitchen. He found soap and a towel on the central table beside the tub full of used but warm water. He sloshed into the tub and washed away every trace of cave water and maple sap while the goose baked.

When the sun went down, four clean people sat at the table. Ann divided the goose and stuffing onto four plates. She also transferred the precious goose fat from the roasting pan into a jar. As she ate the succulent meal, Ann felt happy. She decided that hiring Eli had brought them very good luck. Sally, however, felt uneasy and agitated as darkness settled in. "I want to light some candles."

"I'll get them." Ann left the dining room and returned with a candle in a holder for each of them.

After everybody was in his or her room, Sally stealthily made her way to Ann's door. She stood in her nightgown holding her candleholder with a lit candle. "Ann."

"What is it, Sally?"

"I feel bugs crawling on me."

"Come in. Let me see what's on you."

"I can't see anything, but I feel them."

Sally handed Ann the candle. She stood beside the bed as Ann examined her.

Ann looked Sally over. She also found nothing, but Ann remembered how upset she and Stephanie had been after their scare in the cave. "Sleep with me."

Sally slipped into bed. "May we leave the candle burning?"

"Sure." Ann put her arm around her sister. Finally feeling safe, Sally slept.

TEN

After the sun was up, Eli needed to see to the cougar. He asked the girls what they wanted to have done with its skin. Stephanie thought they should hang it on the wall as a trophy but was concerned that it would remind Sally of her ordeal in the cave. Sally did not feel that way. "Eli shot it. He can do whatever he wants."

Ann decided. "Eli should butcher the animal and tan the hide, so he has to remain at the house." She asked, "Which of you girls wants to go with me to get the sap?"

Sally loved to ride in the forest. "I'll go."

That suited Stephanie. She wanted to watch Eli skin and butcher the cougar. She was sure he would do it expertly.

The sap bucket wasn't heavy. However, it

was so big that it took all of them to maneuver it onto the wagon. Ann hooked up Samson and left with Sally. Beside the cliffs at the maple grove, Ann and Sally poured the sap from the small containers hanging on the trees into the giant bucket in the wagon. As they clamped down the lid, Sally tried to estimate the final quantity of syrup it would produce.

At home, Stephanie watched Eli skin and butcher the cougar. She wrapped the best cuts of meat in butcher paper and took them to the underground stone-lined cellar stocked with ice they had harvested from the creek that winter. She went back to the barn to cut the remainder of the cougar meat into strips and to be close to Eli while he scraped every trace of flesh from the cougar skin. She finally sliced the last piece of meat. "Are you finished?"

Eli put down the knife. "Just now."

"Good. Help me carry these to the smokehouse."

Eli stacked baskets and followed. "I'll get the wood. Do you use different wood for smoking?"

"The only wood we have is from the trees Papa felled two summers ago."

Eli carried wood into the smokehouse and then hung cougar meat strips with Stephanie until they heard the jingle of Samson's harness. Ann steered the horse to a small shack, unhooked Samson, and took him to the paddock. She walked back across the yard and looked into the smokehouse. "That's more meat than I thought you'd get." Ann held out a bottle of matches. "Eli, since you shot the beast, do you want the honor of starting the fire?" Eli took the matches and lit the tinder. The fire grew and filled the building with smoke. "Eli, I told you there would be a lot of work. The next task is already at hand. Are you ready?" Ann paused for his reply.

"Lead on." Eli followed the three girls into the sugar shack.

Ann touched a three-sided stone fire pit. "Make a fire here."

Eli went for another armful of wood. He arranged the wood in the low, open-topped enclosure in the center of the one-room shed. Out of the corner of his eye, he watched the precision of the dance of the three sisters. They wove around each other as if they knew precisely where the others were going. They never even bumped each other or anything else in the tight space. They poured sap by the bucketful through a cloth into the large flat cooking pan that Ann positioned over the fire pit.

The low sugar concentration of black maples meant that it would take a lot of sap to make a decent amount of maple sugar. Ann hoped the massive amount of sap of the first collection would continue for the whole season. When the pan was a third full, Eli started the fire. Hour after hour, they worked in the house, chopped wood, stirred the liquid over the fire, or skimmed the foam off the top as the sap condensed. The sun was low on the horizon when Ann went to the house with the matching cooking pan that they would need to complete the last steps of the process in the kitchen. Stephanie yelled across the yard, "Eli, we don't need any more wood tonight."

He walked to the shack and leaned the axe against the inside wall. "Anything else I can do out here for you ladies?"

Stephanie picked up a stack of hot pads. "We need to filter the syrup before the final cook-down. Help us pour it into that big pot."

Sally positioned several layers of cheesecloth over the cast iron pot to make a concave catch basin that she tied in place with a rope. The three of them picked up the condensing pan and poured the syrup.

Eli noticed that the syrup matched the golden color of the end-of-the-day sunlight that filled the shack. The small amount of liquid sugar compared to the considerable amount of sap they had when they started surprised him. "I never knew it took so much juice to make so little syrup."

Stephanie looked at the light shining through the falling fluid. "It's beautiful, and it does take a lot. Some years when the sap didn't run, we got only a gallon of syrup from the whole season. I think we'll have a couple of quarts just from today." Stephanie put the empty pan on the shelf, and Eli put out the fire while they waited for the syrup to filter through the cloth into the pot.

Sally untied the rope and held the cheesecloth as Stephanie and Eli removed the heavy pot. Sally quickly pulled another container under the cloth to catch the little bit of syrup she knew would continue to drip. As Stephanie and Eli placed the pot on the kitchen stove, Stephanie felt there was hope for their survival.

Ann sent the others away but stayed in the kitchen to start the final cook-down. "I put warm water in each of your rooms. Get cleaned up before you come to the table."

Sally remained in the kitchen for a moment. "What do you think? We got a lot."

"Yes, we did. Let's pray that the nights stay cold and the days stay warm, so it continues."

"It's going to be a lot of work, but it's so worth it. I can smell the maple. It makes me want some right now."

Ann put on her heavy apron and long gloves. "Me too, but it's too hot, so go clean up."

Sally didn't want the syrup ruined during the final step. As she left, she called back, "Keep a close eye on the syrup, and make some candy, please."

Ann's cougar stew simmered as she stirred the maple. When the maple sugar ran off her spoon in a long thick string, she thought it was condensed and hot enough. She dropped a small dollop into a bowl of cold water. A smooth ball formed. She took it out and mashed it between her thumb and finger. It was squishy but didn't remain a flattened disk. It was ready. She poured most of the syrup into the big pan she had brought in from the sugar shack.

While the syrup in the flat pan cooled, Ann continued to heat the liquid in the cast iron pot until a thick layer of tiny bubbles formed. The next glob that she dropped into the water congealed into threads. She took one out. It was flexible. It was just right for making soft candy.

They needed the molten maple sugar in a much smaller cast iron teapot with a narrow spout that could control the flow of the liquid into the small holes of the candy mold. As Ann filled the teapot, Stephanie walked into the kitchen. "I'll pour it into the mold."

Eli entered the room just as Stephanie got on her long doeskin apron and long doeskin gloves. Stephanie cautioned him. "Stand back. This will give you a horrible burn if it gets on you." Eli stayed out of splash range and watched as Stephanie filled the heart-shaped hollows carved into a wooden block.

Stephanie lowered the empty teapot into the washbasin of warm water.

Steam erupted as Sally came into the kitchen. "How much maple syrup did we get?" She made her way through the small cloud to the large pan of syrup.

"Two and a half quarts, plus what Stephanie poured into the candy molds." Ann went into the pantry to retrieve the rack of sugar molds.

Sally spooned a small amount of syrup into the bowl of test water. "It's ready." She donned her maple-sugar-making outfit before she used a long-handled wooden spoon to stir the cooling syrup in the flat pan. As Sally stirred out the last of the water, Eli watched the liquid syrup turn into soft granules.

Ann washed the blocks of wood that fit together to make cone-shaped holes that could each hold two cups of compressed maple sugar. Stephanie clamped the cleaned sugar molds halves together.

Eli asked, “Do we have enough to fill all six holes?”

“I think so.” Ann brought over the freshly cleaned upper frame.

Sally spooned the last of the maple granules into the mold. Eli asked, “May I?” Ann handed Eli the top. He aligned it and tightened the wooden screws. The thick wooden disks pressed into the tops of the holes and compressed the maple sugar into cones that could be stored for years when dry.

Ann quantified the day’s labor. “We got four pounds of sugar cones plus the candy.”

“That’s good, right?” Eli carried the full rack of cones into the pantry.

“It’s wonderful. Good work, everybody. Now, it’s time to eat supper.”

ELEVEN

"I hope cougar is yummy." Ann carried the stew to the table.

Stephanie brought the pot of sassafras tea to the table. "The stew smells good."

"I've never eaten cougar." Eli sat in the same place that Sally had assigned him the first night.

Ann ladled supper into each of their bowls. "I stewed it a long time. I hope the meat will be tender."

Eli chewed a chunk of meat. "Two days and the third wild animal I've eaten. Not too bad."

Sally pondered and chewed. "What do you think it tastes like?"

Stephanie quipped, "Cougar," and drew laughter from the others.

Ann finally finished her first piece of cougar and started on a second. "I don't know what's made me more tired: chopping wood, working by the fire, or chewing this cougar meat."

Sally giggled. "I'm developing great jaw muscles."

Stephanie shared her cougar-eating thoughts. "If we cut the meat into smaller pieces, we might be able to eat it." Eli snickered and cut a chunk of meat into pieces the size of peas. "Not that small." Stephanie poked him in the ribs.

Ann cut hers into teeny pieces and put a spoonful into her mouth. "Eli is right. I can swallow these whole." They all laughed. Ann stood up when their bowls were empty and dipped the ladle back into the pot. "Get your knives ready. Everybody needs to eat more food while we have it." Between the comments about the quality of the meat and the laughter, they managed to eat the whole pot of stew. Ann rewarded all of them with one maple candy.

Stephanie knew Ann would make them eat all the cougar meat over the coming days. "We have sausage casings. They've been in the pantry for two years and might not be good anymore, but they might be usable. We can mix three parts of cougar meat with one part fatback bacon and some of the spices we picked from the herb garden and run it through the meat grinder. We can make sausages to smoke. Ground meat wouldn't be tough or chewy, and smoked sausages will last longer."

The cougar and the fatback bacon were the only meat they had. Sally was all for a tastier way to eat either type of meat than the ways they had consumed them over the last two days. "I'll be glad to make them tomorrow."

TWELVE

The four settled into a comfortable routine. Neither Sally nor Ann told the others that Sally slept with Ann or that they left a candle burning every night. Each day, they got up early and did the morning chores. Two of them went up the mountain to gather maple sap while the others chopped wood. When the sap gatherers returned, they chopped. The two left at home started cooking the sap. In the afternoons, they also worked on other projects, checked the squirrel traps in the woods behind the house, fished, or hunted ducks at the creek that ran across their land. The days they didn't get some other meat, they ate cougar sausages or cougar jerky.

Eli enjoyed the trips to the maple grove.

Sally always wanted him to talk about things that interested him. He thought she was genuinely interested. He also felt that she was still upset with him for getting them to go into the fissure in the cave.

Ann always took the time to show him the places and things of interest she had discovered in the area. One day, they lay on the ground with their feet touching and arms stretched out as far as possible, but they still didn't equal the diameter of a giant bristlecone pine. He liked the way she saw the world. Ann thought the world was a treasure waiting for discovery. Also, Eli could see that Ann cared deeply about Stephanie and Sally. He believed that she would protect them with every ounce of her being. If ever in a battle, he wanted Ann on his side.

He liked being with Stephanie best. She had the gentlest manner, the most pleasant spirit, and she didn't insist on having her way. Stephanie was full of information and shared it without hesitation but always humbly. They all expressed their appreciation for the helpful things he did, but he felt that Stephanie saw the real him. Eli thought she liked what she saw and accepted him just as he was. When he looked at her beautiful face, he saw the man he wanted to be reflected in her eyes.

That month, they ate meagerly and more wild food than Eli thought he would have ever eaten in his entire life. He tanned the cougar skin, helped to make maple sugar, and got the equipment ready for planting. He also repaired the broken chair and the broken harness. Eli knew they needed more food. Intending to suggest that they trade it for provisions, he cleaned up all the tackle that was too small for Samson.

By the time the maple sap quit running, they had eighty pounds of maple sugar cones and a few pounds of both soft and hard maple candies. All four of them were grateful for the bountiful harvest of maple, but they were also tired of processing sap and extremely glad it was over. Stephanie and Eli put the equipment away for the season. Stephanie slid a cleaned pot into its place. "Tomorrow is Ann's birthday. Sally and I want to make Ann a birthday meal. We need you to get her out of the house for most of the day."

At supper, Eli attempted to put the plan into motion. "Ann, you know where all the interesting things are around here. Now that we've finished making maple sugar, would you take me exploring?" Ann agreed without any argument. She knew what Eli was doing. She was more than happy to let her sisters enjoy preparing for her birthday.

THIRTEEN

The next day, when Ann took Eli to see Rock House Cave, she didn't bother to ask her sisters if they wanted to go. Sitting on Samson, they rode into the hundred-foot-wide, open-fronted cave. Five more horses with riders could have sat one on the other without touching the roof.

Indian drawings from the past covered the many large natural coves in the giant cave. The fact that a whole tribe had once lived on Ann's land always gave her hope. If the land had provided for an entire tribe of Indians, she knew it could provide everything she and her sisters needed. She wished she would meet one and learn their secrets for survival.

Eli and Ann dismounted and walked to an

alcove at the back of the deep cave where rock steps led up to a spring. They enjoyed a refreshing drink of water and filled their canteens before letting Samson drink. Eli looked into one of the tunnels in the cave. "Where do these go?"

"You know we can find out. Your leg bumped our light all the way over." Ann untied the lantern. She handed it to Eli to light while she tied a rope to Samson and took him to the entrance of one of the tunnels she had previously explored. Ann knew they didn't need the rope, but she thought it best to use one. Tied to the other end of the line, they traveled the winding but non-branching passageway until they exited into the sun high on a ledge on the other side of the ridge.

Ann and Eli enjoyed the view while they ate a dinner of boiled eggs and drank water from the spring. After eating, they followed the rope back to Samson. Ann stood close to one of the lower cave drawings. "What do you think this is supposed to represent?"

Eli looked at the drawing resembling two

hooks linked together. "Almost looks like hands holding each other." They studied many of the ancient and more recent markings on the walls. "Obviously, Indians lived here. It would have been a perfect place. It's strange that I can't decipher what these drawings symbolize. Things couldn't have been that different for the Indians than they are now."

"It is odd that they're so unusual."

"I'm glad you brought me here."

Eli didn't need to thank Ann. Stephanie and Sally never wanted to explore with her. She was glad he enjoyed it. To Ann, having a companion exploring with her was an excellent birthday gift, but she wondered if it was time to go home. "Are you ready to head home?"

Eli wanted to see everything he could and thought they should be gone longer. "Unless you know of something else we can look at that wouldn't take too much time."

Ann assumed that meant they needed to

spend more time away. “It wouldn’t take long to see where Spadra Creek comes into the valley off Low Gap Mountain.” They rode over. Robins flitted from one leaf-bud-covered oak tree branch to another. The stream gathered water and speed as it came down the mountain past masses of the tiny white blossoms of spring beauty flowers. They enjoyed the beauty of the season for several minutes before they started back.

When they got home, Eli called out, so the girls would know they were in the house. Sally dashed across the sitting room to put a blindfold over Ann’s eyes. She led Ann to the dining room, where she removed the scarf. Their best dishes and glasses beautifully graced the table. Hot green pea porridge cooked with other dried vegetables, biscuits, fried fish, and roasted duck decorated the table with an imperial cake as the centerpiece.

“How lovely and so much food! I appreciate you making this meal and getting me out of the house." They happily enjoyed the delicious meal together. Since it was the end of the month, and Ann wanted to be faithful to her agreement with Eli, she asked him, "When do you want to go to town?"

"Tomorrow. May I take some maple sugar to give to my father?"

Ann had already thought about what to do with the maple sugar. "We should keep forty pounds to last us until next spring. That would leave ten pounds for each of us to do whatever we want. I want to come with you to town. Do you think your father would trade the used horse tackle you cleaned for food?"

Sally spoke up, "Let's all go and find out."

They convinced Ann that everything at the farm would be safe unattended for a few days, so they could all go. That evening, they packed the wagon with the maple sugar, the harnesses for the smaller horses they no longer owned, the broken harness that Eli had repaired, and all the tackle that wouldn't fit Samson.

FOURTEEN

Since Eli wanted to spend as much time with his father as possible, they woke early and rode toward the town Ann hadn't visited for nine years.

***

Since she was ten, Ann had been obligated to help alleviate the massive work at the farm. Ann had been too young to go all the way to town alone to trade their cheese and eggs for the things they needed. Therefore, their mother went to town every spring with her two youngest children to keep them out of the way of the two left at the farm.

Each fall, their mother had traded ham, pork chops, tenderloins, bacon, and sausage from the hogs their father had slaughtered, butchered, cured, and packaged. Sally and

Stephanie had always sat in a chair in Yate's Mercantile while their mother styled their hair with a silver brush. Ann's mother had never fixed Ann's hair into a fancy hairdo. Ann had never worn her hair any other way than hanging loose, pulled back in a ponytail, or plaited into a braid. All she had ever been was a hard-working farm girl.

***

On their way to Harmony this spring morning, Ann felt excited that she was finally getting off the farm and going to town.

As he pulled the wagon, the muddy March soil coated Samson. When they stopped at Yates Mercantile, Samson had become the earth in horse form. Eli jumped off the wagon. He reached up to help Stephanie, then Sally, and lastly, Ann. All of them were completely able to get off of and onto a cart on their own, but Eli wanted to attend to Stephanie. It would have been awkward if he had then declined to do the same for the other two. Therefore, they had an unspoken agreement to all be helped.

Eli swung open the door. Before the bell announced their arrival, he yelled, “Pop.”

Mr. Yates hurried out of the back room. “I’m so glad to see you. I hope you’ll be able to stay a while.”

Eli stood in the store and hugged his father. “We’ll leave late tomorrow.”

“Will you be staying with me?”

“Of course, I don’t want to miss a minute with you.”

Tom Yates let go of his son and walked over to the girls. “Hello, Stephanie. Hello, Sally. You must be Ann. Welcome to Yates Mercantile.”

Ann replied cordially, “Hello, Mr. Yates.” She thought Eli and his father looked so much alike. Both had dark brown eyes and hair and well-developed muscles from carrying the heavy sacks and other items in the store. The only difference was that Tom was thirty-seven, and Eli was seventeen.

“Pop, I have a gift for you, and the girls have some items to trade.”

Mr. Yates strode out the door to the wagon and pulled back the cover. "What's all wrapped up over there?"

Sally chimed in, "Maple sugar we made."

Eli gave his father one of the packages. "This is a gift from me for your personal use. The rest is for trade or sale. What do you think, Pop?"

Mr. Yates decided he needed to take a better look at the trade items. "Help me carry everything inside." He carefully examined three harnesses, two bridles, two horse blankets, two saddles with bags, and two pack saddles. "These are all in good condition. Don't you need them?"

"I sold two of our horses to some men passing by. These won't fit Samson."

"Must have been the same strangers who came to town. They busted up the saloon before the sheriff threw them in jail. Next morning, he ordered them to leave and not come back. They high-tailed it out of here."

"We were lucky they didn't steal our

horses or hurt us." Stephanie purposefully shivered to reinforce her comment.

Tom considered what the girls usually purchased as he wrote the value of the items the girls wanted to trade. "I'll give you thirty-six dollars for all the horse tackle if you want money, thirty-eight if you want to trade and two cents a pound for the maple sugar.

Ann thought about what she needed in the way of money versus goods. "We'll need money for meals and a room at Joe's Saloon tonight. How much will we need for that?"

"Nothing; you girls stay here with us."

"We can stay at the saloon perfectly well." Just as her father always had, Ann insisted they provide for themselves.

Mr. Yates could see that Ann was a strong-willed young woman. He countered forcefully, "Nonsense. I insist you stay here. We have an extra room with a large and a small bed. Eli can sleep with me, and one of you can use his room if you want separate beds."

Ann's sense of fairness would not let the Yates take them in just because Eli worked for them, especially because she was very glad to have Eli helping at the farm. He was strong, skilled, and competent, and never complained. He worked well beyond what she expected. Ann felt she should be doing something thoughtful for Eli and his father and not taking advantage of them, but she didn't want to offend Eli's father either. "We'll use the one room if you deduct for the room and the meals as part of the trade."

"I'll deduct one dollar a day for the room and your meals."

Ann would have paid more at the saloon, but she had never been anywhere but her home and didn't have any idea what was appropriate. She inquired of her sisters if that was all right with them. They weren't going to question Ann's judgment and were happy to stay with the Yates. Ann agreed to stay, then looked around the store to decide what to get.

Stephanie and Sally already knew what was there and didn't bother. Sally walked across the room to the short glass counter and picked up the silver brush. She lovingly swept it through her hair. Mr. Yates saw a tear shimmering at the edge of her eye. He knew it was more than Sally's love for the glistening brush set.

***

He remembered the day thirteen years before when Sally's mother had brought her newest baby into the store for the first time. The shiny silver had caught Sally's attention. While lying in a basket on her mother's arm, she had reached out and grabbed the glistening object. "Oh! No!" Sally's mother had tried to capture the mirror but hadn't moved fast enough. The mirror slid away. Mr. Yates and Sally's parents had expected to hear the awful sound of shattering glass. Thankfully, the mirror fell into the basket, where Sally lay happily with the mirror in her possession.

Her father's sigh of relief had been so loud that Mr. Yates had heard it across the room. Sally's father sternly warned his wife to control their baby. "That was almost the end of me. Keep that child away from the counter."

During Sally's early years, her mother carefully kept her daughter's hands away while the child looked at the glittery objects. When the girls were several years old, Mr. Yates gave his permission to use the brush set. "I think the girls are big enough to sit still. If you want to brush their hair with the silver brush, you may. Just be very careful."

After that, as soon as Sally entered the store, she went straight to the gleaming items she loved and carefully picked up the brush and mirror. "Please, Mama, brush my hair for a few minutes." Sally hadn't needed to beg. Their mother happily did what she could to bring them joy, so she brushed her youngest daughter's hair into a shimmering swirl of waves while Sally watched in the mirror.

Being generous, Mr. Yates had always left a sliver of ribbon by the brush. "I'm going to throw that scrap of ribbon away. Why don't you take it?"

Her mother would tie the ribbon in Sally's hair. "See how beautiful you are."

Sally always very carefully placed the mirror back on the counter. "It's the ribbon." Proudly wearing the ribbon, she would gather supplies and bring them to the counter.

Mama would ask, "Stephanie would you like me to brush your hair?"

Already in a position to take her turn, Stephanie had always replied, "That's for children. You know I don't have time for that."

To which her mother would say, "We have plenty of time, come over here."

Since her mother had always insisted, Stephanie would happily leave the items she had gathered and go to the stool where her mother stood with brush in hand. She would pick up the mirror and watch. Stephanie had told her mother, "When we have enough money, I'm going to buy this brush set for Sally."

That wasn't likely, but she hated to break her daughter's heart. "I know how much Sally would love it. Maybe we can get it next year. Right now, we only have enough to buy our supplies. That is if Mr. Yates will trade for our cheese and eggs."

"As always, I want all your cheese and eggs." Tom had watched Stephanie's golden hair transform into starlight wrapped in a French bun.

Stephanie's mother pinned the hair in place with two of Tom's ivory combs. She told her middle daughter what she thought, "You're so beautiful. You're a princess."

Stephanie had looked into the mirror but had seen just a girl. She had taken the combs out of her hair and handed them back to their owner. "Thank you for letting me try them on."

***

They all knew Tom had been happy to let them have a simple pleasure that cost him nothing. He knew they barely eked out a living. Even after years of work, with only one man to do the hard physical labor, the farm hadn't been very productive. They never had spare money. There wasn't any other way that the family would ever have been able to use a fancy brush, look into a high-class mirror, or create stylish hairdos.

FIFTEEN

On the current spring day, with that same brush, Sally brushed her hair only a few strokes, then gently laid it down and let out a big sigh. Stephanie felt much happier than she had the last time they had been in the store. She went to the brush set. "Let me brush your hair, Sally."

Sally picked up the mirror and watched. "I miss Mama brushing my hair." The sunlight streamed through the storefront windows and brought out the reddish hues in Sally's chestnut hair.

Stephanie complimented her sister, "Your hair is gorgeous in this light."

Ann thought they should be practical. "Don't you want to decide what to get?"

Stephanie kept right on brushing Sally's

hair. "I already know what I want, and I want Eli to get it for me."

Eli wondered what she would buy with her twenty cents for her share of maple sugar. Stephanie placed her order. "I want a peppermint stick. Eli is going to give it to me, and I'm going to eat it right now."

Ann and Eli broke out in laughter. Tom Yates and Sally looked at them as if they'd lost their minds. Sally wanted to understand what was so funny about asking for a piece of candy. "Did we miss something?"

Explaining as little as possible, Eli replied, "It's just some ancient history." He got two peppermint sticks from the jar, which he presented while on bended knee. "Stephanie, I am pleased to present: one peppermint for the present and one for the past, both compliments of me."

"Much obliged," she accepted the offering, "you're forgiven." Stephanie's gorgeous smile called out to Eli's heart. As if it had been only yesterday, Stephanie, Ann, and Eli remembered what had happened so many years before.

***

Stephanie had begged their parents for candy. "Can we have peppermint?"

Hoping to convince their father, Ann had chimed in, "Please, we've been good girls!"

"I can at least buy my angels a piece of candy. Tom, pack five peppermint sticks."

Stephanie had whined for immediate satisfaction. "I want mine now."

Their father put the candy into the bag. "Wait, if we eat them now, they'll get covered with dust."

To Stephanie, that meant she wasn't getting the candy, so she had stealthily slipped a peppermint into her pocket. Tom's young son, Eli, had not missed Stephanie's maneuver. He didn't have permission to help himself to candy. Right in front of him, another little person had taken candy after she had been told to wait, and that wasn't fair. He followed her out the door. When they were out of view, he had grabbed the candy and run away.

Ann had been the next person out the door. She saw her sister sitting in the dusty road crying. "What's wrong?"

"That horrible boy took my candy."

"I'll tell Papa. He'll get it back."

"No, Papa told me to wait, and I snuck one. Promise you won't say anything."

"All right, I won't. Next time, do what Papa says. This wouldn't have happened if you had." Even at that early age, Ann believed in being responsible and didn't like it when others weren't. She was mostly sure doing things willy-nilly would cause problems. To Ann, the candy-stealing incident had been proof of that fact. The idea had lodged firmly in her mind.

For the next few years, every time they were in the store, Stephanie had whispered to Eli that he owed her a peppermint stick. Eli couldn't just take a peppermint stick to give to Stephanie, and he surely wasn't going to tell his father that he had stolen from a customer. Besides, he knew Stephanie would have to confess to tell on him, so he had always told her he didn't owe her anything. Eventually, Stephanie had realized that Eli wasn't going to replace the peppermint and had stopped speaking about it.

***

SIXTEEN

Ann stopped thinking about the past and handed Sally the list she had just written. "Here's what I think we should get."

Sally barely glanced over the items before she passed the list to Stephanie. "It's close to what we usually get. It's fine."

"You know what's best, Ann." Stephanie handed Ann the list without looking at it.

"With my share of the maple sugar and the tackle, we should be able to get what's on this list and pay you for the room for two nights and for our meals, including breakfast the morning we leave. Please double-check that I have it right." Ann handed Tom the list.

Eli inquired with surprise and joy, "Two nights?"

"We should ride back in the morning. It will be safer to travel through the mud in the light of day." Also, Ann knew how much she missed her folks. She wanted to give Eli and his father more time together.

Mr. Yates instructed his son, "Take the wagon around back and Samson to the stable."

Eli stepped outside and retrieved their small bags. He placed them on the floor just inside the door. "I'll take them to your room when I get back."

"Thank you," the girls replied in unison.

Mr. Yates looked over Ann's list. Two hundred pounds flour, fifty pounds lard, fifty pounds various dried fruits, fifty pounds dried vegetables, a hundred pounds dried beans, a hundred pounds oats, a hundred pounds cracked corn, ten pounds salt, one pound pepper, a hundred pounds rice, a hundred pounds cornmeal, a hundred pounds candles, three pounds saleratus, seventy pounds bacon, and three peppermint sticks. Tom laid the list on the counter. "How is Eli doing?"

"He's been a great help. We wouldn't have been able to make all this maple sugar without him, and he fixed that harness." Ann pointed.

"Plus, he shot a cougar." Stephanie then asked for her favorite item. "Will you trade my share of maple sugar for canned peaches?"

Ann added, "He's helped with many other things as well. He's been a great blessing. I don't mind telling you; I prayed all winter for God to help us. First, those men came and bought our horses. That gave us the money to buy the supplies and the seeds we bought this spring. Then, Eli showed up to help us. To be quite honest, it's not just the work. I think he brought us back to life."

Under her breath, Sally said, "I'm still mad at him," but she agreed that he had brought them back from despair.

Stephanie sucked her peppermint. "I think he's wonderful. I mean a wonderful help."

Mr. Yates added up the cost of the items on the list. The value of Ann's items was almost enough. He told Ann the final tabulation. "Your trade will pay for all this, the room, and the meals. I'm glad Eli has made such a difference for you girls. I knew he would work hard. Let me show you your room."

The girls picked up their bags and followed Tom through the store's side door into the attached house. They went through the kitchen into the living area and then left to the guest room. It was a small room with a dresser and two beds. There wasn't much room to maneuver, but they thought it was completely acceptable. They stepped into the room while Tom returned to the kitchen to put potatoes on the stove.

When Eli returned, they sat in the living room and drank English tea. Tom Yates told stories about young Eli. Each time, Eli said, "Pop, not that story," but he didn't actually mind.

The girls also told stories about each other until Tom stood up. "Eli, listen for the bell. I'll go fix supper." He didn't have to tell Eli to listen. They could hear the bell everywhere in their home, but the store was Tom Yates' life. It was important to him to attend to it properly. Every day, he went into the store, puttered around, dusted, and made sure everything was in its place.

Ann got up with him. "I'll help"

"That would be nice." In the kitchen, Tom cut slices from the smoked beef on the counter. Ann sliced bread from the loaf Tom had cooked the previous day and then placed it on the table along with fresh butter, jam, and the potatoes Tom had slow-roasted. "Eli, lock up the store and come to the table. Girls, come on in." Eli put up the closed sign, closed the shutters, locked the door, and went back into the house. The girls and his father already sat at the table, but Eli's regular place was empty, waiting for him.

Tom couldn't remember when he had

enjoyed a meal as much. The same food in the presence of Eli, Ann, Stephanie, and Sally changed everything. Too soon, supper was over. They moved back to the living room.

After only a short time, Ann said, "Girls, it's time we retire for the evening."

Sally started to say that she wasn't the least bit tired, but then she saw the look on Ann's face. They excused themselves and made their way to their room. Sally closed the door. "What's up, Ann?"

"We should give Eli and his father time alone. I'm sure they've been missing each other."

"You're exactly right. I'm so glad you thought about that." Stephanie put her boots in the corner.

Seeing how much Eli and his father loved each other reminded Sally how much she loved her parents. "I miss Mama and Papa." Two of them were going to sleep in the same bed. Sally made sure she was one of them. In her nightgown, she climbed into the double bed. "Which one of you is going to sleep with me?"

Ann told her sister, "Stephanie, you pick. I'm happy either way."

Stephanie slipped on her nightgown. "I'll sleep with Sally."

Ann lit a candle. "Good night, love you both to the moon and back."

SEVENTEEN

After breakfast, the three girls left Eli with his father. They walked the boardwalk past the private homes of folks they didn't know. When they came to a building with a sign that read, *school,* they stopped and peeked in the window. Young people of various ages sat inside with their backs to the window. The teacher didn't want to draw her students' attention to the window, so she acknowledged the sisters with only a slight nod. Betsy knew who owned the faces outside her window. Within minutes of their arrival the day before, every person in town knew that Eli had come home with the Williams girls and that the oldest one had even come to town.

Curiosity was thick, but no one dared to

barge into Tom's store to gawk. The sound of boots on the wooden planks of the boardwalk alerted everybody that the girls were out walking. When Ann turned from the schoolhouse window, she saw the curtain in the house across the street quickly move back into place. Ann told her sisters as they continued down the street, "The folks here are watching us, so look sharp."

Sally looked around. "I don't see anybody."

Stephanie replied, "They're peeking out, hoping we don't see them." She stood with her sisters at the end of the boardwalk and looked at the street that was just as muddy as when she had fallen the previous year.

Sally didn't like the conditions either. "Maybe we shouldn't cross."

Ann encouraged her. "It doesn't look deeper than our boots. I think we can do it. Besides, Samson is in the stable on the other side. We should see how he's doing. We can stop and come back if it gets too deep."

Sally agreed to try. Slowly lowering her feet until they reached the solid ground below the mire, she crossed the street, and came out of the mud in front of the livery. "I'm glad I got across without getting any in my boots." As Sally stomped the mud off, her sisters stepped onto the boardwalk beside her. The proprietor, who worked at his forge with the large doors open, looked up. Samson looked too. He saw his owners in the doorway and called to them with a loud neigh.

The blond-haired man in his late thirties with the muscles you would expect to see on a man who pounded iron all day greeted them. "Come in. Samson is well. He's a fine horse."

The girls entered. Ann pointed to each of them. "I'm Ann Williams. These are Stephanie and Sally, my sisters."

"Pleased to meet you. My name is Smithfield Wyman but call me Smitty. Are you going to be in town long?"

It suddenly occurred to Ann that Samson's board wouldn't be free. She thought about what she would have to remove from her list to cover the cost. "We'll be leaving first thing tomorrow. How much will you charge for boarding and feeding our horse?"

"Two bits."

"May we work to pay for it?"

Stephanie held up her pointer finger. "One moment, please." She motioned for her sisters to follow. Outside, Stephanie whispered, "What can we do for a blacksmith?"

"You don't have to do anything. I could muck out the barn or chop wood for the forge. If not, we'll have to give up supplies to get the money. We need everything. I really should have thought about this more. I should have told Eli to make the best deal he could and to get as many supplies as possible with the money."

Sally firmly believed in Ann's opinions. "I'll help if he'll let us."

"You're right, and we'd be working if we had stayed home."

They stepped back into the combination barn and blacksmith shop. Ann knew it could use mucking by the strong smell of manure. Trying to look capable, Ann strode to the bellows where Smitty sharpened a plow. "Is it possible for us to work to pay for Samson's keep?"

"What can you girls do?"

"We can muck out the stalls and chop wood. Probably other things, but I don't know what kind of work a blacksmith needs."

"You can start by mucking. As you can smell, I haven't done it for several days. Go change then come back."

"We'll be right back." The sisters hurried back to the store. They stepped up onto the boardwalk after they had once again crossed through the mud. Ann told them, "Leave your boots out here."

Stephanie already had one boot off. "You don't have to tell us the obvious."

Smitty watched the girls clean out two stalls each and then form a line. Each moved a shovel-wide section of manure to the far end of the barn, where Sally shoveled it into the wagon. The other two moved the next two lines of manure. When they got to the end of the barn, Stephanie took over shoveling into the cart, and Sally helped Ann push more of the mess to the cart. Ann shoveled the last batch into the cart. Smitty was impressed. They never even talked about how they were going to accomplish the task. He didn't know they had done the same thing in their own barn many times. Sally put the shovels back. "What next?"

"Wood chopping. Do you see the woodpile out back?"

"I do." Sally got two of the axes hanging on the wall. "Come on, Stephanie. This will be easy. These are very sharp."

Wood was ready to be stacked when Ann finished mucking. Before she joined her sisters, she asked, "Where do you want us to put the wood?"

"Now that the stall is clean, put it in there." Smitty pointed.

"Perfect." Ann walked to the pile of split logs.

Smitty moved to the other side of the anvil to pound a wagon wheel rim. He watched the three, with a perfect system, rotate through the aspects of the labor. Bring the wood to the chopping block, split it, and then move it into the stall. They rotated through many rounds until they had chopped and stacked the wood in the stall.

Smitty's wife saw that the girls were in the barn, and she wanted to meet them. She devised a plan. First, she prepared dinner. Then, being a woman frequently in a barn, Mara put on her calico dress hemmed to be a foot above the ground and her boots fit for walking in a sloppy barn to implement the next step. So that the girls covered in mud, manure, and sweat could wash, she took a pitcher of warm water and a basket with an enamel basin, soap, and towels into the livery. She sat them on the worktable. "Hello, I'm Mara, Smitty's wife. I think he's working you much too hard. You should have something to eat."

The girls walked across the stable toward the attractive woman wearing her red hair in a bun. She had a lovely smile on her face. Ann, Stephanie, and Sally introduced themselves as the woman poured water into the washbasin and laid the bar of soap beside it. She left the stack of towels in the basket. "So nice to meet you. Everybody clean up."

"You girls go first." Smitty continued to shape the wagon wheel. Sally washed her face, arms, and hands as Mara returned to the house and then brought out a second basket filled with dishes, glasses, and silverware. She put it in the side room Smitty used to conduct business and then walked back to the house.

Ann washed her hands and arms, then emptied the water too dirty to clean her face into the field behind the barn. Mara came back out and placed a third basket with fried chicken, mashed sweet potatoes, green beans cooked in bacon grease, and apple pie on the table beside the dishes. Sally leaned over the basket of food and inhaled deeply. "That smells heavenly. I'd be happy to set the table."

Smitty asked his wife, "Honey, will you bring out more water?"

"I'd appreciate that, Sally." Mara went into the house and quickly returned with two more pitchers. She put one by the washbasin but carried the other to the table with the food. With clean water from the pitcher, Ann washed her face, then her arms and hands again. Stephanie and Smitty repeated the procedure as Mara brought fresh water. When they were all clean enough, they sat down to eat.

Mara poured lemonade from the pitcher on the table, then sat down and asked so many questions that Smitty felt embarrassed. The girls knew they were news in an otherwise mundane life. They felt the same. They enjoyed the conversation and asked just as many questions of Mara and Smitty.

By the end of the meal, Mara was the possessor of a lot of knowledge about the girls that she knew she would enjoy sharing with the other people in town. She respectfully asked, "The other folks will want to know about you and what we spoke about. Would you mind if I tell them?"

Ann answered, "Feel free. It's the least we can offer for such an excellent meal."

"May I have another slice of pie?" Stephanie held out her plate. "What spices did you use? This is superb."

"It's not the spices. It's the apples. When we came here, Smitty planted the apple seeds we brought from my parents. I always thought they were the most delicious apples ever. I guess you do as well."

"I sure do!" Stephanie took back her plate filled with a second piece.

"What's next, Smitty?" Ann scraped up her last bite.

"You girls are very efficient. I've never seen anything like it. The amount of work you accomplished is truly impressive. I think you've earned Samson's keep already."

"We have? That's marvelous!" Sally pushed her stool back from the table.

Ann wanted to hold up her end of every deal. "Are you sure? I don't want to cheat you."

Smitty was satisfied with the trade. "I'm sure, but come talk with me anytime."

Mara hoped to know the girls better. "Me too."

Stephanie politely excused them, "Mara, thank you for the delicious meal. We need to take a bath."

As they turned the corner at the door, Stephanie heard Mara say, "What nice girls! I wish we had met them sooner."

"Let's walk down this side." Sally started up the boardwalk.

They strolled back to the store past a sign carved with the words *Doctor Gridley*. "Here's the doctor." Ann pointed at the sign.

"Here's where they drink. I'm glad we aren't staying here." Sally looked at the sign with the word, *Joe's,* that hung over a set of swinging doors. They were at the end of the walkway, so they waded back across the muddy street. Ann opened the door to make the bell ring.

Eli entered the store in a flash. "Oh, my word!" He held his nose. "What on earth happened?"

Stephanie explained, "We shoveled manure at the livery for Samson's keep."

Sally removed her second boot. "We met Smitty and Mara. Mara made us an excellent dinner. I enjoyed it very much."

Too late, Eli said, "I had already made arrangements for Samson."

Ann brought them back to the pertinent topic. "What's done is done. We need to take a bath, but we don't want to track manure all over your home."

"Go around to the back." At the back door, Eli told them, "Go into the shed. I'll bring your bags, a ten-gallon tub, soap, water, and towels." Eli brought them everything inside the tub except the water. "I'll keep bringing water until you tell me to stop." Eli handed water to Ann, who stood outside the shed covered in manure. Ann took the water inside. As her sisters washed the mess from their bodies, fate placed its hand over their lives. People who would not come together peacefully approached Harmony.

EIGHTEEN

The first man arrived at Harmony on an Appaloosa horse. The lone man wore a coat of elk, deerskin pants, a deerskin shirt, and moccasins. A long sharp knife hung from the belt fastened around his coat. He tied his horse outside the only place he saw to get a meal and a room. He walked inside and leaned his rifle against the bar. "I'd like a hot meal and a room for the night."

"It'll be two bits. If you want seconds on the food and a hot bath, that's a dollar."

The traveler handed the man a coin. "Two helpings, the room, and the bath."

"Coming right up. By the way, I'm Joe." The saloon owner went to get a serving of dinner.

Before he took a seat at the bar, the man

took off his coat and strapped the belt with his knife back around his waist. As he enjoyed his first plate of food, a group of men who had been in Harmony before rode into town.

The men left their horses in Smitty's corral and walked up the boardwalk. Their spurs jingled as they walked toward the place they remembered served good, strong whiskey. The man leading the pack slammed the doors hard against the wall. He didn't pay any attention to the other person in the saloon as he ordered in a loud, demanding voice, "Bottle of whiskey for me and the boys."

Joe remembered the men. He wasn't happy. As he stated the cost, Joe moved his rifle into a more accessible position behind the bar. "That'll be seven cents." He placed the bottle and seven glasses on the bar in front of the man he wished was not in his saloon again.

One of the men at the table yelled, "Get over here with that whiskey, Hank."

Hank slammed a Spanish Piece of Eight on the bar. "Bring us food too." He grabbed the bottle and glasses and carried them to the table where his men sat. "To being in a ^$&%&*% town," Hank stated his excuse for a toast and filled their glasses. The men clanked their shot glasses together and gulped the whiskey.

An exceptionally tall man seized the bottle. He cursed out his reason to drink as he poured the dark amber liquid into their glasses, "To the XO&$JJR trail." They downed another round.

The skinniest of the men raised his glass. "To $%&**% easy women." They all thought that was worth two shots. The bald man clanked his glass hard into the others and splashed whiskey onto the table.

Hank laid into him. "#$$^ %&$# $$&*(^(%&% (^%*%. You're wasting whiskey, you *&*%**_&^%."

Being older and knowing they had money in their pockets, the bald man thought it wasn't worth getting upset. "Don't pitch a conniption fit; just pour more."

Hank turned the bottle upside down and refilled the glasses, covering the table with just as much liquor. They tossed back shots as they toasted every topic that came into their minds.

Eli heard the language coming from the saloon. He didn't like it. He went into his house, got his rifle, propped it against the shed, and then brought more buckets of water from the storage barrel in the shop.

Across the road in the saloon, after many toasts replete with foul language, Joe arrived with four plates of stew with all the doings. He put them on the table. A young man with a square face and dark hair pulled over a plate. "This one's mine."

Hank glared at the man and informed him belligerently, "No, it ain't, Roy."

The young man shot up, pulled his brows down, and leaned forward menacingly. "Why is it yours?"

Hank stabbed his knife into the tabletop between the plate and the man trying to claim the food. "Cause I'm older, and I said so."

"Take it easy, boys. I don't want more trouble. I'll have the rest out here full chisel." Joe hurried off to get the other plates of food. When he got back, the men had polished off the bottle of spirits.

Happy again, Hank commanded the barkeeper, "Bring us another bottle." He gave his men permission to take a plate. "Eat up, boys." He continued scarfing down the savory stew he had taken from his brother.

The commotion in the saloon got louder. Eli became very concerned. "Hurry up. I don't know what's going on across the street. There's no telling what may happen. I don't want you girls out here undressed."

Ann tried to finish cleaning up as quickly as she could. With Sally behind, Stephanie stepped out of the shed, already clean and dressed. "We hear the cussing."

Sally, like her sisters, had never heard such language. "That's horrible."

The barkeeper didn't immediately get Hank another bottle of whiskey. Instead, he gave the man sitting at the bar another plate of food before he went to the backside of the bar. Hank looked at the person Joe had served before him. His face twisted with rage. "Ain't no stinkin' Indian sittin in here with me!"

Joe froze where he stood. *This isn't going to be good.*

Hank's statement made his tall companion's alcohol-soaked brain realize that an Indian sat in the same room. The man came around from the backside of the table. "It's 1839, an all you murderin' scum supposed ta be outta Arkansas. Get up an haul your sorry, worthless #$% back ta Indian Territory, or I'm gonna put a bullet through your skull." With drunken logic, all the men in Hank's gang yelled insults. They tried to get a reaction, so they could shoot the Indian, who silently scowled into his second helping of food.

Eli wanted the girls to be safe. He perceived a substantial potential for harm. "Go to the house. Tell Pop to take you to the storage room and to stay with you. Tell him I want him to keep you safe. Get rifles and ammo on your way down." They complied immediately.

Eli cornered the store as Smitty came up the boardwalk with a rifle in his hand and his sheriff's badge on his vest. Eli signaled to him that he was going around to the back of the saloon. Smitty nodded that he understood. The other townsmen also heard the yelling and followed behind their law enforcer.

The sisters hurried into the house. Sally called out, "Mr. Yates, Eli said to get your guns and ammunition and take us to the storage room."

Knowing the three sisters were bathing in his shed, Mr. Yates had waited in his house. "What's going on?"

Stephanie divulged what little they knew, "Cussing and yelling at the saloon."

"Should I go help?"

Sally was afraid. "Eli said he wants you to take us to the storeroom and protect us."

"Just show us the room. We can take care of ourselves." Ann tried to shoo Tom away.

Stephanie nodded toward Mr. Yates. "Ann, Eli wants his father here with us!"

Ann got the message. Both her sisters and Eli wanted Tom to be with them. "Get your guns and take us to your storage room."

Tom took them to a shelf in the kitchen. He amazed them when he slid over a jar on the bottom shelf, pulled up a lever, and swung out the whole shelf. "I have guns and ammunition down below. Watch your step on the stairs. I'll bar the door."

They went through the door and immediately descended wooden stairs through an earthen passageway. At the bottom, they found themselves in a small underground cave they surmised was under the backyard. Cheese wheels, as well as salt-cured and smoked meats, hung from wooden racks. Crates of items for sale and personal use sat neatly stacked in the cold underground bunker. It made an excellent place for storage but an awful place for girls with wet hair.

Upstairs across the street, yelling insults wasn't getting the reaction Hank wanted. He attempted to force the Indian to react with a different method. He picked up a chair and slammed it on the table. A wood shard planted itself in Joe's cheek, and another speared into the Indian's left arm.

Joe reached under the counter. One of the ruffians noticed the move and saw the piece of wood in Joe's face. He figured the barkeeper was going for a gun and dropped his hand to his revolver. Smitty stepped into the saloon and aimed his rifle at the outlaw about to draw.

The other townsmen trained their weapons on the strangers, including the one at the bar who continued to eat while blood ran down his arm and dripped onto the floor. Joe stood behind the counter with his rifle pointed at the man responsible for the piece of chair protruding from his cheek.

Smitty warned the short bald man, "Don't draw, or it'll be the last thing you do. I told you all not to come back." Smitty calmly but forcefully issued instructions to the leader of the gang, "Hank, put that chair leg down very gently." Hank's knuckles turned white as he clenched the chair leg. Time ticked by as everybody waited for the other's next move.

Down in the storage room, Sally whispered, "It's just too cold down here, and I can't hear what's happening."

"That's the point. When the door is closed, you can't hear anything outside, and nobody can hear what's happening in here."

The girls shivered.

"Let me help you get warm." Tom offered his arms. They huddled together, but that didn't solve the problem. The girls shook so violently that Tom could hardly keep his arms around them. "We can't stay down here. Let's go to the top of the stairs. It will be warmer. We can stop while we're still underground."

In the saloon, Hank proved that some men are just too belligerent to survive. Strangely, his expression changed from anger to relief. He turned and flung the chair leg. Smitty dodged as Hank pulled his revolver. Six bullets from the men of Harmony slammed into Hank's body. The outlaw slumped to the floor. All his men went for their guns.

Roy screamed, "You killed my brother, you sorry, no good cockroaches!"

In the stairwell to Tom's storage bunker, Ann stated what they all heard. "That was a lot of shots!"

Stephanie backed down the stairs. "Oh God, please keep Eli safe!"

Smitty tried to stop any further bullet trading. "Put your hands in the air and keep them there. Do not be stupid like Hank." Smitty again reminded them of what he had told them the last time they were in Harmony. "I told you not to come here again." The six friends of dead Hank took their hands off their guns and put them in the air. "You at the bar, get your hands up where I can see them."

The Indian put the last bite of food in his mouth then held his fork in the air. *I'll use this as a weapon if I have to.*

Across the street, Sally added to Stephanie's prayer, "If you're there, protect them this time."

Tom bitterly stated, "He won't help. I know He doesn't care. He let my wife die."

Ann refuted the statement, "I don't know what's going to happen, but God is listening, and He does care!"

"Maybe we should go help." Stephanie started up the stairs again.

Tom stopped her. "They've got enough to worry about without us getting involved."

While they waited several tense minutes, Stephanie repeatedly begged God to keep the people of Harmony safe.

Smitty and Joe kept their rifles trained on the outlaws. Smitty issued instructions to the other men of Harmony. "Men, get their guns." Smitty looked at the man on the barstool, facing the wall with his hands in the air while blood ran from his arm into his armpit and down his side. "Put all the guns except his in the blanket. You at the bar, don't move a muscle, or you'll join Hank." Smitty returned his gaze to his men. "One of you men, take his rifle and that fork and get that Arkansas Toothpick off his belt."

The Indian signaled his permission to the one man he was willing to let take his knife and gun, the other man whose blood was leaving his body because a piece of chair had made a hole in him.

Crimson flowed from Joe's cheek as he pulled the chair shard from his face. He took the fork from the Indian, untied the belt with the knife attached, fetched the rifle, and deposited them behind the counter.

The other men gathered the weapons of the six people in the back corner of the room. Smitty offered the men an opportunity to leave alive. "I'll send your guns out of town before you; then you can leave if you go peacefully. When you find your horse, you'll have your weapons back. We will shoot you if we see any of you anywhere near here again. Do you understand?" The other six members of the Hank Butterfield Gang confirmed that they understood.

Smitty kept his fully-cocked rifle aimed appropriately. He ordered nobody in particular, "Get a large blanket." Joe laid his rifle at the end of the counter. He left the room and returned with a blanket. Smitty told him what to do, "Open it up on the floor." Joe spread it out as Smitty spoke to his other men. "Saddle up one of their horses. They're down at the corral. Bring it here. We'll tie their guns on and run the horse out of town."

One man left the room. Another tied up the corners of the blanket with the outlaws' guns inside and carried the blanket out the door. Smitty ordered the troublemakers out of the saloon. "Walk out of here real slow."

Harmony's men kept their guns aimed at the members of the Butterfield Gang as they went out the door. Roy stayed where he stood and stared down at his bullet-riddled brother. *That's why he pulled his gun. He only needed control for a second. Be at peace, Hank.*

Eli listened from the other side of the wall and waited to be their ace in the hole if needed. Smitty commanded Roy, "Get moving, or I'll shoot you where you stand."

Begrudgingly, Roy complied. "Since you insist!" He rounded one of the tables on the side closest to the counter. As he passed Joe's rifle, he grabbed it and slammed the butt as hard as he could into the head of the Indian, who immediately crumpled.

Before anybody could react, Roy lunged at Smitty and sent them both reeling. The rifles held by both men slid across the pine floor worn smooth by years of saloon customers. As he went down, Smitty's head slammed into the edge of the table behind him. He lay on the floor, unmoving. Roy scrambled for a rifle to take revenge for Hank's death.

I have to stop Roy from getting a weapon. Eli sprang from the back room, knocked Roy to the floor, and stood over him with his rifle barrel pressed between Roy's brown eyes. "You better pray Smitty wakes up, or Joe will be cleaning your brains out of this floor."

Outside the saloon, the rest of the Butterfield Gang remained held at gunpoint. Doc Gridley knelt beside Smitty and opened his eyelid to look at his pupil. The light brought Smitty back. "Let me up." Smitty motioned Eli away. "Roy, it seems that stupid runs in your family. If that Indian is dead, you're going to hang for murder."

Roy spat out, "It ain't murder! It's vermin removal!"

Smitty hated prejudice. He jerked Roy off

the floor. "Eli, help me get Roy out the back." They muscled Roy to the jail and shoved him into a cell. The door clanged shut.

"That's a satisfying sound." Eli brushed his hands against each other as if to rid himself of the six-foot-tall muscular man who glared back retaliation from inside the cell.

"Yes, it is!" Smitty tucked the key into his vest pocket before they walked back up the road to join the others.

Still in the stairwell, Ann strained to hear. "Surely they would come and tell us if it's over."

Tom decided to divulge another one of his house secrets. "I have peepholes. Keep behind me." He led them into the living room and turned off the lights before he took a picture off the front wall and uncorked two holes. "One's to look through. The other is to shoot. There's some behind each of the pictures."

Stephanie took a position at the other set in the living room. Sally whispered, "I saw two pictures by the stove." Ann nodded. They made their way to the kitchen.

A group of men stood together in the street with drawn guns. Eli and Smitty joined them. Smitty told the outlaws their options, "What's it going to be? You can join Hank in Hell or Roy in jail if that's what you want."

The short bald outlaw begged, "No, sir, we don't want neither of them choices. If ya let us go, we'll leave for good."

"Is the horse ready?" asked Smitty.

"I've got it right here." A man stood behind their sheriff, holding the reins.

Smitty tied the guns on tightly and then smacked the horse on the rump. "Get going!" The horse streaked off. At the end of their gun barrels, the men of Harmony marched the men of the Butterfield Gang to the corral.

Tom decided it was safe. The girls followed him outside as the men went out of sight at the other end of the street.

At the corral, Smitty directed his men, "Saddle their horses."

Mara ran across the muddy street to join Tom and the girls. Very relieved that it was over, other women stood on the boardwalk but didn't allow their children out of their homes. Mara told them what they wanted to know. "Everybody is fine. I counted them."

With great relief, Stephanie hugged Mara and spoke a quick prayer, "God, thank You so much for listening and keeping everybody of Harmony safe. Amen."

NINETEEN

The four women and Tom stood in front of Yates Mercantile and peered through the open saloon doors at scattered tables and chairs. Mara urged them, "Let's go look in the saloon."

Tom issued a warning, "Keep your eyes open."

A few of the other women from town joined them. They stepped inside the saloon and gasped at the sight. Two men lay dead on the floor in a pool of mingled blood. There was so much blood that worry filled their minds. Mara asked nobody in particular, "Who else is hurt?"

As if Mara had asked her specifically, Betsy replied, "I don't know. How would I know?"

Sally reported what she found. "There's a lot more blood on and behind the bar."

Tom followed the trail of crimson to an open closet door. "Must be Joe's."

The doctor's wife, Nellie, thought differently. "All this blood can't be his. There's also some on the edge of this table." She walked to one of the bodies. "With this many bullet holes in him, I'm sure he's dead. He looks like he's smiling."

Ann knelt beside the man lying next to the bar with a piece of wood protruding from his arm. A deep gash on his head still bled profusely. She put her fingers to his neck. A weak pulse still beat. "This man isn't dead! We need to stop this bleeding. Tom, we need bandages. You can charge it to me." She stretched the man out on his back.

Tom returned quicker than greased lightning with a box of bandages. He pulled some and handed them to Ann.

Ann wrapped several tightly around the man's head and then looked at the piece of wood in the man's arm. "We need to get this out and his shirt off." Ann sat in the blood with the dying man's arm across her lap. She looked up at the one woman she knew. "Help me hold his arm." She turned her gaze to Tom. "You pull it out." Ann held the man's arm at the shoulder. Mara had it just above the elbow. Tom pulled. The large wood fragment came out with a sucking sound. Ann pulled at the man's shirt. "Help me get this off." Mara circled to the other side and knelt on the floor. Being careful and gentle with his injured head, they took off the Indian's shirt.

Nellie, the doctor's wife, gave instructions. "We need to stop the blood flow. Tie a bandage up here around his arm." Tom handed a cloth strip to Mara and another to Ann. Ann wrapped the fabric around the injury while Mara tied hers tightly above the wound.

"That's the best we can do for now." Ann laid the man's head in her lap.

Nellie suggested, "Can we get him to my place?"

Tom knew it was what they needed to do. "Let's try."

Laura stood outside the saloon and looked in. She didn't like the look of the blood-soaked Indian. "We shouldn't bring a criminal into our home."

"You don't know anything about this man to know if he's a criminal or not, and he needs help. We're taking him." Nellie held onto the Indian at the shoulder of his injured arm. Mara took hold of him around the shoulder of his good arm. Sally and Stephanie each grabbed a leg, and Tom and Ann slid their arms under his waist.

"On three, you ready?" Tom locked hands with Ann.

They all said, "Yes."

Tom called out the count, "One, two, three, lift!" Together, they raised the man, walked out the door and down the street to the doctor's house. Reluctantly, Laura held open the door to her home and then the door to her father's office. Curiosity drew the rest of the women who had not dared to go into the saloon. With their children in tow, they followed into Doc's house.

The outlaws stood beside their saddled horses. For the second time that year, Smitty commanded the Butterfield Gang to mount up, leave, and never come back. The men kicked their spurs hard into their rides. As the women closed the door to the doctor's office, five horses shot out of the corral and galloped away with five riders on their backs. Smitty stated what every one of them already knew. "Keep your eyes open. I don't think we can trust them." The scallywags picked up the trail of the horse that wanted to escape the abuse it had received from its current owners and had followed its instinct to go to the place where it had known love and care.

Doc issued instructions as they walked to the saloon. "Bring the Indian to my place. Joe and Smitty, I also want to look at you."

Smitty entered the saloon. The Indian was gone. Strangely, his shirt lay inside out in the blood and mud smeared across the floor. "What happened to him?"

"Danged if I know. Maybe he crawled away." Eli searched for clues.

Doc scratched his head and pondered. "If he came to, why did he take off his shirt?"

Smitty looked around the room. Bloody, muddy footprints went in every direction. At the door, he saw small footprints, mostly exiting. He followed them out the door. "I think the women took him to Doc's place."

Doc opened his front door and found every woman and child in town crowded inside. "You have the Indian, Nellie?"

"Yes, dear, in your office."

Doc ordered everybody out. "Everybody go home." Nobody made a move to leave. "At least let me in." They stepped apart.

As Doc entered his office, Nellie gave him a status report. "He's severely injured. He can't have more than a drop of blood left inside."

Smitty came into the room behind Doc. Mara threw her arms around him. "Thank God you're alive. Are you hurt?"

He gently and briefly kissed his wife's lips. "I'm fine. Doc just wants to check me over."

Doc begged for space, "Except Smitty, Mara, and Joe, everybody clear out of my office."

After they had brought in the Indian, Ann, Stephanie, Sally, Mara, and Tom had remained in the room with Nellie. Ann held the Indian's head in her arm as she tried to get the unconscious man to drink water. She started to leave. Doc stopped her. "Keep getting water into him." Ann dribbled water into the man's mouth. When he swallowed, she poured in more.

Doc looked at the injured arm with a blood-soaked, but not dripping, bandage. He gave instructions to his wife. "Wrap more bandages over this one. Let the tourniquet loose for a minute then tie it back. Let me look at his head." Doc carefully removed the dressings and examined the gash. "That was quite a sockdolager he got. He's going to need a lot of work. Honey, wrap his head back up as tight as you can."

Doc directed his conscious patients to chairs, "Smitty, sit there. Joe, you sit over here." The men sat where instructed. "Let's see what we've got here." Doc examined the back of Smitty's head. He looked at his eyes. "Do you feel dizzy, fuzzy-headed, or sick in your stomach?"

"Not dizzy or sick, but I have a headache you wouldn't believe."

"You need stitches. I'll get you sewed up. Then you can go home, but don't sleep until late tonight. Mara, you keep him awake and treat him extra good. Watch him real close, and let me know immediately if anything seems wrong. Agreed?"

"I promise."

Nellie didn't need her husband to direct her. She had helped him for so long that she already had a washbasin ready to clean the wound and a straight razor in her hand to cut the hair away. Doc stepped over to look at Joe. The puncture in his cheek went all the way through. Joe had pulled out the hunk of wood, but splinters remained. "You're lucky that shard hit your jaw at an angle just right to skin your gum but not knock out your teeth. Do either of you need an antifogmatic before I get started?" Doc held out a bottle of whiskey.

Smitty never drank. "Just sew me up."

"Nellie needs to shave around the wound."

Joe stalled. "I'd better have that drink. I think I'm going to need more help. You can work on me second."

This time, Doc did instruct his wife, "Get as many splinters out of Joe as you can while I sew up Smitty."

Nellie finished shaving the injured part of Smitty's head as Doc threaded his needle. Doc carefully sewed up the gash on the back of Smitty's head. To disinfect the best way he could, Doc poured whiskey over his work.

Smitty jumped up. "How about warning a person first!"

"Sorry. Mara, take Smitty home. Don't forget what I told you."

"Much obliged, Doc. We'll remember." Mara took her husband's hand. She and Smitty squeezed into Doc's crowded foyer.

There was something else Smitty needed to handle before he went home. "Earl, bury Hank and the Indian when he dies. I'll pay the expenses."

Nellie turned to Doc. "I removed all the splinters I could find. Joe's an excellent patient. He held his cheek back while I worked on his gums. I know it hurts."

Doc poured another shot of whiskey and handed it to Joe. "Swish this around in your mouth as best as you can, then spit it into the basin."

Joe took the antifogmatic, emptied it into his mouth, and swished. Whiskey sprayed out his cheek, so he put his hand against the hole and tried to swish again. Bloody whiskey sloshed against his hand and dribbled down his cheek.

"That's good enough."

Joe spit the whiskey still in his mouth into the basin. He made a request, "One to go down?" Doc poured another shot. Joe drank it down. He held the glass out for a few more before he said, "Ready."

Doc worked on the inside of Joe's cheek. Joe put down more shots before Doc started on the outside of Joe's cheek. Joe requested and received more whiskey. When the last few stitches went in, Joe was out cold. Doc opened his office door. "Carry Joe home." Except for Ann, everybody left when the men took Joe to his room at the saloon.

Ann had gotten several glasses of water into the man when Doc told her it was time for her to leave. Caught by the emotions of holding a dying man in her arms and trying to save his life, Ann couldn't let go of her concern for the Indian. She stayed while Doc and Nellie worked on the Indian for what seemed to be forever.

When Nellie finally opened the door, she smiled approvingly and called Ann over. "I thought you might still be here. Come in. Lawrence wants to talk with you."

"Nellie told me what you did. You may have saved this man's life. If you hadn't stopped the bleeding and gotten all that water into him, he would have died in a few more minutes. His skull is cracked, but I don't think it pushed in. There probably isn't any brain damage, but I don't know for sure. I cleaned and stitched his head. The wound in his arm is deep, but there are no severed muscles or tendons. I stitched the puncture closed. Even so, it's most likely that he won't live. You can sit with him, but go home and get clean first."

Ann didn't know why, but she felt very grateful. "Thank you for everything, Doctor. I'll be back." After she had bathed in the shed for the second time that day, Ann went to Doc's and sat beside the Indian. She trickled water into his handsome mouth. She talked to him and prayed to God to spare him. From time to time, his eyes fluttered. She believed that he heard her.

TWENTY

While the man lay in bed, barely surviving, the horse that Smitty had run out of town ran across the countryside carrying the ruffians' guns. In a few hours, the horse arrived at its destination. It stood outside the barn and called. If the girls had been home, they would have heard its loud whinny, but they weren't there. It wasn't long before the men it had tried to escape caught up with the horse. They untied their parcel of guns and then beat the horse for running so far before stopping.

The short bald man recognized the place. "You think we bought this horse here last winter?"

Ben confirmed, "I reckon so, Charlie."

Al, the tall one, suggested reconnoitering,

"I think there's just girls here. Let's see if anybody's home."

Gus remembered. "That's right. Hank didn't let us bother 'em last time, but he's not here now." Hank was the only person Gus had ever respected. There was something about Hank. He had been strong, rough, demanding, and downright mean, but he had kept them all in line in a way that didn't upset them. Gus didn't care about anybody, but somehow, the way Hank did things seemed right. He had no problem doing what Hank had wanted. Gus convinced himself that he felt the way Hank told him to feel. Now that Hank was gone, Gus didn't know how he was supposed to feel. Mostly, he felt angry. Right then, he felt lustful and rubbed himself suggestively.

Charlie warned Gus, "We want 'em ta let us in, so act nice, or I'll beat the hide from your skinny body."

Gus didn't cotton to being threatened.

All five men stood at the front door, but

Charlie knocked. They waited. Gus ordered Charlie, "Knock harder." With no internal impulse control, he immediately beat at the door with the butt of his newly reacquired gun. No more than a few seconds passed. Nobody came to the door. Even though Charlie had assumed leadership of the gang, Gus didn't care what Charlie wanted. He pressed Charlie, "Ain't nobody home. Check if the door's open."

Charlie turned the knob. The door opened. "Hello in the house."

They barely waited. "Nobody's here." Gus pushed past Charlie. Charlie went right behind Gus, followed by the rest of the men.

Pete, the smallest of the gang, said, "Don't mess things up. They'll be back, and we don't want 'em to be on guard."

Gus replied sarcastically, "Anything you say, Pete."

They walked across the foyer, then the living room, into the dining room, and on around into the kitchen. Al opened the kitchen door leading to the outside, poked his head out, and looked around. Ben opened the other door, saw that it was a pantry, and notified everybody, "I found food."

Charlie came over and looked in. "We need ta check everywhere first." He closed the door. They went through the fourth doorway from the kitchen back into the living room. Gus stopped at the fireplace. He opened the lid of the music box on the mantelpiece and wound the spring with the key. He stood there and listened as it played. Even though Charlie urged them to continue exploring, the other men stayed and tried out the furniture. When the music stopped, they crossed the entry hall to the doors on the other side of the house. Not even slightly aware of the interpersonal dynamics of the men with him, Charlie directed Pete and Gus to go together. "You two go in that room." He, Ben, and Al went through the other door. All five of them entered the same room that spanned the house.

Pete looked around the room. "Must be a workroom."

Being careful that he didn't set Gus off, Ben gently jammed his elbow into Gus's arm and snidely replied, "That's pretty clear from all the tools an such."

They followed Charlie back into the hall and up the staircase. Charlie turned toward the balcony left of the open space to the floor below. Because he didn't want to be around either of them, Charlie sent Gus and Pete to the matching balcony on the right. "Go that way."

Gus and Pete didn't have any reason to do anything different. They went to the right-hand balcony and strolled halfway across before they went left through the door. They entered the hall between the four bedrooms over the living room, kitchen, and dining room.

Charlie, Ben, and Al walked along the left balcony, where there were two doors. Charlie pointed to the door at the far end. "You two go in that door. I'll go in this one." This time, they entered two separate rooms over the one large workroom below. A thick powdering of dust covered the floor, bunk beds, dressers, washstands, chamber pots, and the pot-bellied woodstove. Charlie pulled out a dresser drawer full of sheets and blankets.

Across the house, Gus found female clothes in the first room. He blurted out, "This one's a girl's room."

Pete examined the room across the hall. "This one too." He moved on to the other room on the front side of the house and looked at the clothes folded in the bureau drawers. "This one must be a man's room."

Gus went into the room at the end of the hall on the backside of the house. "Another girl's using this room. I should give her some company."

"So there must be a man here with the girls."

Gus mocked Pete as they met back in the hall. "You think so?" Gus held out a long pole that he had brought from the wardrobe of the last room. "Found this." Gus used the hook on the end of the pole, caught the latch in the hall ceiling, and pulled down folding stairs.

They climbed into a large empty room. In the middle of the room were two chimneys. A wood stove, not used in decades, stood between them. Beyond them, in the far wall, two doors led to the other half of the house. The room's walls matched the roofline of the house. They angled in slightly for four feet then came in sharply the top two feet. "This floor probably goes all the way ta the other end a the house." Pete didn't harass Gus, who would have done so to him after a statement of an obvious fact.

Charlie shut the dresser drawer in the bunkroom at the backside of the house and called out to those in the front room, "Let's see what's upstairs." They ascended the stairs on that side of the balcony.

Al, being six feet five inches tall, bent

down to get through the door at the top of the stairs. He hit his head anyway.

"You moron." Ben went through the doorway tall enough for people of normal height. Charlie followed him into a room filled with open doors. Just to the left of the entry door, they saw a woodstove. They looked into nine empty rooms of different sizes. The largest room was six by six, but most were four by six. Around the far side of the chimney, they found a closet with several shelves, upon which lay sixteen small padlocks with their keys. On the left side of the room, a hall turned back toward the center of the house. They found six more small storage rooms on the right side of the corridor. At the end, they came to a door that Al couldn't open.

Ben knew he was the strongest of the bunch. "You can't pull bending over like that. Let me by." He pushed Al aside. Ben couldn't budge it either. "Must be locked from the other side."

As Charlie and his group examined

farmhand storage rooms, Gus and Pete crossed the large room at the top of the pull-down stairs. Pete froze and whispered, "I hear somebody."

"You scared little man; I shoulda pushed your tiny little body inta that well when I had the chance. It's gotta be the others, ya idiot!" Gus called out loudly, "What's over there?"

Ben turned his head and looked at Al and Charlie. "I hear Gus." He spoke to Gus through the door, "Storage rooms."

"There's one big room over here. This door is padlocked. The other looks like it locks with a key."

"How'd ya get in?"

"Come up through a ceiling hole."

"Can ya open the lock?" Charlie wanted to learn as much as possible about the place.

Pete tried the knob. "No."

Charlie instructed Pete and Gus, "Go back ta the kitchen." He told the men with him, "Let's go."

Al expressed his discomfort as they exited

the attic, "I don't like it up here. It's too short."

Ben explained, "If ya weren't a giant, ya wouldn't a had this problem."

Downstairs, Gus stopped and wound up the music box again. As he listened, the scowl on his face became a look of serenity. To the man who had never felt peace, the music sounded how he imagined it would feel. Deep in the back of his mind, Gus longed to find some.

Charlie went into the pantry. He took cougar jerky from the bag, five cougar sausages, and several handfuls of dried apples from the bushel basket. He handed out the food. "It's not much, but eat up." Charlie then ordered Pete, "Get water." He pointed to the barrel.

Pete remembered the china. He put five nice glasses on the dining room table and then walked to the water barrel with a pitcher. "We oughta leave soon. We don't know when they'll get home."

Gus countered the suggestion, "We can each take a watch an sneak out one a the doors if they come back."

Pete started back to the dining room with the water. "But we don't know which way they'll come."

Gus wanted to get on Pete's nerves and tried to start a row. "Coward." He pushed up into Pete's space. Pete walked around him with the water. Because he wanted to sleep in the bed of one of the girls, Gus pleaded, "We can keep watch an' stay in the house."

Dust covered the bunkrooms. Charlie, therefore, assumed nobody had been in or would be going into them. Hence, nobody would know that anybody had been there. He decided they could stay inside if they slept in the bunks.

Pete acquiesced. *If them girls are comin' home taday, it'll be soon.* "I'll take the first watch." He walked out of the house. *They're all idiots. I don't know why I stay with 'em.* Pete obsessed over the stupid choice as he moved the horses and ammo boxes to the thick cover in the woods behind the house.

Gus carried the music box to the bunkroom. After the twentieth time they had listened, Charlie hollered, "Don't wind that thing up again, or I'll bust it."

Gus protectively stashed the wooden box between him and the wall. He lay on the bunk with his loaded revolver out. *Anybody who tries to hurt this will end up with a hole in him. I hope Pete tries.*

TWENTY ONE

Stephanie went to the doctor's house. "Ann, are we going home this morning?"

"Yes, I'll be there in a few minutes." Ann stroked the cheek of the unconscious man. "I don't know who you are or even what kind of person you are, but I hope you're a good man, and I hope you live." She prayed, "God, watch over him and heal him," then she called out, "Nellie, Doc, I'm leaving."

They came into the hall. Nellie reached for Ann's hand. "We'll take care of him. Do you want us to let you know what happens?"

"I don't know him. There isn't any reason for me to know, but we'll ask the next time one of us is in town. Help him the best you can." Ann left the man with a hole in his arm, a cracked skull, and very little blood, in the hands of God and the doctor.

Ann arrived at the store. Tom informed her of a problem. "I think you made a mistake on the list. You wrote one hundred pounds of candles. You must have meant one hundred candles. I owe you a little money."

"It wasn't a mistake. Please pack them. What do I owe you for the bandages?"

"Nothing. I gave them to that man, not you."

Ann told him sincerely, "I'm much obliged for everything. I can see why Eli is such a nice young man. He takes after his father." She walked to the wagon and silently prayed, *God, show Tom Yates your love and comfort. He's mad at You because his wife died. I know how hard it is because of Mama and Papa. Help him.*

Eli hugged his father. "Love you, Pop. See you next month."

Tom placed a crate of candles with the rest of the supplies. "I hope it will be a very uneventful visit."

Eli walked to the wagon, "Me too."

"We appreciate you keeping us safe." Sally hugged Tom.

Stephanie took her turn. "Everything really, but especially for letting Eli help us."

"Take good care of each other." Tom waved goodbye.

TWENTY TWO

Late the same morning, the men in the Williams' house woke. Gus made sure that Pete knew he had been wrong. "See, ya yellow-bellied coward, ya can't catch me any better than ya can catch a weasel asleep."

Ben didn't need to harass Pete. He felt hungry. "Let's get somethin' ta eat."

Gus's belly also called out for food. "I'm on your tail."

Pete disputed everything Gus suggested, mostly because he thought Gus was always wrong but also because he was sick and tired of everything about the man. "We need to wait ta see what Charlie wants ta do."

Gus threatened Pete, "I'm sick a your sniveling. I'm gonna tie ya up an leave ya here."

Pete knew what Gus wanted since they came into the Williams' house. "Then ya wouldn't get your slimy hands on them girls."

Gus shoved Pete into his bunk. "You're right. I'll kill ya an give ya ta the vultures." He left Pete rubbing a knot on his head.

Ben followed Gus. "Maybe we should."

Pete heard what Ben said even over the melody of the music box that Gus carried down the stairs. Steaming with anger, Pete stomped down the stairs and out the front door. He saw the wagon across the field and ran back into the house. "They're comin'."

Charlie and Al scrambled out of bed, pulled on their boots, and stumbled down the stairs. Gus and Ben had just gone into the pantry when they heard the warning. Before they jetted out the kitchen door into the woods behind the house, they jammed sausages and dried apples into their pockets and stuffed jerky into their mouths. Pete flew out of the house behind them. The music box, back on the mantel, finished its melody as Al and Charlie hurried through the kitchen.

Charlie saw the open pantry door. He darted over to close it. Cougar jerky and dried apple pieces lay scattered on the floor. "#$% #&# %$." He picked up the evidence that somebody had been in the house and crammed the food into his pocket. As he closed the pantry, the wagon came around the corner and stopped at the kitchen door. Eli propped the two rifles that the girls owned and the rifle he had just brought from home against the side of the house.

Pete whispered angrily, "I told ya we shoulda left. Now, Charlie's caught, an it's all Gus's fault."

Charlie scuttled rapidly across the floor into the dining room on his hands and knees. He made it out of the kitchen as Eli opened the door. "You want us to hand everything to you or put it on the table?" Charlie recognized the voice of the one who had threatened to blow Roy's brains into the floor. Charlie couldn't remember if the floors squeaked or not, but he had no other avenue of escape. So they wouldn't see him through the kitchen door, he tiptoed across the living room along the front wall. Luckily for Charlie, James had built the house well. Not a single board made a sound. Undetected, he made it out through the workroom door. He paused at the edge of the house and peeked around the corner to be sure they wouldn't see him. The way looked clear. He dashed into the woods.

Charlie told his gang what he had discovered. "That's the cur what said he'd splatter Roy's brains across the floor. He must be one a 'em what shot Hank. We oughta get even."

Pete stated his usual cautious type of suggestion, "We oughta leave. Nobody knows we've been here. We won't have any problems if we leave."

Hank had kept the gang running smoothly. Al already felt them falling apart.

He wanted revenge. "We can't let 'em get away with killin' Hank."

Gus had the same thought in his mind that he always had. "If we kill him, then we can do whatever we want with them girls for as long as we want."

In their hiding place in the woods, they argued about the best thing to do. They could shoot them all easily enough, but Gus desperately wanted to get control of the girls alive. The other men didn't object to keeping the girls alive until they were done with them, but they thought it was more important to take out Eli. None of them thought he had a right to live when Hank was dead and Roy was in jail. The problem was, if they shot Eli, the girls might shoot back. They didn't know their abilities, and none of them wanted to take a chance of dying, so they watched Eli and the girls unload their supplies.

Ann knew what they had just bought was not enough. "We should plant the vegetable garden. The seeds are from two years ago, but some should grow."

Knowing plowing was one of the upcoming chores; Eli had already checked the plow and found the blade sharp. He assumed it had sat unused since their father had sharpened it two years earlier. "The plow is ready to use."

Sally passed Ann the candles. "Should we start today?"

Stephanie hefted a bag of flour onto her shoulder. "I think we should."

"After we're done unloading, we'll see what's what." Ann wanted vegetables to eat as soon as possible. They put up the only provisions they would be able to buy until fall. They took all the rifles when they moved the wagon into the barn.

Pete tried again. "At least two a the girls must know how ta shoot, or they wouldn't've taken all three guns. We should forget about 'em an leave." None of the men moved from their places of observation.

Stephanie unhooked the horse and went to get the brush. Sally searched for the seeds. "Where would Papa have put them?"

"I remember he always brought a wooden box to the garden." Ann reached for a wooden box on a high shelf. She placed it on the bench, slid off the lid, and took out several papers folded into fat packets. She attempted to decipher the faded writing. "I have no idea what this says, but it feels like seeds inside." Ann passed one to Stephanie.

Stephanie opened it up. "Maybe you can tell what we have. You must know more about seeds than we do." She pushed the packet toward Eli.

"I'll see what I can figure out." Eli examined the contents.

"Let me look." Sally crowded with the others around the packets of seeds as Ann laid them out on the bench. Sally decided she wanted to make it into a game. "Let's keep track of what we each think. We can see who got the most right when the plants come up."

Ann didn't see any harm in guessing, and it would make Sally happy. "Why not? But I think Eli will get the most right."

After much discussion and examination, they decided they had beans, beets, broccoli, cabbage, carrots, leeks, onions, melons, parsnips, peas, okra, spinach, turnips, and squash. They had never planted this early. Stephanie didn't know how soon they could plant these types of seeds. "What can we plant today, and what has to wait?"

Eli knew the answer. "We can plant everything except the melons. Are we going to plow the garden today?"

"Yes, let's get Samson hitched to the plow."

Stephanie led the horse to the backyard. Sally placed the packets of seeds back in the box. Ann brought the rifles and laid them beside the garden plot. "I'll go first because Samson is used to me. Eli, I'll show you how to do this then you can help pick out the rocks." Eli watched as Ann plowed and explained the process. He verbally repeated the instructions correctly, so Ann sent him to help remove rocks. An hour later, Ann and Samson had turned half the garden. She decided it was time for Eli. "It's your turn."

Eli wasn't sure how prepared he was, but he walked to the plow. "I'm ready."

They switched places. Ann stood beside the rifles. She watched Eli battle the plow as he tried to keep it upright and run it straight. She told him the secret. "Let the horse do the work. Just keep the plow vertical. Samson will pull straight." Eli continued to struggle. Ann continued telling him to let the horse do the work until she decided he would have to wear himself down before he would figure it out. She left him on his own. She picked up rocks and tossed them out of the garden, but she continued to observe.

In only half an hour, Eli's arms were too tired to muscle the plow. Samson took over the work. Eli discovered how much better that worked, and Samson was glad the friction from the rear decreased. An hour later, when they had finished the plot, Eli had just about figured out how to do it. Ann hinted at what she wanted next. "It would be great if we got the little field plowed today."

Eli replied, "Just tell me exactly where," but he wondered if he would have the strength.

"Girls, do you want to plant or walk with us?"

Stephanie picked up the box of seeds. "Sally, unhook Samson. We'll let him graze while they're gone."

"Come with me, Eli." Ann picked up one of the rifles.

Gus realized the four were separating. "Maybe we can catch some of 'em while they're apart."

Pete couldn't fathom how Gus could be so ignorant. "None of 'em are gonna let us walk up ta 'em, but if ya want ta get shot, go on."

Gus didn't want to wait, no matter how dangerous it might be. He thought he could accomplish capturing one of them. He stood up. Charlie grabbed his arm. "Be patient. Let's follow them two leavin'. Since we wanna kill one of 'em anyway, we'd have a better chance with them two."

"But I want the young one." Gus pulled out of Charlie's grip. Pete tackled him.

Gus was furious. Pete prevented him from going after what he wanted. "I'm gonna kill ya." He shoved Pete off.

Sally thought it was a waste of time to walk to the field just to look. "Ann, he'll see it when we go. Let's plant this garden." Ann picked up a spade and a packet of seeds and stepped into the garden. "You too, Eli, plant up there." Sally pointed to the front and winked at Stephanie.

Eli decided on the carrot seeds. He and Ann got down on their knees to plant. Stephanie saw Sally scoop up a handful of soil. She gathered a batch. Together, they slung their soft gooey handfuls at the backsides in front of them. The mud made a big splat and spread nicely across their bums.

Ann felt the mud hit and immediately knew what was going on, "You little scallywags!" She scooped up a handful of dirt and returned fire.

Eli quickly realized that Stephanie and Sally had declared war. "I see how it is!" He gleefully joined the battle. All four rolled in the mud, screamed, laughed, and enjoyed the fun. Anybody watching would have thought the people in the garden had lost their minds. The people in the garden didn't know that the men Smitty had run out of town the day before were watching them.

They had flung all of the freshly plowed rock-free mud at least once before Ann ended the battle. "Truce! Let's clean our faces and get this garden planted."

Sally informed her oldest sister, "We won!"

Ann put her arm around Sally's shoulders. "I think so too." They cleaned up enough to see what they were doing, crawled back into the mud, and planted their seeds in the well-mixed soil. Neat lines of planted seeds graced the garden when Ann asked for a volunteer. "Who wants to get dinner ready?"

Sally always enjoyed cooking. "I'll do it."

"All right, you're on cooking duty." Ann drew two buckets of water to wash the dirt off their arms and hands. They pulled off their muddy shoes on the porch before going to their rooms. Sally, however, went to the kitchen, got the big water pots, hung them in the fireplace, and filled them with water. She threw more wood on the fire and stirred up the flames. Before long, Ann entered the kitchen in clean clothes. "We could have a quick meal of cougar sausages. Then, if you're willing, you can prepare supper while we work in the field. What do you think?"

"That's fine with me."

Ann went into the pantry to get sausages. "I thought there was more than this."

"I don't know how many were left."

Ann saw Stephanie and Eli crossing the

living room. "We're going to eat a quick meal, so we can get today's plowing done before dark."

"I'll be right back." Eli did an about-face and went back up the stairs. He returned quickly. "Smitty wanted to do something to thank me for stopping Roy. I told him he didn't need to do anything, but he insisted. I asked for a whole cheese because I want it to be for all of us."

Ann handed him the butcher knife to carve slices. "That is very thoughtful and generous." They each ate one slice of cheese with their one cougar sausage. Eli, Ann, and Stephanie put their plates into the washbasin. Gus saw them take only two rifles when they went to the barn.

TWENTY THREE

Sally washed the dishes, looked out the kitchen window, and hummed to herself. From the cover of the woods, Gus watched her. *This is working out just right.* Gus felt an emotion he rarely felt; happiness.

Ann opened the barn door. “Stephanie, please hook up Samson.” Ann went in and pulled a wooden contraption toward the plow. “Eli, hold up the plow.” Under the plow, Ann slid a small platform that hung low below the axle of its big wheels. She lowered the hitch over the pull pole and pulled a leather strap through the hole to hold it.

Eli looked over the contraption. “Did your Uncle James make this?”

Stephanie bragged about the uncle she

had never met. "Yes. It makes it much easier to get the plow to the field. He was such a smart man."

"Samson likes it, and since today is his first day plowing this spring, we'll turn the small field. The ground is softest there, and there are fewer rocks. We can do a harder field tomorrow." Ann knew it would make no difference to the horse, but she believed it would make a difference to Eli.

Stephanie agreed it was best to do the field farthest away first. After a fifteen-minute walk at a steady pace, they arrived. Eli put down the rifles and started in where Ann told him.

Gus informed the other members of the Butterfield Gang of his intentions or at least what he wanted them to think. "I'm going to see what's in these woods." He walked away, but he didn't search the woods. He searched for the best approach to the house.

After many passes across the field, working the plow fairly well, Ann stopped

Eli. She didn't want to work Eli too hard, cause him to quit, and leave them to do all the work alone again. "Let's each take a turn. Stephanie, you haven't taken a turn today. Are you willing to go next?" Not knowing what Ann was thinking but also wanting Eli to remain at the farm; Stephanie happily traded places with him.

After Stephanie had plowed out of hearing range, Eli confided to Ann, "You're right; letting Samson do the pulling is easier for both of us."

"Papa told me the same thing when he taught me, but I was only ten. I didn't have any choice. I couldn't have done a thing if Samson wasn't pulling."

Much to his dismay, Gus discovered there was no good way to approach. Through the windows, Sally had a good view of the wide field that surrounded the house. All on his own, Gus made a rare wise choice. To avoid getting shot, he decided the best plan would be to wait until Sally was in the workroom then cross at the other end of the house to the kitchen door.

Sally stood in the kitchen looking out the window at the woods she loved. She started the bread as she contemplated improving supper over cougar sausages.

Far away from Sally, Stephanie plowed a large portion of the field before Ann took over. Ann and Samson had plowed together for nine years. They knew exactly how to accomplish the most plowing with the least effort. Before the sun shone directly into Ann's eyes each time she headed west across the field, they had turned over almost all of the dirt. "The sun is blinding me. I can hardly see what I'm doing."

It wasn't the first time Stephanie had heard the same complaint. "And you complain about it every spring. You know to look at the ground and not ahead. You have only two more passes to finish."

Ann knew she always complained, and she knew it never stopped the light from getting into her eyes, but she complained anyway. However, she did know what to do. As always, she continued the job. Relief and satisfaction filled her when she finished the field. "It'll be dark in an hour. There are still too many rocks to get them all out today. Let's hook up the cart and go home."

Eli took the cart to the edge of the field and dumped the rocks. Then, serenaded by Rose-Breasted Grosbeaks, they trudged back to the house. When they neared the house, they smelled the baking bread and picked up their pace. In the barn, they unhitched the one who was most responsible for all they had accomplished that day. He went straight to his stall and waited for his pay. Stephanie brushed him down, Eli drew water, and Ann brought hay and oats for doing such good work.

Ann entered the workroom. "We're back." They heard no reply. A stack of towels sat beside the washbasin. The water beside them was barely warm. Ann reached for a pitcher.

She accidentally bumped the handle. All the water jugs crashed against the counter on their way to the floor. She jumped back as broken ceramics and water flew in every direction, "Ahhh!" Water soaked the front of her blouse and trousers, covered the counter, and ran onto the floor. Strangely, the commotion didn't bring Sally into the room.

Stephanie picked up the pottery. "This one only has a broken handle. These two are ruined."

"I'll get the pitchers out of the bunkrooms and get more water." Ann exited the room. A minute later, she stood at the balcony railing. "Come up here, right now!"

Eli grabbed the rifle, leaning against the workbench. "Go up. I'll get Sally." Stephanie took the other and hurried up the stairs. Eli headed to the kitchen.

"Come here." Ann directed Stephanie's attention to the evidence trampled into the floor.

Stephanie peered past her. "Oh no, I'll

check the other room." She walked down the balcony and opened the door. What she saw filled her with fear. "It's the same over here. How could we have left Sally alone?"

Ann followed the trail out of the room. "Same on the stairs to the attic." Afraid of what she would find, Ann reached for the attic door.

Stephanie stopped her. "Don't open the door until Eli gets here."

Eli came up the stairs. "What's going on?"

"Where is Sally? Did you find Sally? Oh, Ann, how could we have done this?"

"Done what?" Sally's head rose into view.

Ann's fears evaporated. "We were afraid you had been hurt."

Sally stepped onto the landing. "I'm fine. Why think something happened to me?"

"Somebody was in here. Footprints are everywhere, and there were fewer sausages."

Stephanie put her hands on her hips and a perturbed expression on her face. "Why didn't you say something?"

"I did mention it to Sally, but I figured I remembered wrong."

Sally proposed a possibility, "Maybe it was some hungry people who are gone."

Eli doubted that was what happened. "More likely those varmints we ran out of town. If they're still here, they'll be in the woods." He peeked out the window.

In a state of high irritation, Gus threaded between the trees back to his gang. He had seen only two rifles carried away with the three people who left. He had figured they left one because the girl in the house knew how to use it. Sally had stayed in the kitchen, where she would have seen him approach. When Sally had finally left the kitchen, the others were back with a good view of the house. Gus never had a chance to dash for the house to grab Sally.

Eli was afraid he was right. He looked intently into the woods. "I saw movement. I can't tell who or what, but something is definitely in the woods."

TWENTY FOUR

Ann immediately issued orders, "Act as if you're behaving normally but be careful of what they can see through the windows. Bar all the doors as you pass them. First, we put all the guns and bullets in Stephanie's room. Afterward, Eli, go to the workroom. Stay in there out of view, but stand where you can see me at the kitchen door.

"Sally and Stephanie, stand out of view next to the living room windows that face the woods. Don't close any shutters until we're all in position. I'll go to the kitchen doorway. When you see my signal, you two close and bar the back shutters, run across the room, and lock the front shutters. Eli, close up the back window first then go to the window by the door and then to the front. I'll be in the kitchen, so I'll get those shutters and the ones in the dining room.

"If they're watching, they'll see the shutters close. If they have bad intentions, they'll come at us quickly, so run upstairs as soon as you secure your downstairs windows. Eli, get the bunkrooms. Get the back one first. Sally, you get the window right at the top of the stairs then run to Stephanie's room and close those shutters. Stephanie, go to my room before you go across to Eli's. By then, I'll be up there to shut the front balcony shutters. Whoever gets there first, secure the shutters in Sally's room.

"Make sure you do not change the order. Close up as quickly as you can then we'll meet in Stephanie's room. Everybody understand?" They each acknowledged that they knew what to do. "Let's get at it."

Stephanie stopped them. "Wait. We can't forget the most important thing."

"What?" Eli didn't want to give the scoundrels a chance to get any further time advantage.

"We pray. God, You have all the power, and You know what's happening here. You know we love You and that we are your servants. Protect us."

Eli added, "And, if You will, punish them."

"Help us be strong and wise," Ann asked for what she thought they needed.

Sally concluded, "Amen."

They barred the doors, got their small arsenal set, and went to their stations. At Ann's signal, they flew into action.

Gus had believed he was going to have his way with Sally. He was furious that he had decided to wait until it was safe and had then failed. Gus saw the shutters close. He was sure he wasn't going to let the four in the house have time to lock him out. He fired on the house and hollered, "They're on to us." Not knowing what was happening; the other men grabbed their guns and charged to the edge of the woods.

In the house, Eli heard Gus's yell

immediately followed by the first shot. "They're coming! Fly!"

Even though Eli had not fired a single shot during the saloon fight, the outlaws considered everybody from Harmony to have killed Hank. They weren't going to let Hank's killer live. If the girls had to die with him, then they would. The men outside let loose a barrage of lead at the house. Bullets slammed into the house, embedded themselves in the mortar, or ricocheted off the stones. Since there was no way they could close the exterior shutters, window glass shattered everywhere.

Ann darted through the dining room door to the side window. She slammed the shutters shut and threw the bar into place. As she turned toward the front window, a bullet penetrated the closed kitchen shutter and sailed through the house. The glass in front of her exploded. She dropped to the floor. Liquid dripped from her face. Expecting to see a bloody hand, she wiped her cheek. Her mind screamed with relief when she saw only sweat.

Immediately, Ann resumed her appointed rounds. She closed the shutters and secured the bar that held them shut. Cautiously, she crawled across the living room and then flew up the stairs. Ann saw the closed shutters at the top of the stairs and turned to the front window.

Eli came out of the bunkroom. “I’ve got this one.”

Ann warned him, “Be careful! Their bullets can go through the shutters.” She ran to the hall door that led to the bedrooms. Both her sisters sat against the stone wall in Stephanie’s room. Stephanie pushed a pile of glass out of the way and signaled Ann to stay low. Ann joined them at the wall. “Everything already closed?”

Bullets blew the remaining shreds of Stephanie’s shutters into a million worthless pieces. Lead and wood zinged past. Stephanie hung her head. “No, there are too many bullets. I’m afraid to move.”

"What's open?"

Stephanie confessed with tears, "I didn't follow your directions. I didn't go to your room first. Instead, I came into my room first, Sally's room second, and then I went to Eli's room. By then, too many bullets were flying to go into your room. When Sally got here, I yelled for her to get on the floor and crawled in here with her. I'm sorry. I messed everything up."

Ann comforted her sister, "It doesn't matter. The shutters aren't stopping the bullets anyway."

When he arrived at the hall door, Eli saw bullets, glass, and wood whiz across. He dropped to the floor, afraid of what he might see. He peeked around the lower edge of the door into the room. Stephanie yelled over the thundering of the guns. "Come in on your belly."

Eli probably knows how the bullets can get through our thick wooden shutters. Ann asked, "What kind of guns do you think they have?"

Eli confessed, "I have no idea."

"There are so many bullets. There must be millions of people out there. We don't have a chance." Sally's tears rolled down her cheeks.

Even though he also thought they weren't going to make it, Eli attempted to comfort Sally, the other girls, and himself, "They have to come across the open field. We can pick them off as they come."

Under the pressure of trying to keep her family alive, Ann only thought realistically. She didn't help comfort anybody. "Except we can't look out the window to see."

Useless information popped into Stephanie's mind. "If there were holes in the attic like your father has in his house, we could see what we're up against."

After thinking about what Stephanie said, Ann nixed the plan. "Right here, we're behind a stone wall. Up there, it's only wood. It wouldn't be safe."

Eli didn't see any other possibilities. "I'll go. They probably don't think anybody is up there for that very reason and won't shoot that way."

They cowered behind the stone wall as bullets continued to fly in. Stephanie glumly pointed out the futility of the plan. "There aren't any holes."

Eli contemplated upon how he could make a hole. "I thought I saw a hand drill in the workshop."

Maybe we should make a hole in the attic, but the men outside will realize what we're doing. Sally asked, "Wouldn't they hear the drill?"

"I don't think they would hear a drill. I can barely hear you. Besides that, the sun will be going down soon. If I'm going to see anything, I have to get started."

Ann didn't consider the choice long. "To have any chance, we need to do something now. They'll surely come as soon as it gets dark. They can't climb up here to get in, but we need to guard the downstairs windows. Since we have three rifles, we can stand behind the wall next to the window and shoot three of them before we need to reload.

"That could work if they don't come in too fast or circle to the front. We need to know how many are out there." Ann tried to take a quick peek out the shutterless glassless window. She saw nothing but drew a massive volley of bullets that slammed into the ceiling. Plaster broke loose and flew in every direction. A huge chunk smashed into the washstand and chamber pot below. Ann dropped. She huddled on the floor behind the wall. "That won't work."

A sudden lull in the attack left a scary silence. Assuming everything in the world was just as it was supposed to be, the grosbeaks resumed singing. Inside the house, they knew they still had a problem and pondered. Maybe the men outside were trying to trick them into showing their faces. They needed to find out everything they could, but there was no way any of them was going to try to look out again. "I'm going to drill the hole."

Stephanie begged, "No, it's too dangerous. Don't try." Eli crawled out of the room.

Due to the silence, Ann no longer believed that Eli would be able to drill a hole. However, since Eli was going to try, she also had something she had to do. She whispered, "I'll be back," then slid out of the room on her belly. Once in the hall, she made her way on her hands and knees.

Ann arrived at her door. "Help me, God." She slithered into her room. The dresser was in front of the open window. Ann knew if they shot at the chest of drawers that it would not stop the bullets, but she had no choice. What she needed was in the top drawer. Therefore, she sat with her back to the dresser, raised her hand to the handle, and pulled. The drawer squeaked thunderously. She dropped sideways to the floor and waited nervously to see if the people outside had heard. There was no response. She sat up again, hoped to prevent squeaking, and pushed up with one hand to raise the drawer a little. She slowly pulled as she begged, "Please, God, let me get it."

When the drawer was almost all the way out, she put both hands in the middle of the underside of the drawer then pushed up and forward. The drawer slid out. She held it above her head for a second, rotated her hands, and lowered the drawer to her lap. She felt around in the clothes, scrambled by the bullets that had passed through. As soon as she had it in her hand, she quietly put the drawer on the floor and slid back out of the room.

Eli returned with the drill. Ann met him in the hall and opened her hand. "They would be able to see you pull down the stairs in the hall. This key opens the door at the top of the stairs on this side of the balcony. If you're careful, they can't see you go up that way." Ann passed Eli the key and turned toward her sisters.

Stephanie pulled Ann in so she could stay low. "You gave it to him?"

"Yes, pray."

Since Ann had already sent Eli on the

mission, Stephanie did as asked. "God, it's me again. Thank You for keeping us safe so far. Please continue to keep us safe. Close the ears of whoever is out there, so Eli can make a hole. Show Eli what he needs to see, and bring him back to us safely. Amen."

Ann wholeheartedly added, "Amen."

Sally didn't believe God cared. He had destroyed her family when He had let her parents die, but she also said, "Amen."

The key turned in the door's lock. Ann expected the worst. "That must have been heard for miles." Once again, there was no response from outside.

Eli's footsteps crossed above them. They heard a thud. Stephanie guessed, "He must have put his rifle or the drill on the floor."

Everybody inside and outside heard a low raucous noise in the distance. It grew loud. Eli started drilling. Soon, the sound was almost deafening. Thousands of blackbirds cawed as they took up roost in the woods. The girls covered their ears.

The drill went through the side of the roof. Eli peeked out. He had never seen so many birds. Like black leaves, they covered the leafless trees in the woods. He turned his focus and counted five men on the ground at the edge of the woods. Their guns lay beside them as they held their hands over their ears. White splotches of bird droppings splattered the outlaws.

Eli heard the tall man holler, "Shoo, go away." The man rolled over and shot more birds than Eli thought was possible without reloading. Birds fell dead to the ground, and masses of blackbirds took flight. Other birds immediately refilled the vacated spots. The horde was so thick; they didn't make a dent in the coverage.

The bullets they fired into the air did the only thing possible; they returned to earth. One plowed through the tall man's shoulder. "I'm hit." He scrambled to his feet. All the outlaws agreed that the time had come for them to make their getaway. They tried to get to the horses. Eli knew legs were not supposed to go the way theirs were. He heard them scream in pain as they slipped in the deepening mass of white.

Inside the attic, the sound of the birds reverberated at an excruciatingly loud level. Eli had the information he needed, and there was no way the outlaws could hear anything going on in the house. He didn't worry about making noise as he hurried out of the attic.

The girls huddled together in Stephanie's room with their hands over their ears. When he joined them, Eli passed on what he had found out. "It's the five we ran out of town. The birds poop-bombed them."

Ann wasn't sure she understood. "What?"

"They were lying in the woods. I saw the bird's poop dropping on them. God must have a real sense of humor." Eli snickered as he tried to peek out the window. "They're going for their horses and sliding everywhere. I think they're trying to get away."

The four inside stayed down as their attackers carefully made it out of the woods with their guns blazing. The birds cawed their irritation deafeningly. The outlaws galloped across the poop-free meadow around the house. When Eli and the girls couldn't hear the guns over the birds, they looked out the front window. Five men, painted entirely white, rode away on completely white horses as fast as they could go. After the men had gone, the birds became silent sentinels in the woods.

TWENTY FIVE

Ann hugged her sister. "God answered your prayer, Stephanie. We need to thank Him."

Sally felt incredibly thankful, "God, thank You so much for sending the birds to save us. Maybe You are there, and maybe You do care. Amen."

Eli voiced his opinion, "What a bunch of idiots! They shot into the air directly above themselves. I wouldn't have thought anybody could be that ignorant."

"Do you think they'll come back?" Sally asked.

Eli knew the men had a long ride to get help for the one with the bullet in his shoulder. "Not tonight. They have to find a doctor."

Stephanie added assurance, "The birds will let us know if they come back tonight."

Ann, however, didn't want to assume. "Let's look over the house. We need to secure it as well as we can." She was afraid of what they would find. However, she knew they had to do everything they could.

Stephanie described the state of her room. "The shutters and window glass are demolished. The washstand and chamber pot are smashed, but the rest of the furniture stayed safe behind the walls."

Across the hall, Sally called out, "The only things damaged in my room are the window and shutters.

Glass crunched under Ann's feet as she went into her room. "My dresser has a million holes. The end window is intact. The glass is gone in the other. It's a good thing you didn't close the shutters, Stephanie. They're fine."

Eli checked his room. "The end window is good. The furniture looks undamaged, but the window and shutters on the front side of the house have been shot up."

Ann frowned. "I hope we have a bedroom we can use. Let's check the bunkrooms. Maybe we can sleep in there."

On the balcony, the shutters and windows on both sides of the house were rubble. Eli stated his opinion of the state of the house, "This is awful." They walked into the back bunkroom, where Eli put the stovepipe back together.

Ann examined the holes where bullets had perforated the shutters. "Only three holes."

"Here's one of them." Sally picked at the bunk bed.

"The other two bullets are embedded in the wall." Stephanie walked to each of them.

"I hope nothing in the front bunkroom is damaged." Ann walked into the last room and breathed a sigh of relief. "We'll stay in here tonight, but let's try to secure the downstairs first." They made their way back to the stairs. Ann stopped before descending. "Hold the banister and be careful. There's a lot of broken glass and wood on the stairs."

At the bottom of the stairs, Eli repeated his earlier statement, "This is really bad."

Ann knew that was true but didn't want to hear it. "Stop saying that."

"Well, it is!" Stephanie looked at the demolished windows in the sitting room on the woods side of the house. They walked past the undamaged front door that the wall of stones behind the stairs had protected. Stephanie opened the living room shutters closest to the stairs. "Not many bullets made it across the room, past all the furniture, and through these shutters."

Ann stood beside the couch. "It looks like all the rest of them are in this sofa."

Eli crossed the room. "Not all of them. The sitting table and both chairs by the window, as well as your Ma's rocking chair, are in splinters."

Sally opened the shutters of the window

next to the dining room, looked toward the broken windows across the room, and then looked into the dining room. "The angle of attack and the stones of the fireplace must have protected this window. There's no damage at all." She looked into the dining room again. "I don't know if I can bear it without our china." Sally walked to the china cabinet.

Eli followed her. He glanced in. "None of it looks broken." Sally moved the dishes around as Eli turned toward the table. "I see a bullet embedded in the edge of the table, and the top of the chair in front of the door is gone."

On the front side of the room, Stephanie looked at the floor. "It's lying over here. The shutters don't have a single hole, but glass is all around the chair top." Stephanie opened the shutters. "How on earth did this glass get broken when there isn't a hole in the shutter?"

Ann explained the mystery, "A bullet hit

it before I closed the shutter. The glass exploded in my face."

"Are you all right?" Sally asked with concern.

"You've been looking at me. You can see that I'm all right."

"I just want to be sure. I'm so glad you weren't hurt." Sally went into the kitchen. "I had just put the bread on the counter when Eli got me. Now, it's nowhere. Those horrible men blew our bread completely to dust."

"I hope the rest of the food is all right." Stephanie opened the pantry door. White and yellow powder covered everything. She stepped in with the exploded flour and cornmeal bags. "Look at this. Bullets are lying on the floor." She bent over and picked them up. "Some are in the pantry wall on the dining room side." She poked at one of them. It fell out of the wall and joined others already in the basket below. "Here's more in the basket of dried apples." She picked them up and then turned toward the door. "And strangely enough, some bullets are even in the back side of the pantry wall on the kitchen side."

Eli pointed to dents in the metal pails of lard. "They must have ricocheted off these buckets."

Sally counted holes. "The pantry wall has thirty-four holes on the outside and twenty inside in the dining room wall." She walked back into the dining room. "It's amazing that none of them got all the way through."

"There are holes in some of these sausages, but I think we can still eat them. I'll get the bullets out." Eli dug out the slugs.

After examining the kitchen, they checked the workroom. Eli found one broken glass pane and one hole in the shutter, but he couldn't locate the bullet. All the other windows and the door were unscathed. Eli stated his deduction, "I'm sure this room is so well off because they knew we weren't in here and didn't bother to shoot this way."

"How many windows are completely

gone?" Ann started counting on her fingers as she named the windows.

Stephanie had already been thinking about it. "The glass isn't going to help us. As far as the shutters down here go, they're all workable except the kitchen and the two back living room windows."

We need protection. Eli said, "Let's move the undamaged shutters from upstairs."

Ann looked out toward the woods. "All right, but we need to reinforce our defenses further. We should move furniture up against the windows."

Sally feared that the men would return. "Let's get started."

It took two people to raise a single shutter off its hinges. Eli carried one down the stairs with Stephanie. "These shutters aren't thin. It's amazing that they were able to shoot through them."

Stephanie wondered how only five men had wreaked so much havoc. "What kind of guns do you think they used?"

"I don't know, but I'm going to find out."

The four of them carried the shutters, one at a time, down the stairs and remounted them on the lower windows. An hour later, except in the room where they planned to sleep, they had all the exterior shutters closed and locked. The interior shutters from upstairs were in their new positions downstairs, with a large piece of furniture or a workbench against each window.

Sally started up the stairs. "I'm plumb tuckered out. I can barely move."

Not wanting to use the blankets and sheets that the men of the Butterfield Gang had used, they took the bedding from their shot-up bedrooms to the bunkroom. Ann lit a candle before they climbed into the beds.

Eli was not taking a chance with their lives. "Good night, girls." He stretched out on his bunk to be comfortable while he stayed awake and listened for warning sounds. He was much too drained.

TWENTY SIX

Eight human eyes flew open at the sound of the cawing of thousands of blackbirds and the flapping of twice as many wings. "They're back!" Eli jumped down from his bunk, darted to the window, and cautiously peeked out. He didn't see any people, but he did see the vast horde of blackbirds flying away into the morning sun. Eli told the girls hiding under the bunks, "It's only the birds leaving."

Stephanie slid out from under the bed. "Should we go tell the sheriff what happened?"

Sally cowered under the bed and cried. "They're going to come back and kill us."

Eli turned toward the girls. "The one with a bullet in his shoulder needs a doctor, and they can't go to Harmony. If they do come back, it won't be for several days. Right now, we're probably safe if we stay here or go to Harmony."

Ann felt afraid. "It isn't wise to be out in the open, and we should secure the house and get things fixed as best as we can."

Stephanie pulled her resistive sister out from under the bed. "How can we fix the windows?"

"I don't know. We can't buy more glass." Ann left the bunkroom and went to her room to get ready for the day.

As she prepared breakfast, Eli told Ann what he thought they should do about the windows. "Just like we did last night with the shutters, we could use all the good window sashes and glass panes from upstairs to fix all the broken windows down here."

"That's a great plan. Can you do it?"

"I can, and I saw wood out in the barn that I can use to make new inner shutters."

Sally came into the kitchen. "It's a good

thing winter is over." She flipped the few flapjacks they had rationed for breakfast.

After breakfast, they carried the broken furniture into the workroom to repair later. They chopped up what was left of the non-repairable furniture and shutters for the woodpile. Except for those in the bunkrooms, it took every window sash and every individual unbroken glass pane from upstairs to fix the downstairs windows.

While Eli rebuilt windows sashes and moved glass panes, the girls cleaned. Stephanie and Sally swept glass, plaster, and wood shards out of the bedrooms, through the hall, then down the stairs to the lower floor. Ann swept from the kitchen, through the dining room, then across the living room and entry hall into the workroom. Sally wondered aloud, "Could we get the glass melted back into panes for less money?"

Ann reminded her of their primary problem, "It doesn't matter. We don't have a single penny."

"I'm going to keep it anyway, just in case." Sally knelt to separate the glass.

"You're wasting time," Ann snapped.

Sally didn't like Ann's response. "Don't throw it away. I'll figure out something later. Just leave it alone."

Ann saw the determination in Sally's eyes and consented even though she believed it would give false hope about something that would never happen. "Sweep everything into the corner."

Over in the pantry, just as if she were mending a sock, Stephanie darned the holes in the flour and cornmeal sacks. Afterward, she cleaned everything and salvaged all the flour and cornmeal she could. Sally and Ann straightened up the dining room and living room.

At the end of the day, the windows had intact glass panes and almost perfect shutters on the lower floor. All the broken but hopefully fixable furniture sat in the workroom. It looked like nothing had happened except for all the demolished nick-knacks, the many bullet holes in the walls and furniture, the broken ceiling in Stephanie's bedroom, all the gaping holes upstairs where there should have been windows, and the massive pile of rubble in one corner of the workroom.

Eli sat at the table and ate his one cougar sausage, a slice of cheese, and some of the new loaf of bread that Sally had cooked. "Other than bullet holes everywhere and the open windows upstairs, it doesn't look too bad."

Sally named the ruined item that upset her the most, "Except all of the things they destroyed, including Mama's music box that has a bullet hole and won't play anymore."

"Why did Smitty let them go?" Stephanie asked.

"They hadn't broken any laws at the time, but I promise you girls that I'm going to kill any of them I see. I don't care if they're breaking the law or not."

Ann replied, "They've certainly broken the law now. They tried to kill us, and they destroyed our property."

The following two days, the rain poured. The closed outer shutters on the upstairs windows kept out most of the water. Eli used the hardware from the broken shutters and boards stored in the barn to repair the inner shutters or build new ones. The girls brought in pails of lime plaster they mixed up in the barn. They patched all the bullet holes and the ceiling in Stephanie's room. At the end of the third day, the house was back together as best as they could repair it.

Ann stated her plans for the next day. "If the rain stops, we should go to town."

Eli suggested, "We should keep the extra-heavy shutters on the outside closed and locked. We should also close and lock the inside shutters and put the furniture against the downstairs windows again. With the house well secured, we could leave and stay in town."

Ann poured sassafras tea. "I disagree. We should not abandon the farm. Besides, we can't secure the house. We can only bar the doors from the inside, and we'd need to get out through a door."

Sally pleaded with Ann, "But we need to be safe. We can do what Eli said. We can block the downstairs windows, bar the doors, and then go out one of the upstairs windows."

Ann tried to reason with Sally, "How would we get back in? We need to come back to plow the fields and plant. With all the birds' droppings that washed out of the woods and over the fields, we should get a good crop if we can get it planted."

Eli liked Sally's idea. "I think we can secure the house. We can go out a window because I have a ladder we can bring when we come back."

Stephanie thought about going out a window. "The windows are too high."

"How much do you weigh, Sally?" Eli thought he had the answer.

"Ninety pounds, I guess."

"I'm sure I can catch you if you jump."

Sally remembered the time in the cave when Eli had assured her that his plan would work. "I don't know."

"How many pounds have you seen me carry?"

Stephanie knew of one amount for sure because she had watched him. "You carried two hundred pounds of corn to the wagon."

Ann had an idea. "Maybe we can make the distance shorter by bringing the wagon over."

Stephanie trusted Eli. She decided she would do it. "If we put the sofa in the wagon the long way up and lean it against the house, it would just about go up to the bunkroom window. I'm willing to climb down if everybody else holds it still, and Eli is there to catch me if I fall. Once I'm down, we can put the sofa in the barn or take it in the wagon."

Ann gathered the empty supper dishes

and stood up. "We need to secure the house, go tell Smitty, and come back home. So, if the sofa goes high enough, and we can get it stable, then if you're still willing to climb down, we'll do it in the morning."

TWENTY SEVEN

Tom sat on the porch outside his store and enjoyed the beautiful, sunny spring day. He heard the sound of a wagon and wondered who was coming. He didn't even consider that it might be his son back so soon until he saw the giant horse. There was no mistaking Samson. Worry suddenly filled his mind. The wagon came to a stop in front of him. "Hello, son. Hello, girls. What brings you back so soon? Is everything all right?"

"No, Pop, things are not all right." Eli stepped down. He held his hand out to Stephanie.

"What's wrong?"

Ann explained, "Those men who Smitty drove out of town attacked us at the farm."

That upset Tom. "What?"

Stephanie added, "And they went into the house while we were here."

Eli picked up the story, "When we realized that somebody had been in the house, we tried to close the windows and doors, but they saw us and came for us with guns blazing."

Sally again named the ruined object that devastated her. "They ruined a lot of our things, including Mama's music box."

"We thought we were at our end, but then a huge flock of blackbirds came. I'm telling you, Pop; I've never seen so many birds. They landed in the trees and started pooping. The idiots shot at the birds directly above them. One of the bullets came back down and hit the tall one. They could barely get to their horses fast enough. They slid all around in the poop. If they weren't so dangerous, it would have been hilarious. They rode off covered in bird poop. I bet they still smell."

Ann expressed her puzzlement as Eli helped her out of the wagon. "I don't understand why they attacked us."

"I don't either, but you should report this to Smitty," advised Tom.

Eli helped Sally down. "We're going now."

The five of them walked to the other end of town, where Smitty pounded iron at the forge. As they walked into the livery, he put the object back into the fire. "Well, I'll be. Why are you back so soon?"

The girls and Eli told Smitty the story with all the details. After hearing the story, Smitty altered his plans. "I was going to wait until the circuit judge arrived to try Roy for attempted murder. Since we need one now, we should go to Fort Smith and get that judge instead. We better form a posse, capture those men, and bring them here."

Ann voiced her happiness and relief. "Attempted murder? I'm so glad the man didn't die!"

"Despite Roy's efforts, Doc says he's going to pull through. I need to go look at your house."

Ann realized they had made a mistake. "We've already put most of it back together."

Smitty chastised them, "You should have come here and not touched anything."

Ann accepted the blame. "I know you're right, but I was afraid to ride out in the open right after it happened. I didn't want to leave the house open to any person or animal that came by either."

"Well, it's done now. I'll finish up then we'll go." Smitty pulled a red-hot horseshoe out of the fire.

"I'm going to check on the Indian. I'll be quick." Ann walked to Doc Gridley's house and knocked.

Nellie opened the door. "Ann! What a pleasant surprise. Did you come to check on your man?"

"He's not my man, but I have come to check on him."

"Come into the waiting room. I'll let him know you're here." Nellie left Ann in the foyer. She went to the bedroom where the Indian was recuperating and knocked.

"Come in."

"She's here! She came to see you!"

He knew which woman. Several times, he and Nellie had spoken about the woman who had saved his life. "Bring her in."

Nellie left the door open and fetched Ann. "Here is Ann Williams." Nellie continued to stand beside Ann.

The man encouraged her to leave. "Thank you, Nellie."

"You're welcome." Nellie took the hint and left.

Ann had not expected to hear perfect English come out of the Indian's mouth. The man's blue eyes surprised her too. She had expected to see dark brown Indian eyes. Nellie had completely shaved away the man's long, blood-covered hair. Above the bandage around his head, the lighter skin of his clean-shaven head gleamed in the sunlight streaming through the window. Ann was tempted to laugh. She did not, but it brought a beautiful smile to her face. "I'm glad to see that you're recovering."

"I understand that's due to you."

"Dr. Gridley and Nellie did much more than I did."

"The doctor tells me there wouldn't have been anything for him to do if not for your care. Thank you very much for saving me from the undertaker."

"You're welcome."

Neither one knew what to say next. An awkward silence filled the room until Ann spoke. "So, as you already know, my name is Ann Williams. What's yours?"

"My father calls me Swift Hawk. My mother calls me Noah."

"What nice names. May I call you Noah Swift Hawk?"

"Yes, I like that."

"I'm sorry I can't stay. I have to leave with the sheriff, but I wanted to check on you. I'm glad you're going to be all right." Ann turned to leave the room.

"Why are you going with the sheriff?"

"The same men who attacked you attacked us and shot up our house."

"Those, lowlife yellow-bellied… I won't even say what they are. Are you going to be safe?"

"I don't know. We think they went to Clarksville. One of them shot himself. Smitty's taking a posse after them."

Eli called from the street, "Ann, we're ready to go."

"I have to go."

"Be careful. I hope I'll get to see you again."

"I hope to see you again too." Ann hurried away.

Noah walked to the window in his hospital gown and watched Ann get on the wagon. "Nellie, bring my clothes."

"You're not well enough to leave."

"Yes, I am."

"You may pass out if you exert yourself."

"I want to see what they did to the Williams' house. Please, Nellie. I won't exert myself."

"If Lawrence were here, he wouldn't let you go."

"That woman may not be safe. I owe her my life. Please. Give me my clothes."

Nellie could see that she wasn't going to stop him. "At least let me bandage your head and arm better before you leave, and promise me that you'll go easy on yourself."

"I promise that I'll go easy on myself."

Nellie added more layers of bandages. "I'll bring your clothes. I cleaned and mended them."

"That was very nice of you. How much do I owe you?"

"Five dollars."

Noah handed Nellie the money. "I appreciate all you and Doc did for me." He walked to Yates Mercantile to buy a hat to protect his head but found the store locked tighter than a drum. He went back to Nellie. "I need something to cover my head."

"I have a bandana."

"That should work fine." He tied it around his bandaged head, got his horse, and rode out of Harmony.

TWENTY EIGHT

It wasn't long before he saw the wagon ahead. He didn't want to scare them, so he called out a greeting, "Noah here. May I join you?" Everybody turned toward him. He repeated himself, "Noah here. May I join you?"

Smitty sat on his horse and faced the approaching man but turned his head toward the people with him.

Eli wanted to get to know the man. "Fine with me."

Ann replied with concern but also with a smile. "He should be back in town recovering. Since he's here, tell him to come on."

Smitty hollered, "Come on in."

Noah rode up to the wagon. "I hope you

don't mind. I feel like I should know what those men did to your farm, and I want to go with the posse."

Ann didn't want Noah to do what Roy had failed to do. "You almost died. You shouldn't be riding in a posse."

Smitty corrected Ann, "It's his decision, not yours." He turned to Noah. "At the first sign that you're not doing well, you have to go back to town. Do you understand? We can't be doctoring you."

"Yes. I promise." Talking and getting to know each other, the group rode to the house.

Ann drove into the barn. "This is the ruined sofa."

Stephanie held out her hand. "I'll put up Samson."

Eli helped Stephanie down, pulled the ladder off the wagon, carried it over, and leaned it against the house. He went through the window that Stephanie had come out of that morning. Eli walked down the stairs and unbarred the workroom door. Everybody entered the dimly lit, shuttered-up house.

"There's half the house." Sally pointed to the big pile of glass and other debris in the corner of the room.

They opened the shutters and again described everything that had happened. They showed Smitty, Tom, and Noah the repaired bullet holes, the ceiling still filled with drying plaster, the windows with only shutters, and the hole Eli had drilled through the attic wall. To find out if anybody knew what weapon had so much power, Eli asked, "What kind of guns do you think they used to blow apart the shutters like this? The bullets went through them with no problem at all."

"Don't know of any gun that can do this, but it's good to know they have guns like that before we find them." Smitty stood on the wet floor and looked through the hole in the attic as he recited the law. "It's clear they were intending to destroy this house for the purpose of injuring and in a spirit of vengeance. The law says a person or persons committing this kind of crime shall suffer death by hanging."

Ann wanted the outlaws to get what they deserved. "All of them should hang. Not only for what happened here but also for what they did to Noah."

"We'll get them. I'll gather up the posse and ride out in the morning. Eli, are you coming?"

"If the girls stay in town, I will. If not, somebody needs to be here with them."

Stephanie didn't want Eli to go. She immediately repeated what Ann had said the night before, "We can't leave the house." When nobody else said anything, she added, "We need protection and manpower around here."

Everybody could see Ann thinking it over. She asked, "What is the likelihood that they're still around our farm?"

Noah reasoned. "If they didn't leave

immediately, they surely would have left by now. The wound from the bullet covered in bird dung is most likely infected. They have to get to a doctor. I doubt if they could make it in time."

Smitty and Tom nodded their heads in agreement. Ann stated her decision, "Then we'll stay here and plant corn. We need Eli." Ann turned to Noah. "We could use another person. If you want to stay and help, I'll pay you the same as Eli. Ten dollars for each month's work, paid when we sell the harvest, plus room and board until then."

Noah looked into Ann's eyes and believed she was sincere, but he had reasons why he didn't want the men who did this to the Williams' farm to get away with it. "Right now, I have to go with the sheriff. I'll come back afterward. If you still want help at that time, I'll work for you."

"I will." Ann walked with them back to the horses. Tom, Smitty, and Noah mounted up. Before they rode away, Ann told the men,

"Be careful but find them and bring them back so they can hang."

When they were out of sight of the house, Noah told Smitty and Tom that he was going to look around but would be in town before morning. He shifted into Indian mode. He became Swift Hawk as he looked for clues not washed away by the rain. Not far away from the farm, he found where the men had made camp the first night. He found no indication that they had been able to clean themselves. The bandits would've had to get to the Arkansas River to wash. They had left camp going in that direction. Noah knew enough for the moment. He rode back to Harmony. It was well past sunset when he knocked on the doctor's door.

Doc opened the door. "I'm glad you're back."

"I sure am tired. Will you look me over?"

Laura heard Noah talking. She had been glad when the Indian had left. Now he was back. She locked her bedroom door.

Doc examined Noah's injuries and then chastised him, "Nothing's wrong. It's just your body telling you that you shouldn't be up."

"Roy tried to kill me. The rest of his gang tried to kill the woman who saved my life, and they did a lot of damage to the Williams' house. I'm going to find them and bring them in."

"I understand. I'm also going. It's likely that more than one of you is going to need me. Tonight, eat the rare steak and blood pudding Nellie put by your bed, drink as much water as you can hold, and get as much sleep as you can."

"You're a good man, Doc, and Nellie is a good woman. Goodnight." They went to their beds. Shortly after he lay down, Doc was asleep beside his wife. Noah had been in situations that were more dangerous and had felt calm. This night he felt unsettled and slept fitfully.

TWENTY NINE

Noah thought it would be better not to create additional problems by displaying his Indian heritage. He went to Tom's store, bought an outfit of white man's clothes, and redressed in the back room.

Tom looked at the blue-eyed man without a lick of hair under his cowboy hat. "If I didn't know otherwise, I'd swear you were as white as me." Tom locked the door behind them.

Smitty joined Noah, Tom, and the other men of Harmony: Clyde, Clyde's grown son Zachariah, Earl, Horace, and Dr. Gridley, who had already gathered in the livery. "I need one of you to bring the judge from Fort Smith."

Tom volunteered for the safe excursion to

Fort Smith. He rode into the forest toward Horsehead Creek.

The other men took the Spadra Creek Trail south toward the Arkansas River and the Butterfield Gang. They traveled fifteen easy miles then searched along the river. Earl found the campsite of the men they suspected had shot up the Williams' farm. "I think this is it."

Noah examined the riverbank beside the deep, slow-moving water. "Several horses and men went into and out of the water."

"Can you tell which way they went?" Smitty squatted beside Noah to examine the tracks.

Noah replied, "Several sets of hoof prints go west beside the river."

Before they left Harmony, Doc had already assumed the outlaws had gone to the only other civilian doctor they could reach within a week. It seemed certain now. "They must be going to Clarksville. They're probably there by now."

Smitty looked west. "If we ride hard and don't stop, we can make it there by tomorrow night."

Noah didn't want to push himself or his horse. "We don't need to do that."

Doc agreed and added his two cents worth. "I doubt if they'll go anywhere else."

Smitty mulled it over. "All right, we'll spend the night here." They camped in the same place where the people they were tracking had stopped.

The following day they traveled across the beautiful Arkansas landscape. Above them, a few wisps of white clouds streaked the blue sky. Beside them, large fish swam in the clear Arkansas River. When they stopped for the night, they caught black crappies and rainbow trout, which they cooked over the campfire as a tasty addition to the beans and coffee they brought from Harmony.

The afternoon of the third day, on the hill overlooking Clarksville, they stopped to plan their next move. Smitty looked at the town through a spyglass. "If they're watching for somebody to come after them, the only one they won't know is Noah. None of them saw his face. He should be the one to go into town and see if they're there and what they're doing."

Noah was happy to accept the assignment. "I don't know how long it will take, but I'll be back to let you know what I find out, so wait here." The outlaws had not seen Noah's face, but Noah hadn't seen the men they were tracking either. He was going to have to ask around without giving himself away. Noah thought if he found their horses, he would have the start of his trail. He guessed that the horses his quarry had ridden might still carry traces of their encounter with the birds.

THIRTY

Noah checked Arabella in at the livery and quickly identified the animals. Even after their bath in the river, they still reeked. Noah turned his horse over to the stable hand and held his nose. "That smell is awful. What happened to those horses?"

"Don't know. The men came in and acted like they didn't know they stank to the high heavens, and they didn't ask me to wash their horses either."

"I'm going to vomit. Direct me to a place where they won't be."

"They took the sick one to Doc Baker. The rest of them must be staying at the saloon. I smelled them in there. The only other place to go is Mable's. It's the green house."

Noah stroked his horse's neck. "How much to feed Arabella and give her a bath?"

"One bit."

Noah handed the man twenty-five cents and then went off in search of a green house. He looked at the sign over the door. It read *Mable's Place. Come on in*. The bell on the door rang as Noah stepped inside. A large woman in her forties wearing a plain blue dress and a food-splattered apron entered the front hall. "Welcome. I'm Mable."

"Do you have a room available tonight?"

"Yes, it's thirty-five cents. If you want 'em, supper and breakfast are twelve cents each. Pay in advance."

"One night, supper, and breakfast." Noah handed the woman two bits and a dime. Mable removed a penny from her apron pocket as she led her guest to the room. Noah took the set of keys. "Keep the penny." He went into the room and discovered why Mable had given him two keys. He pulled the curtain aside, looked out, opened the other door, and stepped onto a balcony.

Noah didn't like having two doors into his

room, especially when one allowed direct access to the room from the outside. He casually looked over the town and thought about asking for a different room but chose to walk the balcony before deciding.

The balcony went all the way around and had a set of stairs to the street below. At ground level, a matching porch circled the house. Access to his room was much too easy, but the saloon was clearly visible, the room faced the hill where the posse waited, and there was a good view of most of the street through the window. Since every room opened to either the porch or the balcony, he decided to keep the one he had.

Noah pulled a chair outside, leaned against the wall, and pulled his hat down low as if asleep in the sun. For about an hour, Noah watched the street from under the brim of the hat and pondered what reason he should give for coming to Clarksville. He decided he would say that he was looking for passage upriver. That way, he could ask about people and look around town.

The street remained vacant, so he carried the chair back into the room. He closed and locked both doors before he walked to the saloon. "Shot of whiskey."

The barkeep put a small glass in front of Noah but held the bottle of spirits. "One shot."

Noah put one of his rifle's bullets on the bar. "Who should I talk to about going up the river?"

The barkeep poured. "Try John Freeman."

Noah slowly turned the shot glass. "Where can I find John Freeman?" As if expecting to find the man in the room, he looked around the bar. Groups of two or individual men occupied a few tables. Four men sat together at the table beside the piano.

"He's not here. You might find him over at the barbershop. He likes to play checkers with Moses."

Noah walked to the piano with his whiskey and tapped a key. A single note drifted into the room. He cocked his head as if contemplating the sound he had created. In reality, he listened to the men behind him.

One of them was more unhappy than usual. Trying to save a man's life had interfered with what he wanted. "Ya see, Charlie. I told ya he wasn't gonna make it. We shoulda shot Al an' buried him at the river. Then we coulda gone back an' helped ourselves ta them girls."

That comment confirmed that Noah had found the men who had shot up the farmhouse, men who had tried to kill the woman who had saved his life. The same gang of outlaws had tried to kill him for no reason other than the fact that he was an Indian.

Charlie snapped, "Shut up, Gus! Go pay the undertaker ta bury Al."

Gus wasn't doing anything for anybody but himself, nor was he going to stop pressing the subject of his current fixation. "Then can we go back? We can catch them girls an have a little fun."

Noah strongly desired to turn around and shoot all four of them. He didn't want them getting anywhere near the Williams girls, but shooting them like that in public would be considered straight-out murder. Instead, he continued to listen as Pete suggested a better plan. "Go find a whore, an' forget 'em. We should get outta here while we can still go home."

Gus waved a revolver in Pete's face. "I'm sick a your yapping. If ya don't shut your bone box, you'll be taking an earth bath."

Pete stopped talking. *You think you're gonna kill me, but I'm gonna kill you.*

Ben said, "We gotta break out Roy."

"Don't tell me what we gotta do, Ben." Charlie slammed his empty glass on the table. "I'm tired o' the arguin'." He swept the money to bury Al into his hand and stalked toward the door.

Noah had heard enough. He was sure he could secretly eliminate the man. Noah turned to follow Charlie, but he didn't know for sure what Charlie had done or planned to do. Roy was the one man he knew was guilty. Gus was an entirely different matter. Noah changed his mind. He put his shot of whiskey on the table in front of Gus. "Have a drink on me."

Gus raised the glass toward his benefactor. "Much obliged, mister." Noah looked at the faces of all the men at the table but memorized the face where he knew evil dwelled. He studied the man's black eyebrows drawn down to his squinting brown eyes and the crease in the skin between them put there by thirty or so years of unhappiness and anger. The wrinkle stretched smooth across Gus's round face as he let the whiskey flow down his gullet.

Noah went to the stable. His horse neighed a greeting when she saw him. Noah spoke to the stable worker. "I'm going to the river."

"I washed your horse just like you asked. She sure did like it."

"I can see that she's happy." Noah mounted and rode out to tell the posse what he had discovered.

"Al is dead. They're ready to shoot each other. I heard them talking about possibly going back to break out Roy. The one they called Gus wants to go back and have his way with the Williams girls. I am not going to let that happen no matter what. They're still trying to decide what to do. Charlie left to pay the undertaker. I think he's the one in charge now. He doesn't seem to be doing a very good job of it."

Smitty told Noah, "Go back, find out, and let us know what they decide to do."

"You see that green house?" Noah pointed.

Smitty looked through his spyglass. "Yes."

"Keep watch on the door all the way over on the left on the second floor. If I put the chair out on the left side of the door facing you, they're going back to Harmony to break out Roy. If I put it on the right facing down the balcony, they're going to the Williams' house. If I turn it around and lean it against the rail, they're not going back our way."

Zachariah thought, *we probably don't have to do anything.* "We could just let them kill each other."

Horace asked, "And deprive ourselves of watching them hang?"

Smitty told his men, "Listen well. Proper justice is mandatory. They will get a fair trial." However, he did believe the men were guilty. "Then, we'll watch them hang."

THIRTY ONE

Just before sundown, Zachariah looked through the spyglass. "He put the chair on the left."

The men in the posse watched throughout the night. Nobody left Clarksville until early the following day. "Noah's coming." Horace took the coffee Smitty exchanged for the spyglass.

When Noah arrived, they had broken camp and sat on their horses, ready to do whatever was necessary. Smitty held out a tin cup of hot coffee. "You want this?"

"I already had breakfast."

Horace saw a group of riders leave town. "Give me the spyglass." He studied the group. "It's them."

Smitty dumped the coffee on the ground,

tucked the cup into his saddlebag, and ordered his men into position. "Doc and Zachariah, get behind those rocks. Horace and Clyde, go over there behind that boulder. Noah, lay on top of it. Earl, ride up the trail around the corner. When you hear my signal shot, come riding back this way. I'll come up from the rear. Since we'll have them trapped, they should surrender. Everybody move into position."

Soon they heard the clickity-click of horse hooves on the rocky trail as Charlie, Pete, Gus, and Ben rode up the hill, oblivious to the trap.

Pete's hand rested on his gun. *Charlie an' Ben won't know what happened 'fore Gus is dead. Ben said they oughta kill me when we was at the farm. Maybe I'll take out Ben too. I think I'll go ahead an' shoot all of 'em.* Pete dropped behind. *I'll do it when we get far enough away from town.*

They rode past Smitty without seeing him in the mountain crag. Smitty slowly moved his horse forward and drew his gun to fire the signal shot. Pete pulled his revolver to put a hole through Gus's head.

Blam!

Pete was confused. *I didn't squeeze the trigger.*

Gus, Ben, and Charlie swung around at the sound of the shot from behind. There sat Pete on his horse with a drawn gun. Gus glared at Pete. &^*)_ *^$&#. *I know why ya got your gun out.*

Smitty galloped full throttle up the trail. *Please realize you're surrounded and surrender.* The men hiding beside the trail fired rifles into the air as they sprung their ambush.

Pete scowled at Gus. *Shoot him,* he told himself. A man rapidly closed in from the side. Pete turned and pulled the trigger.

The close-range blast blew Horace backward out of his saddle. Charlie, Ben, and Gus pulled their guns. Gus pointed his gun at the sheriff from Harmony, but there was a man he hated much more than Smitty. He shifted his aim and fired.

Pete's eyes flew wide open as a bullet hit

him dead in the heart. *I knew I shoulda shot him,* was Pete's last thought.

Zachariah rushed into the melee, not knowing that Pete was already dead. Since they were not supposed to kill any of the accused men, Zachariah used his horse as a weapon and rammed the rider in front of him. The impact slammed Pete and his horse into Ben and caused the shot Ben pulled off to go above Doc's head.

Ben's horse went down to the sound of breaking bone. Ben was extremely ticked off. *#$(^%^*%#%^@%^&. I just bought this horse, an' now it's done for.*

Charlie heard somebody farther up the trail. He twisted around just as Earl rode into the chaos. Charlie's men constantly bickered and fought against each other and him. He was wound tighter than a clock before they had even left town. Now people were attacking him. He wanted to kill everybody, including his own men.

Earl rounded the corner and saw Charlie's

rifle swing toward him. *Holy Mother of God!* He reined in his horse. Tiny bits of rock flew into Earl's face as the bullet ricocheted off the rocks in front of him. The horse veered into the cliff. Earl and his horse went down.

Charlie drew a bead on Earl pinned down under his horse. "One flea on my *^& gone."

Earl saw the rage on Charlie's face. *I'm dead.*

Noah jumped from the boulder. "You're a sorry excuse for a man!"

Charlie flew off his horse with Noah's body attached. The two men tumbled down the rocky trail. Charlie screamed, "Indian vermin! I'm gonna make sure you're dead this time!"

Gus gloated over Pete's demise, *so ya planned ta kill me. Just as I promised, I killed you.* Clyde charged toward Ben but thundered past and used the butt of his rifle to slam Gus off his horse. Gus hit the ground.

Doc jumped off his horse and pressed his revolver into Gus's forehead. *This is what I'd rather do: pin a man down and not hurt one.*

Even in all the confusion, Ben realized that it was over. He threw down his gun. "I surrender. Don't shoot me."

Earl could barely believe he was alive. He shoved his horse until it got back to its feet. The horse moved off his leg, but the pain stayed. He continued to lie on the ground.

Clyde and Zachariah saw that the fight at the top of the hill was over. They feared that it might still rage below. They raced down the trail and found both men lying motionless. Blood flowed from Noah's shiny, hairless, hatless head. Charlie lay a few feet farther down.

Zachariah knelt and felt for a pulse. "Noah's alive."

Clyde looked at Charlie and vomited. Zachariah started over. "You all right, Pa?"

Clyde held up his hand to stop him. "Charlie's head is cracked open against the boulder. We better not move either of them until Smitty and Doc look this over." They ran back up the trail. Clyde blurted out the news. "Charlie is dead. Noah is unconscious and hurt, but Zachariah felt a pulse."

Smitty securely attached the bridle of Charlie's horse to his own horse. The Butterfield Gang's capture may have cost the lives of his friends. He made doubly sure that they could not escape. As he tied Ben's hands to the saddle's pommel, Smitty issued his orders. "Zachariah, get a rope. Be sure to attach Gus's horse to yours before you get him on it. Tie his hands to the saddle. Doc, check Horace and Earl before you go down to Noah and Charlie." Doc knelt over Horace. Smitty desperately hoped he hadn't gotten Horace killed. "Is he dead?"

"No, thank God, but he's shot through the gut. We need to get him to town."

Doc started toward Earl. Earl waved him away. "Horse only broke my leg. Noah's still recovering from almost dying. Go check on him."

Doc hurried down the trail. He hadn't wanted Noah to get out of bed and feared that he wouldn't find him alive. He saw Noah kneeling beside Charlie. *Thank You, God.*

Blood streamed over Noah's face and ran down his neck. "I didn't do it, Doc. I remember that I jumped at him, and we started rolling. After that, I don't remember anything until I woke up over there. Charlie was already like this."

"Sit on this rock. Let me look at you." It only took a few seconds for Doc to see the damage. "You've ripped apart the stitches in your head, and look at all these cuts and bruises on your face. You've probably also knocked your brains around inside that stubborn head of yours. You've ruined all my hard work stitching you up the last time. I told you to stay in bed. Now I have to sew you up all over again. Take off your coat. Let me look at your arm."

A single shot rang out. Noah stood up. *There's still a problem. I need to help.* "What's happening now?"

Doc stopped him. "You're not going to do any good in your condition. Sit down!" Noah took off his coat and sat. A fresh bloodstain soaked through his shirtsleeve. "You see, your arm is open again."

Smitty led the group down the hill toward Clarksville. Earl sat on his horse with his crushed leg dangling. Horace held his stomach as blood ran over his hand onto his saddle and out of his back onto his horse. Ben sat tied up on Charlie's horse. Even captured, Gus looked cocky. Pete's horse carried its rider's body draped over its back. The other men came behind, leading Doc's and Noah's horses.

The patches of blood on Noah's shirt grew. "What was that last shot?"

"Ben's horse broke its leg. We tried to push the body off the trail. Eventually, someone will have to do something with it."

Clyde and Zachariah put Charlie's body beside Pete's. They rode into Clarksville to the inquisitive and shocked stares of the folks in town.

THIRTY TWO

Sheriff Lemuel Slade of Clarksville crowded every one of the men from Harmony into one of his two jail cells. Gus and Ben sat uncrowded in the other. Dr. Gridley and Clarksville's Dr. Baker ministered to the wounded in the crowded cell. The doctors knew there would be an investigation. They examined everyone carefully and wrote very detailed notes.

Sheriff Slade started the investigation while the evidence was red hot. As sheriffs of close by towns, he and Smitty were acquaintances. Sheriff Slade took Harmony's sheriff away for questioning. "Tell me everything you know about this."

Smitty explained, "We were tracking five men wanted for attempted murder and destruction of a home back in Harmony. I intended to capture them alive. I thought if we surrounded the men that they would surrender. They didn't. I have another member of the Butterfield Gang in jail for trying to murder a different man. I sent a man to get Judge Atwood. They should be on their way to Harmony. You might as well send somebody over to Harmony to bring him here."

"Maybe I will. I'll decide what to do as I go."

Smitty continued the story and omitted nothing.

After Noah, Earl, and Horace were as stitched up and bound up as they could get them, the doctors examined the deceased. Once again, they notated their findings in detail. They dotted their last I, crossed their final T, and loaded the bodies into a wheelbarrow. Dr. Baker escorted Dr. Gridley back to jail. "Sorry, Lawrence." He opened the cell door.

"I understand." Dr. Gridley compliantly joined his fellow townsmen.

Dr. Baker wheeled Pete and Charlie down the road. The undertaker looked at the corpses. "Yesterday, that man paid me to bury his friend. He gave me extra to put the man in my best coffin. His friend is so tall unless I break his legs, I don't have one that'll fit him. I have to build one."

Dr. Baker knew it wasn't pleasant to have bodies above ground for very long, and it would take time to make three coffins. "Do you have any already made that will fit the other two?"

"Not good ones. When they started the bank, I figured somebody would try to rob it, and I'd end up with a bunch of bodies, so I made a stack of pine boxes. I never imagined I'd have more than one any other way."

"Build a long box for Al. Charlie paid for it. I'll get the Sheriff to ask their friends what to do with these two."

Several minutes later, Sheriff Slade arrived

at the undertaker's house with the answer. "Their friends said, 'The men who killed them need to pay to bury them.' Of course, everybody denies killing them. Since it happened during Sheriff Wyman's law enforcement attempt, he decided to pay to bury them in pine coffins."

"A dollar each to dig a hole and bury them."

"That's what I thought." Lem handed over two dollars.

The undertaker was very happy, not that three men had died, but that he had earned four dollars in under twenty-four hours.

A few days later, Sheriff Slade completed his investigation. He had spoken to all the men from Harmony and the accused men. He had questioned all the folks from Clarksville who knew anything related to the incident, and he had examined the trail. Lem declined to have the judge brought over. "Smitty, take everybody to Harmony and deal with it there."

Later, at the insistence of both doctors, he changed his mind and allowed Earl, Horace, Noah, and Lawrence, at their own expense, to recover a while longer at Mable's Boarding House.

Smitty, Zachariah, and Clyde left with Gus and Ben in custody.

THIRTY THREE

Three days later, they rode into Harmony. The women and children came out of their homes and looked for their men.

Nellie didn't see Lawrence. "No!"

"Where's Horace?" Tears streamed down Betsy's face.

Clara clutched her hands to her chest. "Not Earl."

Smitty calmed them, "It's all right. They're all alive in Clarksville. Doc is taking care of them. You three come into the jail. Patty, take all the children to your house."

The men pulled Gus and Ben off their rides. When they were on their feet, Smitty walked them to the jail. Nellie, Betsy, and Clara followed.

Patty hugged her husband and son.

"Come along, children." The three of them ushered the children to their home.

"Ladies," Smitty thought it best to give the women the news without worrying about anybody fainting, "please sit." Smitty escorted Ben and Gus to the empty cell in the room at the back of the jail. Roy sneered as Ben and Gus walked in. Roy had thought they were going to break him out. Now, he knew that wasn't going to happen. "Good job, boys."

Smitty went back to the front room. He explained to the women, "Doc is fine. He stayed behind to look after the others. Horace is shot through his gut but was doing fine when we left." Horace's wife, Betsy, cried uncontrollably and couldn't speak. Smitty spoke next to Clara, "Earl's leg is smashed up pretty bad. His horse fell on it. They put it back into place the best they could and bound it up." Clara also cried but felt relieved that her husband was alive and didn't have a hole through his middle.

Nellie cared about her patient. "What about Noah?"

Before Smitty could answer, Tom walked in with Judge Richard Atwood of Fort Smith. Tom made all the introductions. Judge Atwood shook Smitty's hand last, "Tom took me straight out to the Williams' farm. What's wrong with those girls?"

"What do you mean?" Smitty asked.

"They're as skinny as a rail."

Tom explained, "They don't have enough food, and Ann is too proud to let anybody help."

"Eli doesn't look like that."

"The parents of the girls died two winters ago. They've been trying to survive on their own. Eli just started working out there."

"Oh." Judge Atwood contemplated, *if Sheriff Wyman did catch the men who did this, I'll find out everything those girls need and make sure they get enough money.*

Smitty turned to Nellie. "Since you asked, Noah jumped on Charlie and busted open the stitches in his arm and head when they rolled down the hill." Smitty looked at Clara. "Noah saved Earl's life. If he hadn't knocked Charlie off his horse, Charlie would have shot Earl sure enough."

Clara squeaked, "Can we go see them?"

Judge Atwood answered before Smitty had a chance. "You need to stay here and wait for them to get back. You ladies, go on home." After the women left the room, Judge Atwood spoke with Smitty, "I want to hear your version before I talk to anybody else."

Smitty related his long tale about the first time the accused men had come into town with the rest of their gang. He told the judge about the second time the men were in town and had caused the fight in the saloon. He explained why they had killed one man and put another in jail, repeated what Eli and the girls had told him, and described what he had seen when he went to their house. Last, he related what had happened during the trip to Clarksville and their failed ambush.

The judge let Smitty tell his story without interrupting then loudly notified the sheriff. "I'll talk with everybody else tomorrow."

"All right, I'm going home." Smitty followed Judge Atwood out of the jail.

All the way to the edge of town, Judge Atwood's footsteps sounded loudly on the boardwalk. At Joe's Saloon, he didn't go through the swinging doors. He slid around to the back, sneaked to the jail, and stood outside the window. Gus declared, "I'm telling you, Roy."

Judge Atwood couldn't believe his ears. *Please don't let it be!*

Inside the jail, Gus spun his tale of lies. "We was trying ta get away when they shot Pete in cold blood. Then, they jumped Charlie an slammed his head inta a rock. That sheriff set us up. He tied our guns ta the horse we bought from them girls last winter an made it run away. He knew it would go ta their house. We tracked it there late the next day. The one who said he was gonna blow your brains inta the floor was there. He shot Al when we was coming up ta their house ta get our horse an guns. We vamoosed outta there. The sheriff told us we couldn't come back ta Harmony, so we went ta Clarksville. That bullet hole in Al got infected. He died over in Clarksville." Gus purposely didn't tell Roy that a flock of birds had run them off or that they had stupidly shot bullets into the sky above themselves.

"Exactly." Ben had seen Gus shoot Pete, but Gus was his friend, and Pete was irritating. On top of that, he wasn't confessing that he had thrown down his gun and surrendered like a lily-livered coward. "What we gonna do, Roy?"

Roy was very unhappy with the latest developments. "Be quiet. I'm thinking."

The judge couldn't tell from the few words. *What if it's him? Surely, they would tell the truth to their own man. They don't know I'm listening, and there is no reason for them to lie to each other.* The judge quietly slipped away from the window. *I knew this was going to happen someday. I hope it isn't him.* Judge Atwood couldn't make himself go in the jail to find out.

The next morning, Judge Atwood walked into the back room of the jailhouse. *^*%$*^%$#& &%$. It figures.* "I don't know who is who, so state your names."

Richard doesn't want anybody to know that we know each other. "Roy Butterfield."

"Benjamin Rowe."

"Gus Hutchinson"

When Smitty walked into the jail with breakfast for the prisoners, Judge Atwood had already heard what Roy, Ben, and Gus had to say. "I'm going to Clarksville." Before he departed, he took the plates off the tray Smitty held and passed them through the slot to the men in the cells.

Instead of leaving, the judge spied on the people in town and again listened outside the jail window.

THIRTY FOUR

After gathering all the intelligence he could in town, Judge Atwood went to the Williams' farm. Unknown to Eli, Ann, Stephanie, and Sally, the judge secretly scrutinized them. *Those girls are much too slender. They sure play a lot, but I guess they are getting work done. I'm glad Roy was locked up and wasn't involved with whatever happened here.*

The judge then searched the countryside around the Williams' farm. He didn't see any evidence of bird droppings or find any dead birds in the woods. However, he did find the place where the accused men had camped. He looked at the closed exterior shutters on the backside of the house. *I don't see any bullet holes. If the place were as shot up as Tom said, some bullets would have hit the shutters. The shutters in the woodpile looked chopped with an axe not shot up.*

That night, the judge saw something that did not sit well with him. *Eli is going into the same room as the girls.* He waited and watched. *He's not coming out. He can't be sleeping with all three of them.* He watched all night. In the morning, all four came out of the same room. *He's sleeping with all of them.*

The judge decided he had discovered all he could around Harmony.

THIRTY FIVE

The twenty-mile trip to the Arkansas River from the Williams' farm was easy to ride at a slow gallop. At the river, Judge Atwood searched for the campsite of the accused men. When he found it, he slammed his hat to the ground. "!@#^#&* $&^% &*%^$%^. Why would they muck up this place unless they're covering up? Maybe Roy, Gus, and Ben are telling the truth."

He picked up his hat and dusted it off. The drawn-down eyebrows and pinched-together skin between his eyes remained on his face. Even though the site was already ruined, he moved up the river to camp for the night. The judge hurried to make up the time he had spent in Harmony and rode all the way to Clarksville the following day.

Before he rode into town, Judge Atwood examined the trail where the men had fought. Over the next few days, Judge Atwood heard the accounts of Sheriff Lemuel Slade, Dr. Baker, John Freeman, the stable hand, Mable, Cyrus the bartender, and the other men in the saloon the day Noah arrived. He walked back to Mable's boarding house. *I'll take careful notes of the accounts of Dr. Gridley, Earl, Horace, and the Indian.*

Judge Atwood mulled it all over. Questions spun around in his mind. *Why did they disguise the Indian Roy supposedly hit in the head as a white man? Why did the Indian lie about wanting to take a boat upriver, and why did he really want his horse washed? What was his actual reason for riding out of town? Why did he never talk to John Freeman? Why did he go to the piano, play a single note, and then give Gus a shot of whiskey? Why are three of the accused men dead and the people of Harmony only injured? What reason could Ben and Gus possibly have had to attack the Williams sisters? Why is Roy always in trouble?*

THIRTY SIX

When Harmony's men left Clarksville, Judge Atwood chose not to travel with them. Instead, the judge gave Sheriff Slade instructions. Not long after, he left Clarksville alone. He followed behind the group and tried to stay out of sight but within hearing.

He wasn't as stealthy as he thought. Noah's habit was to keep a close check on his surroundings. He thought it was peculiar that the judge didn't want to travel to Harmony together. He decided to be especially vigilant. After only a short while, he saw the judge sneaking around them, but he didn't alert the others. He thought it would be better if everybody acted normal.

The injured men suffered as they traveled over the rough trail. Earl's splinted leg bounced against the side of his horse. That caused pain in his leg and hip, and it caused the horse to perceive the command to go faster. For several miles, Earl fought his horse until it realized it was not getting a signal to go faster but only had something bouncing against its side. Horace hurt all the way through from front to back. Noah's head pounded. His arm and all his new cuts and bruises ached.

They decided to stop for the night long before reaching the river. Doc looked them over. Even though they felt awful, he pronounced them all in satisfactory condition. Doc built a fire, cooked beans, cut and fried chunks of bacon, and made coffee. The coffee was ready first. The wet heat relieved the injured men's discomfort to a small degree, and they drank it thankfully. Doc brought out a large loaf of bread to sop up the bean mixture when ready. He broke it into four pieces and set the bread beside the fire to toast.

Horace shared his painful condition as

they sat around the fire. "I hope we don't run into any cougars or bears. I'm sure I can't jump on my horse fast enough to get away."

Earl looked Horace in the eyes. "Don't worry. Your life is not in jeopardy. It would eat me since I can't even get to a horse."

They all laughed. Noah put his hands to his head. "Don't make me laugh. It makes my head hurt even more." He shooed a bug away from his face. Soon, other insects attracted to the fire's light buzzed around them. The four men waved their arms frantically and tried to drive them off. Judge Atwood stayed hidden on the other side of a boulder. He watched from the dark and silently laughed.

Doc swatted something flying in from the side. His hand hit something much bigger than a bug. "What was that?" Accompanied by another, the flying creature circled back into camp to chase bugs. The next instant, a colony of Ozark Big-Eared bats swooped in to partake of the insect feast by the fire. The men saw the lumpy faces, sharp teeth, inch-long ears, and foot-wide wingspan of the bats as they darted past the fire. On each trip back for another mouthful, the bats zinged past the judge, then dived and weaved around the fire in pursuit of supper.

The men in camp hit the ground. Noah yelled, "Put out the fire!"

Horace, being closest, flipped the pot of beans onto the fire. He poured the last of the coffee on the remaining embers. For good measure, he also poured the coffee in his cup over the fire. The bats ate up the bugs that didn't fly away quickly enough and then left in search of another supper offering. Horace continued to lie on the ground. "Let's leave the fire out. I doubt I'd survive another bat visit."

Doc didn't want his patients to have to fight off another wave of insectivores. "I agree."

Horace clutched his stomach. "Maybe we would have been better off with a bear."

Earl looked at the bean, bacon, dirt, ash, and coffee sludge coating the logs and chunks of bread in the fire pit. "I guess it's going to be a hungry night."

Doc examined his patients for complications caused by the bat ordeal. Everybody passed inspection, so they laid out their bedrolls and tried to sleep.

The next day, Doc and his patients broke camp early and went on their way. The river came into view as they rode down the east side of the ridge. Far below, a colony of beavers chewed down trees, gnawed off branches, and dragged them into the water. As they descended, the men watched the critters build a dam a short way up a creek that ran into the Arkansas River below. When the men got close enough for the beavers to notice them, the lookout slapped his wide, flat tail on the water. Every beaver plunged into the water and hid out of view under the surface. The men continued down the hill and then rode beside the river on the flat trail that provided no cover.

Judge Atwood decided to join the men ahead. He hung back out of view until the others were far ahead and then rode out as if he had only just caught up. He called out from a long way back, "Hello, men!"

Noah knew what was going on. The other three men turned in surprise and called for Judge Atwood to join them. All four greeted him warmly into the group.

They continued toward Harmony until mid-afternoon when Earl insisted that he could not travel farther. They stopped and set up camp. Earl apologized, "Sorry, Judge, you can push on. I hurt too bad to ride any farther today." Judge Atwood declined to go on alone.

Earl expressed his concern while Doc examined his leg. "I hope my leg will heal right. I need to be able to walk. I don't know how I'll take care of my family if I can't walk. I've hardly slept from worrying about it."

Doc assured Earl that he would be all right. "Your leg will heal fine."

Everybody knew that gut wounds frequently killed, and Horace was worried. "Doc Baker said the bullet went right through. He said I'd be fine even though I'm torn up. I think I'll be all right if I don't get rotten inside. What do you think, Doc?"

Doc inspected Horace. *His back is sewn together like a patchwork quilt.* "I agree with Dr. Baker. You don't need to be worried. I'll keep a watch on you anyway. You'll all be fine, but take it easy and give yourselves time to mend, especially you, Noah."

"Why, especially me?" Noah acted indignant.

"Because you need to, and you probably won't. Earl and Horace have wives who will make them."

Horace confirmed. "My Betsy is one great woman, but you better do what she says."

The judge chimed in, "You aren't dead like Hank, Al, Pete, and Charlie. You're all lucky."

Horace got a sinking feeling in the pit of

his stomach, and it wasn't from the bullet hole. He did not like the tone the judge used. He stood up. "I'm going to set up my bedroll." He walked away. *I'm blown almost in half, and he thinks I'm lucky.*

The other three men noticed it as well. Earl looked at Noah. "Will you help me up?" Noah helped Earl get up and then hobble to his horse. As Earl got his bedroll, he whispered, "What do you make of the judge?"

"He's followed us the whole way, kept out of view, and spied on us."

"Why didn't you tell us?"

"I didn't want the judge to get the wrong opinion if we weren't acting normal."

"It's too late for that. I think he already has the wrong opinion."

"It looks that way to me as well."

Noah carried Earl's bedroll and helped him back to the group. "Where do you want me to put you?"

Even though the trail had been much

smoother that day, Earl's leg throbbed. The leather straps binding it to the board were so tight that he thought his swollen leg would pop. He didn't want to take another step. He needed to stretch out his leg, rest his back and hip, and be still. "This is as good a place as any. I have to lie down." Noah helped Earl to the ground before he got his own blankets and tarp. He laid them in the only unclaimed spot.

The three weary, injured men stretched out next to the fire. It was a long uncomfortable night of hurting, fretting about the future, and worrying about what the judge was thinking. Morning finally arrived. The men weren't sure if they were glad that the night was over or unhappy because they had to get on their horses and ride.

Horace mounted up for the last leg of the journey. "It hurts to ride, but I want to get home."

Earl wanted to be home as much as

Horace did. "I'm not sure what I want to see more, Clara and the children or my bed." Only a few hours into the day's ride, Earl whimpered, "I can't ride anymore."

The judge pressured him, "Yes, you can."

Earl begged, "I can't. Please, I have to get down."

Horace hurt terribly from front to back, but he wanted to be home. He encouraged Earl, "It's only a little farther. You can make it."

Noah reined in Arabella. "I'm sure we can make it, but we don't have to. Why don't the rest of you ride to town and come back with a wagon? I'll wait here with Earl. He's about to fall out of his saddle from pain, and I want to stop too. I feel completely worn out, my head is throbbing, and my arm aches."

Doc concurred, "You're right. I'll stay with you. Let's get Earl down."

Some or all of these men might have killed Al, Pete, or Charlie. Judge Atwood wasn't going to let any of his suspects get away. He stated his condition, "Only if you stay without horses."

Noah wasn't going anywhere and knew Smitty would take good care of Arabella. "Fine."

As they maneuvered him off his horse, Earl let out a pain-filled screech and passed out. Horace found a soft spot out of view of the trail. He spread Earl's bedroll and added his own on top before Doc and Noah laid Earl on the pallet. Doc got his bag, Noah got his bedroll and rope, and then Judge Atwood and Horace led away the horses of the men they left behind.

THIRTY SEVEN

Doc untied the leather straps around Earl's leg and took off his boots. "I'm glad he's out. I need to take another look. I'm also glad Judge Atwood is gone. He makes me nervous." Doc removed Earl's trousers. "You see the lump here? I think that's a piece of bone working its way out."

Noah got closer. "His leg looks awful."

"You don't look well either. Can you make a fire?"

"I can do it. I saw some wood not far from here."

Thirty minutes later, Noah pulled a load of wood up beside Doc. Earl's leg was open from his knee to his ankle. Several bone fragments lay on the ground.

Noah looked at the inside of Earl's leg. "Did you get them all?"

"I think so. I had to cut Earl's leg open to see what I needed to do. I removed the little pieces and aligned the big pieces correctly."

"When it heals up, will he be able to walk?"

"He wouldn't have been able to because the bones are partially shattered, and none of them were in the right position. It's a good thing we took this trip. Without all the bouncing, I wouldn't have opened up his leg and wouldn't have known that things weren't right until after the bones had knit together wrong. He'll heal up just fine now."

"I hope so." Noah untied the wood.

By the time Doc finished stitching Earl's leg together, the fire burned brightly. Doc removed a flask of whiskey from his bag. He poured some onto a clean cloth, applied it over Earl's incision, and splinted his leg again.

He turned his attention to Noah. "Sit over here. Let me take a look at you." Since he knew Noah had just pulled a big load of wood, he checked his arm first. Blood oozed from the wound, but the stitches had held. Doc doused a fresh bandage with whiskey and wrapped it around Noah's arm before he removed the bandage from Noah's head. Those stitches were also in place, and there was no fresh blood. Doc looked at his eyes. "Do you feel dizzy or sick in your stomach? Are your ears ringing? Do you have a headache? Do things look clear or blurry?"

"I'm exhausted, everything is blurry, I feel like I'm going to vomit, the world is spinning, and my head feels like it's going to explode."

Doc took a swig of whiskey. He handed the bottle to Noah. "Take a big swallow or two. That should help."

Noah took a large gulp and then gave the bottle back. Doc soaked a clean bandage with the last of the whiskey and wrapped it around the stitches in Noah's head. "Lie down and rest."

Noah was more than happy to comply. He

couldn't remember a time when he had felt so tired. He had barely stretched out before he was fast asleep. Doc stood watch.

As soon as he arrived in Harmony, Judge Atwood went to the Williams' farm. "Come to town early tomorrow, and be prepared for an extended stay."

Ann asked, "May we come back to the farm to check on the house and do chores?"

"All of you have to be at the trial. You can't go riding off across the countryside."

After the judge left, Ann closed the door. "All right, let's do everything now. Fill the water barrel in the kitchen and all of the wood boxes. We need to close and lock all the shutters except the windows in the bunkroom where we sleep."

Eli added, "And we should barricade the windows down here again."

Sally came into the living room with a basket. "Since we won't have time to prepare breakfast in the morning, we should go ahead and gather all the eggs now. Tonight, we should boil every egg we have, pack them all with a loaf of bread, and also take a gallon of water."

Ann authorized her. "Get started."

Stephanie followed Sally out the door to get an armload of wood. "We should load the breakfast basket and our travel bags into the wagon before we go to sleep."

A few hours later, a cart approached Doc. When Doc saw Smitty in the driver's box, he stood up and waved. "Help me pick up Earl."

Smitty straightened out the layers of comforters laid there by Clara and Nellie to make the ride more comfortable. They placed Earl gently in the wagon then Doc woke Noah. "Smitty's here to get us."

Noah picked up his pallet, tossed it on his side of the comforters, and climbed in. The gentle motion returned Noah to sleep. Earl never woke during the move.

While Earl and Noah slept, Doc told Smitty what he knew about Judge Atwood's investigation at Clarksville and his suspicions that the judge was coming to the wrong conclusion. He related everything that had happened on their journey home, including the surgery he had just completed on Earl's leg, and showed the bone fragments in his pocket. Smitty said that he also had a bad feeling about Judge Atwood. They discussed their concerns about the upcoming trials until Smitty pulled up to the back of Doc's house.

Nellie came to the door with a lantern. At the request of Smitty, Clara also waited at the doctor's house. She looked at her husband lying unconscious in the wagon and fretted. "How is he? What can I do to help?"

"I did some surgery on his leg. I think he'll heal up fine, but I want him here for a while before he goes home."

"Can I hug him?"

"Of course you can. Let us get him into bed first. Then, be very careful of his leg."

Judge Atwood was also there but not at the request of anybody. He issued one command, "Give me the keys to the jail." Smitty didn't like the feel of it but handed over the set he had in his pocket. The judge took the keys and left Smitty and Doc to get Earl out of the wagon and into the house without his help.

Noah got out of the wagon and picked up a handful of blankets. Nellie stopped him. "Put that down. Go straight into the house and get in your bed." Noah hurt too much and felt too tired to argue. He knew Nellie genuinely cared about his well-being. He was glad to go into her home to recover, so he did as told. He found a tub of warm water, soap, a towel, fresh bandages, clean nightclothes, and a hearty bowl of soup in his room. Once out of the tub, he dried off, wrapped the bandages around his arm and head, sat on the bed in the nightclothes, and ate the soup. As much as his body hurt, he equally felt cared for.

Judge Atwood lay on his bed at Joe's Saloon. *I always thought Hank was going to get*

*Roy killed, not himself. Poor Roy, he was so close to Hank, and Roy's friends are dead too. Roy, Ben, and Gus are probably guilty as hell, but I'm not going to kill Roy because some *&%^% Indian didn't stay where he belongs. This whole thing stinks to the high Heavens, and these people will know it. I wish there was another place in town big enough. If these people take matters into their own hands, there is a lot of merchandise in the store they could use as weapons. I'm going to have to empty it and keep tight control. D@^^ Roy. He's never been anything but a problem.* Judge Atwood felt as nervous as a long-tailed cat in a room of rocking chairs.

THIRTY EIGHT

After the sun had come up, Judge Atwood walked across the street. He asked Tom to clear out Yates Mercantile to set up a courtroom. After delivering his instructions to Tom, the judge told every citizen in Harmony to be at the store with a small chair when the sun was at its zenith.

Eli and the girls arrived in town early. They put the wagon behind Yates Mercantile. Stephanie, Sally, and Eli took Samson to Smitty's livery. Ann went straight to Doc's to check on Noah. "Good morning, Nellie."

Nellie didn't wait for Ann to ask. She knew why Ann was there. "I'm under orders. I can't allow anybody to visit Noah."

Ann's eyebrows pulled down. "Noah is the victim. That sounds like he's the suspect."

"I'm sorry. You can't see him."

"Please tell him that I called." Ann walked to Yates Mercantile and told her family what had happened. They all agreed that it didn't seem right. The sisters, Eli, and Tom spent the morning moving everything off the store's floor into the house or the storeroom.

In case he had to flee, Judge Atwood wanted easy avenues of escape. Late that morning, he returned to the store and gave further instructions. "Move the shortest counter to the left beside the storeroom door. Leave only enough space between the counter and the wall for a platform big enough to put a small but stable chair on top." He laid his gavel on the mostly glass counter. "Put a chair in front, facing the judge's bench, and three next to the wall by the back entrance."

Strangely, even though none of it was in the way, the judge ordered, "Take everything off the shelves, and get it all out of here." Noon approached as they moved the last items out of the store. Folks arrived and jammed in. Judge Atwood entered through the back door and took his seat. He tapped his gavel to call everybody to silence.

He stated the charges. "People of Harmony, we are here today to determine what happened in the town of Harmony on March 12th of 1839. The charges are the attempted murder of Noah Swift Hawk by Roy Butterfield and the murder of Hank Butterfield by the men of Harmony. Judge Richard Atwood, presiding."

Shocked by the charges, the people voiced their concerns. Smitty stood up and stated what was on everybody's mind. "Hank wasn't murdered. Where did this charge come from?"

Judge Atwood hit his gavel on the counter. "Everybody is to be silent unless speaking as a witness." Talking continued. "Come to order." He pounded his gavel. "Come to order. Unless you are speaking as a witness, be quiet. Do you understand?"

When the judge got everybody quieted down, he called out, "Bring in the men from jail."

Before Smitty could get to the door, a group of unknown men led Ben, Roy, and Gus into the room through the back door and put them in the defendant's seats at the back wall. Not caring if anybody thought he was incompetent for not knowing what was happening, Smitty asked, "What's going on, Judge?"

Judge Atwood rattled off his preplanned answer, "I asked some men from Fort Smith to help with these proceedings."

Smitty looked at the men dressed in civilian clothing. He knew military men, and these were definitely soldiers.

Stephanie looked at the men in the defendant's seats. "Aren't those the men who bought our horses last winter?"

Ann had stood at the door and spoken with Hank but had also looked at the people riding double. "I reckon so."

Judge Atwood called his first witness, "Sheriff Smithfield Wyman, come to the witness seat." Smitty struggled to make his way. "Raise your right hand and place your left hand on the Bible." One of Judge Atwood's men stood beside the chair and held out a Bible. "Do you swear to tell the truth, the whole truth, and nothing but the truth? So help you God."

"I do. So help me God."

"Tell us what happened on March 12th of 1839." After Smitty had explained what happened, the judge asked, "Do you believe that the men of Harmony had no choice but to shoot Hank when he threw the chair leg?"

"They didn't at that second, but—"

Judge Atwood cut Smitty off. "That will be all. Please go back to your seat." Smitty didn't get to say that Hank had drawn his gun after he had hurled the chair leg.

"Joseph Pinckney. Come to the stand."

Joe made his way to the witness stand, took his oath, then gave his testimony. "Hank and his men came in and asked for whiskey and food. They became belligerent toward Noah, who only sat at the bar eating his food dressed in Indian garb. Hank yelled insults, then picked up a chair and slammed it on the table."

Joe raised his hand and forcefully brought it back down in front of him. "A piece of the chair hit me in the cheek, and one went into Noah's left arm." Joe showed the judge his cheek. The stitches were gone, but the bright red scar was not. "I had just pulled my rifle from under the bar and trained it on Hank to force the man to calm down when Smitty and the others came in." Joe held out an imaginary rifle and aimed it at the store door.

"So, you thought you could control the situation after Hank broke the chair?"

Joe confessed, "At that moment, I did."

"How many times have you stopped a fight in your saloon?"

"A few times, but they weren't nothing like this one."

Judge Atwood had heard what he wanted everybody to hear. "Thank you for your testimony. Please take your seat."

Joe navigated back to his seat, upset because the judge had made him say something that wasn't entirely accurate.

"Noah Swift Hawk. Take the stand." Noah worked his way to the front, placed his left hand on the Bible, and raised his right hand. Judge Atwood asked, "Does swearing on the Bible mean anything to you?"

"Of course it does."

"Why would it mean anything to you?"

"Because it's the Word of God."

The judge thought it was true of all Indians and stated as a fact, "The God of the Bible isn't your god."

"Yes, He is. God is the only true living God. He is the creator and sustainer of everything."

The judge told Noah, "You don't know anything about Him."

Noah refuted the accusation and informed

the judge of reality. "I've read the Bible many times. I know about Him. I'm swearing on The Word of my God to tell the truth." He sat down to end the discussion.

Sally whispered, "What was that about?"

Ann remembered that she hadn't been allowed to visit Noah. "I think the judge is trying to make Noah out as a bad person."

"State what happened March 12th of 1839."

"I had traveled a long way. I planned to eat a meal and rest for the night then ask about the place I wanted to find. I was sitting at the bar, not bothering anybody, when some men screamed for me to leave. I had paid for my meal, and I was going to eat it. I didn't want any trouble, so I ignored them. I heard the chair crash and felt the pain in my arm. I thought about throwing my knife into the throat of the man who had injured me, but I told myself to remain calm and not respond."

"So you wanted to kill him?"

"For a second, but the sheriff and his men came in and were handling the situation."

"So you don't take care of your own problems?"

"That's not what I meant. I didn't want to make things worse. My mother taught me always to be under control and not to be the one to raise the level of conflict. As much as it is up to me, be at peace with others. God says that too."

"Did you tell Roy that Hank deserved to be dead, and you were going to make sure they all died?"

"I never said a single word."

"Was anybody close enough to know you didn't speak?"

"Joe was."

"That's all. Go to your seat."

The judge continued the proceedings until he had heard the testimony of all the men who were in the saloon except Eli and Earl. Earl because Doc Gridley insisted he was not able to leave his bed or testify.

"That will be all for the prosecution."

Eli stood up. "What about my testimony?"

"You weren't in the room."

"But I heard everything."

I don't want to hear anything from a man who sleeps with three women at the same time. You're barely more than a boy, and that's what you're doing. "Sit down and be quiet."

It became evident to everybody that Judge Atwood wasn't looking for the truth. Roy especially, but also Gus and Ben, looked smug as if they expected things to go well for them. The rest of the people of Harmony felt quite concerned about the direction of the proceedings. The judge called the next witness, "Roy Butterfield, take the stand."

On the Bible, Roy swore that he would tell the truth then sat up straight in the witness chair and looked the judge directly in the eye. He laced his fingers together and carefully placed his hands on his lap. He then related, in perfect English, what he wanted Judge Atwood to believe. "Before we came to town, that Indian attacked us and took one of our horses."

Noah stood up. "That's a bald-faced lie! I've never had any dealings with those men. Arabella is mine."

"You are out of order." Judge Atwood pounded his gavel on the counter.

Highly agitated, Noah sat down. Nobody was taking Arabella from him.

Roy calmly continued his story, "Even though the sheriff had ordered us not to, we came to Harmony because we tracked the Indian here. When we saw him, we told him we wanted the horse back. He said, 'You pale-faces can't have the horse, and if you try to take it back, I'll scalp you.'"

Noah shot up. "I never said anything."

Joe stood up at the same time. "I was there. That never happened!"

Judge Atwood wavered. *Roy is lying through his teeth. I shouldn't let anybody get away with bald-faced lying.* Then he told himself, *I'm sure the heathen is guilty of something. I don't care about him, but the folks here obviously do. I need to make sure everybody feels completely compelled to do as I say.* He pounded his gavel. "I will have order."

Noah sat down, but he steamed with anger. Roy continued, "It wasn't in the saloon. We treated him very respectfully and told him we were going to the law."

Noah stood up again. "He's lying."

The judge glared. "If you speak out one more time, you are going to jail."

Roy continued, "So that's why, when we saw him in the saloon, Hank told him we weren't going to sit in the same room with him. He wouldn't even turn and look at us respectfully or say anything, so Hank slammed the chair. He didn't mean to hurt anybody. Hank just wanted to make that Indian do something. When Joe pulled a rifle on us, Charlie put his hand on his gun, so he could defend us.

"Then the whole town came in and told us that we couldn't defend ourselves. Hank threw the chair leg down, and every one of them shot him. He didn't do anything to deserve killing. When the sheriff ordered us to leave, I stood there broken up because Hank was dead. I wanted to stay with Hank, but Sheriff Wyman said he was going to shoot me if I didn't leave the saloon. I tried to get past the Indian. That's when he said that Hank deserved to die, and he was going to make sure the rest of us joined him. I hit him to protect us."

Noah started up again, but Smitty held him down. Noah whispered, "I never said anything."

The judge led the witness, "So, it was self-defense when you hit the Indian?"

"Exactly. I tried to make a run for the door because the sheriff said he was going to shoot me. I bumped him, and we fell. I tried to get my rifle, so I could get away, but Eli jumped me. He also said he was going to kill me. Then, the sheriff got up and said he was putting me in jail. I cooperated and went with him. I've been in jail ever since, and I never ever did one thing wrong."

"Thank you for your testimony, Mr. Butterfield. Please go back to your place."

The judge then called Ben, who said, "The sheriff tried ta make us think he was letting us go, but he ordered his man ta tie our guns ta a horse he knew would lead us right inta a trap. We bought that horse last winter from them girls." Ben pointed at Ann, Stephanie, and Sally. "That horse ran right ta their house. We followed it ta get our guns. The one who said he was gonna blow Roy's brains inta the floor shot Al when we was walking up ta the house cause they wanted that horse back."

"Thank you. Please take your seat, Mr. Rowe. Gus Hutchinson, come to the witness chair." Gus stood before the bench. "Take the oath then tell us what happened on March the 12th of 1839."

Gus swore to tell the truth. He then told the judge what he wanted him to think had happened. "That Indian took Hank's horse. We followed him ta get it back. When we saw the Indian, we toll him we wanted our horse. He just walked away an' went inta the saloon. Hank wasn't gonna let him get away with it, an' he toll him that in the saloon. Next thing you know, the people o' this town killed Hank. They tried ta make it look good, but it was cold-blooded murder. Then, they ran us out a town ta protect that Indian like no decent white person oughta do."

The sun dipped below the horizon as Gus finished his testimony. "That will be all for today. Court is adjourned." Judge Atwood pointed at his men with his gavel and waved it toward the jail. "Take the accused back to jail. Everybody go home. We'll reconvene here two hours after sunup."

That night, Eli, Tom, and the girls talked about the trial while they prepared and ate their evening meal. They couldn't fathom why, but they all agreed that the judge was biased. They expected the judge was going to find Roy not guilty of attempted murder, but they didn't have any idea what he was thinking about the death of Hank.

Ann led them in prayer, "God, guide Judge Atwood to make the correct decisions."

Tom didn't believe any God was listening.

THIRTY NINE

As soon as everybody was in the store, the court convened. "People of Harmony, we are here this morning to determine if Noah Swift Hawk is guilty of horse stealing on March 12th of 1839, Judge Richard Atwood presiding."

Noah stood up. "I did no such thing. I've never stolen a horse. Arabella is mine."

Smitty stood up beside Noah. "You can't just make up a charge."

Judge Atwood banged his gavel on the counter. "There will be no speaking out in this courtroom unless you are on the witness stand. Roy Butterfield, Benjamin Rowe, and Gus Hutchinson have alleged horse stealing by Noah Swift Hawk. A court of law hears presented cases to determine what happened.

I can't decide in advance what is or is not true."

Smitty knew the judge was right. "Go ahead," he sat down, "Sit down, Noah."

"Roy Butterfield, take the stand. You are still under oath. State what happened March 12th of 1839 before you entered Harmony."

"We had just woken up when that Indian sneaked into camp and cut out one of our horses. We heard something, so we grabbed our guns. That's when he attacked us, but he couldn't win, so he rode away on the horse."

"How did he attack you?"

"You know, he jumped on us with his knife."

"Did you or any of the others get any injuries during the fight?"

"No."

"Why not?"

"He couldn't get at us because there were more of us."

"Whose horse did he take?"

"It was an extra one with us."

"Why did you have an extra horse?"

"It was carrying our supplies."

"Where are your supplies?"

"They got lost."

"Thank you. Please go back to your seat."

When Gus and Ben testified, they also said that Noah jumped them with a knife. When he couldn't get the best of them that he rode away on the horse.

Judge Atwood then called Noah to the stand. He reminded Noah that he was still under oath, but he did not ask Noah to give his testimony. Instead, the judge interrogated him.

"When did you take the horse from Hank Butterfield and his friends?"

"I never took a horse from them. Arabella is mine."

"What did you take from them?"

"I never took anything from them. I never saw any of them until we were in Clarksville."

"You must have seen them."

"Then why did I have to figure out who they were?"

The judge ordered Noah sternly, "I ask the questions in this courtroom. You do not. Don't do it again."

"I can prove that Arabella is mine."

"Tell me what happened at their camp."

"I was never at their camp, so there's nothing to tell. I came to town by myself on my horse that I rode all the way from Indian Territory."

"I've heard enough. Take your seat."

"I can prove that Arabella is mine."

"I told you to go to your seat."

Noah looked at Smitty as he walked to his seat. "Sorry." He let out a loud whistle. From down at Smitty's stable came the sound of crashing and splitting wood as Arabella tried to kick her way out of the stall to get to Noah, who then whistled a double whistle. The commotion ceased. Noah loudly informed everybody in the room, "That," he paused, "was MY horse!" The judge glared at Noah.

He wanted to throw him in jail for that maneuver. Judge Atwood determined that he was right to believe that the Indian was a troublemaker, but he felt sure that he knew what had happened. He moved on to the next charge.

"People of Harmony, I will now hear the case of the alleged attack on the Williams' house on March 13th of 1839. The charges are the destruction of the Williams' house, attempted murder of Ann, Stephanie, and Sally Williams, and Eli Yates by Gus Hutchinson, Charlie Cobb, Pete Drake, Alvin Ives, and Benjamin Rowe, and the murder of Alvin Ives by Eli Yates, Judge Richard Atwood presiding."

Once again, the folks were shocked. Smitty wondered how things had gotten to this place. He didn't know when or how a charge of attempting to murder Al had come in. Tom glanced at Ann and Stephanie. They had their eyes closed, but their lips were moving. He knew they were silently calling out to their God. Tom wondered *if God IS real, will He listen to them? I hope God is there, and I hope God will hear their prayers. I can't lose Hattie and Eli.*

***

Tom remembered when he and Hattie had been young. He had been a Christian man like his folks. They had wanted him not to marry a woman who wasn't a Christian. They had said, "Don't be unequally yoked." It didn't matter. He loved Hattie. He had planned to pray every day for her to become a Christian. He believed God would help her do it.

When Eli came along, he was sure she would see the miracle of their baby and realize that only God could design something so perfect. She didn't. Hattie told Tom that she would never believe, that he was wasting his time, and to stop reading the Bible. He didn't. He continued to read the Bible and thought that she would see the truth eventually. Every day, he prayed for Hattie to give her heart to God.

When she contracted cholera, he prayed to God to save her. The day she died, Tom decided God wasn't there, or He didn't care about him and Hattie. He put his Bible on the shelf. He had never picked it up again.

***

Today, as Tom heard the charge of murder against Eli, just as it had when Hattie had died, his heart overflowed with fear and loss.

The judge broke into Ann's silent prayer. "Ann Williams, come to the stand."

Ann swore to tell the truth, but she believed the truth would be twisted into something that wasn't true no matter what she said. She silently prayed, *God, please help me to say what you would have me say.*

"Tell me what happened on March 13th of 1839."

Ann pointed toward Roy, Ben, and Gus. "Last winter, I did sell two horses to those men and the other men with them. The horse may have gone to our house when they ran it out of town, but we weren't there. We went home the morning of the thirteenth. That was the day after the incident in the saloon. Late in the day of the 13th, we realized that somebody had been in the house.

"We assumed they were the same men Sheriff Wyman had run out of town. We didn't feel safe, so we tried to secure the house by barring the doors and closing the shutters. As soon as we started closing the shutters, people shot at our home. They hit the house so much that they destroyed the shutters and the windows, which allowed access into the house. We thought whoever was outside was surely going to kill us, so we prayed for God to help us.

"Thousands of screaming blackbirds flew into the trees and pooped so much that they completely covered the whole woods behind our house in sloshy white goop. The men in the woods shot at the birds above. One of the bullets they fired fell back to earth and hit the tall man in his shoulder. They slipped around getting to their horses then rode away."

Judge Atwood considered. *God isn't real, but if He were, He would not send a flock of birds to defecate on people to run them off.* "Miss Williams, did you see this yourself?"

"I didn't see what the birds were doing, but I could hear them, and I saw the men ride away covered in white."

"Were you ever unable to see what the others in the house were doing?"

"There were times when we were in different parts of the house, and I couldn't see what they were doing."

"Was Eli always with one of you girls?"

"No, he closed the shutters in a different part of the house, then he went to get the drill, and he also went up into the attic alone."

"I didn't see any bird feces or dead birds behind your house, but you want me to believe that God miraculously sent a flock of blackbirds that you didn't see to save you?" *I can't believe this woman. She has no morals.*

"Yes, but–"

"That will be all. Go back to your seat." Once again, Judge Atwood cut off the testimony of the witness.

As Ann passed Smitty, she whispered, "He didn't let me say that I did see the birds later."

Judge Atwood called Stephanie and then Sally, who both gave the same testimony as Ann. He confirmed with both of them that they had not seen the birds pooping, the men firing into the air above them, or a bullet falling from the sky into Al's shoulder.

Judge Atwood had to allow the accused an opportunity to defend himself, so he called his next witness, "Eli Yates, come to the witness seat and take your oath."

Eli swore to tell the truth, the whole truth, and nothing but the truth.

"Tell your story."

"Starting with what happened in town or at the farm?"

Since everything was tied together, the judge decided to listen to it all. "In town."

"So I could come in from behind if we had to surround them, I hid in the back room and listened. When I realized that I needed to keep Roy from shooting Smitty, I jumped him and kept him down with my rifle while Doc examined Smitty."

"So, you admit you jumped on Roy."

"Yes."

"What did you say to him when you were keeping him down?"

"I told him to hope Smitty was all right."

"What were your exact words?"

"You better hope Smitty is all right, or Joe will be cleaning your brains out of the floor."

"You admit you threatened to kill him?"

"Yes, but I didn't mean that."

"When you told him that Joe was going to be cleaning his brains out of the floor, you had no desire to kill Roy?"

"I planned to shoot him if I needed to."

"So, you made a plan to kill at least one of the men with Hank Butterfield?"

"Not like that. It was only right then."

"What happened at the Williams' farm?"

"We discovered that somebody had been in the house when we saw footprints in the bunkroom. We tried to secure the house, but someone fired on us from the woods. There were so many bullets that we thought there must be more than just the men we ran out of town. The barrage of bullets had shattered the shutters, so we had to do something to keep anybody from getting into the house.

"We couldn't look out the windows to see how many men were there or where they were located. We decided that they probably wouldn't be shooting at the attic, so I went up there, drilled a hole, and peeked through.

"I saw five men and six horses. Also, birds filled every tree in the woods. They dropped their feces and quickly covered everything below. The men tried to make the birds leave by waving their arms and then by shooting at them. Al hollered that he was hit. They got on their horses and rode away."

"Were you in the attic alone?"

Eli answered truthfully, "Yes."

"Would you have been able to shoot Al from the attic?"

"No. There was only one hole, and I was looking through it."

"Did you take your rifle to the attic?"

"Yes."

"Would you have been able to fit your rifle barrel through the hole and shoot it?"

"Yes, but I couldn't have seen where to aim."

"That will be all. Go back to your seat."

The judge called Ben and Gus, who repeated the story from the day before; they followed the horse to the Williams' farm, where Eli shot Al when he walked up to the house.

When they finished telling their lies, the judge spoke. "Thank you for your testimonies. We will break for dinner. Go to your own homes, stay there for two hours, and then come back. Take the prisoners to jail and feed them."

Extremely concerned, Tom put together a meal. "Judge Atwood is not trying to find out what happened. He wants to make it look like Eli shot Al."

Ann turned her back to the window and whispered very softly, "The judge's men are outside listening." She added at normal speaking volume, "He didn't do it. I'm sure the judge knows that."

"He hardly seems to want to hear what we have to say." Stephanie discreetly motioned that she heard what Ann had said.

Sally didn't hear Ann's warning. "What can we do? Everything's going wrong."

Ann spoke words only the appropriate people would understand, "Eli may have to see the Indian with the rope," she walked past Sally to get the water pitcher and whispered, "We're being watched again."

Eli understood that Ann meant for him to hide in the cave. "If I have to, I will." They sat at the table and ate glumly then nervously waited for the court to reconvene.

FORTY

Doc helped Earl into the courtroom and propped his leg up as well as he could in the crowded room. When everybody was back in Tom's store, the soldiers brought Roy, Ben, and Gus over from the jail. The judge came into the room and called the court back into session.

"People of Harmony, we are here to determine what happened at Clarksville on March 24th of 1839. The charges are the murders of Pete Drake, Alvin Ives, and Charlie Cobb. Judge Richard Atwood, presiding. Sheriff Smithfield Wyman, take the stand. You are still under oath. Do you understand?"

"Yes."

"Be seated and tell me what happened on March 21st through March 24th of 1839."

Smitty related everything that had happened and ended with, "Noah told us that the men were going to either break out Roy, or rape and possibly murder the Williams girls, or just move on."

Drawing in practically all the oxygen in the room, everybody in town gasped, especially Ann, Stephanie, and Sally. They had no idea that rape was in anybody's plan. Eli glared at Ben and Gus. Nobody was going to hurt any of the Williams girls if he had anything to do with it.

"Did you yourself hear any of the men say that they planned to break Roy Butterfield out of jail or wanted to rape or murder Ann, Stephanie, or Sally Williams?"

"No, Noah told us."

"If you didn't hear them yourself, it's just hearsay and not admissible. Continue."

"Before he went back to town, Noah told us he would send a signal to let us know what they decided. At sundown, Noah signaled that they were going to try to free

Roy. We watched all night. Nobody left town until the next morning. Noah rejoined us before Charlie, Ben, Gus, and Pete left town. We thought we could ambush and catch them before they drew a gun.

"I fired the signal shot when they were in position. As I raced up the trail, I saw Pete shoot Horace clean off his horse. Then, it was chaos. Horses and people fell everywhere. Noah and Charlie rolled away down the hill. Ben threw down his rifle and surrendered." Roy glared at Ben.

Smitty continued, "We got all the men and bodies onto horses and rode into town."

"Was anybody not involved there?"

"No."

"Please take your seat."

One by one, the judge called the men from Harmony to the stand. He told Earl, "Take your oath and give your testimony from your seat."

Earl promised to tell the truth and then reported his recollections. "Charlie almost shot me as I rode around the corner of the trail into the fight. I reined in my horse when I saw his rifle swing my way. My horse fell, and the shot missed me. I was completely sure that Charlie was going to kill me because of the expression on his face and because my leg was pinned under my horse."

Clyde said, "Zachariah and I ran down the trail. Both Noah and Charlie were unconscious. Zachariah felt Noah's neck, and I went over to check on Charlie. Charlie's head was smashed open like a pumpkin. We went back up and told the others what we saw then got everybody on horses and rode straight to Sheriff Slade."

The judge called the last witness, "Noah Swift Hawk, take the stand. You are still under oath. Tell your story."

Noah sat in the witness chair. "I didn't know what the men looked like. I needed to find them without them realizing that I was looking for them. I thought the four men at the table were likely to be the people we were looking for, so I went to the piano to listen to them. I heard them say that Al was dead. They argued about what they should do next. Gus drew a gun on Pete right there in the saloon and told him to shut up, or he would shoot him. I went and told the men what I had found out. After that, I went back to town and discovered that they had decided to leave in the morning to break Roy out of jail. I put out the signal and then went to bed. In the morning, I rode out to join the men in the posse."

"Why did you pretend to be a white man?"

"I'm not pretending. I'm as much a white man as I am an Indian man, but I put on those clothes because I didn't want them to recognize me."

"Were you planning to take revenge for the injuries they gave you?"

"None of them did it."

"I asked if you were planning to take revenge for the injuries they gave you?"

"No."

"Why did you ask to have your horse washed?"

"Because the stable hand told me that some men had come in with horses that smelled awful. He was upset that they hadn't asked him to wash them. I knew Arabella would like it, so I paid him to wash her."

"Why did you play one note on the piano?"

"I wanted to get closer to the men to find out if they were the ones I was looking for and to hear what they were talking about. Since I don't know how to play the piano, there wasn't any sense to play more than one note."

"You want me to believe that story? If you can't play, you would not have gone to the piano at all. Go back to your chair."

Everybody squirmed. It was obvious that Noah was in trouble, but they didn't know what to do about it. The judge motioned one of his men over. He didn't want anybody else in the room to know what he was asking, so he whispered, "How much longer until they get here?"

"I don't know."

The judge announced a break, "The court will recess for fifteen minutes." He hit his gavel on the counter and motioned for his man to follow him as he left the room. "They should have been here by now." The judge switched his topic of concern and asked for a report. "What did you find out about the people here in Harmony?"

"We haven't heard anything to make us think they're lying. They all believe you're not listening to what people are saying and that you're twisting things around."

"I'm not twisting anything. That boy is sleeping with all those girls, and that's why they're covering up that he shot Al. Besides, God doesn't send a flock of birds to save people, and no guns could have shot through those thick shutters. They must have shot up everything themselves and chopped up those shutters with an axe. And there sure isn't any Indian who is going to get away with killing white men in my court of law."

"Yes, sir. I understand." Lieutenant Warren Lampson realized the people were right about the judge. These were hanging offenses. He walked out of the room to contemplate what he should do.

Fifteen minutes later, there were still no new arrivals. The judge wanted to wait for them. He looked into the courtroom but didn't see the lieutenant. He motioned another of his men to come over. "Is everybody back?"

"Earl and the doctor haven't come back."

Judge Atwood thought that was his opportunity to stall the proceedings. "Go get them. We aren't reconvening until everybody is here."

Five minutes later, the private came back. "Dr. Gridley says Earl is not coming back today. I told them they are ordered to come, but they won't."

"Private Jeremiah Pratt, are you telling me that a soldier can't get a doctor and a man with a broken leg to do what he says?"

"No, sir. I'll have them here right away."

Lieutenant Lampson heard the exchange. He joined Jeremiah on his way back to the doctor's house. "I'll go in. You wait out here." The lieutenant knocked.

Dr. Gridley came to the door. "I told you that Earl is not able to sit over there anymore today."

"I understand. May I come in?" Doc stepped aside to let the man enter. "Where can we speak privately?"

"Step into my office." Doc used his best bedside manners. "How may I help you?"

"I'm not sure. The judge has people coming from Clarksville. That's fine with me, but I get the feeling the judge is not looking for the truth."

Doc thought the soldier might be setting him up. "Surely a man such as Judge Atwood would be seeking the truth."

"When I came here, I would have agreed, but now I don't think so. He said that Eli Yates is having relations with all three of the Williams girls, and that's why they're protecting him. He said there is no such thing as God sending birds to save the day and that no Indian is getting away with killing white men in his court of law."

Doc's jaw dropped open. "How many of your soldiers feel the same?"

"None that I know about."

"What do you suggest?"

"I don't know, but I'm not going to allow him to hang an innocent man. If we could keep the people from Clarksville from getting here for another half an hour or so, I might be able to get him to adjourn until tomorrow. That'll buy us some time to try to figure something out."

Doc offered, "I'll go hold them up."

"The judge expects to see you and Earl in the courtroom immediately."

Clara left Earl's bedside and quietly made her way across the house. She opened the door just enough to slip into the room. "Maybe I can help. I ride my horse bareback and without a bridle all the time. Nobody is concerned about me. They won't even notice that I'm gone. I'll go hold up the people from Clarksville."

Doc wanted to be sure that she understood. "Earl will have to go back to the store. He's hurting very badly."

"He's going to have to go anyway. I told him what you two were talking about, and he said he wants to go back over."

"All right, let's try, but be careful." With a lot of commotion and complaining, Lieutenant Lampson, Doc, and the soldier waiting outside helped Earl cross the street. Everybody watched them come to Yates Mercantile as Clara rode unobserved out of town.

Earl settled in as comfortably as possible. The lieutenant went to tell the judge that everybody was present and that he could convene the court. The judge had hoped they would refuse until the witnesses from Clarksville had arrived. Now, he had to call the court back into session. He asked Ben, Gus, and Smitty to retell their stories and made Noah explain everything he saw and did a second time. The judge motioned Lieutenant Lampson over. "Is there any sign of them? It's been forty-five minutes. They should have been here long ago."

"Maybe it would be best to adjourn until tomorrow."

The judge decided he was not going to be able to catch anybody off guard and gave up waiting. "Court is adjourned. Everybody go to your home. We will reconvene two hours after sunrise tomorrow." He slammed his gavel on the counter and stormed out the back door.

FORTY ONE

Confused and concerned, the people made their way to their homes. Later that evening, Doc stepped out of his house. The young soldier, who earlier had tried to get him to go back to the courtroom, stopped him immediately. "Please go back into your house, Doctor."

"You've heard everything we've been saying. You know I have patients. I need to check on Horace."

"Well." Jeremiah mulled over the situation. *I don't want to be responsible for a man not getting medical treatment.* "I have to come with you, and you need to make it quick."

Dr. Gridley knocked on Horace's door. "I'm here to see how you're doing. May I come in?"

"Sure," Horace invited him in.

Doc went into the house. His escort attempted to follow him in. "I'm sorry, son. Wait outside while I examine my patient." He closed the door in front of Jeremiah. Then he carried on a loud conversation about his examination while quietly whispering his concerns about the judge, the lieutenant's visit, and Clara's secret ride to delay the people Judge Atwood had summoned from Clarksville. "I want you and Betsy to be prepared. We're prisoners in our homes, and we don't have a plan. This may go terribly wrong."

"Should I tell anybody else?"

"If it's not completely safe, don't take any chances."

Doc told Horace loudly, "You're healing very nicely. I'll see you tomorrow." Doc stepped out of the house and let the soldier escort him home.

Sally saw the soldier try to keep Doc in his house and then walk him to Horace's house and back. She told the other four, "First, they were spying. Now, they're treating us like prisoners."

Tom became more concerned. "The judge wouldn't be confining us unless he thinks we're the guilty ones."

Stephanie was sure Eli was in trouble. "I know the judge thinks Eli shot Al. They'll hang him for murder. We have to get him out of here." She started to cry.

Eli put his arms around her. "It's going to be all right, Stephanie. It won't come to that. They'll surely think I'm guilty if I run and hide." Nevertheless, he wasn't completely putting aside going to see the Indian with the rope.

They were not the only family who had noticed the soldier escort the doctor to Horace's house. That was one of the reasons for Doc's trip to see Horace. He hoped that people would realize that they were prisoners.

Shortly after the doctor returned home,

the group from Clarksville arrived. The townsfolk, as well as the soldiers and the judge, came out into the street to greet them. Clara slipped into Smitty's stable, dismounted, and mixed into the crowd unnoticed.

Smitty turned. "What's going on, judge?"

"I asked these people to come here for the trial. I want to get all the facts."

Smitty thought *the judge is up to something,* but he said nothing more.

Judge Atwood saw to the needs of his Clarksville witnesses. "Joe, put these folks up and feed them. The court will pay the expenses."

"Come on in. I'll get you to your rooms." Joe ushered them into the saloon. As a good innkeeper, he thought, *what will I feed so many at this hour?*

The judge ordered, "All of you go home."

As the others made their way back to their houses, Clara slipped into Smitty's. Mara almost jumped out of her skin when she saw somebody in a dark corner of her sitting room.

Clara immediately assured her that there was no danger, "It's me, Clara."

Mara asked, "What are you doing?"

"Act like I'm not here."

Mara and Smitty sat in their chairs, picked up a book, listened, and occasionally turned a page.

Clara explained about the lieutenant's visit to the doctor's house and repeated what Doc said the judge had told the lieutenant. She divulged that she had sneaked out of town to let the people coming from Clarksville know what appeared to be happening with the trials and to stall them. The folks from Clarksville were skeptical but agreed to wait to go into town and promised to be observant during the proceedings. Clara conveyed to Smitty and Mara that, as far as she knew, there were no definite plans about what to do.

Smitty spoke from behind his book,

"Thank you for being brave. Let's see if we can get you to Dr. Gridley's house." He put down his book. "I'm going to check on the prisoners."

Smitty opened the door. Just as he suspected, a soldier stood outside his door. "Stay in your house, sir."

"What do you mean by this? I'm the sheriff. You can't tell me what to do in my own town, and you certainly can't keep me from checking on my prisoners." He stepped out of his house onto the boardwalk.

"Yes, we can, and we will."

Smitty insisted, "I demand to speak with Judge Atwood right now." The other soldiers came over in case they needed to restrain the man. "Am I a prisoner here?"

Smitty yelled so loudly that everybody in town heard. Most of the town's people already suspected that something was wrong. Now, they knew for sure. They stepped out of their houses. Clara joined them.

The judge tried to cover up. "Everything is fine. Nobody is a prisoner. Let the sheriff go to the jail. I don't know why you stopped him. I told you to ensure that the town is safe in case anybody tries to free the prisoners."

The soldier who had stopped Smitty stepped aside. "Go ahead. Sorry for the misunderstanding, Sheriff. "

Private Jeremiah Pratt was sure his fellow soldier did not have his orders wrong. Jeremiah had the same understanding of their orders as the soldier who had tried to stop the sheriff. He had recently done the same with the doctor. The chance that every one of them had misunderstood was just about impossible. He went to talk with the lieutenant after everybody was off the street. "Sir, may I speak to you?"

"What's on your mind?"

"Sir, I apologize for getting my orders wrong. Please explain my orders."

The lieutenant asked, "What's your opinion about your orders?"

"I doubt that we all misunderstood."

"Are you saying that something doesn't seem right to you?" The lieutenant probed.

"Sir, yes, sir. Very strange, sir." Jeremiah didn't want to be insubordinate, but things weren't right.

"At ease, Jeremiah, there is something wrong."

"What's wrong, sir?"

"Judge Atwood doesn't seem to be seeking the truth, and he may sentence the wrong people to hang."

Jeremiah relaxed slightly. "I was thinking the same thing, but it's not my place to question orders."

"Let me tell you about orders. Yes, you obey your orders. Sometimes, they may seem harsh or don't make sense, but you follow them anyway. But when your God-given conscience tells you something is plainly wrong, you must do what God would have you do."

"I agree, sir. That's why I came to you."

"You're a good soldier to come to your commander for clarification. We can't take action on an assumption. He may or may not knowingly sentence innocent people, but we must be prepared to go against his sentence if we have to. I'm not going to hang an innocent seventeen-year-old boy, no matter what his relationship is with those girls, or hang a man just because he's part Indian."

"What should we do?"

"I don't know. Do you know if any of the other men would be with us?"

"Jesse and Will already told me they thought the judge was twisting things. Maybe Ernest as well, but I'm not sure about him."

"Tell Jesse and Will to be looking to me tomorrow and to follow my lead."

Judge Atwood sat in his room and thought over all the evidence, which was almost non-existent, and about the testimonies, of which there were a lot. He knew Gus and Ben were lying. Some things

Judge Atwood was sure were lies, and some he didn't know what to think. He knew he didn't believe for one second that a giant flock of birds had arrived at the Williams' farm. Atwood didn't yet know what had happened on the trail at Clarksville. That was why he had asked the folks from Clarksville to come to Harmony.

The judge remembered the day Indians had killed his brother. He had thought they were going to end him as well. He had been terrified. When the murderers went free, he had been furious. That was why he had become a judge: to make sure that people received punishment for what they did.

He thought about all he had done to help get the Indian Removal Act passed. They had to get the Indians out of Arkansas for this very reason. They were murderers, and they were holding the white man back. He had worked long and hard to get the Indians removed, not just for himself but also for his wife and her mother. Now, one was here, possibly stealing horses and threatening to scalp white men. He fell asleep thinking about Indians scalping white men.

FORTY TWO

Two hours after dawn, Noah walked into the store. Ann stopped him. "Sit here by the window." Noah put his chair down and sat beside Eli. The three remaining members of the Butterfield Gang, and the people of Harmony, Clarksville, and Fort Smith all squeezed into Yates Mercantile. The space in front of the judge's bench narrowed to barely more than the space taken up by the chair and a set of legs. Because nobody wanted to be close to the defendants, the distance between them and the rest of the people remained as wide as the day before.

Judge Atwood banged the gavel on the counter and called the court back into session, "People of Harmony and Clarksville, we are here today to determine what happened at Clarksville on March 23rd and 24th of 1839. The charges are the murders of Pete Drake, Alvin Ives, and Charlie Cobb. Judge Richard Atwood, presiding. Sheriff Lemuel Slade, step forward. Raise your right hand and place your left hand on the Bible. Do you swear to tell the truth, the whole truth, and nothing but the truth, so help you God?"

"I swear on the Bible to tell the whole truth. So help me God."

"Sheriff, tell us what you know about the incidents at Clarksville on March 23rd and 24th."

Sheriff Slade related the same facts as previously stated by the men of Harmony. He ended, "Sheriff Smithfield Wyman, Dr. Lawrence Gridley, Noah Swift Hawk, Earl Carpenter, Clyde Eggleston, Zachariah Eggleston, Horace Devine, Gus Hutchinson, and Benjamin Rowe rode into town with the bodies of Charlie Cobb whose head was cracked open and Pete Drake who had a bullet wound to the chest. They came directly to me. I locked all of them up before I got Dr. Baker to look at the men with Dr. Gridley."

The judge inquired, "Could Noah Swift Hawk have beaten Charlie Cobb's head on the rock?"

"There was only one blow to Charlie's head. I believe the pool of blood farther up the trail formed where Noah lay on the ground. The two men were not close enough to have been interacting at that point."

"Was any other person in a position to have smashed Charlie's head against the rock?"

"There was no indication of any struggle in that part of the trail, so I don't believe anybody hit Charlie's head against that rock."

"Which of the men would have been in a position to have shot Pete?"

"I can't determine exactly who was where because the trail was scuffled in all directions. However, if Charlie, Ben, Pete, and Gus did not see any of these men until they were upon them, their assailants must have been hiding. That would mean they had to have been shooting from the side. The bullet went straight into Pete's heart. It must have been somebody directly in front of him on the trail. I believe it could only have been Charlie, Ben, or Gus because they would have been the only men in that position."

"That's all. Thank you."

Judge Atwood called Dr. Elmer Baker, who took the oath and sat in the witness chair. "Dr. Baker, first tell us what you know about Alvin Ives."

"They brought Alvin Ives to me with an infected gunshot wound in the shoulder. His clothes and those of the other men smelled dreadful. I cleaned and examined Al's wound. It was apparent that the substance in the wound was an infectious agent. The infection was already in his blood. He had a high fever and was delirious. He repeatedly said, 'Make the birds go away,' and 'Make the birds stop screaming.' There was not a bird anywhere around. He was too far gone to save."

"What was the angle of the wound?"

"He had a wound in his shoulder. The bullet hole went in the front, straight through, and out the back."

"Did you find any substances in the wound?"

"There was some foul-smelling white matter in the front. I don't know what it was. The wound in his back had dirt in it."

"What can you tell me about Pete's injuries and cause of death?"

"Death resulted from a single bullet to the heart. It was a frontal straight-through shot."

"Last, what were your findings about Charlie?"

"Death was caused by a blow to his head which broke his skull and smashed it into his brain. There was one location of impact. Tiny bits of rock were present in the brain matter."

"In your opinion, did somebody hit

Charlie with a rock or smash his head against the rock?"

"I went up the trail and looked. The rock is too big to pick up. It's an unmovable object. The location of impact on the rock was low. There was only one place with blood and brains, although there was spatter radiating from the point of impact. I don't believe a person could have forced his head into the rock at that location. My opinion is that the impact occurred as he rolled down the trail."

"Thank you for your helpful information, Doctor. Please take your seat." Dr. Baker sat down before Judge Atwood went on. "I don't believe I need any further testimonies." He issued orders to his soldiers. "Men, close all the doors." He waited until the room was secured. "I will now render my decisions on the matters before me. In the case of the attempted murder of Noah Swift Hawk, I find Roy Butterfield not guilty."

The room immediately filled with loud

complaints that the verdict was wrong. Judge Atwood beat the gavel on the counter until he regained silence. "I believe Roy Butterfield acted in self-defense against an Indian who threatened to scalp him as well as self-defense against the people of this town who had just shot his brother and, by your own admission, had told him twice that you were going to kill him. However, Roy Butterfield, you are ordered never to molest, harass, or cause any damage to Noah Swift Hawk, and you are ordered never to come within fifteen miles of Harmony under penalty of being shot to death if found within that radius.

"As to the death of Hank Butterfield, I find the men of Harmony guilty of overreacting and unnecessarily executing lethal force while protecting the peace in their town. I don't find this to be murder, but it was very bad judgment. I order the citizens of the town of Harmony to pay one hundred dollars of restitution to Mr. Roy Butterfield under the assumption that over several years

Hank Butterfield would have contributed money toward the maintenance of life for himself and his brother, Roy Butterfield. Restitution is to be paid before court is adjourned."

The people didn't have that kind of money. On top of that, they thought Roy didn't deserve it. Commotion and shouting filled the room as the people of Harmony protested the verdict. The judge slammed his gavel against the countertop. "Come to order now!" He pounded the mallet on the counter until he got control. "As to the attempted murder of Misses Ann, Stephanie, and Sally Williams, and Mr. Eli Yates, I find Benjamin Rowe and Gus Hutchinson not guilty."

The room erupted again. The townsfolk couldn't believe how every charge could be so misconstrued. Judge Atwood hollered, "Come to order!" He slammed the gavel on the counter. The glass front of the counter exploded. Glass flew into the room and pierced the people. Startled screams and screams of pain filled the room. Blood ran from cuts, and pieces of glass protruded from bodies. "Administer aid." The judge hurried into the storage room and locked the door.

Dr. Gridley instructed Nellie, "Get my bags, all the sutures, and all the bandages."

Tom and Eli walked toward the door into their home to get bandages. The soldiers blocked the doors. Lieutenant Lampson stood by the door into Tom's house and barked out orders, "Let the woman go. Everybody else, sit down."

Jeremiah guarded the front door as commanded by the lieutenant. He stepped aside and let Nellie pass. In her house, she threw on her nurse's apron and loaded it up. She filled Doc's old bag with items she knew they needed, got Doc's regular bag, and then hurried back. She and the two doctors removed pieces of glass, stitched them up, and bandaged the significant cuts. Everybody else dressed minor injuries.

Judge Atwood remained alone in the back

room. He had never experienced so much opposition. He knew it was happening now because he was doing the wrong thing. He felt emotionally drained by the proceeding that had dredged up pain from his past. He felt shame at having caused injuries to the people of Harmony and Clarksville, the soldiers he had brought from Fort Smith, and even the men accused of causing all the chaos. He didn't know if he could face the people and continue.

Emotions and concerns swirled in his heart and mind. His decisions about these cases were going to affect his family drastically. He absolutely could not go home and tell his wife that one brother had been shot dead, and then he had hanged her other brother. He surely didn't want Roy to come to Fort Smith for revenge if he executed Ben or Gus. If that happened, he might be forced to hang Roy right in front of Edith.

Judge Atwood didn't believe that God exists, and even if God did, He wouldn't get birds to do his bidding. On the other hand, he found it hard to believe that starving girls would have purposely vandalized their home to the extent that theirs had been damaged, even to protect Eli. The Williams sisters very obviously needed help, not heaped on difficulties. Frustrated and angry, Judge Atwood paced in the small space and wished his brothers-in-law had never come back into the area. When Lieutenant Lampson knocked on the door and said they were ready for him to continue, he forced himself to go on.

"I am deeply sorry for the injuries inflicted on you by the breaking of the glass. There will be no charges to you. I will pay all the medical expenses. However, you must maintain control. Please, may I get your agreement to be calm?"

Everybody nodded and spoke agreement.

"Benjamin Rowe and Gus Hutchinson, you are ordered never to come within fifteen miles of the Williams' farm, or Ann, Stephanie, or Sally Williams, or Eli Yates.

You are not to molest or harass them in any way. You may be shot without further court proceedings if you are seen within fifteen miles of the Williams' farm.

"In the matter of the theft of a horse by Noah Swift Hawk, I find him not guilty. Arabella is the property of Noah Swift Hawk. She has always been his, as evidenced by her obedience to his commands. Nor do I believe he took any other horse, nor was there any previous encounter between Noah Swift Hawk and Hank Butterfield, Roy Butterfield, Charlie Cobb, Benjamin Rowe, Gus Hutchinson, Pete Drake, or Alvin Ives. Noah Swift Hawk, Roy Butterfield, Benjamin Rowe, and Gus Hutchinson, you are all ordered to stay out of shooting distance of each other. You are not to harass or harm each other in any way."

Noah could not believe his ears. He had been sure that Judge Atwood was prejudiced against him and would sentence him to hang. Ann was also surprised. She felt an enormous emotional relief but braced herself for what Judge Atwood would decide about the attack on their home. *Please, God, guide him to give me the money I need.*

"In the matter of the destruction of the Williams' house, I believe there are no guns that can blow heavy shutters to shreds. If men attacked with weapons that powerful, the four in the house would be dead. I do not believe that a giant flock of birds flew in to save them or that any man would be so ignorant as to shoot directly above himself. I did not see any bird feces or dead birds around the house when I investigated, but I found a campsite near the house.

"I believe the damages to the house were self-inflicted by the Williams girls and Eli Yates as a cover-up for the shooting of Alvin Ives. Gus Hutchinson and Benjamin Rowe are found not guilty. Still, they are again ordered never to come within fifteen miles of the Williams' house, their lands, the town of Harmony, or any of its citizens under penalty of being shot on sight if found within this radius."

Stephanie didn't have time to cry for herself. She was sure Eli would have to hide in the cave. She, along with Tom, Ann, and Sally, had made a plan for Eli to break the store window with his chair and escape while they blocked all attempts to go after him. That was what they all wanted, and that was what they all expected Eli to do. After Judge Atwood's comment, they were sure Eli would have to run. Ann whispered, "Be ready. Take Noah with you." Desperate pleading rose to the heavens. Eli stood up and moved behind his chair.

"In the matter of the murder of Alvin Ives, I find Eli Yates guilty of shooting Alvin Ives in the shoulder." Eli's fingers turned white as he gripped the chair. He adjusted his stance, looked at Noah, and whispered, "Follow me." Judge Atwood continued, "Eli, Ann, Stephanie, and Sally Williams made up the story of the attack. They then shot up their house and chopped the shutters with an axe to cover up the shooting of Alvin Ives. However, I do not believe the shot to the shoulder killed Alvin Ives directly but that the infection killed him. Eli Yates did not directly cause the infection. Therefore, it was not murder. I find Eli Yates not guilty of the murder of Alvin Ives. Since we do not know of any next of kin, no restitution is ordered."

The town let out a collective sigh of relief but steeled themselves. Judge Atwood might find Noah, Smitty, Earl, Clyde, Zachariah, Horace, Doc, or all of them guilty of the murder of Charlie and Pete.

Judge Atwood is going to pin everything on Noah. Eli remained prepared to help.

"As to the murder of Charlie Cobb, I find that death was caused by hitting his head on the rock. Noah Swift Hawk did cause Charlie to roll down the hill, but his death was accidental, not murder. Since we do not know of any next of kin, no restitution is ordered."

Noah wanted to jump with joy but was not off the hook. He waited for what the judge would say about Pete, and so did Eli.

The judge continued, "As to the death of Pete Drake, it is evident that Charlie Cobb, Benjamin Rowe, or Gus Hutchinson shot him in the heart purposefully and premeditatedly."

The lieutenant and his men would not have to intervene and breathed relief. Eli relaxed his grip on the chair.

Ben and Gus squirmed, and sweat rolled from Gus's brow. *Judge Atwood knows I shot Pete. He's going to hang me until I'm dead.*

"However, we cannot prove which one it was, and since Charlie Cobb is already dead, I will lay the murder on him. Benjamin Rowe and Gus Hutchinson are ordered to be released."

Gus jumped up and shouted, "Hallelujah." With their eyes, the townsfolk shot daggers into Gus. Gus was oblivious. He didn't care what they thought, anyway.

The people turned their gaze to the judge. He did feel the accusations from their eyes pierce his soul. *I'm no better than the judge who let my brother's killers go free. I just let the guilty get away with their crimes, and I'm forcing the citizens of Harmony to pay restitution to the culprit. How insulting can I be?*

Judge Atwood's conscience refused to allow him to think about the Williams sisters as he summarized his orders to the defendants. "Roy Butterfield, Benjamin Rowe, and Gus Hutchinson, you are ordered never to come within fifteen miles of the towns of Harmony or Clarksville under penalty of being shot to death on sight if seen within this radius. Benjamin Rowe and Gus Hutchinson, you are ordered never to come within fifteen miles of the Williams' house or lands under penalty of being shot on sight. Ann, Stephanie, and Sally, if you see either of them on your farm, kill them. Do you understand me?" He waited for an answer.

The girls replied, "Yes, sir, we

understand." They wondered why Judge Atwood had told them not that they had permission but to shoot the men, period.

"Roy Butterfield, Benjamin Rowe, and Gus Hutchinson, you are ordered not to harass or in any way molest Noah Swift Hawk, Eli Yates, Ann Williams, Stephanie Williams, Sally Williams, or any other citizen of Harmony or Clarksville, under standard penalty depending on the circumstances.

"Citizens of Harmony, you will all be escorted to your homes to gather what money you have. Only the men are to bring it back to this court. The women and children are to remain at home. The division of the payment of the restitution due to Roy Butterfield will be settled among yourselves."

Even though the people of Harmony did not think paying restitution was fair, they were relieved that Judge Atwood had found all the innocent not guilty. They were euphoric that they would not have to fight the judge, his soldiers, Roy, Gus, and Ben. At the same time, as they trudged to their homes, Harmony's citizens were furious that they had to hand over their meager funds.

Tom hated giving Roy anything, but the judge had found Eli not guilty. He was willing to give every penny he owned for that.

Smitty rankled with vexation over the way the law had been twisted. Giving money to Roy rubbed salt into the wound, but he got his money anyway.

Doc and Nellie were angry and exasperated. As soon as they entered their house, Nellie made a suggestion. "Write up a bill for medical services rendered by you, me, Dr. Baker, the other folks of Harmony, and everybody else who saw to those injured by the glass. Make it one hundred dollars. Let that low-down good-for-nothing judge pay the restitution."

"That's high. There were many injuries, but it won't come to that amount, and the soldiers from Fort Smith who helped are not citizens of Harmony. Neither is Dr. Baker or the other folks from Clarksville who helped."

"You could try. Give him the bill and see what happens. It could at least cover part of the money."

"I will, and I'll also bring our money. I want to get this awful mess over and done with."

Doc wrote the bill while Nellie got their money. Clara handed Nellie the only dollar she and Earl owned, the dollar Earl earned for burying Hank. "We were going to pay you with this, but since Earl was the one who picked the horse they tied the guns to, he wants to put it toward the restitution. Somehow we'll earn more money to pay you for caring for Earl."

Nellie added the dollar to her money and took it to her husband. Doc walked out the door with the money and the bill for services. As ordered, the women remained at home with their children. They fretted about whether or not the town would have enough to pay the restitution and worried about what they would do without what little money they'd had.

The soldiers escorted the men back to the store where Judge Atwood still held court in open session. Tom called all the men of Harmony away from the eyes and ears of the judge and his soldiers. "Men, come into my house." The soldiers took up positions and guarded every exit from Tom's house. After all the men of Harmony were inside his home, Tom closed the door between the store and his kitchen. "I don't think they need to know anything about our finances. I'm going to take you where nobody can hear us."

Tom opened the kitchen shelf door and led the surprised men down the stairs into the cave. Horace, Clyde, and Zachariah felt infuriated to be giving what little they had to Roy but went ahead and put the four dollars they had between them on Tom's storeroom table. Doc spoke up, "Before we go any further, let me tell you Nellie's suggestion.

She said we should give Judge Atwood a bill for medical services for one hundred dollars."

Smitty said, "I think it's worth a try. What about the rest of you?"

Horace saw a problem with the plan. "I'm sure Judge Atwood doesn't have that amount of money with him."

"He said he would pay the medical expenses. I wonder how he was planning to do that." Clyde scratched his head and pondered.

Zachariah stated his opinion. "He was probably planning to go to Fort Smith and send it back."

As a storekeeper who always dealt with the issue of owed money, Tom thought they should try it. "Money owed is as good as money owned. Give him the bill. I'm going to make one for my counter."

Joe reminded them that more money was due to a citizen of Harmony. "Judge Atwood owes three dollars and four cents for five days and fifteen meals for himself and his soldiers' rooms and meals. If they stay tonight, it will be five people for three nights. That is four dollars and eighty cents. Nine meals each would be five dollars and fifty-five cents more. Also, he said the court would pay the expense of our neighbors from Clarksville, so that is five more people. It's already too late to leave today. That'll be another night and three dollars and seventy cents more. Five meals each are three more dollars. It all comes to twenty dollars and nine cents. Tom, you have something I can use to write up a bill?" Tom handed Joe a sheet of paper and a quill then pushed the ink bottle between them.

"Let's have the money ready, just in case." Smitty placed his seven dollars in the pile on the table. Tom added thirty-two dollars and sixty-six cents. Doc put the thirty dollars and fifty cents in his pocket onto the table. Joe placed eleven dollars and twelve cents on the pile of money. Smitty counted the money on the table. "That's only eighty-five dollars and twenty-eight cents. We don't have enough."

Noah emptied his money pouch. Ten dollars and three cents more lay on the table. "Everybody has been so good to me, and this is my fault, so even though we still only have ninety-five dollars and thirty-one cents, I want to add this."

"We only have what we have. Let's go." Smitty slid the money off the table and put it into his pocket.

Eli knocked on the girls' bedroom door. "We're going back."

Ann opened the door. "Do we have enough?"

"Only ninety-five thirty-one, but we've got Doc's bill, Joe's bill, and our bill."

"What's going to happen?"

"We don't know." Eli closed the door.

The men went into the courtroom and took their seats. Smitty stood and spoke for the town. "Honorable Judge Atwood, is an agreement made by a court official binding on all parties?"

Judge Atwood snapped back, "Of course it is! Stop stalling, and get on with it."

"Your Honor, what is the law concerning the payment of debt?"

Thinking they were trying to get out of paying the restitution, Judge Atwood figured he would tell them the law to encourage them to cough up the money. "The law states: if a debt is owed and requested to be paid and the debtor will not pay the amount owed, then the debtor will be placed in jail until the last penny of the debt has been paid."

"Is Lieutenant Lampson required to enforce the law?"

The judge reached the end of his patience. "Yes, he is, and if you don't turn over the money right now, I will order him to throw every man in this town into those two cells across the street!"

"At this time, I have a request for payment for medical services ordered by you to be paid by you, a request for payment for lodging and meals that you ordered for yourself, your men, and your witnesses from Clarksville, and a request for reimbursement for damages to the counter." Smitty handed the judge the three bills.

"Who thought this up?"

Smitty avoided the question. "Pay what you owe."

"I don't have this kind of money on me, and this medical bill is higher than it should be for what Dr. Gridley did. This is nonsense! Pay the restitution!"

"You did not say that you would pay only Dr. Gridley. Every person who applied a bandage or washed a cut administered medical assistance and will be paid for their service."

"This is sheer nonsense! I never told you I would pay immediately."

"Lieutenant Lampson, did the Honorable Judge just say that the law states: 'If a debt is owed and called due, but the debtor will not pay the amount owed, then the debtor will be placed in jail until the last penny of the debt has been paid.'?"

The lieutenant understood. "Yes, he did. Do you require me to execute the law at this time, Sheriff?"

Smitty presented the judge with a way to come to terms and save face. "Perhaps we can be reasonable about this payment. I think the law allows for a transfer of debt. What do you say, Judge Atwood?"

"I do remember that law. I think that is an excellent alternative. I hereby rule that the restitution of one hundred dollars due to Roy Butterfield be transferred to me, Richard Atwood, in lieu of a cash payment for medical services ordered by the court. And, since you insist, I'll negotiate a fair price for the counter replacement with Mr. Yates, and I'll go over to the saloon and settle up with Mr. Pinckney."

The judge struck the broken counter with his gavel to finalize his ruling. The remaining pieces of glass dropped out of the frame and pinged against the broken glass below. "Court is adjourned." The judge threw his gavel on the floor and escaped.

Getting away while they could, Roy, Ben, and Gus left seconds after.

FORTY THREE

Lem congratulated Smitty, "That was a masterpiece of legal maneuvering, but you had better keep your eyes open. Those three are as guilty as I ever saw, and I'll bet they're still looking for trouble."

Smitty put his hand in his pocket and jingled the town's money. "It's strange that they pulled the wool over Judge Atwood's eyes so handily."

Lem agreed, "He's a pretty sharp fellow. I have never before seen that happen. There's got to be something else going on."

Smitty called the men over. He gave the money in his pocket back to its owners. The men enthusiastically slapped each other on the back. Everybody in town had their money, and they were all safe.

Eli walked over to Noah. "I thought you and me were goners for sure."

"They wouldn't have hanged anybody from this town. I got upset, but honestly, I was very controlled. I could have been different." Noah insinuated that he could have taken other avenues of action.

"Ann came up with a plan for us. If it came down to it, I was supposed to break the store window to get away, and she told me to take you to our hiding place."

Noah glanced at Ann conversing on the other side of the room. "That girl has grit. I'm glad we didn't have to do that, although I would like to see that location sometime."

Eli divulged the location, "It's where the Indian with the rope is hiding."

"What Indian is hiding around here?"

"It's our secret. You'll understand when you see it." Eli left Noah and joined Smitty and Lem by the window, where he pointed down the road. "Did you notice that Roy followed Judge Atwood? I think we ought to find out what they're talking about."

Smitty looked at Lem, who nodded in affirmation. The three slipped out the back door. Noah looked where Eli had pointed. Just a second before they moved out of view, he saw Judge Atwood and Roy together. Noah checked on Arabella on his way to observe the meeting.

Since they were free to do what they wanted, and they wanted to know what happened, the women went to the store. They felt the proper thing to do was to ask another woman and not interrupt the men, so they questioned Ann, Stephanie, and Sally.

Doc brought Earl to the store but told him he would take him back home as soon as he started to feel uncomfortable. Ann looked across the room to catch a glimpse of Noah. He was gone. Eli, Smitty, and Lem were not in the room either. She turned to Mara. "Will you excuse us for a moment?" She took her sisters by the hand and motioned for Tom to join them.

Sally walked into Tom's kitchen. "What's

wrong, Ann?" Tom came in behind her and closed the door.

"Eli, Smitty, Lem, and Noah are gone."

Tom advised Ann not to worry, "Let's trust them to know what they're doing."

Sally didn't see a problem. "I'm sure they have a perfectly good reason to be gone, and everything is fine."

Stephanie thought *Eli would have told us he was leaving if everything was normal*. However, she decided to agree with Tom. "Let's just go back to the store and trust them." Ann felt something was wrong but went back into the store and tried to feel calm.

Eli and Lem stole across the road and then made their way toward the back of the building where Judge Atwood and Roy were hiding. Smitty circled at the other end of the road. *It's not two minutes since Roy's release, and we're right back where we started.*

Not suspecting that people had already crossed and were closing in from the rear, Roy popped his head into the street to see if anybody was leaving the store. Smitty, Lem, and Eli crept as close as they could and listened. Roy threatened the judge, "I know you think you're not going to give me that money because you're married to Edith, but you are, or I'll come to Fort Smith and cause you a heap of trouble."

"You'll get your money. Why do you always have to be in trouble? See where it got Hank. Now I have to tell Edith that Hank is dead. As rotten as the two of you are, I don't know why she loves you."

"But she does, so be good to little brother because I'll be coming to dinner real soon."

"Don't bring Gus or Ben."

"I'll see about that. Right now, I'm going to shoot that sorry horse that got us into this mess." Roy strode out into the street.

The judge caught Roy's arm and yanked him back. "If you want to shoot that horse, wait until you're long gone from here. There's only so much I can save you from."

"It's my horse. I'll shoot it when and where I want, and don't jerk me around."

"If you kill that horse in town, these folks might take matters into their own hands and shoot you. For once in your life, don't be stupid."

"Don't call me stupid. I'm not stupid. Didn't I talk perfectly this whole time?"

"So don't act stupid. Ride out of town and stay away from here. Take those horses and do what you want somewhere else." Roy stormed off. The judge leaned against the wall of Smitty's house. "I ought to shoot him myself and hope Edith never finds out." He continued to hide to regain his composure before wrapping things up with Joe and Tom.

Smitty, Lem, and Eli slipped away and met at the back of the store. Noah joined them. "I heard everything."

Eli asked, "What should we do?"

Noah started, "I've been thinking–"

Lem interrupted, "If you stir this up, it's not going to bring anything but trouble."

Eli wanted some amount of proper justice. "I agree, Lem, but Roy busted Noah's head.

He almost killed him, and his gang shot up the Williams' house. Those girls are missing nine windows. They don't have the money to replace them, and those no-good lowlifes get to walk away. It's not right."

"I don't need revenge, Eli, but I agree that it's not right for the girls to take all the loss."

Smitty expressed his concern, "You're right. We paid that fine with injuries inflicted when the glass broke, but we'll heal. Joe and Tom are going to be paid. The girls got nothing. They won't be able to stay in their house this winter without those windows, and they need food something awful."

Noah shared his plan, "I'm going to try to convince Roy it's better to sell that horse than kill it. I want to give it back to the Williams girls. It's not much, but I hope it will help."

Eli knew it would. "We'd get more corn planted and earn more money."

Smitty had to enforce Judge Atwood's ruling. Therefore, Noah's plan couldn't work. "You're supposed to stay away from them."

"That's why I was hoping Sheriff Slade would talk to them." Noah held out his money.

"But that's all you have!" Eli exclaimed.

It was obvious that Eli cared about his welfare. Noah smiled with brotherly affection. "I'll be fine. I'm going to take Ann's offer to work."

Lem hoped there would be no further trouble. "Then we agree to try to buy the horse and let Roy, Ben, and Gus ride out of here?" They all consented. Lem took Noah's ten dollars and three cents. "It's not much for a horse, but since it's one Roy doesn't want, maybe he'll agree." He went to find Roy.

Noah, Smitty, and Eli quietly entered the store and rejoined the group. Maybe the others didn't see them return, but Tom and the girls did. Ann was still upset that they had gone off and gotten into she didn't know what, but she was glad they were back in one piece. Even though nothing appeared to be about to break out into chaos, Ann felt apprehensive.

The people from Clarksville stayed in the store and socialized with the people of Harmony. Tom and Joe walked across the road to the saloon to make the necessary arrangements with Judge Atwood about the payments due. The women hugged their husbands and each other and told everybody how glad they were that nobody had been sentenced to die and that none of them were in jail or penniless.

Noah joined Horace to find out if he was healing well. After several minutes of talking with Horace, he moved on and worked his way around the room until he had positioned himself next to Ann. "Miss Williams, may I have a word with you?"

Ann turned to him. "Of course."

Noah looked into Ann's green eyes. *Amazing!* "Is your offer of a job still open?"

"We need help, but you should be recovering, not working."

"Yes, ma'am. I thought I would stay at Doc's another week then I could come to your farm."

Ann held out her hand to ratify the deal with a handshake. "Then I'll be looking for you in a week."

Gus, Ben, and Roy were under orders to leave town immediately. They stood in the corral, saddling their horses. "I told ya ta trust me, didn't I?" Roy gloated over their triumph but didn't tell his friends his secret. Lem strolled up to the corral. "What do you want?" Roy asked belligerently.

"I'm in need of horses. Since you have extra horses, I thought you might sell them."

Ben prodded Roy to make the sale, "We need money. We don't need them horses."

Roy itched to shoot the horse that had run off and gotten the boys killed. He blamed the horse instead of the men who had chosen to attack the house.

"They're just gonna be trouble." Gus didn't want to put effort into caring for a horse that wasn't even carrying him.

Roy decided to consider the proposition. "How much you willing to pay?"

Sheriff Slade offered what Noah had given him, "Ten dollars and three cents."

Roy thought the Sheriff had to be joking. "Are you serious? I can sell them for thirty dollars each."

"Eleven dollars and three cents," Lem added a dollar of his own.

"I'm not selling you three horses for eleven dollars."

"What about one, but I get to pick it?"

Gus repeated, "We got no money, an it's a long way ta home. It's only one."

Roy counteroffered, "Eleven dollars, three cents, and your spurs."

"You've got a deal." Lem handed Roy the money. Since he wasn't a greenhorn, he kept his eyes on the three men while he took off his spurs and gave them to Roy. "I want this one." Lem reached for the horse Noah wanted.

"Wait a minute! I didn't know you were going to pick that one!" Roy snatched the reins.

Lem reminded Roy, "You agreed I could pick the one I want."

Flustered and upset that he wouldn't get to kill the horse, Roy sputtered, "I didn't say you could have the bridle."

"You're right." Lem took off the bridle, handed it to Roy, and then led the horse away by its mane. He took it to Smitty's barn and put it in the stall with Arabella.

Ten minutes after Roy, Judge Atwood rode out of town. Lem remembered what Clara had told him about the judge spying on Doc and the injured men traveling back to Harmony. He figured the judge was planning to do the same to his brother-in-law.

When Lem entered the store, Noah turned for silent confirmation and felt jubilant when Lem nodded his head slightly up and down. After the sun went down, the folks of Harmony went to their homes. The soldiers and the folks from Clarksville spent another night enjoying Joe's excellent supper and rooms.

FORTY FOUR

After the first sound sleep he'd had in weeks, Noah went to apologize to Smitty. "Good morning, friend. I'm sorry about what I did. I didn't see any other way to prove that Arabella is mine. If you let me use your tools, I'll repair whatever damage she did to your stall."

"She's an exceptional horse. I wouldn't let anybody take her either, especially not those men. Look at all the injuries on the Williams' horse. They should be hung for that alone."

"It's uncalled for to treat a horse like that." The two men tried to examine the injured horse, but it stayed on the opposite side of Arabella. "He's not letting us get close. I'm surprised he let Lem touch him to bring him here." Noah gave up. "Let's see what I need to do to repair this stall."

They circled the stall and looked at the wooden slats. "I made the boards thick to keep in horses that might want to get out. I think your new horse needs more help than this stall."

Noah led Arabella out of the stall into the corral. His rescued horse followed her. When they were safely out of the way, Noah chiseled off the sharp spikes of wood that Arabella had kicked out. Because Noah wanted Ann's horse to see that he was safe, he decided to wash Arabella. When Noah could, he poured water over both horses. By the time Arabella gleamed, her stall mate had decided he enjoyed the fresh water and allowed Noah to pour buckets of water directly over him as well. Noah drenched the horse repeatedly. He washed off the caked-on blood-soaked dirt and looked for signs of infection.

That week, while he recovered at Dr. Gridley's, Noah worked with his horses. The horse he had bought back from Roy remained skittish, but it sensed that Noah was safe. It let him dab ointment on its injuries. By the end of the week, both horses happily let Noah approach and rub them behind their ears.

The day Doc told Noah he was well enough to leave, Noah dressed in the white man's clothes he had purchased at Tom's store and attached his knife to his belt. Feeling sad to be leaving the home of such fine people but excited to be going to the Williams' farm, Noah closed the door to his room at the Gridley's house. He walked into the living room, where Doc, Nellie, and Laura sat working on a jigsaw puzzle. "How much do I owe you?"

Nellie declined to take any money. "You already paid for our medical services for the injuries Hank and Roy gave you. Smitty paid for all of the people injured as a posse member. After the trial, you've been a friend visiting. A person doesn't pay for visiting."

"You truly are good friends. I appreciate all you've done for me."

Doc issued his discharge orders, "Remember, if you feel anything is wrong, come here immediately. And take it easy for a week or so more."

As Noah went out the front door, Nellie added, "Come visit us."

Earl had gone home, so Noah went to see how he was getting along. Clara gave Noah a gift. "You saved Earl. I found a beehive. Everybody else seems happy to let me tangle with the bees. I don't have any problem. When I smoke them, they don't get agitated."

Earl made a promise. "I owe you more than honey for saving my life. If a time comes when you need a favor, find me. If I'm able, I'll see to whatever you ask."

"You two don't owe me anything. I'm glad I was able to help get those men captured."

"Take the honey anyway, and remember I'm here if you need me. I hope it goes well working out at the Williams' farm. Give them our regards."

"I'll remember. I'll tell them." Noah took the honey and went to the store. Clyde and his son Zachariah were there. "Tom, I'm going to be leaving shortly. You said to come and see you."

"Would you wait just a minute? I'm explaining how I want the counter built when they make my new one." Tom and Clyde continued to discuss and draw on the paper on top of an unbroken counter.

Zachariah poured a scoop of nails onto the scale. "Where you heading off to, Noah?"

"I'm going to work for the Williams girls. They need help, and I owe them."

Clyde folded up the drawing he and Tom had made. "I'd like to help. I wish we had never sent those men after their guns like that. We could ride to the farm to help plow and plant, but we don't have a way to get our harnesses and plows out there."

Tom had an idea. "Ask Horace if he'll let you use his wagon."

"Good idea." Zachariah put the nails in a sack.

"I'll be back soon." Noah went with Clyde and Zachariah to talk with Horace.

Horace and Betsy were happy to loan the wagon. Even though Noah didn't expect Horace to plow, Horace explained, "I'd come help if I didn't hurt."

Betsy added, "And didn't have a hole through your middle."

"The use of the wagon is what we need." Noah placed the honey from Clara with his Indian clothes and rifle under the wagon seat.

"I'll get our equipment ready. Bring the wagon to my place." Clyde left with Zachariah.

"Be there soon. Much obliged, Horace." Noah left Horace's home and went back to the store.

Tom asked, "Are you going to use Arabella to plow?"

"I've been thinking about that. She's never done it. It'll depend on how she takes to it."

"Take these two harnesses. I don't know if either of your horses will be any good for plowing right now, so tell Ann I'll take the standard usage fee only if she uses them and only after she sells her harvest. Tell her exactly what I said, or she won't use them."

"I'm sure these will help. I'll tell her." Noah took the harnesses. "I'm going to Smitty's."

Tom handed Noah a small package. "Tell Eli I love him, and give him this."

Before he went to get his horses, Noah placed the two harnesses in the back of the wagon and tucked the package from Tom inside his bundle of clothes. In the barn, Smitty offered Noah a batch of the medicated liniment they had used on the injured horse. "It's for the horse, but it's also good for people."

"We appreciate it." Noah put some of the medicated cream on his arm and head before gently scratching his horses behind their ears. He patted Arabella on the withers then led both horses to Horace's wagon. Smitty walked with him and slid the medicated cream next to the honey. Without a fuss, Arabella allowed Noah to put her in the harness. Since she didn't mind wearing the harness, Noah asked her to try something new. She cooperated nicely, pulled the wagon to Clyde's place, and then halted. Zachariah added two harnesses and helped Clyde load the plows.

Noah headed out of town. He looked back at his friends and waved goodbye. After he let James know about his family and the farm, this was where he wanted to live.

The Williams' horse walked beside Arabella with a soft cloth around its neck tied to a lead rope attached to the wagon. The problem was that it would not walk behind the wagon. Since it would only walk up front beside Arabella, the rope dragged dangerously close to the wagon's wheels.

Noah stopped, shortened the line, and attached it to Arabella's harness instead of the wagon. As they got closer to the farm, the ears of his new horse perked up. The horse pranced in anticipation. Noah was afraid it would try to dash off while still tied to Arabella, so he got off the wagon again, detached the long lead rope, and buckled on a short one that wouldn't trip the horse if it ran. Noah walked the last mile on the other side of Arabella, holding the untied lead rope. He hoped that the horse would stay with him. When they were in sight of the house, the horse neighed loudly.

Samson's ears perked. He knew that whinny and neighed his reply. Eli and the girls didn't know what had gotten into the horse. "What's Samson doing?" Eli continued to plow, but Samson wasn't paying attention.

"I don't know," Stephanie replied.

"I hope it's not those horrible men." Sally looked around for a place to take cover.

"It's probably Noah. It's been a week, but I don't understand why Samson would care."

"We have the advantage. We can shoot them as they come over the rise. Get your rifle." Eli unhitched Samson. The horse ran away, whinnying. The girls and Eli lay in the field with fully cocked and primed rifles trained on the slight hill.

Sally asked, "Why did you let Samson loose?"

"If there is shooting, we don't want him stuck to the plow with no cover."

They heard Samson before the other whinnies that followed. Samson's head came over the crest of the hill first then Noah's eyes. He saw four rifles ready to fire. He stopped. "Noah here. Don't shoot me."

Ann stood up. *It's curious that Samson cares about Noah.* She saw two more horseheads rise into view. Their horse saw them. Noah felt a sudden jerk and dropped the lead rope.

"Dusty!" Sally put down her rifle. One horse and three girls raced to each other. You couldn't have seen a happier reunion, even if it was between a horse and human girls.

"How did you get him?" Ann asked jubilantly.

"I can't believe it!" Stephanie exclaimed.

Dusty didn't have any jitters about

touching the girls. They could barely stay on their feet because he rubbed against them so hard.

"I asked Lem to buy him for me."

Sally insisted they drop everything else. "He's hurt. We need to look after him."

Ann agreed, "You're right. Eli and Noah, please get the plow into the wagon." They didn't have to lead Dusty. He stayed close to his family as they went to the barn. Ann looked at Noah as they walked. A fuzz of oakbark-colored hair covered his head. She remembered the sun gleaming off his shaved skin and smiled. With his short hair, blue eyes, and new outfit, she would never have guessed that he was the same man she first saw with long, blood-soaked hair, wearing blood-covered buckskin clothes.

They opened the barn door. Dusty trotted into his stall. When Noah unhooked Arabella, she went straight to Dusty.

"Noah, help me get water. Grab that pole with the buckets." Eli picked up the other set.

He enjoyed explaining the procedure. "Look how it's set up to draw twice as much. Isn't that nice?"

Noah pulled up his set of buckets. "It does make it easier." He looked over the pulley system before they walked back to the barn and poured the water into the watering troughs. The girls already had hay in the stalls. "Smitty sent some ointment for Dusty. I'll get it." Noah got the wooden bucket of strong-smelling goop. He removed the lid and handed it to Ann.

"Wow! If it doesn't heal Dusty's cuts, at least it will have cleared our sinuses." Ann turned her head away and held the bucket as far away from her nose as she could.

Stephanie carefully dipped a cloth into the bucket. "Did Smitty tell you how thickly to apply this?"

"He said to put it on like this." Noah demonstrated by applying more to the injury on his arm.

"It's going to be hard to get it on without

hurting him." Sally applied the salve as carefully as possible.

They managed to get all of Dusty's injuries covered with ointment and then walked out of the stall. Arabella came out right behind them.

"I understand, girl. It's really strong." Even though Arabella wasn't going to get far enough away to make a difference, Ann opened the door to a different stall.

"I'll get more water." Noah went to the well while Eli forked hay into Arabella's new stall. They brushed down the uninjured horses and then went to the house and cleaned up.

Ann fried bacon. Stephanie and Sally put freshly baked bread, cheese, and stewed fruit on the table while Noah and Eli went to get the honey. "Your father told me to tell you that he loves you and asked me to give you this." Noah handed Eli the package.

Eli unwrapped the paper. Inside were five peppermint sticks. "My Pop never lets me have free candy! I appreciate you bringing it to me." To Eli, the candy meant that his father loved him more than he loved anything else. He planned never to eat the peppermint sticks, so he could look at them and know how much his father loved him.

Noah couldn't carry all the jars of honey, his clothes, and his rifle. "Put those in your pocket and take some of this honey."

Noah followed Eli into the kitchen with his arms full of honeypots, his clothes on top, and his rifle wedged under his arm. Eli deposited the honey he carried on the counter.

Sally hurried to Noah. "Let me help." She took Noah's clothes. "I'll put these in the living room."

Noah was sure he wouldn't be able to put anything on the counter without breaking some of it. "I appreciate that, Sally."

Ann extracted the rifle, and Stephanie took some jars. They set the honey beside the other containers.

"These are from Clara and Earl. I'll bring one to the table." Noah picked up a jar and followed Ann into the dining room. Stephanie and Eli came in and sat in their regular positions.

"We have five plates again!" Sally happily set the fifth plate on the other side of Ann. "You sit here, Noah." Sally sat in her favorite place by the kitchen door. "I haven't eaten honey for such a long time." She put a spoonful on her plate.

Noah took a helping. "Me neither. I'm looking forward to letting it drip through the bread and licking it off my fingers."

"How did Clara and Earl get it? Why did they give it to you?" Honey flowed over the edge of Ann's bread. She slid her plate under her bread to catch it.

Noah explained that it was a thank you gift and told them the story about Clara tending the bees and gathering the honey just as she had told him. Afterward, he informed them that Zachariah and Clyde wanted to come to the farm the next day to help plow.

"Why do they want to do that?" Ann scraped the honey off her plate into her serving of fruit.

"Your house was damaged because the men of Harmony ran Hank's gang out of town right to your house. They shot it to pieces, it's not completely repaired, and you all went through a terrifying experience. Everybody feels very badly about it. They want to do what they can to make it better for you."

After getting no restitution, Ann decided it didn't matter what her father had taught her about providing for herself. She had to think about her sisters and find a way to feed them. That meant she had to let people help. "That's very thoughtful and appreciated."

Sally pointed out the flaw, "It doesn't fix our windows."

Even so, Stephanie believed they couldn't do anything but live each day as it came. Therefore, they might as well be thankful for what they received. "Let's trust God that

He's working it out and be grateful for the help He's sending."

Eli said, "I guess that's why you have the harnesses and plows in the wagon."

"Clyde and Zachariah are going to ride out here on their horses. The equipment will already be here. We'll load everything back on Horace's wagon tomorrow when they leave, and they'll return it to town."

Eli suggested a plan, "If Clyde, Zachariah, Ann, and I each plow one field, that will be the last four fields that Ann hopes to get planted. Noah, Stephanie, and Sally, you can come behind us and plant the seeds."

Ann had worked the farm for almost half her life. "We probably can't plant the field tomorrow, but having all the fields plowed would be a huge help. We'd only have to pick out rocks and plant seeds after tomorrow."

Noah had never plowed an inch of ground but had come there to help. "I can plow."

Ann refused to let him. "I want you to be able to continue helping. Killing you off plowing won't accomplish that." She added softly, "I'm sure you'll do plenty after you heal more."

Stephanie told them what she thought. "We can cook lots of eggs in the morning. Let's cook plenty of bread."

"I'll help you get started." Sally picked up dishes.

"What will we do for dinner and supper?" Ann gathered more of the empty plates.

Noah asked, "What do you have?" *It couldn't be much since we just ate almost nothing.*

Sally called out, "We have cougar meat!"

Noah followed them. "Why do you have cougar meat?"

Stephanie explained, "Eli shot and butchered it. We dried some into jerky, made some good sausages, and have some raw pieces in the ice house."

"I doubt if the meat in the ice house is

good. Besides, I made stew, and we almost worked our jaws off chewing." Ann admitted her cougar meal failure.

Noah offered his skills, "I have a good recipe for tough meat. If any is still usable, I could make it."

"I'd rather not waste it. I'd be tickled pink if you could make it into something worth eating. I'm going to make sassafras tea. If anybody wants some, take your cup with you to the living room." Everybody took his or her cup, so Ann brewed a big pot. She carried it into the living room, poured for everybody, then sat and enjoyed her honey-sweetened tea.

Noah brought up something he had wondered about since he had heard the horse's name. "How did Dusty get his name?"

Ann told the story, "When Sally was little, every time Papa and I came back from plowing, Sally would say the horse was dusty because he was covered in dirt, so we just took up calling him Dusty."

Noah said, "I like it."

The four talked about nothing in particular for the rest of the evening, got to know more about each other, and relaxed until bedtime.

The girls retired to the front bunkroom. Eli took Noah to the back bunkroom. Doc had told Eli that Judge Atwood had gotten the idea that he was sleeping with all the Williams girls because they had slept in the same room. Therefore, after returning to the farm, Eli had removed the unbroken glass from the back bunkroom's top row of panes and inserted them into the three broken sections below. Then, he had fitted wood into the holes to keep the insects out and make the room usable.

Noah placed his clothes in one of the bureaus, leaned his rifle against the wall, put his knife under his pillow, and lay on the bunk in his home for the summer.

FORTY FIVE

Ann started the morning chores extra early. As they went from task to task, Ann stayed close to Noah and explained what she wanted. Stephanie inspected Dusty and applied a heavy dose of ointment. The pungent aroma made it impossible to stay in the barn.

They quickly loaded everything onto the wagon. Samson pulled it out of the barn into the fresh air. Arabella clamored to escape. Dusty didn't want to be around the smell either. He hadn't figured out that the scent was on him. Stephanie opened both stall doors. Dusty saw his harness that Tom had returned for the plowing and walked to the wagon. Stephanie speculated. "I think he wants us to hitch him up."

"Obviously, we can't." Ann shoofed Dusty

into the paddock with Arabella. She closed the back barn door and walked out the front. "Oh, my word!"

Six people rode toward them across the meadow. The cloud of dust they kicked up billowed around them when they stopped at the barn. Not only Clyde and Zachariah but also Smitty, Mara, Tom, and Nellie arrived dressed to work. Mara jumped off her horse. "When Tom told us what Clyde and Zachariah planned, we decided to help. The others have to tend to children and such but wish they had been able to come."

"Would you show us where we can take these?" Nellie untied her cargo of baskets.

Ann was more than happy to show her guests to the kitchen. "Of course. Follow me."

The group entered the house. The girls and Eli informed them that only one window pane had been broken in the workroom. They reported the extensive damage to the living room as they passed through.

Everybody crowded into the kitchen. Ann told them, "Put the baskets on any counter."

Nellie looked around. "What a beautiful kitchen." She placed her baskets on the butcher table. "I have two jars of gooseberry jam, a pound of freshly made butter, a cheese quarter, and two gallons of milk in this basket." Since Nellie was the current owner of the cow that the Williams family had previously owned, Nellie was the provider of everything made from milk. Nellie opened another basket. "This basket has bread and bacon."

Mara knew everybody would like what she brought. "I brought coffee, sugar, and apple pies!"

Stephanie asked hopefully, "With your special apples?"

"Yes, and this is from Clara and Earl." Mara opened a basket of eggs carefully packed in bran flakes.

"My contribution." Tom plopped down his big basket filled with a large smoked ham, a pot of prepared mustard, and dried apricots in all the extra space.

Clyde and Zachariah put four gallon-sized-jugs of apple cider on the counter. "Patty sent these."

"This is so very thoughtful!" Ann felt overwhelmed by their generosity.

Mara informed the girls of their plans, "We'll help you cook all the meals today, and we'll also help get as much of the corn planted as we can."

Ann spoke what was wedged in her mind. "That will be so very wonderful!"

Sally got them started on the meal. "I'll beat the eggs. Which of you will get the other doings ready?"

All of the women helped prepare and carry the food to the table. After many years, people once again filled every chair in the dining room. Stephanie stood. "May I say the blessing?"

Ann was glad to let her sister do so. "Absolutely."

"Our Heavenly Father, I thank You for these wonderful people. I don't know when I ever felt happier. Keep us safe as we work today. Bless everyone with blessings overflowing from Your abundance in glory. May the work and fellowship of today bring You glory and honor. In the name of our precious Savior, Jesus, I pray. Amen."

"Amen," rose from every mouth and heart at the table. Ann believed that laughter and friendship filled and healed the house as they ate and talked.

After the meal, Eli called the men to the bench in the workroom. "I want to show you something." He put the stopper into the washbasin and poured in water. "Gather around." He motioned for them to come closer. "Watch this!" He pulled the plug.

"Where is it going?" Zachariah asked.

"Come on. I'll show you." Eli led them to the back of the house. "It goes out this hollow wooden tube and drains out behind those pines. There's also one in the kitchen. We use only water and soap in them and wash clean water through the kitchen tube every day."

Zachariah looked over the contraption. "That's pretty smart, I'll say."

Eli stated his opinion, "Their Uncle James built a lot of clever things."

Clyde stood beside Eli. "I remember that James was a smart man. We wouldn't have Harmony if it weren't for him hiring workers for this farm."

Smitty examined the water conduit. "I agree."

Before they got the horses ready, Eli showed them different things around the farm that fascinated him. The women cleaned up from breakfast and then carried dinner to the wagon. Samson pulled it loaded with dinner baskets, empty buckets, wooden troughs, plows, and the big sap bucket full of water.

Clyde, Zachariah, Smitty, and Tom's horses wore harnesses. Eli told them how he thought they should divide the work, "I think Clyde, Zachariah, Smitty, Pop, and I should plow. The rest of you can plant." Noah felt perturbed that Eli again suggested he stay with the women.

Leaving Arabella and Dusty behind in the paddock, they went on their way to the first field. Dusty ran circles around the paddock's edge then charged straight across and flew over the fence. Arabella saw the escape and followed. On the correct side of the fence, they galloped to their owners. Sally rubbed the horses behind their ears. "I guess we better let them come with us."

Zachariah said, "We don't need to worry about the horses roaming loose. We won't have a hard time tracking Dusty. We can smell him for miles."

Noah agreed. "Let them come, Dusty's not going anywhere without us, and Arabella won't leave unless I tell her to hide."

Ann had no problem with the horses joining them. "Let's go." All the horses and people resumed the trek to the fields. Ann remembered how her mother had always asked their father for help. Her father always knew her mother appreciated and needed him. Ann tried to treat everybody the way her mother had. She could see that Noah didn't like being coddled, but she felt he still needed to take it easy. After all, his skull was broken. Ann thought of a solution. She added another field to her plan and made a request. "I need strong men in the lower field. It's been fallow a long time. I'm sure we'll need to remove big stones."

Noah accepted immediately, "I would be glad to help you." They walked to the first field.

Ann asked, "Who wants to plow here?"

Tom spoke up, "I'll work it."

Ann stated the plan for the day, "The rest of us will go on, but we'll meet back here at noon." They unloaded a plow and a water trough beside the field and put all the food baskets under the large, close-by tree. Ann used a water bucket to fill the water trough, scooped out one more bucket full, and placed it under the tree with the food. "This is for you to drink, Tom." She put a big ladle in the bucket. They moved on to the next field.

Tom hitched his horse to the plow and started it through the ground. He hadn't turned over a field since he had left home to begin his life with the woman his parents opposed. He hadn't seen his parents since he was a young man. As the plow broke the ground, it brought him back to those days. Tom realized that he missed his folks.

Clyde took the following field. They left him and his horse water just as they had for Tom. He also thought back to the past when, as a young man, he had hired out to James and plowed the very same field. He had decided that plowing wasn't for him. He had asked James if he could help build the house, and James had allowed him. He had learned carpentry as they built the house and furniture.

Zachariah remained in the following field.

Since there wasn't much call for carpentry lately, he had been working for another farmer in the area. He knew what he needed to do. He hitched up the plow and immediately made deep, straight furrows.

Smitty took the fourth field. He had also started out plowing on James Williams' farm. However, every time one of the horses threw a shoe or a plow needed sharpening, James had asked Smitty to take the horse to the farrier or the plow to the blacksmith. Smitty had watched the men work. It wasn't long before he had asked if he could try. First, he had tried to form horseshoes. He picked up the skill easily. By the third year, Smitty reshod the horses, sharpened the plows, and repaired any broken metal items right there at the farm. *It was stupid and unnecessary to have lost all of those men by forcing the Indians to move.*

They got to the last field and changed Samson over to the plow. Ann had not even imagined that they would be able to work all the fields. She hadn't originally planned to plant this tract. It was low and usually marshy in the spring. The nearby creek kept the Eastern gamagrass lush and filled the whole area with tough grassroots. She and her father had left the field fallow almost every year. Even though the previous winter had been frigid, they hadn't gotten much snow. *It might be workable.* She examined the soil. Happily, the ground was dry enough to plow.

Mara and Nellie's horses and Dusty and Arabella grazed on the nutritious gamagrass as Samson and Eli plowed. The two had become very comfortable with each other during the last month of plowing. However, in this field, man and beast struggled to cut furrows through the Arkansas grass that'd had years to sink its roots into the soil.

Ann was the first into the furrow to toss stones out of the field. As the groove grew longer, others joined her. Even with all of them clearing out the rocks, they didn't get to the end of the first row before Eli started to plow the next furrow. Stephanie and Mara decided they wanted to work together and moved to the second row. Nellie and Sally worked the third row. Noah and Ann finished row one. Noah walked over to row four. Ann followed him. "After all these years, you'd think the rocks would be gone, but there's a new crop of them every year."

"Strangely, that also happens back home. I guess God keeps us in good health by providing a work plan."

Ann laughed. "Oh, so that's what it is. Well, I'm glad you're helping us with ours."

"I'm happy to be here or anywhere for that matter. I came close to being on the other side of the ground."

"Yes, but you didn't have to come help us. You could have continued to wherever you were going."

"I was coming here."

"You were? Why?"

"I should have told you this before, but there wasn't a good time."

"Well, I guess you better tell me now."

"Your Uncle James sent me."

"You know James? Why did he send you? Does he want his farm back? Is he all right? What is he like?"

"Whoa, one question at a time." They continued to remove rocks as Noah explained, "James and his family were fine when I left. Your uncle came to my village. I noticed that his eyes held the sky just like mine. I went to look at his eyes and listen to his stories about a different kind of place. I repeatedly asked him to tell me about this place until I could see it in my mind. I dreamt of this farm. I felt that I knew it. James wondered all these years if anybody from his family had come to his place. I asked him why he didn't go find out. He told me he would not leave his family, and they might be hurt if he tried to take them with him. I asked why anybody would hurt them. He said the white people in the east would know they were Indians, and white people didn't want them in Arkansas. My mother is white, and she loves me, so I didn't understand why others wouldn't love us. Your uncle said he never understood why, but he knew it was true. Last year, I told him I had his eyes and hair and could find out what had happened. I asked him to tell me how to find it. He did, so I came."

"I think what the government is doing and what Roy did to you is horrible. I don't blame James for leaving. My folks always told us what happened was wrong, but they were happy they had the farm. I'm glad you came. When are you going back?"

"I don't know when I'll go back, but I will. After I tell James about this place, you, and your family, I want to come back here. I like the people here. You all know I'm an Indian, and you're my friends anyway."

"I agree that the folks here are wonderful. Look how they're helping us. Now that I know these folks, I wish I'd known them sooner."

Noah and Ann reached the other end of the field. Stephanie and Mara finished their row just ahead of them, but several more plowed rows awaited rock removal. Stephanie jokingly scolded Ann and Noah, "Come on, you slowpokes. Stop gabbing and get to work."

"Yes, Ma'am." Noah walked to a new furrow.

Ann announced the news. "Noah knows Uncle James. He came here to find us."

Sally stopped working. "You do?"

"Tell them what you told me."

Noah didn't want to bore Ann. "Are you sure you want to hear it all again?"

Stephanie begged, "Please tell us about him."

Noah agreed to tell the story as they worked. They moved closer together, with Noah in the middle. The sun rose high as Noah repeated everything he had told Ann and added even more information about James and his family. They arrived at the end of the tale as they arrived at the far end of the field for the third time.

Ann unharnessed Samson. Because she didn't want to push Noah into something he might not want to share with everybody, she asked him, "Noah, would you mind telling everybody about James during dinner?"

Noah loved to talk about his friend James. "I wouldn't mind at all." They headed toward the first field. The horses followed.

When they arrived at the designated dinner location, Tom only needed to plow a few more rows to complete his field. Eli and Noah picked rocks out of the soil as Tom plowed. The women laid out two large tablecloths in the shade under the tree and unpacked the baskets. After everybody had arrived, they each took a plate of ham, cheese, bread, butter, jam, honey, and apricots. Sally put out a bowl of the maple candies that the girls and Eli had made that spring. Ann passed the pot of mustard to Tom. "Noah has news to share."

Everybody wanted to hear about James and his family, so they lingered over the meal. Noah took a cup of cider and once again told everything relevant that he knew about James Williams. Tom, Clyde, and Smitty also shared their experiences with James.

The day became one of sharing and bonding as a community, not just a day for work. After they swallowed the last crumb of food in the basket and drank the last drop of cider in the jug, they packed the dishes and tablecloths. Ann told the others what she thought was the best plan for the rest of the day. "When the sun is three fingers above the horizon, we'll stop and bring the wagon around to get the plows. That should give everybody time to eat supper and get back to town before it gets too late."

Tom wanted to spend more time with his son. He also wanted to continue to help the Williams sisters. "If you have space for me to stay, and I wouldn't be a burden, I can stay overnight and help tomorrow."

Ann quickly accepted, "You wouldn't be a burden at all. We would love for you to stay."

Mara looked at Smitty with questioning eyes. She liked all of the girls, especially Stephanie. He knew she wanted to continue to help them. "We can stay as well."

Stephanie chimed in, "That would be wonderful, and maybe Mara will teach me her apple pie recipe."

Clyde felt on the spot, but he didn't want to cause his wife any concern. "I don't want Patty to think something happened to us."

Nellie said, "I should go home tonight."

"I'm gonna stay, Pa. Tell Ma that I'm here." Zachariah wanted to finish the field he was working. Also, Ann was an attractive and delightful woman. He wanted to stay and get to know her. The only other female in town even close to his age was Laura, and she rebuffed him every time he tried to talk with her.

"Do you have enough space?" Clyde

didn't want to create a housing problem for Ann.

"One of the men will have to stay in a room with only shutters and no glass. The mosquitoes would get in. Everybody else can fit into the bunkrooms."

Noah offered to be the one, "I can stay in the other room."

It's very considerate of Noah to give up his bunk. Ann didn't want to impose. "I'd love for anybody to stay who wants to, but I don't want to take you away from other things you need to do."

Clyde ignored the comment about doing something else. "The field I plowed is done. Nellie and I will head back to town when Zachariah's field is finished. I'll let Horace know the wagon will return tomorrow."

They broke into groups and walked to their assignments. Mara and Sally went with Smitty. Even though Zachariah had plowed most of his field before dinner, several others joined him, so they could finish faster and have plenty of time to get back to town. Nellie wanted to leave directly from Zachariah's field, so she went with Ann to the barn. They got Nellie's horse, saddle, and bridle, along with Clyde's saddle and bridle. Noah and Clyde got the travel platform and pulled Clyde's plow to Zachariah's field.

Tom joined Stephanie, who had chosen to stay with Eli. Eli and Tom worked the plows. Stephanie tossed rocks as the three of them talked and enjoyed each other. *This is my family,* popped into Eli's mind. He looked at Stephanie's blonde hair tied in a ponytail falling over her shoulder. She stood up to throw a handful of rocks, turned her head in his direction, and saw him looking at her. She looked into his eyes with a mischievous smile and casually tossed a rock. Eli thought *I don't think anybody could ever be more desirable. Stephanie is so sweet and beautiful.*

Clyde decided to leave the last two rows of his son's field for Zachariah to plow. He stopped and unhitched the plow from his horse. "It's time for me and Nellie to go."

Ann stopped working. "Don't you want to eat supper before you go?"

"I want to let this old nag take it easy going home."

"I can't tell you how much I appreciate your help. It's made a world of difference." They led both horses to the trough for a long drink of water. Clyde and Nellie gulped down a ladle of water from the people bucket, mounted up, and waved goodbye to very grateful friends.

FORTY SIX

Tom and Eli finished plowing the lower field. Throughout the day, every time Samson emptied the water trough, Stephanie had replenished the water from the creek. This time, Eli took Samson to the creek to let the horse drink as much as it wanted. After it had enough, they hitched Samson to the wagon, loaded the plows, and headed over to the field where Smitty, Mara, and Sally worked.

Smitty's field was one that the Williams family had worked every year. It didn't have nearly as many rocks as the lower field. Smitty, Mara, and Sally were sitting on the pile of rocks waiting for the wagon. Once they loaded the plow in the wagon, they went to join Noah, Zachariah, and Ann. As soon as the wagon pulled up, they stopped clearing their field and loaded the two plows. At the barn, Ann opened the door. "I can't tell you how happy I am. We got so much done."

Eli picked up a water bucket pole, handed it to his father, and then took the other. "Come with me."

Sally carried hay into the stalls of the horses that hadn't grazed all day. "I would never have believed we would get two fields completely ready to plant in one day."

"And another one almost cleared and two more plowed." Stephanie unhitched Samson.

"What's the plan for tomorrow?" Smitty led his horses into one of the stalls.

Ann put Arabella and Dusty in separate stalls. "First, let's decide what would be best for supper."

Smitty looked out the rear door of the barn. "It's a warm day, and I noticed a big watering trough behind the barn. I might wash off and shake out my clothes."

Ann took the lid off the ointment bucket.

The intense aroma immediately filled the barn. Sally waved her hand in front of her face. “Wait until we’re done in here.”

Ann placed the lid back on, which did nothing to eliminate the smell that had already escaped. “It’s fine with me, Smitty, but it’s only the end of April. The water won’t be warm. We have a big tub in the kitchen, but somebody will be getting supper ready. We also have ten-gallon tubs in each of our old rooms.”

As Noah went past Ann with a pitchfork full of hay, he quietly offered to prepare the cougar meat. “I can fix that meal we talked about last night.”

Ann didn’t want to insult Noah or imply that he wouldn’t make an excellent meal, but she dreaded another cougar meal like the stew she had cooked. “Would you mind if we have another meal like dinner?” Noah assured Ann he wasn’t upset that she preferred ham. Ann asked the whole group if they minded a repeat of dinner. The others all said that suited them fine. They watered and brushed the horses but left Ann to put the ointment on Dusty.

In the house, Sally gave everybody a towel and a bar of soap. Each headed off to their designated places to wash as the sun went under the horizon. Stephanie lit candles and helped Ann and Sally make up all the beds. When everybody rejoined to eat, the sun was long down. They feasted on more food from town by candlelight and planned what to do the following day. Then, since they no longer had enough seats in the living room, they drank hot sassafras tea at the dining table and continued to talk until they retired to their beds.

Noah lay in the room Eli had used before it lost its windows. He heard a buzz and flipped the sound away. It returned. He waved his hands and orchestrated a symphony of sound played by minuscule tormentors honing in on his warm body. The shutters failed miserably at keeping out the infernal little creatures but very effectively kept out every trace of fresh air. He swatted away the mosquitoes that surrounded him. He squashed them when they breached his defenses and made contact. The tiny, perfect strategists easily won the battle. Noah finally surrendered. He decided he might as well open the shutters across the hall and in the room where he lay. Even though it gave the bloodsuckers unrestricted access to his flesh, Noah at least had fresh air. It was a blessing when he finally fell asleep.

After his night feeding the mosquitoes, Noah found a cloth draped over a corked bottle on the floor just outside his door. He rubbed the liquid on all the itchy welts left behind to remind him of his defeat.

Noah strolled into the kitchen as Ann slid bran muffins into the oven. He held out the bottle. "Thank you for the witch hazel."

"Keep it for now. You might want to put more on later. I didn't get to thank you for staying over there, but I want you to know I appreciate you doing it. I know the nasty little creatures had their way with you last night."

Noah liked that Ann acknowledged the sacrifice he had made. "You're welcome." He went to the barn to help with the morning chores. They watered the animals, chopped a pile of wood, and put another dose of ointment on Dusty. It hadn't been long since Noah had gotten Dusty back, but the horse had already healed quite a bit. Noah believed it was as much due to Dusty's happiness as the smelly goop.

Zachariah carried bucket after bucket of water to refill the barrel in the kitchen. On each trip, he told the women in the kitchen, "Another bucket of water for the lovely ladies."

Each time, one of the women said, "Much obliged, Zachariah." After the morning's work, everybody enjoyed the last of the eggs and bacon from town, along with bran muffins, butter, jam, milk, sugar, and coffee.

Smitty bit into a warm muffin. "It was just like this when James was here. So we didn't have to come back to the house, we took dinner out with us during the day. Besides that, Algoma didn't want all that dirt tracked into her house. Everybody came together at this same table for breakfast and supper."

Sally asked, "Is Algoma James's wife?"

"Yes. She told me her name means valley of flowers. She was just like a flower: very beautiful."

Stephanie said, "It's a lovely name."

Mara drank the last swallow of coffee in her cup. "Shall we get these dishes cleaned?"

Eli stood up. "Who wants to help get the hoes and seeds?" All the men followed him. The women cleared the table and washed and dried everything.

The night before, they had decided they would all work together and start in the field by the creek. Since cleaning up took longer than getting their supplies, the men started to the field carrying the hoes and seeds that the girls and Eli had previously separated into smaller sacks.

Noah, however, went back to the house to let the women know that the other men had already left. He entered the kitchen and found the women eating apple pie. “I caught you.”

Ann bribed him. “There wasn’t enough for everybody, so we didn’t pack it. I’ll give you the last of it if you keep our secret.” She held out the pie pan containing the last slice.

Noah promised, “I won’t refuse apple pie. Your secret is safe with me.” He gobbled up the pie. “I came in to let you know the others already went to the lower field with the seeds and hoes.”

“We’re almost ready to go.” Stephanie packed bread into the basket. Ann and Sally put the last cleaned dishes into the china cabinet. Mara washed the pie pan and fork, pulled the plug, and watched the water leave the basin.

Ann walked to the kitchen door. "Let's take the path through the cedars.”

Stephanie and Sally both agreed. Mara was happy to go whatever way they wanted. Noah deduced it must be pleasant since all three sisters liked it and agreed to the proposed path of travel. They walked into the woods behind the house.

The blackjack oaks waved their three-fingered leaves high above their heads. Mockingbirds mimicked the songs of the robins and yellow-rumped warblers as they sat among the white dogwood blossoms. The white flowers of scattered wild hydrangeas mirrored the white blossoms of the dogwoods. Post oak, black walnut, and hickory trees added to the canopy that shaded the path. As intruders in the forest domain, they passed sassafras trees, pawpaw trees, and hollies. Hairy poison ivy vines climbed trees and covered them with their leaves as they tried to reach the sun. May apples poked their umbrella leaves through the virginia creeper that covered the ground. A bobwhite called from its hiding place as they came to the stand of cedars.

Ann stopped and breathed in the scent. "It's so clean and refreshing here. Let's enjoy the magnificence for a few minutes."

Noah stood beside Ann. *It's good that Ann likes nature.*

Dappled light filtered through the towering, seventy-foot cedars as Cedar waxwings flitted among the branches. The aroma of the forest tantalized their senses as they soaked in the glory. A rabbit hopped into a patch of ferns and nibbled the fiddleheads. Noah whispered, "If I had my bow and an arrow, I could get us that rabbit to eat this evening." Since he didn't have a bow or arrows, they enjoyed a few minutes of rabbit entertainment before they continued down the path. "I could make a good bow and arrows out of cedar. If you allow me to cut a few branches, I'd like to make some this summer."

Ann readily gave her permission, "That will be fine. I believe you will respect the trees."

At the edge of the woods, Noah held out his arms, halted the group, and pointed to the creek across the field of bluestem grass. Joining Arabella at the water was a deer with its rump facing them. Its white tail flashed. Reddish brown fur showed in splotches as it shed its winter coat. Antlers covered in velvet sprouted from its head. Noah asked, "Shall we have venison?"

All the women nodded their heads in affirmation. They had prepared before they left the house in case Roy, Gus, and Ben decided to visit them. Each of them had rammed a fresh charge of powder and a lead ball into the barrel of their guns, cleaned the touchhole, put primer powder in the pan, and closed the frizzen to keep in the powder. The only thing they didn't do was cock the rifles. Since he now planned to shoot, Noah cocked his rifle, aimed, pulled the set trigger, and asked the deer's spirit for permission to take its life. "Deer Spirit, you walk on Mother Earth as I do. I ask for this animal for food.

May I have it?" The deer raised its head and looked at the group standing at the edge of the woods but remained by the creek.

Crack!

The deer dropped.

Noah saw the men in the field grab their rifles. He hollered, "Noah taking a deer!" They waved and walked toward the creek. The two groups joined by the fallen animal.

"Good shooting," Smitty congratulated Noah, "I didn't even know it was there."

Eli looked down at the dead animal. "I thought I saw two horses walk to the creek."

"The deer must have walked over with Arabella. All the other horses are over there." Stephanie pointed at the horses grazing in the meadow.

Other than the ham and the small amount of cougar in the icehouse that probably was no longer edible, they had no meat. Ann was very glad to have venison. She complimented Noah, "However it got there, it's lucky for us that you saw and shot it."

Arabella trotted over to them, shadowed by Dusty, calm and happy again. Reeking of its fresh dose of ointment, Dusty went right to Sally when she called. "He's healing well with this miracle goop."

"It's working well for me too." Noah showed everybody his injuries. "I've been putting a little on when I'm sleeping and washing it off in the morning."

Eli pinched his nose shut. "I know."

Noah draped the hundred-pound white-tailed deer over his shoulders. "I'm going to hang this on that big tree at the edge of the woods."

Ann watched him walk away. She thought he was strong and skilled and liked that he had respected nature and asked for permission before shooting the deer.

Noah went just inside the edge of the woods. He slid the deer off his shoulders onto the ground and asked the deer's spirit for forgiveness, "Thank you for giving your life for us. Please pardon me." He drew his knife from its sheath, slit the deer's belly, scooped out its entrails, and cut its hamstrings. He punctured the vein on the side of its neck close to the head and then tied the deer's hind legs with one of his rawhide strings. Noah broke the smaller branches off a sturdy branch at the right height. Before he joined the others planting corn, he raised the deer, slid on its legs, and then situated the carcass to allow the earth to drink the blood.

The field was only a few acres in size, but the thick grass roots blocked every stroke of the hoe. Smitty wiped his brow. "I hope this grass doesn't choke out your corn."

Ann thought about it. "It probably is going to be a nightmare keeping the grass down. I guess I shouldn't have tried to use this field."

It took the nine of them four difficult hours of fighting and pulling out the entangling roots to get the field planted. After the last seed was in the ground, they ate on the creek bank. The water babbled as it flowed by and soothed their nerves frayed by their battle with the field. The sunlight filtered through the branches of the trees growing by the creek and cast a green glow over them. The horses grazed nearby in the waves of grass ruffled by the slight breeze.

When they had finished their meal, everybody felt rejuvenated and ready to plant another field. With hoes, pails, and empty dinner baskets, they ambled to the other field, prepared for planting. It was twice the size of the previous plot, but the ground was much friendlier. They easily hoed a trough and sowed the seeds while talking about the days when James had been there and the events of the last month. It seemed like less time, but it took another four hours to plant the field.

Ann felt very happy about the amount of work they had accomplished. "Should we head in?"

Smitty wasn't ready to stop for the day.

"The field we worked was almost done. Mara and I will help clear that one before we head home."

Zachariah wanted to stay. "I'll help too."

"No problem for me to keep working." Tom hadn't yet asked for what he hoped.

Stephanie looked toward the creek. "We should get the horses now. They might founder if they eat more of this grass by the creek."

Eli offered, "I'll go with you and bring the deer up." Stephanie held out her hand to invite Eli along. They went off to get the horses. The others walked to Smitty's field.

When Eli and Stephanie arrived with the horses and the deer, they found everybody lounging beside a small mountain of stones. "That was quick work."

Sally stood up. "We're going to the barn to get the wagon ready."

At the barn, Eli retrieved the deer draped over Samson and put it on the same pegs where he had previously hung the cougar.

Stephanie led all the horses into the paddock and closed the gate.

"There's still some ham left. I'll go get it." Ann started toward the house.

Tom wanted to spend more time with Eli and knew the girls could use more help. "I don't want the ham, but I would like to stay longer."

Eli chimed right in. "Sure, Pop. That would be great." No sooner were the words out of his mouth than he thought; m*aybe I shouldn't have given permission since permission isn't mine to give.*

Stephanie felt it would be wonderful if Tom stayed on. "That would be so nice. Please do."

Eli smiled. *Stephanie always thinks the same as I do. I shouldn't have been worried.*

They loaded Clyde and Zachariah's plows and harnesses into the wagon while Zachariah hitched up his horse. Tom placed his two harnesses into the wagon with the others. "Please put these in the shed behind the store."

Smitty saddled their horses while the women gathered the baskets brought from town. Zachariah put his saddle and bridle in the wagon. He hoped to win Ann's appreciation. "I'll come and help again if you'd like."

Ann didn't realize his objective. "I'm much obliged for all your help. It's so kind of you to offer, but I can't possibly impose on you anymore." Zachariah unhappily looked at Noah, standing beside Ann.

Stephanie hugged Mara. "Thank you again for the recipe. Next time one of us is in town, we'll get those apple seeds."

"Double thanks to all of you." Ann felt very grateful. She believed they might be beyond fighting to survive. When they sold the corn, they could buy plenty of food and even repair the windows. However, she first had to find a way to feed everybody all summer.

Tom encouraged the others to keep working. "I think we can get that field planted today. Do you want to try?"

Noah knew the sooner they got the corn in the ground, the better. He picked up a ten-pound sack of seeds. "I'm up for it."

Eli got a second sack. Sally pulled the barn door closed. They walked back to the field they had just cleared. Just under three hours later, they gathered up the tools and seed bags. They left the third field they had planted that day as the sun went under the horizon.

Sally confessed what she thought as they walked to the barn. "I guess maybe God is taking care of us."

Ann put her arm around her sister's shoulders. "Why are you thinking He's taking care of us?"

"I didn't believe there was any way possible to plow, clear, and plant those fields. I thought we would be lucky to plant two or maybe three fields this year if we worked very hard. You and Stephanie have been praying every night for God to help us plant every field and have an abundant harvest. I said, 'Amen,' but I didn't believe it would happen. Then we had Eli, and we made all that maple sugar. With Eli's help, we planted the littlest and the main cornfield, but we are at the end of the corn-planting season. I thought we would get the third field planted, but that would be it. Then, Noah and all the people from town came. In two days, we've gotten five fields plowed, three planted, and only two left to clear and plant. Those people never helped us for all the years we've been here. God must have let everything happen so they'd help now that we desperately need them. If we hadn't done all these fields, that probably would have been the end of us."

Stephanie agreed, "I think you're right. God made the bad things work to make a good thing happen." Eli, and especially Tom, pondered the idea of God working bad things into something good. They put the tools up, brought the horses into the barn, and brushed them down.

Ann contemplated upon the next thing

that she needed to accomplish. That was supper. She decided on the best way she could feed all of them. "Let's make split pea soup."

Stephanie liked more than just peas in her pea soup. "We can also add ham and some of the dried vegetable mix we bought."

"Sounds great." Eli tasted the soup in his mind.

Ann made up her mind about something else she had been considering. "Noah, I think Papa's clothes will fit you. I'd like you to have them."

Noah owned only one set of clothes appropriate for his current living situation. "That would be wonderful. These clothes sure need washing."

"Come on. I'll show you what we have." Ann led Noah to the room that had been her parent's room. She laid two sets of work clothes and her father's Sunday-go-to-meeting clothes on the bed, placed his boots on the floor, turned, pulled open a dresser drawer, and got out her papa's cotton and wool unmentionables and socks, a belt, and a pair of suspenders. She had already given her father's heavy overcoat to Eli when they had explored the cave, but she put her father's lighter coat on the bed. "I'd like you to have it all."

"This is very generous, Ann. Are you sure?"

"I'm sure. I'll bring you some warm water to wash as soon as it's ready." Giving her father's clothes away finalized that he was gone. Ann's heart ached. She escaped the room.

Stephanie and Sally started the fire in the stove to heat the large pot of water to cook pea soup. It was night when the soup was ready. Even though the moon would be full in only a few days, it was dark in the house. They ate by the light of candles again. Ann looked at Noah sitting at the table in her father's clothes. They fit him perfectly. He looked just as handsome as her father had, and he seemed like he was just as good of a man.

Noah looked at Ann too. Her dark hair curled around her face. Before he knew Ann, he had never seen eyes like the forest. Her eyes were so enticing. He contemplated her generosity and pleasant nature as he ate. After supper, Ann served tea in the living room. She poured hot tea into Noah's cup. He told her, "Thank you," with his words and eyes.

"You're welcome." She blushed under his gaze.

Noah watched Ann pour tea. He thought she was beautiful and gracious. That night, as he lay in his bed, curiosity about what kind of woman she might be continued to intrude into his attempts to sleep.

FORTY SEVEN

After a sleepless night, Noah got out of bed and prepared himself for the day. At the breakfast table, Sally asked, "Noah, will you help me weed the vegetable garden?" As they pulled weeds, Sally filled Noah in. "We have a competition to guess what we planted. I hope you'll join. It's not too late to guess."

Noah wanted to participate fully in life on the farm he had dreamed about while growing up, and he could already identify some of the plants. He thought it curious that some plants were randomly scattered around the garden. Pointing at sections of the garden as he walked around, Noah shared his predictions, "These are onions. These are carrots. These have to be beans. Over there are turnips. This is a cucumber patch. …"

"I'm glad you're part of the contest. We'll tell the family what you think tonight."

Noah enjoyed working with Sally. He thought she saw through the cloudiness of life. He found her innocent and refreshing. After the mid-day meal, Eli, Tom, and Stephanie weeded the rest of the vegetable garden. Noah and Sally went with Ann to remove rocks. By nightfall, the five of them had weeded around all of the tender new vegetables and cleared one more field.

A drizzle of rain prevented work in the fields, so the following day, the men went to the barn to butcher the deer while the girls started a marinade. Eli brought out the cougar hide.

Noah asked, "Why do you have it wrapped up in the barn?"

Eli told about the day he shot the cougar. "… I know Sally hasn't gotten over it. She's afraid in the dark. Don't mention it, but they keep a candle burning every night. I don't think she'll ever forgive me, and I feel horrible about it. I wish there was something I could do to make it up to her. One thing's for sure; I'm not going to do anything to remind any of them about that day or cause them any hurt ever again."

"I don't think Sally is still mad at you. She brought up having the cougar meat and didn't seem upset to me. Is the cave the one that has the Indian with a rope? I wonder if we could see the cave."

"I don't know. I won't upset Sally any more than I already have, but I'll try to talk to Ann privately."

"Go ahead and put the skin away. Will you scrape the hair off of this deerskin and tan it?"

"Sure." Eli helped carry the deer.

Noah started skinning with the knife that he always carried on his belt. Before Tom went outside into the drizzle to chop wood with Eli, he told Noah that he'd help cut up the deer when it was ready. Just before the rain started to pick up, the girls brought the marinade into the barn. Ann tried to run between the raindrops to the sugar shack to get the two large sap-condensing pans.

Except for dosing Dusty with liniment, the girls did their chores in the barn while Noah skinned the deer. Eli and Tom carried all the split wood into the barn before they joined Noah, who cut off an already-skinned leg. He pushed it over to Tom, cut off the other front leg, and handed it to Eli. At the request of Noah, they sliced the silver skin off the meat. When the girls completed their other chores, they removed the sinew from the other parts of the carcass. Once it was off, they cut most of the meat into thin slices to drop into the marinade. Some large pieces they kept whole to smoke as a roast.

Noah completed the first part of the task. "There, the skin is off." Eli switched chores. He carried the skin to the far end of the bench. Noah carved off and handed a back strap to Ann. "We'll eat this tonight."

"Mmm, Mmm. Do you want it in the

marinade?" Ann held the long muscle from the deer's back over the pan.

Noah removed the other back strap. "Yes, and put this one in there with it." He cut the rest of the animal into sections. The parts he didn't want to marinate or smoke, they wrapped in butcher paper. Ann hurried through the increasing rain to the icehouse with several packages of venison. Noah followed with more. "This smells awful. We need to get this old meat out of here."

"You're right. I don't want this lovely venison to pick up the rotten odor. I'll get a shovel and bury it."

"I'll help." Noah removed the cougar packages while Ann was gone. She returned with two shovels. Together they buried the reeking meat. Noah was impressed that Ann dug a deep hole in the pouring rain without complaining. That night, while the rest of the venison marinated in the pans in the barn, they enjoyed a back strap roast.

FORTY EIGHT

Ann sat in her bunk in the dim morning light and looked at the fields that had turned into mud pits. She decided they should stay out of them.

When they started the day's work, Tom, Eli, and Noah went to the barn. They made a mixture from the deer's brains to rub into its hide.

Sally hung meat in the smokehouse with her sisters. "Would you finish? I want to help with the deer hide."

Ann stopped her. "We should let them work on it without us."

"Why?"

"Sometimes, men need to have only other men around. I think Papa missed that when he got me instead of a son."

"That's silly."

"Sally, don't go over there. Listen to them. You don't even have to hear what they're saying. Just hear the way they sound together."

She listened. "I guess they sound happy."

"Right, we'll have plenty of time to be with them later and learn how to tan a deer hide."

"They wouldn't be mad if I went over there."

"They wouldn't, but let them enjoy each other."

"Humph." Sally went back to hanging meat.

A few days later, they planted the prepared ground and then cleared and planted the last small field. That evening, after cleaning up, Tom walked across the sitting room to the kitchen. He heard Eli talking and stopped. Ann took bread from the oven as Eli asked, "Is there a possibility for Noah and me, without upsetting Sally, to go to the cave?"

"All the fields are planted. I don't mind if you go, but I don't know how you would do it without her knowing."

After they were all in bed, Tom brought up the subject with Eli and Noah. "I think you two should say that you're going with me to town, and we can all go see the cave. Afterward, I'll go home, and you two can come back here."

"Pop, how did you know about that?"

"Fathers always know what their children are doing."

"You do always seem to know what I'm doing. What would we say as to why we're going with you?"

Noah didn't like the plan. "We'd have to be gone all day because that's how long it would take to go to town and back. I don't want to leave the girls alone that long. I'd rather not leave them alone at all."

They heard a knock. Eli called out, "Come in."

Sally came into the room holding her

candlestick. “These walls aren’t designed to keep out sound. Go see the cave. Just because I don’t want to go doesn’t mean you can’t. It doesn’t upset me. I’m not a baby.”

Eli pleaded for forgiveness, “I don’t want to cause you any hurt, and I’m sorry I got you to go through that hole.”

“It’s all right, Eli. I was terrified in that tunnel, but I knocked my lantern over, not you. I shouldn’t have told you that I would never forgive you. I wasn't rational at the time.”

Eli walked to Sally, put his arms around her, and hugged her tight. “Every day, I’ve felt horrible that I hurt you. I was afraid you would never forgive me.”

“I forgave you a long time ago.”

Tears filled Eli’s eyes. “I love all you girls. That means a lot to me.”

Ann and Stephanie had followed Sally and stood in the doorway. They quickly walked over and put their arms around the two of them. The next second, Tom and Noah stood with them in the middle of the room. They all shared in Eli's healing of forgiveness. Eli kissed Sally on the top of her head and then Stephanie and Ann on the cheek.

After a minute, Sally said, "You're going to suffocate me." She kissed Eli on the cheek. "We love you too. Get back to bed, and tomorrow go see that cave."

Ann and Stephanie followed their sister. "Good night." Ann closed the door to the men's room.

Stephanie sat between Ann and Eli at the breakfast table and looked down at her plate. She had heard what Ann had said to Sally about letting the men do things without the women, but she wanted to go. "Would it be all right if I went to the cave?"

"It's fine with me. I'll stay here with Sally."

Eli helped Stephanie get on Samson with him. She leaned back against his chest. "Hold me tight. I don't want to fall off."

Eli pulled her close. Tom got on his horse, and Noah rode Arabella. Dusty wasn't healed enough to ride, but he wanted to go, so they let him.

Ann asked Sally, "What special thing would you like to do today?"

"Let's picnic in the woods, look at the wildflowers, and read."

"Sounds wonderful. Let's start some bread before we go."

With their dough in pans in the kitchen and their dinner basket packed, they walked into the woods. The cedar waxwings sang. The red squirrels scolded them and performed acrobatics in the trees as Ann and Sally ambled to their favorite spot. They encountered a black rat snake just around a bend in the trail. They stopped and watched it consume its prey. The snake's jaws unhinged to work a Gray-necked chipmunk into its mouth. With slow but steady progress, it undulated around the meal it had captured until the rodent was a bulge inside its body. Once it had completed the task, it slithered into the undergrowth.

At the cedars, the girls lay on their backs and enjoyed the green glow and pleasant aroma. Ann shared her thoughts, "Every time I come here, I think about how much God loves us to give us such a glorious place."

"I agree. This is the loveliest place on earth."

After soaking in the ambiance for a time, Sally brought their books out of the basket. She handed one to Ann, opened the other, and read until the sun let them know it was time for dinner. Ann pulled out two large cloth napkins, which they spread across their laps and then divided their small dinner. After they had eaten, they ambled to the creek, took off their shoes and socks, and dipped their feet into the cool water. Sally wiggled her toes. She kicked water on Ann, who returned the splash. Soon, they were both drenched and giggling. Next, they strolled to the field they had planted before the townsfolk arrived and examined the little green corn bodies that had pushed up out of the soil.

Ann noticed the weather changing and made a quick decision. "The wind is picking up. It's probably going to rain, and those clouds are coming fast. We better head home." Because they were at the field farthest from their house, they left at a brisk walk. The wind whipped up quickly. They sprinted across the land.

Suddenly, black clouds filled the sky, the rain broke free, and the thunder crashed. Before them, a lightning bolt flashed to earth and incinerated a small lone tree. Ann ordered Sally, "Lie in the field."

They dropped to the ground and lay on their bellies with their arms across each other's backs as the rain drenched them. Twenty minutes later, the storm had passed and raged over Harmony. When the last drops fell from the sky, the girls got up. Mud splattered them from their faces down to their boots. They looked at each other, pointed, and broke out in wild laughter. "I love you. I'm glad you're my sister." Sally hugged Ann.

Ann repeated what their mother had always told them, "And I love you. All the way to the moon and back." With their arms around each other, they continued home. No one was there, so the girls stripped off their muddy clothes and boots by the door.

They stirred up the fire in the kitchen and put four big pots of water in the fireplace. Not waiting for warm water, they thoroughly washed their faces, arms, and hands with lye soap and a bucket of water taken directly from the water barrel. When clean enough to touch it, they kneaded the dough. After the dough was back in the pans to rise again, the two sisters pulled the tub out from under the butcher table and transferred room-temperature water from the water barrel to the tub. Ann added heated water. "You go first," she told her sister.

Sally wasted no time getting into the warm, soothing bath. She soaped up. "That was some storm, but I wasn't afraid because you were with me. It was exciting."

"It was exciting, but I was afraid. Do you want me to wash your hair?"

"Sure. It felt much nicer when Mama washed my hair than when I did it."

"I thought so too." Ann rubbed the bar of soap in Sally's hair and then scrubbed. Sally slid under the water to rinse out the soap then raised her head out of the water. "Out you go. It's my turn." Ann wrapped a towel around Sally. "Go get dressed."

Ann had almost finished washing when Sally came back and offered to return the favor. "I'll wash your hair."

"That would be wonderful." Sally rubbed soap from the top to the end of Ann's long hair and massaged Ann's head. Ann sighed, "It's Heaven on Earth." When Sally finished, Ann went off to get on clean clothes. She sat by the window in the bunkroom to slip on her house shoes and saw the others riding across the meadow. Halfway down the stairs, Ann stopped when Noah came into the foyer.

"What happened? I see muddy clothes by the door."

Ann downplayed the storm, "Just a rain shower."

"I don't think so. We waited inside the cave until that storm passed. It was fierce. Lightning hit one of the maple trees. That was the loudest sound I've ever heard. My ears are still ringing."

"Did you see it happen? That must have been frightful."

"We did. That huge tree split. I've never seen that kind of power before. I understand why my people revere the thunder god."

"It's the one God, not a thunder god, who holds the lightning in His hands."

"I know. I see why they came to believe in the power of thunder and lightning."

"I agree with that." She didn't tell Noah about the lightning striking the little tree in front of her and Sally. Tom, Eli, and Stephanie came in the door. Ann asked, "What did you think of the cave?"

Eli looked around to be sure Sally wasn't close. "It was as impressive as the last time."

Noah explained what they did, "We didn't go all the way since you can't cross the gap in the trail, but I went into the crack and got the rope free."

Tom held a coil of rope. "It's the most incredible place I've ever seen."

"I agree!" Noah stood at the bottom of the stairs and looked up at Ann.

"What about the skeleton?" Ann took a few more steps toward him and spookily wiggled her fingers in Noah's face.

Ann looked so beautiful and enticing that he wanted to scoop her into his arms. Of course, he did no such thing. "He's still there guarding his domain."

"There's a bathtub of water for anybody who wants to use it." Ann walked toward the kitchen. Noah followed her across the living room. When everybody was clean, the dough was ready. Ann put the bread into the oven. While the venison stew simmered and the bread baked, they sat in the living room and drank sassafras tea.

"There's nothing like the smell of baking bread." Tom drew in a long breath.

Eli agreed, "It smells delicious."

Tom sighed, "My mother cooked bread every Saturday. I miss her. I should have gone back to see her."

In the morning, Tom hugged his son and all the girls. "You girls are wonderful. I can see that my Eli is happy."

Stephanie looked at Eli and smiled. "We're in good hands with Eli here." Tom perceived Stephanie and Eli's interest in each other, and it made him happy. He liked the idea of having Stephanie as a daughter-in-law. He thought having all three girls in his family would be wonderful. He also noticed something brewing between Noah and Ann. He thought that would also be a good thing.

FORTY NINE

After Tom left, Noah went into the pantry for a handful of dried apples. He saw how little food they had. He knew it would be a long time before anything in the vegetable garden would be ready to eat. He contemplated and then remembered that he had seen cattails when he had looked around before the posse had gone to Clarksville.

That afternoon, Noah walked into the kitchen with as many young cattails as he could carry. "Come in here, everybody. Get knives, two big baskets from the pantry, all your big pots filled with clean water, a frying pan, and all your laundry baskets."

Stephanie walked away with Ann. "I wonder why we need laundry baskets."

"We'll soon find out," Ann replied.

Eli, the girls, and Noah stood around the butcher table with four plants from the creek in the middle. "We can eat these. Get one, and do what I do." Noah already held one of what his family in Indian Territory thought of as a major vegetable. "First, cut off the roots above this bulge." He threw the tangled mess he removed from the bottom into one of the baskets Sally had gotten from the pantry. The other four did the same.

"Now," Noah broke off one of the new shoots he had severed from the muddy roots. "Make sure you clean everything very well. We can eat these small new growths as is. Peel off the mushy outer part of the bigger ones. We'll cut up the centers and cook them. We only want the white part from down here before the leaves start. Keep all the peeling in the other basket Sally brought over. After the peelings dry, we'll toss them in with the tinder."

While they removed and prepared the sprouts, Noah explained, "Later, we'll crush the big roots and the central bulge we kept and soak them in water for a few hours. When you pour off the water, do it gently. We want to keep what settles to the bottom. It's used like flour after it dries. We'll crush the roots and do it again a few times to get it all."

Once they had completed the first two steps with all the plants, Noah pulled the long leaves off the remaining central stalk. "Put all these leaves in the clothes baskets. The leaves are good for making lots of different things. After you have the bare stalk, cut off this much, and peel it." Noah positioned his knife about a foot up from the bottom. "Cut it into bite-sized pieces. We can fry or boil them like potatoes."

That night, they ate fried cattail shoots and chunks of the stalks with cougar sausages. On the counter in the kitchen, all the cleaned roots soaked in water to extract the starch.

Ann cautiously tried a bite of cattail. "This is tasty."

Two days later, Noah brought wild henbit, dead nettle, and bittercress greens to eat. Ann assigned Noah the duty of finding plants they could eat. He executed the task very well. The five of them ate wild plants and wild game as the vegetables grew. The firm belief that God had sent Eli and Noah to save them settled into Ann's mind.

The corn sprouted. The germination rate was excellent. However, they didn't want to jerk out baby corn plants, so they waited for them to get a few inches high before weeding.

On the third day of May, Eli asked Ann for an extra day off for his birthday. Ann gave her permission, "Sure. What are you going to do?"

"I'd like to explore at Rock House Cave. Anybody want to come with me?"

Even though she would have enjoyed it, Ann declined, "I'll stay here with Sally."

Noah requested, "If it's acceptable, I'd like to go."

"Of course, it's acceptable for you to go." Ann knew her sister would want to go wherever Eli went. "What about you, Stephanie?"

"I'll go if Eli and Noah wouldn't mind."

They didn't. Eli pulled Stephanie onto Samson with him. He brushed his lips across the edge of her ear as she sat in front of him. Noah rode Arabella. Once again, Dusty went along only because he wanted to.

Stephanie rode into the enormous opening that dwarfed the giant horse she sat on with Eli. "I can't believe I didn't want to see this with Ann."

To be sure they would get back; Eli tied the rope around a rock. While Stephanie lit the lanterns, Noah looked at the wall drawings. Eli asked, "Do you know what they mean?"

"No."

Stephanie wanted to explore tunnels, not drawings. "You ready?"

Eli pointed to a different tunnel than the

one he had traveled with Ann. "Let's start with this one."

The three of them started into the hollow side by side but soon had to travel single file. Since it was Eli's birthday, he went first. The surface on which they walked was uneven. For stability, they walked with one hand against the wall and held their lantern in the other until they came to a branch and stopped. Holding their lights high, they peered as far as they could into both tunnels.

Noah noticed something faint on the wall. "Come look." Eli and Stephanie joined him. "It looks like three wavy lines." Just inside the entrance of the other tube, they scrutinized the wall.

Stephanie discovered the remaining bits of pigment. "I found something. It's four-legged."

Noah looked at Eli. "Do we go to a creek or on an animal hunt?"

"Let's go to the creek." Eli led them into the appropriate branch.

Several yards later, the ground became wet. It was just moisture, so they continued until a boulder blocked the path. Under it was a small opening no larger than the fissure in the cave by the maples. The water had increased to a significant flow on the floor.

"We'd have to slide in the water on our bellies, but we can if you want to." Stephanie hoped Eli didn't. She waited for him to decide.

"I want to stay dry. Let's take the other route."

There had been no branches off that section of the tunnel, and they had the rope to follow, so backtracking was easy. They rolled up the wet lifeline and made their way back to the animal hunt route. Noah commented on the drawings. "I guess that water was what they meant by the wavy lines. It's not very descriptive."

Since the tunnel was too narrow to change order, Stephanie followed Noah. "They'd all have known what's in here and only need to know which tunnel has the water."

At the junction, Eli moved to the front and led them in. "I hope the four-legged symbol doesn't mean there are animals in here."

"Me too." Just in case, Noah diligently surveilled to the rear and kept Stephanie safely between him and Eli.

The next choice was a small, high tube with a boulder under the hole so a person could climb in. They found the drawing that identified the path. "I think this one will take us out through a hole to the level ground above. I believe this horizontal line is the ground, and these two radiating lines coming down are this tube." Noah looked at Eli and Stephanie to see if they agreed.

"Could be, but I don't want to crawl if we can walk. I don't want to be too tired to explore other tunnels."

Again, they left the crawling choice behind, unexplored. At the next possibility of multiple paths, the selection was obvious.

Two had a large X, and one had an arrow pointing in. Some other day, they might go into the Xed paths to see what was there. This day they traveled the clear choice. It twisted around until the tunnel abruptly turned to the right. A short distance farther along, it turned to the left.

Eli told those behind him, "I think I see light ahead." Soon, there was enough light that they didn't need the lanterns. The passage became low. They walked stooped over the rest of the way and were glad when they exited through the three-foot-high opening into a clearing.

Fallen over remains of a wall of rocks encircled a clearing. Stephanie stepped over the low pile. "They must have kept animals here." After briefly perusing the clearing, they searched the cliff and found another entrance.

Eli tried to look in. "We could try to go back through this one, except that we have to gather the rope."

Noah looked for markings that might give them a clue. He found two horizontal lines that came very close together in the middle. At the end of the lines was a two-legged stick figure under a half circle. "I think we can get to Rock House Cave, but the passage is very low somewhere along the way."

Stephanie still preferred not to crawl. She suggested they not take the new tunnel. "We have to take up our safety line."

"Let's go. I want to check out another tunnel." Eli led them back into the same opening through which they had arrived. "Ann and I came through a tunnel to a ledge on the backside of the ridge. I remember seeing a small clearing from above, but I didn't see the stones at the edge."

Back in the main cave, they looked at the drawings around the entrances of the tunnels. To the right of the entrance to the passageway they had just navigated, they saw a stick person with a half circle over it. Below it, those who had lived there in the past had painted two wavy lines on the left and a small four-legged animal to its right. Going down the wall, below the animal symbol, were the two diagonal lines with a horizontal line above. Under that were two Xs and an arrow. Farthest down, a circle with a four-legged stick figure inside ended the sequence.

Noah referred to the comment he'd made when Eli had asked him if any of the symbols made sense. "I think I understand the drawings in here, at least the markings by the tunnel holes. Eli, which one did you take when you went with Ann? If we look at that one, we might be able to figure out the meanings of these markings."

Eli showed them which tunnel he had gone through with Ann. To the right of the opening, they found the same symbol for the cave and two horizontal parallel lines to the right and last one line over several two-sided triangles pointing up. Eli pointed at each character as he told them what he thought it meant. "This is the cave we're in, connected to one single tube high enough to walk through. It takes you to the ledge above the trees."

They all felt excited and moved to another tunnel opening. Starting with the symbol for the cave, they examined the markings. Stephanie put her finger beside each mark as she stated what she thought it signified. "This is the cave. You can go to the right at the first division, but there is a place where you have to crawl through a little opening. This symbol for the cave with a horizontal line over it probably stands for the area above this cave. That's where it takes you.

"You should not take the middle route because of the X. The left way is low but not so low that you would have to crawl. When you come to another division, you should not take this one. The other choice is narrow side to side. It will bring you out by the trees."

Eli and Noah believed that she had it right.

Stephanie asked, "Do you want to try this one and see if I'm right? We can take the dinner basket and eat at the trees."

"Let's look at the other tunnels' symbols first." Noah contemplated the wall next to another opening for a short while before he said, "We should not try this one. I think the horizontal line that then comes straight down with a slightly wavy vertical line beside it and then goes on horizontally means there is a drop-off that you will need a rope to go down. We might be able to go down, but it could be hard to get back up, especially because we don't know how high it is."

They looked at all the options and decided to try the one Stephanie had first suggested and found that she was correct about the path to the trees. On the way back, Noah decided to try the tube up to the area above the cave. Eli and Stephanie went on to the cave. To be on the safe side, they left the rope on the ground for Noah. As planned, they went out of the cave to see if they could see

Noah above the cave. He arrived at the edge. "Hello below."

Stephanie waved back. "Hello above."

Eli had investigated the hillside. "You could get down out here, but you have to gather the rope."

"I want to go back that way, anyway. It's a smooth surface, and it was hard to get up, but it will be fun to slide down. I'll see you in the cave."

After Noah got back to the cave, they explored a tunnel they thought would not take them out on the other side but instead go into a large opening inside the ridge. As he stood in the cavern, so large the light of their three lanterns did not illuminate it entirely, Noah wished he had brought paper so they could make a map. He decided he would make one from memory after they got back to the house.

They explored one more tunnel late in the afternoon and then headed home. Stephanie commented on the living conditions in the cave on the way back home. "Indians could have lived in there. With the front being so open, they probably used additional shelter."

Noah had lived most of his life in the kind of dwelling the Indians would have built. "They would have built grass-thatched lodges in there."

Sally was on lookout duty. She saw them coming and let Ann know. Ann dropped the dumplings into the chicken stew. Eli smelled the dumplings cooking and went into the kitchen. An egg custard pie sat on the counter. "How did you know this is my favorite?"

Stephanie confessed, "When your father was here, I asked him what day you were born and what are your favorite foods."

They enjoyed the meal that one of their chickens had given up its life to provide and then sat together in the living room and drank sassafras tea with honey.

FIFTY

That summer, they tended the cornfields, chopped stacks of wood, and stored the logs in the barn. They ate provisions from Yate's Mercantile, Eli's cheese, Noah's honey, maple sugar they had made that spring, vegetables from their garden, wild plants, and game. There was more food than the three girls had eaten for many months.

On Sally's birthday, the 23rd day of June, she announced the winner of the vegetable-garden plant-identification challenge. She ignored the stray plants flung to the wrong parts of the garden during the mud war and declared Eli, the winner. He had gotten everything right except that some of the melons had been cucumbers.

On Stephanie's birthday, August 19th,

Noah completed his bow. He thought the cedar bow turned out perfectly. To go with it, Noah had knapped several arrowheads out of nodules of chert that he had found in the piles of stones they had removed from the fields. From the sinew of the deer, he had braided a bowstring, reinforced the back of the bow, and fastened the arrowheads to the arrow shafts. He stood in the workroom with Eli. "Look how perfectly the bow arches when I pull the string." Noah pulled the string to demonstrate. "That's because of the sinew on the back."

Eli requested, "Let me try.

Noah handed over the bow. Eli pulled the string and let it go.

Twang. The string slapped the inside of Eli's elbow.

"Yow! That hurt."

"I can teach you how to shoot if you want."

"I'd need a bow."

"I can make one for you."

"This bow is impressive. I'd like that."

"I'll do it, and I need some strong, stiff feathers to fletch the arrows."

"I'll keep my eyes open for you." Eli thought that was the least he could do in return.

The summer passed with lots of hard work. As Eli rode Dusty back to the Williams' farm along the faint wagon track from Harmony, he spotted turkey tracks. At the farm, he rode to the vegetable garden. Noah continued to hoe weeds away from the carrots while Eli explained where he had seen the tracks.

Noah believed he knew the place. "I'll set traps. We'll eat the turkey and use the feathers for my arrows."

"I told you I'd keep my eyes open for you." Eli took Dusty to the barn.

Ann picked green beans. "Would you mind if I come with you?"

Noah quickly accepted, "Of course not. I'd love it."

The next day, Noah and Ann rode Arabella and Dusty to the place Eli had reported seeing turkey tracks. Noah quickly found them. He showed Ann how to set a trap and then went off to set other snares. After setting several, Noah returned to inspect the one Ann had struggled to make while he was gone. He squatted beside her. "Good work."

"It's barely set." Ann turned to look at him. Their faces were only inches apart. She felt she could fall into his eyes and be happy there.

Noah stood up and held out his hand. "You should have seen the first trap I set." He pulled Ann up right in front of him. She was in no hurry to move. He touched the side of her face to brush a curl back from her temple then slid his arm around her waist and pulled her toward him. His lips touched hers in a gentle kiss. He stepped back, looked into her upturned face, and brushed his thumb across her cheek. He retreated while he was able to keep from devouring more kisses. "We better get home."

"You're right." Ann mounted Dusty. They rode home, neither knowing what to say.

Just before they entered the house, Noah stopped. "I want you to know that your kiss was very delicious."

"And yours too." Ann slightly touched Noah's hand and then quickly called out, "We've set the traps."

At breakfast, Ann asked Eli, "Since you found the tracks, would you check the traps with Noah?"

"Of course, I'll help."

That wasn't the real reason Ann thought Eli should go. Ann had spent the night thinking about Noah's kiss and had decided it would be better not to go with him alone again. She wasn't sure if she could trust either one of them.

Noah had also thought about that kiss, and he knew it wasn't appropriate. Ann was the boss, and he respected her. He also knew that he wanted more of her kisses.

Eli instructed those staying home, "Stay close to the house and don't go to the cornfields."

Noah walked to the door. "We'll get back as soon as we can. Wish us luck."

Ann assured Noah of what she knew to be true. "What you catch won't be due to luck. It will be because of your skill." A smile spread across Noah's face and mind.

The girls stood on the porch and watched the men ride away on Dusty and Arabella. They could see Noah and Eli talking. Suddenly, they darted off as fast as the horses would go. Soon they were out of view. The girls went back into the house. After cleaning up the breakfast remains, they worked in the vegetable garden next to the house. Stephanie pulled out a spent plant. "September's almost here. We need to hire workers for the corn harvest."

"I wonder where Papa went to get them." Sally placed the onion she had pulled from the soil into her basket.

"Eli will know." Stephanie continued to pull green bean plants that were no longer producing.

"You're right. We'll ask him when they get home." Ann felt happy as she harvested parsnips and beets. They had seeds from all the plants for the following spring and a large store of dried vegetables as well as smoked and dried meats for the winter. They had also eaten all they had wanted during the summer. Their belts were back in the original holes, and the girls' bones no longer showed through their skin. "God blessed us when he sent us Eli and Noah. They saved our lives. We wouldn't have made it through another year alone."

Eli and Noah raced Dusty and Arabella down the wagon trail toward Harmony. Arabella flew across the countryside, barely ahead of Dusty.

"Come on, Dusty. You can do it." Eli squeezed his knees. Dusty ran beside Arabella.

"You're as slow as molasses." Noah drew his legs in tighter. Arabella wanted to win as much as Noah and picked up her speed.

So that Noah would hear him over the wind whipping past their ears, Eli yelled, "Don't get too big for your britches."

They raced until Arabella arrived at the traps ahead of Dusty but only by a horse length. Noah stroked the horse he loved. "There's no horse alive that's gonna outrun Arabella."

Eli got off his ride. "If Dusty hadn't just healed up, Arabella wouldn't have won."

"No other horse has come close to keeping up with Arabella. We've got great horses."

They took off the saddles and rubbed down the horses with grass. Noah attached a short lead rope that barely reached the ground and then took Arabella to a good stand of grass. He dropped the rope to ground-tie her. Arabella knew to stay where Noah left her when the lead rope hung down, and Dusty always stayed beside

Arabella and wouldn't leave if she didn't. Noah tested the wind direction before they went into the woods. They stopped a few yards before reaching the traps.

"When Ann said your skill would be what caught anything, I didn't imagine you were this skilled."

"I didn't either. I never before caught anything not actually snared."

Turkeys pecked at the ground close to the big tom captured in the trap. "How many are there?" Eli counted. "Eleven. Four in snare traps and seven loose."

Noah got the same count. "We caught one tom and three hens, and there are two young males and five hens free."

"We could take the big tom and some hens home and raise turkeys."

"True. We need at least two hens and the tom alive, plus one to eat. The rest of them should survive fine without four of them. Get your piggin' string ready. You tie up one of the hens. I'll get the tom." Noah charged into the flock to drive away the birds not trapped.

Turkeys flew in every direction. With the excess birds out of the way, Noah gently approached the biggest of the birds. It ran but was stopped short at the end of the snare rope around its foot. It darted back the other way. Noah quickly changed direction and grabbed its wing but couldn't hang on. The tom turkey ran the outer circumference of the rope with Noah close behind. It went so fast that before Noah knew it, the tom chased him instead. He remembered that turkeys run faster than humans. He yelled to get Eli's attention, "Help."

Eli wasn't doing any better catching the hen. He dashed over to help Noah, who was up the tree that held the turkey captive. He looked so hilarious in the tree with the tom flapping and flying up at him that Eli laughed. Noah kicked at the bird to keep its sharp beak away. "It's not funny! Well, maybe it is, but get him!"

While the tom focused its attack on Noah, Eli took off his shirt and sneaked up from behind. He threw his shirt over the turkey, dropped to his knees, and wrapped his arms around it. Turkeys that had flown away returned and charged him. A beak pierced Eli's back. He let go and covered his head. The tom darted away when Noah jumped into the chaos. He snatched a hen attempting to eliminate Eli. The rest of the birds changed tactics and raced away. Noah rapidly tied the feet of the hen he had caught. He whipped the cord around its body several times to hold in its wings.

Eli jumped up. "We got one! Let's get more!"

The men worked together. Noah cornered the tom, and Eli grabbed for its legs. The flock defended their leader with their sharp beaks and foot spurs. "We've got to keep them off us." A hen darted away from Noah. Eli grabbed his rifle and shot it. Noah picked it up, discovered a tether attached to its leg, and informed Eli of his error. "You should have killed a loose one."

Not wanting to remove too many of the flock, they went back to chasing, fighting, and distracting, but they didn't get close to catching another, so they stopped and devised a plan. Drive the free turkeys far away, dash back, maneuver the tom up to the tree, close in from both sides, and lunge together. They executed the plan flawlessly. The tom didn't know which way to go, jumped straight up, and tried to fly. Its wings tangled in the branch above. Noah grabbed its legs, and Eli twirled his rawhide strip around them. They dislodged the bird while the tethered turkeys flapped frantically. They had a live hen and the big tom both bound and one dead hen. They only needed one more hen that was alive. The last strategy had worked pretty well. They tried it again on another of the tethered birds. After several attempts, Eli lay across a turkey as Noah trussed it.

One hen remained captive. They already had the three live birds they wanted and a dead one to eat. The problem was that it was difficult to catch them. They didn't want to cut the tether and let it go because it might get caught by the rope and slowly starve. They let the bird calm down. When it again pecked for insects on the ground instead of frantically running, flapping, and jumping, Noah shot it. They mounted up and went home with two dead turkeys, one live tom, and two live hens.

FIFTY ONE

At home, Ann, Stephanie, and Sally completed all the outside chores quickly and then went inside. Late in the day, Noah and Eli still weren't back. Ann sat next to the window, waited, and worried that something had happened. "It couldn't be that hard to retrieve captured turkeys." She finally saw them far across the meadow. "Here they come." All three girls hurried to the porch and watched them approach. Turkeys hung lifelessly from the saddle horns, and Noah held a giant turkey in his lap. Ann walked over to take it from him before she realized it was alive.

Eli held up his two living hens by their bound feet. "We can raise them."

"Stand back." Noah lowered the tom at

the end of its tether. "Let's put the living ones in the barn." The turkey tried to flap and kick so much that it bounced around Arabella's feet. It surely would have gotten loose if its legs and wings had not been tightly bound. Eli lowered the two hens. Noah rode away from the bouncing birds and untied the dead turkeys from the saddle pommel. "Put these in the house. We'll get the horses in their stalls then we can let the turkeys loose in there."

As Eli and Noah brushed the horses, they decided to use one of the stalls as a turkey cage. Stephanie filled the water troughs in all of the stalls. While Ann gave hay to the horses that had been gone all day, Sally fed the chickens and put cracked corn in the food trough of the turkey stall. Samson decided since everybody else was getting food that he needed some and clamored until Ann put hay into his stall. The chickens sat on their roost in the barn and watched.

Noah called Ann to the stall where he

planned to put the turkeys. "Help me hold him while I get him untied." Ann held tight while Noah loosened the string. The tom flapped furiously and beat Ann in the face. Noah yelled, "More help."

Eli, Stephanie, and Sally dashed over and held its wings. So his sharp spurs couldn't gouge anyone, Noah carefully held and untied the tom's feet. When they had the turkey untied, he called out, "Now," quickly pulled the turkey away, gently swung him into the stall, and slammed the door shut. The tom charged the door, but he didn't fly over the top. They repeated the procedure with the other two turkeys.

Finally, all three birds stood in the stall as the tom gobbled his unhappiness. They didn't want the turkeys to fly over the stall wall and get away, so they exited quickly with turkeys, chickens, and horses all safely contained inside the barn.

Stephanie and Ann cleaned and bandaged the injuries received during the men's battle with the turkeys. Ann said, "Tell us what happened."

Eli narrated, "When we got there, the traps had caught four turkeys, plus more were standing around that weren't in a trap."

Noah cut in, "Your trap caught one."

"I thought it was so poorly set that it would fall apart and be useless."

Eli took up the story again, "There were eleven turkeys. Most were hens, but also a couple of young males and the big tom we brought home. We tried to run the loose ones away, but they kept attacking us. It took both of us going after the same bird to get each of the live turkeys."

Noah conveyed their desperation, "They put up one heck of a fight. With them flapping and kicking and pecking and the loose ones attacking us, it's a wonder we got out alive."

Ann joked with Noah, "I can surely see you being taken down by a turkey."

They laughed, but Noah and Eli had been

there. They both knew that wasn't far from the truth.

Sally had eating turkey on her mind and wanted to get started. "We can pluck both turkeys tonight, bake one tomorrow, and smoke the other whole."

"Sounds like a good plan to me." Ann stood up. "I'll start some water heating while we eat. We can scald and pluck the turkeys after supper."

Noah got up with her. "I'll help you."

Sally followed them into the kitchen. "If we all help, we can get it going quickly."

As promised to her sisters when they were in the garden, Ann asked about the help they would soon need, "Eli, do you know where we need to go to hire workers to harvest the corn?"

"They come to Harmony every year. Nobody was there when I left. They should arrive soon."

Even though Eli had come from town only a few days before, Ann didn't want to miss hiring all the needed workers. “Tomorrow, we should go and find out.”

“How much corn do you think we have?” Sally sat at the table, ate beets, and waited for Ann to answer.

“There are lots of ears. I think we’ll get at least a thousand bushels.”

Eli explained how he and his father always handled the corn harvest, “Last year, we bought corn from the farmers for sixty-six cents a bushel and sold it to buyers from Pennsylvania for seventy cents. They won’t take small lots, but they may take a thousand bushels.”

Ann didn’t want to sell directly. “I don’t want to cut your father out. It would be wonderful if we get six hundred and sixty dollars.”

Stephanie helped herself to more greens and felt it was wonderful to eat as much as she wanted. “Not all the money will be ours. We’ll have to pay the workers. How much does that usually cost?”

Eli calculated in his head. "It will probably take ten workers besides us. Two bits and two dollars a week for each would be twenty-five dollars. We'll have to put in a lot of time ourselves to harvest it all in a week."

"Twenty-five dollars isn't bad." Noah placed his fork on his empty plate.

"We have to hire them no matter how much. We can't do it without help." Stephanie looked at Ann to see if she agreed.

Ann turned toward her sister. "I know we do, and we also have to pay Noah and Eli their wages for the summer."

They took the dishes into the kitchen and checked the water. It was boiling. Ann and Stephanie put on their maple processing aprons and gloves and held the turkeys by their legs in the scalding water. Two minutes later, the girls plopped the carcasses on the butcher table. Hot feathers spread across the table, fell on the floor, and somehow made it all the way across the room. Sally, Noah, and Eli gathered them. Stephanie hung the feather and hair-free birds in the pantry.

Ann walked to the workroom with a sack of feathers. Noah followed with the rest in another bag. He wanted her to stay near him. “Help me pick out feathers to use for my arrows.” Ann was happy to do so. They stood close together and separated the sturdy wing feathers. Noah carried a sack of good feathers upstairs and put it with the arrows and the remaining sinew in his bottom bureau drawer. He brought one arrow, two feathers, and his knife to the living room, where the others sipped sweet tea. “May I work on this arrow in here?”

“Certainly, would you like tea?” Ann stood in front of him with the kettle.

“Yes, please. May I use the whetstone that I saw in the pantry?”

“I'll get it.” Ann poured tea into the cup already at the place Noah liked to sit then went to get the whetstone and a cup of water.

“I'll be right back.” Noah retrieved a cutting board from the workroom.

Ann handed Noah the whetstone and water. “May I watch?”

"Yes. Sit here." Noah patted the sofa that the girls had reupholstered with what was left of the curtains after the attack on the house.

Ann got her tea and sat beside Noah. He cut and shaped feather pieces and slid them into the grooves he had cut at the end of the arrow shaft. Eli, Stephanie, and Sally went to bed after a short time of watching what appeared to them as doing the same thing repeatedly but getting nowhere. Ann saw that Noah made minor adjustments, which allowed the arrow to balance better when he laid it on his finger. After a long while, even Ann decided to leave him to his work. When Noah finally completed the arrow, he carried everything upstairs, placed his treasures on the bureau, and settled into his bed beside the back window.

FIFTY TWO

A crackling noise woke Noah. He looked out the window. The woods behind the house were ablaze. "Wake up!" He ran to the girl's room and pounded on the door. "Wake up! We have to get out! The woods are on fire!"

Eli jumped out of bed. *We can escape on the horses.* He glanced toward their means of salvation. "The barn is on fire! We have to save the animals!"

Noah screamed, "Girls, get up!" He looked out the balcony window at the spots of flames spreading across the cornfields. As he urged the girls toward the stairs, a flaming can of oil smashed the front window below and landed in the foyer. Fire leapt across the floor. A man jumped through the opening into the house and darted toward the living room. Everybody upstairs hurried to the front window. The man below ran out the kitchen door with the music box under his arm. He quickly mounted his horse, looked up at the faces in the window, and tipped his hat. He spurred his horse and sped away to escape the conflagration.

Her face white with fear, Sally clutched the window frame. "What are we going to do?"

Noah looked across the girl's room and silently begged, *God, please help me know what to do.* He saw the well and assumed command. "Tie sheets together. We're going out the window into the well."

Stephanie angrily jerked her sheet off her bed. "After all our work, we're going to lose everything."

Ann spread her sheet on the floor. "Throw everything we have in these two rooms into this sheet. We'll take what we can out the window with us."

They quickly gathered everything they could take, put it all on the sheet on the floor, and tied it up. Noah attached one end of the sheet rope to the bunk bed. "Ann, climb down."

"No. Stephanie and Sally need to get out first. I'm not leaving them behind."

"I'll go. God, save us again." Stephanie started down.

The second that Stephanie was down, Sally went out the window. As soon as Sally's feet stood on the ground, she started toward the barn. "We have to let the animals out."

Stephanie captured her wrist. "We can't save them. It's already too late."

"No!" Sally tried to get away.

Stephanie did not let her go. She knew it was horrible, but the fire already burned powerfully at the barn doors. "Even if the animals aren't already dead, we can't open the doors, and we can't get them into the well."

Noah ordered Ann to comply, "If you don't climb right now, I'll tie this sheet to you and throw you out."

"I'm going. You two be sure to come right out."

Ann climbed out the window. She yelled to Noah, whose face she saw watching her climb down, "Come quickly, the fire's spreading across the workroom. Soon you won't be able to get past the window!"

Noah hurriedly told Eli what he needed him to do as quickly as possible once he was on the ground. Noah darted to each bed. Eli barely started down before Noah tossed out the rest of the sheets. "Everybody, tie a sheet around your waist." The girls picked up a sheet and tied it on. Noah pulled the rope of linens back up. He attached the bundle of their possessions and lowered it to the ground. Immediately, Ann pulled at the knot to untie it. Noah came out the window and climbed down the makeshift ladder while Eli pulled the well rope as fast as possible to unwind it from the winch. Ann yanked the sheet corner through the knot and freed it. She moved the bundle out of the way just before Noah reached the ground. Stephanie and Sally grabbed their possessions and dragged them across the yard toward the well.

Ann looked at the barn, the smokehouse, and the sugar shack, all going down in a blaze of fire. She hurried to the well with anger written across her face. Noah explained why he had thrown out more sheets. "Tie your sheet around the rope to lower yourself." He tied the bundle to the bucket bar at the other end of the line. They climbed into the well as flames shot out the workroom window and licked up the side of the house. It was much too hot. Noah didn't have time to tie on a sheet. He had to get into the well immediately. "We have to get in the water quickly!"

Ann could feel the heat of the flames above and knew he was right. "Go faster!"

Stephanie and Sally were already in the water, and Eli was almost there when the barn collapsed and fell across the well. The roof above kept the burning boards from falling on the people below. It also protected the bundle of their possessions that Noah had tied to the bucket bar to prevent the rope from coming through the pulley. Ann arrived at the water and freed herself from the rope. The structure above burned fiercely. Noah knew he was too far above the water to climb the rest of the way down before his support crumbled. "Move out of the way."

Those in the water squashed themselves against the wall. Noah let go and plunged feet first into the deep water. Without the counterweight on the other end of the rope, the bundle tied to the bucket bar dropped. Flaming boards, the pulley, and rope came down behind it.

Eli saw what was coming their way. "Get deep under the water." They sucked in a lung full of hot air and then used the stones of the well to push themselves deep into the water. Their lungs made them return to the surface in a short time. Noah still swam up from the depths. His body screamed for air. He had no doubt, even though he knew he couldn't, that he would soon inhale. He kicked as hard as he could. The second his head broke the surface, Noah sucked in the hot but life-giving air.

Ann knocked burning boards off the sheet parcel. Together, the group got it out of the water and used Noah's bow wedged sideways to keep it above them. They remained safe in the water as the fire raged above. It was a long wait before they felt the air and water getting cooler and saw the light of sunrise.

FIFTY THREE

Ann looked up. "How are we going to get out of here?"

Many times Noah had climbed a fissure in the rock cliff back at his home in Indian Territory. He studied the shaft of the well. It was much wider, but it was the only way out. He tied the rope around his waist. "I can climb out."

They pushed aside the only things they still owned. As tightly as he could, Noah held on to the highest stones he could firmly grip and then pushed off with his foot. He quickly moved his foot up and then wiggled it into a secure place behind him before finding another set of rocks to hold. Noah then did the same with his other foot. Each time he made solid points of contact before moving.

The stones were rough-hewn and provided good ledges to support his feet and good places to get a grip with his hands. On the bad side of climbing jagged rocks, they cut his hands and bare feet. Even so, he climbed and climbed.

In the water below, the other four anxiously watched the death-defying climb and prayed that Noah would make it. Watching filled Ann with so much fear for his life that she could hardly stand it, but she couldn't take her eyes off him either. Ann saw Noah's arms start to shake with fatigue when he still had a long way to go. She could see that he was too far up to drop back down and too far down to make it to the top before his arms gave out.

Noah also knew he was in trouble. He considered his options and then did the only thing that gave them any chance; he kept going. He pulled up with cramping fingers and drew his foot up. It slid back into a very deep ledge. Noah wiggled his foot sideways.

It was wide. He positioned his foot and brought his other foot up to the same stone. With both feet firmly planted, he pushed back and stood with only his toes off the front edge of the large rock.

Noah had not spoken a word as he concentrated on the climb. Now that he was in a good place, he let those below know how he was progressing. "I found a place to stand and rest. I'm about two-thirds of the way."

Ann let out a massive sigh of relief. "Thank You, God."

Noah looked at the rocks around and above him. He couldn't see all the way up, but he mapped out what looked like the best and shortest route for the next several moves. After a long rest, Noah started up again. He was much closer to the top when his arms could no longer take all the burden of raising him. Noah altered his technique to push more with his legs and pull less with his arms. He found he was much less coordinated and desperately hoped that he would find another place to rest. He was almost to the top when he was sure there was no way that he could push himself up even one more time.

"God, I can't make it. I'm so close. Help me."

The sound of a singing grosbeak floated into Noah's ears. He looked up. A rosy breast puffed in and out as God told him that the world was just within his reach. Noah summoned his last drop of strength, forced his legs to raise him, and climbed the last three steps to the top. He lay draped over the top, exhausted and unable to move as the rough stones pushed against his stomach.

"I made it. Give me a minute to rest before I look for something to help get the rest of you out."

Those holding their breath with anxiety and worry finally breathed. Eli answered from the bottom of the well. "Take all the time you need." Eli was strong, but he had watched Noah climb. He knew he would not be able to climb out the way Noah had, and the girls wouldn't be able to do it either. It seemed to Eli that there was only one being who could provide the help they needed. He tried to strike a bargain. "God, it's Eli here. I know I haven't ever talked to you, but if you get us out of here, I'll pray all the time, and I'll believe in you."

After several minutes of lying on the top of the well, Noah recovered enough strength to pull himself out the rest of the way. He looked around. There was nothing but black ash as far as he could see. The barn was gone. He grieved terribly for the animals.

The fire had been so hot that most of the rock walls of the house had fallen over. He couldn't even walk onto the still, very hot remains of the house. Noah wrapped the rope around the well, but it failed to reach the others in the water below. He despaired that he would find anything to allow the others to escape the well.

Noah pleaded, "God, like you did last

night, show me what to do." He still couldn't think of anything he could use to support the rope. He felt desperate.

Something his mother had told him many times popped into his mind. "Work like it's all up to you, and pray like it's all up to God." He determined the best thing to do was to tie the rope to himself. Sally was the lightest. He had to trust God to help him pull her out. Then, she could help him with the next person.

"God, I'm going to try to do this like it's all up to me, and I'm asking and trusting you to give me the strength to do it."

Noah peered into the well. "Sally, while I pull you up with the rope, you need to try to climb like I did and support your weight as much as you can against the rocks."

"I'll try."

"First, tie the rope to our bundle. I'll pull it up and get it out of the way." Noah pulled out what little they had saved from the fire and set it aside. "Give me a minute to rest.

Tie the rope to the sheet. I don't want the rope gouging your skin. I'll tell you when to start."

Ann notified Noah, "We have Sally ready, but rest as much as you need to. You can't let her go once she starts."

Long minutes later, Noah said, "Ready."

Ann silently prayed as her sister started up. *God, don't let Sally fall.*

Sally was almost to the top when Noah knew he couldn't pull any longer. "Can you wedge your feet against the rocks and hold yourself there for a few minutes?"

"I'm at a place where I can do that." She got into a stable position. "I'm ready."

Noah let the rope go and looked into the well. He saw Sally looking up at him only a few feet out of reach. "Tell me when you get too tired."

"I will. I'm doing fine."

After several minutes, Sally suggested, "It's narrower here. If you just keep the rope from slipping, I think I can climb from here."

"Are you sure?"

"I can almost get my hands on the top of the wall already. I think I can do it. Just pull the rope and keep it tight." Sally climbed out with Noah barely pulling. Noah held her in his arms. Several times he repeated, "Thank You, God," before he finally let her go.

Noah called down to the three still in the well, "What next? I'm so tired. I don't think I can pull up another of you."

Eli knew that Noah needed his help. He knew that Sally would try as hard as she could, but she was barely fourteen and wouldn't be enough help. Noah said he would not be able to pull out even one more unless that person mostly climbed out on his or her own. He felt horrible leaving Ann and Stephanie in the well but believed it was the only way. "Noah, if you two can hold the rope in case I slip, I think I can mostly climb like you did. When I'm out, the three of us can pull out Stephanie and Ann."

Noah was afraid. "I might not be able to hold you."

"Rest. We'll wait." Ann didn't want to risk Eli's life.

Stephanie spoke softly with Ann and Eli to keep Noah and Sally from hearing. "It's getting icy in this water. I don't know how much longer we can stay down here."

Ann understood. "It won't do any good if they can't hold us, and we fall."

"Let's wrap these sheets around us together. Maybe that will help." Eli pulled the two girls close. They wrapped themselves together to share their body heat. It barely made a difference.

Noah looked into the well. "We're ready."

Eli separated from the other two, wrapped his sheet under his arms, and then attached the rope. He placed one foot into a groove between the rocks and his other foot against another one behind him, pushed up, reached for a handhold above, and brought his foot up just as Noah had done. Since he was trying to push up with his legs instead of pull up with his arms, he found it hard to stay in position and move again. “Can you hold my weight as I try to pull myself up?”

“Move your hand up, and tell us when you’re ready. We’ll pull at the same time as you move your leg up.” They worked this way, rested for a moment, and then went up another step until Eli arrived at the resting stone. They rested for a long time. When they could go again, Noah and Sally pulled as Eli pushed himself up. They paused and then repeated until Eli climbed out.

“They’re too cold. We need to get Stephanie and Ann out as fast as we can.” Eli looked back down from where he had just come. He knew Ann was not going to leave Stephanie in the well. “Stephanie, you’re next.”

Ann secured the rope. “You can do it.”

“I’m ready, but you’ll mostly have to pull me up.” Stephanie tried the best she could to climb and not make them have to pull. Knowing that Ann needed to get out of the cold water, she tried to climb fast. Her wet foot slipped. The sudden jerk pulled the rope through the hands of those above. Stephanie screamed as she fell.

In the water, believing Stephanie was about to die, Ann screamed, "No!"

Eli whipped his arm around the rope. It slid across his skin and dug a gouge before he got a grip. Even though it was only a second, yards of rope slid past. Frantically, Eli called out, "Are you all right?"

The three above held on while Stephanie got her footing back. She felt the knot on her head, saw blood on her hand, and then wiped it off on her nightgown. "I'm all right."

As if she didn't already know, Eli told her, "Take it slow and be careful."

"I will. I'm ready." Stephanie started up again.

As soon as she was out, they dropped the rope to Ann. Ann's fingers were extremely stiff, and she was almost at the end of her ability to focus. "I can barely move."

Noah called down, "Just do your best."

Ann got the rope tied on and got into position. The four above pulled, but Ann could barely remember what she was supposed to do. She couldn't feel her feet, couldn't get them into the grooves between the rocks, and couldn't hold anything with her fingers.

"Stop, I…" Ann didn't finish her sentence. She didn't know what she was about to say. She dropped and then treaded without knowing why she was trying to keep her head above the water. The next moment, she didn't know anything in her very cold brain.

Noah prayed, "God, You've always been there when I've called. Help me get Ann out."

Sally threatened the men, "We are not leaving her. You better pull her up, or I'll push both of you down there with her."

Eli looked Sally straight in the eyes. "We aren't giving up. We'll get her out."

Noah assured Sally, "There's no way I'm leaving Ann in there." He hollered into the well, "Ann, keep yourself off the sides. We're going to pull you out." He heard no reply. He looked into the well. Ann was gone. "Pull now!"

Noah saw Ann rise from her would-be watery grave. He didn't know if she was alive. He couldn't bear to tell the others that Ann might have drowned. He hated that it had taken him so long to climb out. He hated that he had been too weak to pull the others out faster. He didn't know if he would be able to forgive himself if he had let Ann drown. He pulled in anguish.

The rope stayed tight to the wall. Ann scraped across the sharp rocks. The stones tore and punctured her skin, but more importantly, they banged against her chest and back. The impacts slammed water from her lungs as her body hit rock after rock. Each collision forced out more water and compressed her heart. They drew her up across a razor edge that cut through her nightgown, sliced her back, and then her leg.

She twisted at the end of the rope and slammed into the wall again. Ann's lungs expanded after the compression forced out more water. The air she drew in triggered her breathing response. She sputtered out the last of the water.

Blessedly, she remained unconscious as sharp edges slashed her stomach, wounded her breast, and tore hair from her head. Jagged stones bumped against her body and ripped cut after cut into her bare arms. She arrived at the top cut and bruised all over. Noah slid his arms under Ann's and pulled her out of the well.

They all collapsed to the ground. Noah drew Ann against him and felt her breathing. "Thank You, God." So relieved that she was out of the well, he kissed one blood-covered cheek and then the other. He kissed her lovingly on the lips and felt her kiss him back. He drew his head back and looked into her eyes. "I don't ever want to lose you." Ann wrapped her bloody arms around Noah and kissed him again.

Sally told them, "Get married then you can kiss."

Ann didn't move. She needed to get warm, and she wanted Noah to hold her. The five of them lay cuddled together amongst the charcoal remains of their lives to warm up and regain their strength.

FIFTY FOUR

Noah held Ann close. When she was warm, he got up and lowered a sheet into the water. "Let me clean these cuts." He gently dabbed the blood off Ann's face then wiped the cuts on her arms. "It was Gus who tipped his hat at us. I'm going to find him and slice him to pieces."

Ann assured Noah that she felt the same. "Lord, forgive me, but I hate that man. I'll surely help you skin him."

"He killed our animals." Sally sobbed as she thought about Samson, Dusty, Arabella, the chickens, and the turkeys.

Eli hated the man as well. "Skinning isn't enough suffering for that man."

"I'll help torture him in whatever way you want." Stephanie joined the group's thirst for vengeance. "And why did he take the music box? It doesn't even work."

Noah cleaned all of Ann's injuries that were appropriate for him to see. He handed the wet sheet to Ann. "You girls get out of your wet nightclothes. We'll turn away."

Ann ripped her torn nightgown into strips. The girls tied pieces of cloth around their injuries. Noah and Eli bandaged themselves and also got dressed. Then, wrapped in pink, the five of them went to find out if anything was left of the farm.

The cracked cast iron stove lay worthless in the rubble. The large central chimney still stood, as did a few sections of the walls. The rest of the house, the barn, the smokehouse, the sugar shack, the woods behind them, and all the crops had burned entirely to ashes. Noah stated the horrible truth, "There's nothing left." The home that his friend James had built no longer existed. He felt robbed of the farm he had loved ever since he had listened to James' first story.

Ann looked away from the devastation toward the small white package by the well. "What do we have in the sheet?"

Noah held out his hand. "Let's go see." Ann took his hand. Sally held Noah's other hand and linked herself to Stephanie on the other side. Stephanie joined herself to Eli. They walked across the blackened ground as a single unit filled with anger and grief.

"What have we got?" Stephanie looked over Ann's shoulder.

"We have everybody's clothes except the winter clothes that were in the wardrobes. We have pillows, sheets, blankets, and several handkerchiefs, including the one with Mara's apple seeds inside. We saved all four rifles and two boxes of lead balls, which are useless right now because the gunpowder is wet. We have Noah's turkey feathers and sinew, the cutting board, a tin cup, the whetstone, Noah's knife, his bow, and the arrows he's making. We also have the crossbar, pulley, and rope. I'm glad we saved the tintype of Mama and Papa. We also have two candlesticks, what's left of the two candles, and five peppermint sticks."

Eli sighed. "Not much. It's probably not safe here. We better start walking to town."

Across their backs, each of them carried their share of the burden inside makeshift packs made of sheets. Along with his pack, Noah had his bow and one working arrow. The others carried packs and rifles.

In the midst of the horrible situation, Eli gave them each something he knew they would like. "I know it's not much, but I want you each to have a peppermint." He shared the tokens of his father's love.

"Goodbye, home." Ann stuck one end of the peppermint in her mouth.

Sally took the candy Eli offered. "Are we ever going to come back?"

Stephanie told her the truth, "I don't know."

The five of them walked across the charred meadow. The remains of the grass and flowers crunched under their feet and screamed out their destruction. Every step embedded the desire for revenge until it lodged deeply in their hearts. Sally looked back repeatedly. Tears rolled down her face. Eli put his arm around her shoulders. "You should stop looking. It'll only make you feel worse."

Bitterly, she spat out, "I want to feel worse. I don't want to ever forget how evil that man is."

Ann didn't need to look at the wasteland to prevent her from forgetting the devastation. The image had already permanently etched itself in her mind. Sad, angry, and set for retaliation, they left behind the dregs of James Williams' farm.

Noah trudged along. "We should be able to get to Harmony by this afternoon."

Ann took Noah's hand. "Even though it was very hard to get out, going into the well saved us. We would never have survived that fire any other way." She gently pressed his hand to her cut and bruised cheek. "From the bottom of my heart, I thank you for saving us."

"You saved my life first."

"Yes, but you saved my entire family."

Stephanie believed that Noah wasn't the only one who deserved praise. "And so did Eli. If he hadn't been able to get out and help pull us out, we'd be floating frozen in that well." Noah was glad Stephanie didn't know how close Ann had come to that fate. It seemed that Ann didn't even realize what had happened.

Eli stated emphatically, "I'm just glad we survived, and I'm going to do everything in my power to continue to protect this family."

As she usually did, Sally hit the nail on the head. "We survived as a team."

"You're right. We are a team." Ann liked the thought of the people walking with her being a team and even a family.

The fire, the night awake, and the escape from the well took a heavy toll on all of them.

They walked for a few hours before sitting beside the wagon trail. Noah leaned back onto the grass. "I sure could use a nap."

Sally sat beside Noah. "When did you go to sleep last night?"

"I don't know. We spent a long time in the well before the sun came up."

"You need to rest." Stephanie suddenly felt exhausted. "To tell you the truth, I could take a nap too."

Sally decided all of them should rest. "Let's go behind those bushes and sleep for a while. It's not like we have to get chores done or anything."

"We have plenty of blankets that we can lie on." Noah walked several yards to the bushes covered with clusters of vibrant, azure-blue berries. He looked into the clump of shrubs. Inside, leggy branches created a couple of feet of clearance. The outer shell of leaves, heavily laden with berries, provided good cover all the way to the ground. Noah crawled in and laid out most of the blankets.

The others squeezed together with him in the small space. Eli and Noah took positions on the outer edges, with the girls in the middle. They had barely put their heads down before they were asleep, hidden in the viburnums. As robins sat on the bush above, sang to each other, and ate berries, Ben, Gus, and Roy passed by on their way to check out their arson handiwork.

Ben told his friends, "We need ta stay away. We don't need ta look. There ain't no way anythin's still livin'. Them flames was so high, an' so wide, everybody in a hundred miles must a seen 'em. We oughta stay away."

Gus wanted to see the destruction and gloat, so he pestered. "We gotta know for sure. Besides, don't you wanna see that horse's burned-up bones, Roy?"

Roy had already made up his mind. *They killed Hank an' the boys. Ain't nobody coulda got there yet.* "I wanna know we got even."

When they got to the desolation left by

their inferno, they were shocked and dismayed to find footprints in the ashes. They found tracks at the house, beside the barn, and all around the well. In the wet ashes by the well, it looked like people had lain on the ground. Ben looked into the well. "Weren't any tracks leading inta this pile o' ash."

With much irritation, Gus told them, "But there's prints goin' out. They musta gone inta the well then got away."

Roy grinned from ear to ear. "We burned up that horse an' the others with him."

"Gus," Ben followed the footprints, "ya told us Noah an' Ann for sure saw ya, an' ya think they all mighta, so it ain't all right since they ain't dead."

Gus shadowed Ben and tried to figure out how they could have missed them. "Where'd they get off ta? We didn't pass 'em comin' here, an' there weren't no place for 'em ta hide." Suddenly, Gus had what he thought was a marvelous realization. "We might get them girls alive." Then he had another thought, *an' it'd be real nice ta kill them men up close an' personal.*

Roy advised, "We better track 'em." The three men led their horses beside the tracks that went away from the well. They arrived at the edge of the field of destruction. "Here's the end a the tracks."

Due to the direction of the footprints and the fact that it was the obvious place for them to go, Ben deduced where they went. "They gotta be goin' ta Harmony."

Gus again asked, "How'd we miss 'em?"

"Mount up. We'll look for 'em." Roy swung up onto his horse. The last three of the Butterfield Gang rode across the flat fields. They only saw small patches of shrubs that looked too small to hide five people.

In the Viburnum, Noah woke. He thought about the beautiful woods that were gone and all their hard work on the cornfields that was lost. He felt furious that everybody had been injured getting free from the well. He looked at Ann's sleeping face and gently moved a curl to the side.

Sally opened her eyes and saw Noah move Ann's hair. She whispered, "Do you love her?"

In the burning house, Noah was sure he was not leaving without Ann, and when trying to get her out of the well, he realized how much she meant to him. "I do."

"I'm glad." Sally closed her eyes again.

The sound of approaching horses came from up the road. Sally's eyes flew open. "Who can that be?"

"Be quiet and still." Noah turned to get a better look.

He pulled one of the green blankets over everybody. Only his eyes peered out as he watched Roy, Ben, and Gus. They fixed their eyes on the bush. Noah looked directly into Gus's eyes. He was sure they had detected him. He held his breath and steeled himself for their demise. The men rode on. They were well down the road before Noah notified Sally. "You can come out."

With much apprehension and too loudly, Sally said, "They must know we're alive."

Eli woke. "What's going on?"

Noah told Eli the bad news. "Roy, Gus, and Ben just rode past, coming from the direction of the farm."

"Then they're looking for us." Eli became not only mad but worried as well.

Ann heard every word that Noah told Eli. "Maybe we should track them."

"Good thinking." Noah had previously only thought about avoiding detection.

Refreshed by their nap, they planned while still protected in the bush. They repacked, cautiously crawled out of the bush, and followed their adversaries. Sally told them what had happened while she slept. "I want to tell you what I dreamed."

Stephanie encouraged her. "Go ahead and tell us."

"I dreamed I was a robin in a nest with other robins. Everybody was chirping and happy until an eagle swooped down, seized the other robins, and carried them away. I was in the nest alone when the eagle landed beside me. It told me to get out of the nest. I was too scared, I didn't want to leave, and I wouldn't go. The eagle went away, but it came back with a flaming branch. It set my nest on fire. I didn't know what to do. I couldn't stay in my nest, so I jumped out. I thought I would fall to the ground and die. Instead, I landed in a nest full of eagles. At first, I was afraid they would eat me, but then I realized I was also an eagle. I wasn't alone or scared anymore. Then, I woke up, and I saw–"

"Sally," Noah interrupted, "Umm, how could you have gotten into the eagle's nest?" Sally looked at Noah. He vigorously shook his head from side to side.

Catching his request not to mention their conversation about Ann, she continued. "I saw all of you and realized I do have a new family. I don't know how I got into the eagle nest. It was a dream; things just happen."

Ann analyzed the dream. "I think your dream means we're stronger now."

Eli agreed. "We've gotten through a lot together."

Stephanie looked into Eli's eyes. "I hope we are a family and that we stay together as a family."

"Me too. I really hope so," Sally intensified.

Eli didn't feel that he was on the hot seat. He already knew he was going to marry Stephanie if she would have him. "As far as I'm concerned, you couldn't drag me out of this family with wild horses." He returned the gaze into Stephanie's eyes, which caused a beautiful smile.

Ann changed the subject. She didn't want to apply pressure on Noah or herself. "How will we know when it's time to get off the road?"

Noah was tempted to repeat the same statement, but he didn't think this was the right way to go about what he wanted.

Moreover, he didn't know precisely how Ann felt. He wasn't sure if he was glad she changed the subject or upset because maybe that meant Ann didn't want him in the family.

Eli answered Ann's question. "To be safe, we should leave the road now. We can go into town from the side."

On the eighty-degree late August day, under a sky of solid blue, they started their wide berth off the road to sneak into Harmony.

FIFTY FIVE

As Noah, Eli, and the girls hid in the grass outside of Harmony, the sun took its last look over the horizon. The new moon allowed thick darkness to claim the land. Whatever they did, they would have to do it by starlight.

Eli described the lay of the land, “There’s a shallow wash that comes within a few yards of the back of Smitty’s livery.”

Noah pointed out the problem with that route. “They’ll expect us to come that way or by the main road and be watching. It would be better to keep you women out here in a safe spot while Eli or I go into town alone.”

Before leaving the Viburnum, they had agreed that they would stay together. Now that they were in real danger, Noah worried about the safety of the girls and tried to change the plan. Ann was at the end of her ability to deal with unknowns. Her life was in chaos, and she didn't like things to be out of her control. She insisted that they stick to the plan. It was the only little bit of order in her world. "I won't be left out here not knowing what's happening."

Noah tried again. "It will be much easier for one person to sneak into town and get help."

Ann argued her point. "But we can hide in Tom's storeroom underground. We'd be much safer than we are out here."

Stephanie didn't understand why he even wanted to leave them. "Anyway, what are you going to accomplish by one person going into town and leaving us out here?"

If Noah let these men stay alive, they might eventually succeed in killing one or all of them. Noah wanted to be able to hunt and eliminate their opponents. Even though they said they would like to skin Gus, Noah didn't know what any of them would think or feel if they did kill a man. Noah had never killed a person and had never wanted to hurt anybody except these men. Even though the thought that he shouldn't kill nagged at him, Noah needed to be Swift Hawk. He suggested an alternative, "I don't know. We need to know where they are. Why don't we try to find Roy and the others before we go into town? They have to be out here somewhere. They wouldn't take the chance of going into town and getting shot."

Eli reminded them of the facts about which he felt confident. "They already did take the chance of getting shot. When they rode past us, they were within fifteen miles of the Williams' farm and Harmony, and there's probably at least one of them just outside of town in the wash."

Sally stated what she believed was another of the primary considerations. "It's so dark that it will be just as hard for us to see them as for them to see us."

Noah felt that he was at a stalemate. He

couldn't search with everybody, and they would also be visible if they got close enough to see Gus, Roy, or Ben.

Ann stated another reason it would be safer for them to remain together, "The difference is that we know they're looking for us, but they don't know that we're looking for them."

Noah looked at her. She had stated the obvious. The problem had been that he was only thinking about keeping the girls out of harm's way and not about working together as they had all summer. He decided that he needed to trust them to know how to take care of themselves. Eli knew the most about Harmony, so Noah asked for information, "You're right, Ann. Eli, where do you think they could be on this side of town?"

"Unless they've gotten into a house or the shed behind the store, there isn't any place to hide. I guess they could lie on the ground between the buildings."

"What about the other side?"

"There's the wash we talked about. They could have gotten into a house or the livery or be on the ground between the buildings."

Stephanie whispered, "Did you see that?"

"See what?" Eli asked.

"I saw a flash in the shed." Everybody focused on the shed. Sure enough, a faint light flashed between the boards of the shed. After a few moments, they saw it again.

Noah squinted, "Must be the light from the window, glinting off a rifle barrel."

"We found at least one," Ann suggested a course of action. "We kill this one then look for the others."

Noah still felt it wouldn't be good for any of them to kill a person. "Maybe we should catch him."

Sally wanted vengeance. "We can't. He'll yell and alert the others. Besides, he destroyed everything."

Eli stated something he thought they needed to consider, "It might not be Gus."

"I don't care. They're all guilty," Stephanie agreed with Sally.

Eli disagreed. "We don't know that. Even though they all know about the fire, that doesn't mean they all agreed to set it."

Ann stated their crimes, "We aren't going to get justice around here anyway, and you know it. If they didn't all start the fire, they beat Dusty, and one of them shot Pete. Plus, who knows what else they've done or will do."

"Still, we don't know if they're all responsible," Noah repeated his concern.

Ann informed them, "I know Gus is guilty. If it's him, I am going to shoot him."

They crawled across the field on their bellies with their rifles ready to fire. Ann hoped the powder was dry enough to ignite. If they had found Gus, she absolutely planned to shoot him. Finally, they got close enough to see the outline of the man in the shed.

Eli worried. "It could be Pop. I can't tell." He issued strict orders. "Don't shoot until we see his face. I mean it, Ann."

Ann agreed. "I understand. I doubt your father would be standing in the shed in the dark, but I don't want to hurt him either."

They lay in the tall grass and watched. After several minutes, Ben poked his face around the edge of the shed. He peered into the field he couldn't even see. Ann sighed. "Now it's more difficult." They all looked at her. "You're right. I don't know that Ben's guilty of anything other than stupidity for being with the others."

Relieved that they weren't going to kill at least one of them, Noah told them what he could do, "I think I can sneak up on him and catch him without letting him make a sound."

Eli gave his permission, "All right, but if I see you're in trouble, I'm shooting him."

The girls all confirmed that they were also ready to shoot if needed. Noah slid off his boots. He removed the pink strips of cloth around his cut feet and continued through the grass. Noah remembered that there was a space between the wall and the seed sacks opposite where Ben was standing. As he made his way parallel to the shed, Noah hoped Tom hadn't changed the layout.

When Noah got to the back of the shed, he slid very slowly through the shorter grass and slithered beyond the corner before he stood up and crept to the opening of the shed on the far side of Ben. He waited until Ben poked his head out to look into the field again before he slipped around the corner and into the shed behind the seed sacks. Most of the sacks were gone. He dropped and crawled behind the seed bags until he came to a three-foot wide section open to Ben's view. He was in the dark shadows and couldn't see what was on the far side of the opening. He didn't want to take a chance, so he waited.

In the field, the others were getting antsy. It had been a very long time, and they couldn't see inside the shed. They imagined the worst.

"Maybe Ben saw Noah and killed him. I'm going closer." Ann started to slither forward.

Eli tried to talk Ann into waiting. "Just stay here. Give him time. The reason he can sneak up on a person is that he's patient about it."

Ann felt worried. "I'll keep waiting, but I couldn't stand it if he gets killed."

Sally assured her sister, "It's going to be fine, Ann. Noah won't do anything that might keep him apart from you, not even getting himself killed." She moved next to Ann and patted the pink cloth around the hand Ann was using to keep her rifle trained on the shed.

"Why do you think that?"

"I just know it."

Ann looked into Sally's eyes to gauge her conviction. "I'll be patient, Sally."

Inside, Ben raised his hands above his head and slowly twisted from side to side to stretch his cramped body. Noah darted across the opening when Ben turned away.

He found himself in a maze of crates. Noah navigated slowly and investigated with his hands and feet to know what was there.

An eternity later, Noah stood behind a stack of containers a foot away from Ben. Noah took out his piggin' string and wound one end around his left hand and the other around his right. He reached into his pocket, got his wadded handkerchief, and then stepped up behind Ben. Noah rapidly swung his arms over Ben's head, and then, as they came down, he shoved the handkerchief into Ben's mouth. He pulled the string tight around Ben's neck.

As soon as Ben stopped struggling, Noah let the rawhide strip loosen. Ben dropped. Noah knelt and hogtied Ben with the leather string. He got a second piggin' string and tied it around Ben's mouth to keep the handkerchief plug inside.

Noah put his hand out the shed opening. He waved, and then so that they could see he wasn't Ben, he carefully looked out into the field. In case Ben wasn't the only one on that side of town, the girls and Eli resumed their crawl across the field. When they got into the shed, they stood up and looked around. Ben lay on the ground, tied up and squirming with something tied in his mouth.

"Let me knock." Eli slipped through the darkness.

Tom heard a knock at the back door. It was one of the knocks he and Eli agreed to use if on opposite sides of a door and needed to communicate a secret message. This knock meant: trouble but safe, caution, crack the door. If everything was safe inside, Tom would turn off the light and then crack the door open with his hand on the edge so that his fingers showed on the outside. If trouble existed inside, he would leave the light on and keep his hand inside on the handle when he cracked the door. Tom turned off the light and opened the door just a sliver.

Eli saw Tom's fingers. "Pop, it's me. We need to get in without being seen, and we need to drag in Ben." Noah dragged Ben across the ground.

Tom opened the door just enough to let them pass. "Let's go to the cellar. You can tell me what's happening."

The girls went down first. Right in front of Noah, Tom held tight to the railings to stop them if Ben made them fall. Noah followed with his arm looped through Ben's tied-together arms. Eli had Ben's legs. Ben thrashed as much as he could as they carried him down the stairs. When they were at the bottom, Eli went back up. He closed and barred the door from their side before he rejoined those below. The others were already telling Tom what had happened.

With complete sincerity, Tom declared, "I'm very sorry about what happened."

Sally replied bitterly, "At least we don't need to worry about the windows anymore."

As Ben lay tied up on the floor, he heard the other side of the story. He hadn't wanted to bother the girls. Gus was the one who was always doing these things. He operated out of sheer meanness. Ben saw Gus shoot Pete. He never liked Pete, but he would never have actually killed him. Ben even tried to talk Gus out of burning the Williams' farm. He thought there was no call for it. The girls never did anything to them. He wouldn't have wanted anybody to hurt his folks or his sister. Since Hank had been gone, Ben had come to realize that Gus felt no concern for anybody. Ben tried to get these people to let him talk. He thrashed and tried to say, let me talk. It came out, "lhg mih jaik," due to the handkerchief in his mouth.

With firm conviction and a look that said obey or else, Noah ordered, "Stop it."

They came to the part of the story where they were lying in the field and decided not to shoot Ben. Ben thrashed violently. He had to get them to let him say something. Noah started to drag him into a corner. Tom stopped him. "Let him talk. He can scream all he wants. Nobody can hear what's happening down here." Noah untied the rawhide string and pulled the gag from Ben's mouth.

Ben spilled the beans. "Gus is the one what done everythin'. Gus started up the shootin' at your house, an he's the one what set the fire. I tol him ta leave ya alone. Pete said ta leave ya alone, an' Gus shot him. Roy woulda left ya alone, but Gus just kept on pesterin' about that horse. Thank ya for not shootin' me."

Tom informed Ben, "You're an accomplice."

Ben pleaded, "I didn't do nothin' ta deserve hangin'. Tell Judge Atwood I didn't do nothin', an' I'll tell him everythin' 'bout Roy an' Gus."

Eli divulged Roy's secret, "We aren't taking you to Judge Atwood. His wife is Roy's sister."

"So that's it. When we got away with everythin', I thought it was too good ta be true."

Ann was surprised. "He never told you?"

"He just said everythin' was gonna be all right."

Noah probed for the vital information. "Where are the others hiding?"

"Promise you'll keep me from hangin', an' I'll tell ya."

Noah looked Ben in the eyes. "All we can promise is that we'll let the judge know you helped us. He'll decide what to do with you."

"I can lead ya to 'em."

"Just tell us where they are." Noah rightfully distrusted him.

Tom offered Noah advice, "You can find them without him. Let him hang."

Ben wanted to get every possible advantage. "All right, I'll tell ya. Gus is at the wash, an Roy is outside your house under the boardwalk."

Ann couldn't think of any easy way to extract Roy. "How are we going to get him out from under there?"

Gus had caused so many problems that

Ben hoped they would kill him. He had already had much more than enough of Gus. "Leave him be, an get Gus. He's in the wash right 'fore it bends off ta the left."

Noah turned to Ann. "Will you please stay safely inside with Stephanie and Sally while I get him?"

Ann consented with a condition, "Only if Eli goes with you, so you can protect each other." Noah breathed a sigh of relief. Ann looked into his eyes. "I'm sorry I've been making this harder for you."

"You come at him from two sides. I'll stay back to shoot him if I need to." Tom started up the stairs.

Eli and Noah agreed. To prevent Ben from bothering the girls, Noah tied the gag back into Ben's mouth and dragged him behind a stack of crates. "Leave him there. Don't go close to him."

Stephanie called them all together. "We need to pray for justice." They waited for her to continue. "God, we gather here in the name of Your Son, Jesus, to request Your help. So much has happened we can barely stand it. We ask You not to let the guilty continue to go free and unpunished. Even if You never restore to us any of what has been taken, at least make the guilty accountable. Keep our men safe as they capture Roy and Gus. In Christ's name, Amen."

All understanding that Stephanie had declared them as her men to the God of everything, Eli, Tom, and Noah said, "Amen."

Tom wanted to use his system of knocks. "You girls stay down here but come up and lock the door behind us. Ann, can you remember the code, so you'll know if it's safe to open the door?"

Ann followed Tom up the stairs. "Tell me. I'll remember."

"Three knocks with a long pause between each knock means it's us, and it's safe to open the door. Ten fast ones mean we're in trouble, so open the door cautiously. Two knocks with no pauses between means it's us, but don't open the door. Anything else will not be us."

"I understand. Bring Gus and Roy to justice and come back safely."

When Tom joined, Noah and Eli had the guns ready with fresh powder. They exited the store by the back door. To avoid detection, they crossed the road at the opposite end of town from Roy. Tom and Eli stayed close to the building and went east. Noah stayed on the west side of the wash.

Twenty feet from the spot Ben had specified, Noah dropped. Clinging tightly to the ground, he slithered forward until he saw the top of Gus's head just above the wash. Gus deserved to have it sliced off. Noah drew his knife. As he slid into the wash, he swung his arm in a big arc along the ridge and then across the wash to the other side. Gus screamed. Eli jumped into the ditch on top of the culprit and knocked him flat. Gus lay in a heap as blood poured from his head.

Roy heard the blood-curdling scream.

Richard told these people they could kill us if we came back. I guess they got Gus. Roy dragged himself out from under the boardwalk.

After telling Stephanie and Sally the door signals, Ann had returned to the top of the stairs. She wanted to be faithful to her word to Noah, so she had stopped while still inside but with the door open and her rifle in her hand. Ann heard the scream, slipped to the peephole, and removed the plug. She saw Roy slink across the street toward Doc's house. It was too much.

Everybody in town heard Gus's scream, but none of the others recognized it as human. The men grabbed their guns and peered through their windows. The darkness of the moonless night hid everything.

"Did you scalp him?" asked Eli.

"No, I just cut off a section of hair the size of a bit piece. I probably should have scalped him."

Tom ran to the ditch. "Did you kill him?"

Eli wanted his father safe, not standing exposed in the field. "Get in here."

Noah tied a handkerchief over the top of Gus's head and under his chin. "He'll live. Roy must've heard Gus scream. That'll get him out from under the boardwalk. He'll be coming our way."

Doc tried to see what was happening outside. He stood by the window, loaded a powder charge, then rammed the ball and wadding down the barrel. Roy came into view as he poured primer into the pan. Unfortunately, he didn't have time to close the frizzen before Roy was gone.

In the gulley, Gus revived. Tom put Gus's hand on the top of Gus's head. "Press down if you don't want to bleed to death."

"Am I scalped?"

Noah enlightened him, "Just partly."

As if somebody could save him from the three men around him, Gus stupidly yelled, "Help!"

Eli encouraged him to draw his partner into the open. "Much obliged. We want Roy to come on over."

Changing his strategy, Gus immediately hollered, "Stay back! It's a trap!"

Roy heard Gus's call for help but wasn't about to charge across an open field. He knew it was a trap before Gus yelled out the warning. He stood beside the house and tried to see what was happening without anybody seeing him. He felt a light touch on his ear, heard a rifle cock, and then a woman say, "Give me a reason to shoot you."

Suddenly, seven men surrounded them. Roy looked into the faces of the people who had permission to kill him if he came within fifteen miles of their town. He was definitely within that radius as he stood beside Doc's house. Roy dropped his gun. "I surrender."

FIFTY SIX

"You know the direction." For the third time that year, Smitty marched Roy to the jail of Harmony, Arkansas.

Ann called out, "Smitty's taking Roy to jail."

"We're bringing in Gus. Better get Doc." Tom was glad it was over and hoped it would be permanent this time.

Ann's heart beat frantically. "Please don't let it be Noah. God, please don't let it be Eli or Tom either." She couldn't breathe. She dropped to her knees, laid her rifle on the ground, looked into heaven, and raised her praying hands to her face.

Noah saw Ann backlit by the light from Doc's house. "We're all fine. It's Gus who needs the doctor."

Ann jumped to her feet and ran across the

field. She threw her arms around Noah and knocked Gus loose from his grip. She pressed her head to his chest. "I'm so glad you're all safe." She hugged Eli and then Tom before she warned them sternly. "Don't scare me like that ever again."

Tom apologized. "I'm sorry, Ann. I didn't know you were out here."

Gus felt furious. The person who had just about scalped him had somebody who loved him. Gus knew nobody worried about him. He told himself it didn't matter. The whole world could rot for all he cared.

Doc got his bag and went to the jail. Eli proceeded directly to the store to let Stephanie and Sally know everything was over. The girls heard three knocks, with a long pause between each knock. Stephanie ran up the stairs and shoved the door open. The edge of the shelf hit Eli in the eye. "Thank God you're not hurt."

Eli held his arm across his eye. "I wasn't, but I might have a black eye now."

"I'm so sorry." Stephanie followed Eli down the stairs.

"Don't worry about it."

Ben pleaded with Eli. "Please don't put me in the same cell with Gus or Roy."

"I'm not the jailer." Eli didn't want to drag Ben up the stairs and across the road to the jail. He untied Ben's feet and then tied them back with only enough slack, so he could barely walk but couldn't run. He commanded Ben, "Come peacefully to the jail."

Stephanie and Sally stuck right behind them. When they entered the jail, Doc stood behind Gus, stitching his head. Roy sat locked in a cell. Noah and Ann were telling everybody what had happened at the farm.

Eli opened his hand in front of Smitty. "I'll lock up Ben if you give me the keys."

Smitty handed them over and continued to listen to the story and watch Doc.

Eli opened the empty cell, shoved Ben in, and slammed the door shut. He walked to

Smitty and whispered, "Keep Ben separate from Roy and Gus."

Ben felt grateful. He pulled his bed to the wall away from the other cell.

Doc tied the last stitch in the top of Gus's head. "I think I've become an expert at stitching up heads. How on earth did he get cut like that?"

Noah told the truth. "He got cut like that because I didn't completely scalp him."

"I wish you had." Ann walked over and spat in Gus's face. "You're a horrible excuse for a person."

He wiped the spit with one forearm tied to his other arm at the wrists. Pure evil hatred spread across Gus's face. Gus saw bruises and cuts on every exposed part of Ann's body, and he figured the rest of her was the same. "You spit on me. I wiped it off. You're messed up all over. I won."

Ann stalked out of the building. Noah followed her. "I was going to cut off the whole top of Gus's head. As I brought my arm around, I got the overwhelming feeling that I shouldn't kill him. I don't think God would be happy about it if I had."

"I know it's wrong to murder somebody, but in the Bible, God said to stone people to death as punishment for certain crimes. Sometimes it's not killing; it's justice."

"Forget them for now. They're locked up, we're safe, and standing here together." Noah pulled Ann into the darkness around the side of the jail and looked into her eyes. "I want you to know what I think about Sally's dream."

"I'm listening."

"Wild horses couldn't drag me away from you. I want to be part of this family when the time is right." Noah saw Ann's lips and eyes invite him to love her. She took a short step into his arms and melted into his kiss. They heard the sound of the jailhouse door opening, followed by footsteps on the boardwalk. Ann stepped back. Noah slid his hand down her arm and across her fingers as he stepped back. When the crowd was upon them, they were two people talking.

Doc stopped. "Noah, you're invited to stay with us."

"I'll be right over."

Tom wanted to ensure that the girls were safe. "I insist that you girls stay at my house."

"We will." Stephanie didn't feel like a stranger in Tom's home. He filled the hole in her heart created when her parents had died. She accepted before Ann could say otherwise. Noah, Eli, Tom, Ann, Stephanie, and Sally crossed the street to the store. The other men dispersed to their homes to tell their families the news.

Noah picked up his few possessions tied together in a sheet. "I'm going to Doc's. Goodnight." He pulled the door shut and walked out into the now peaceful night.

Eli searched the house. He opened cabinets, pulled out bureau drawers, and looked in the chest in his father's room.

"What are you doing, son?"

"I'm looking for our Bible."

"Why?"

"I told God that if He got us out of the well, I would talk to him every day and believe in Him. We're out. Now, I want to learn about Him."

"I think you got yourselves out, but I'll get it." Tom got the Bible. Eli opened the book and started reading on page one.

Ann suggested that he read it differently. "You'll understand God better if you start at Matthew."

"All right, then, I'll start there. I'm going to read every day. I wonder what I should say to Him."

Stephanie told Eli how she spoke with God. "Just talk to Him about whatever's on your mind, always thank Him for every blessing, and praise Him for who He is."

"Can I start now?"

Sally assured him, "Absolutely."

"I want to talk to Him in my room. I'll see you tomorrow."

Stephanie said goodnight to the man she knew she loved. The girls excused themselves to bed as well. Ann set up one of their candlesticks and inserted the candle remains. She lit the sulfur match. "There isn't much left of this night. Maybe this is enough to last."

Sally stopped her. "Don't light it. I don't want to see fire in the night ever again."

"I understand." Ann extinguished the match, laid the burned-out lucifer in the candlestick tray, and got into the bed beside Sally. Stephanie lay in the small bed alone and thought about Eli in his room, trying to discover God.

FIFTY SEVEN

As Mara got off her horse, a mist of smoke rose from the still smoldering black wasteland. "This is horrendous."

Sad and angry, Zachariah stood at the edge of the burned-up meadow. "They did this to me too. All our work is ruined. It's infuriating."

Horace's ten-year-old son pulled on his father's shirt. "Papa, I'm afraid they're gonna burn our house."

"They can't burn our house. We have them in jail." Horace picked up his son. The boy wrapped his arms around his father's neck.

Clyde felt more than upset. Not only because of what they had done to the Williams family but because he had helped build the house. "This is senseless and evil."

Smitty saw nothing but ash. He bent over and picked up a handful of it. "We'll have to take them to Little Rock." He let the ash trickle out of his hand.

Ann stated what they all knew beyond any doubt, "We sure can't take them to Judge Atwood."

"It will take at least two weeks." Tom had made the trip in the past.

Ann said, "I see no reason to take the men anywhere. We should try them ourselves."

Stephanie stated their case. "Ben told us that Gus shot Pete. He said that Gus was the one who started firing on our house this spring. We know Gus set the fire that destroyed our farm. We saw him tip his hat at us after he threw the flaming oil can into the house."

Sally begged, "Don't let them get away with this."

Clyde also didn't want the troublemakers to escape punishment. "As sheriff, you're responsible for enforcing the law. They were ordered to stay at least fifteen miles away from this farm, or they could be shot."

Nellie reminded them of an important detail. "That was only Ben and Gus."

Eli asked, "Why do you think that's relevant? We can shoot all of them for being in Harmony."

Ann wanted to rid the world of the one she despised and suggested an alternative. "Gus was ordered to stay at least fifteen miles away from Harmony, this farm, and all of us. He broke every order for which we have permission to shoot him, and Judge Atwood didn't say we could kill them; he specifically told us to kill any of them we found on our farm. I say we kill Gus and then take the other two to Little Rock."

"And they shot my Pa," Horace's son butted in. His littlest daughter sheepishly clung to Betsy's leg with her thumb in her mouth.

Nellie believed none of them would be able to look a man in the eyes and kill him.

She didn't want them even to want to. "Who would carry out the sentence?"

"I'll do it," said Ann, Stephanie, Sally, Eli, and Noah at the same time.

"So you think we should have a firing squad?!" Nellie didn't like it. She and Doc saved lives.

Doc protested. "I didn't sew up Gus's head so you could shoot him."

That comment and what seemed to be Doc's lack of concern about the people who were his friends made Noah feel outraged. "Look at Ann. The stones cut her all over when we pulled her out of the well. Look at the knot and gash on Stephanie's head where she hit it when we got her out of the well. Look at the rope burn on Eli's arm that he got stopping Stephanie's fall. All of us have cut-up hands and feet. Are you saying that's acceptable?"

Doc looked Noah in the eye. "You did that to them."

"It's their fault that we had to get into the

well. It's their fault the barn fell onto the well's roof and set it on fire. We might have pulled the rope, but they made it happen." Noah practically shredded Doc with the angry tone of his voice and his intense stare.

Smitty interceded. "Calm down."

Earl couldn't stand very long because of the Butterfield Gang. He sat on his horse. "It's not right what happened. We all know they're responsible. I say, execute them all."

Joe touched the scar on his cheek. "They're not going to leave us alone; shoot them."

Clara shared her opinion. "I don't want their blood on our hands or any of us to send them to Hell."

Betsy's husband could have died. "They need to come to justice, so take them to Little Rock and let the people there do it."

Zachariah looked around. "We are all witnesses that this whole farm has been destroyed."

Nellie still fought on the side of life. "Only

five people saw Gus, and they saw only Gus."

Ann made her decision. "We'll take them to Little Rock. But I'm telling you, if Gus gets off, I will track him down and shoot him. He will not walk away again."

Sally emphatically assured them, "And I'm helping."

Stephanie also stood with Ann. "So am I."

Noah changed the direction of the discussion. He brought up the next decision they needed to make. "Since we've decided to take them to Little Rock, we have to get them there. Who's going?"

Smitty was first on the list. "I'm the sheriff. I have to go."

Eli needed to be sure that the judge in Little Rock understood what had happened. "The five of us have to go to explain what happened."

"I want to see them pay for this. I don't know anything about what happened here, but I'll go if you need help getting them there." Zachariah offered to go because the destruction made him angry, he felt stifled in Harmony, and he wanted to be around Ann.

Horace's son begged his father, "Please don't go, Pa. I don't want you to get hurt."

Neither Earl nor Horace was in good enough condition to make a long trip. Nobody was surprised when Earl also said that he couldn't go. All the women needed to stay in Harmony to care for their children. Clyde was still building Tom's new counter and Tom had to run the store.

Smitty was glad they declined. "The seven of us will be enough." They made the choice and set the plan into motion. With Noah, Eli, Zachariah, Ann, Stephanie, and Sally, Smitty would transport Gus, Ben, and Roy over a hundred miles to Little Rock.

With all of their friends, the Williams sisters left behind the scorched land that had been their home, praying this time that justice would prevail.

About the Author

Lisa Gay graduated from George Mason University with a Bachelor's Degree in Psychology and from Virginia Polytechnic Institute and State University with a Master's Degree in Education.

All her life, Lisa has had imaginary friends. As a child, they included Mr. Potato Chip, Mrs. Tea Cup, Sally Brick, and a herd of Tom Toms that lived in an invisible hole in her bedroom wall. As she tried to keep pace with her fast-walking father, Lisa always made her family wait for her Tom Toms to catch up before crossing the busy streets of Washington, D.C. We wouldn't want any squished Tom Toms littering our nation's capital; would we? As an adult, her imaginary friends come to life in the stories she writes.

Acknowledgments

To my friends and family, who provided good feedback and encouragement, Hristo Argirov Kovatliev, maker of the beautiful cover, PDPhoto.org for the Scales of Justice (modified), but mainly to the One to whom all glory is due, I am much obliged.

Follow Me Online

https://www.
ChanceandChoicesAdventures.com

Did you like this story?
Please write a review!

https://www.amazon.com/Pray-
Justice-Chance-Choices-Adventure/
dp/1945858001

Chance and Choices Adventures by Lisa Gay

Pray for Justice
Choose Your Consequences
No Remorse
Means of Escape
Torn Hearts
Xida People
Stone Cold
Goodbye Hideout
Along the Way
The Western Sea
Sally's Sketchbook

Books by The Traveler

Provence: a land of lavender and olives

www.ingramcontent.com/pod-product-compliance
Lightning Source LLC
Chambersburg PA
CBHW070537030726
47505CB00001B/62
* 9 7 8 1 9 4 5 8 5 8 0 4 8 *